Books by Talia Wall:

The Nightshades
The Bleeding Hearts
The Oleander

The Oleander

Talia Wall

Trigger Warnings:

Violence, gore, mental health, drug and alcohol references

For those who still hope the world will heal someday.

The Crimson War
February 10, 2055

I DIDN'T THINK MY HEARING OR SIGHT WOULD COME BACK.

Seconds before the blinding white light, a high-pitched frequency pierced the air, like a dog's whistle magnified. It brought me to my knees, and then I flew, carried by a forceful wind as I crashed through every wall, vehicle, and tree.

My head smacked against iron, my body dragged against rough concrete, and my lungs quaked with violent coughs. I blinked until my vision cleared, and the burning pressure in my left arm amplified. I turned my head, and my eyes widened with horror. Blood spurted from my shoulder.

My arm had been replaced by a large, flat piece of shrapnel embedded in the wall.

"N-no," I whimpered, and gazed a few feet further at a lifeless hand poking from under the rubble.

My hand.

I released a vociferous roar with tears squeezing out of my eyes, the pain spreading like the Virus that had wiped out over half the population, then revived us as cursed creatures.

They were supposed to find a cure. Instead...

They gave up on us.

They dropped that bomb to *erase* us.

I had all the time in the world now. No matter how long it took, or *what* it took... I would rise. The Sun Dwellers would rue this day.

PART I

Disturbance

1

STERLING

A glass of fresh blood and a plate of raw steak sat in front of me. Saliva coated my tongue. The nurses shoved pills down my throat every twelve hours, which allegedly prevented the frenzied cravings, but I never noticed a difference.

Silver handcuffs bound my wrists to a metal table, irritating my skin. No one else was in the room, but I sensed them watching me behind the two-way mirror, similar to the interrogation rooms at the Neoterra Police Department. I never thought the roles would be reversed—where *I* became the skittish suspect. We'd prime the room to be too hot or too cold, and wait for hours in hopes that the suspect would fold. The best suspects were Vampyres, because we weren't legally obligated to give them a phone call with a lawyer.

It had only been a week, and the hospital staff had already force-fed me five times, which always resulted in sedating me when I fell into a mindless hysteria afterwards, putting me in isolation for three hours to "reset," and then throwing me into a sterile room like this with a meal in front of me. An incessant cycle.

What they didn't know was that I made myself throw up everything they forced me to eat and drink.

I clasped my hands together and held my breath for as long as possible, so I couldn't smell the temptation.

"Remember what we said, Mr. Shaw." Dr. Nolan's honeyed voice rang through the speaker. "Your goal today is to take one bite, then count to ten with deep breaths. Hold on to something to keep yourself from turning feral."

"I don't want any of it *ever*," I drawled, in case she couldn't understand me.

"That isn't realistic. You're a Vampyre now, and you'll wither away if you don't have any blood. With your pupils dilated, your body is signaling that it wants sustenance. Find a thought, Mr. Shaw, and cling to it."

The fluorescent lights glinted off the fork resting on the napkin. My handcuff chains were long enough to reach across the table and pull the food toward myself, but I kept my fingers laced.

I would've been better off dead. If not for my sake, then for Briar's. I had fantasies all day and night, ranging from escaping this place to snapping her neck in two for what she'd done to me. After everything I went through to rescue her, and *this* is how she repaid me?

"You won't be leaving this room until you do it." Dr. Nolan snapped me back to reality once again.

"Okay? And? I'm already a prisoner here. What difference does it make if I'm in here or out there?" I asked with a sardonic laugh.

"Your room has a bed and more space to roam."

"I haven't slept in three days. The bed is useless," I said, and leaned back defiantly in the metallic chair. "You might as well get your nurses ready."

Vampyre or not, I didn't have to live like one. I'd die before I submitted to this lifestyle.

An exasperated sigh emitted through the speaker before it cut off, followed by Dr. Nolan's clog shoes clumping to the door. Her rose-gold hair cascaded over her shoulders, concealing half of the silver name tag over her white lab coat and baby blue scrubs. I imagined grabbing a fistful of it, smashing her face into the mirror, and draining her veins. I gave her a thin smile.

"What is the problem? Why are you being so resistant?" She folded her arms, revealing a plastic badge dangling from a retractable lanyard at her hip. I pulled the plate toward me with a grimace—not at the sight, but because I craved the uncooked food.

"I never wanted to become one of these *things*. I refuse to live like one!" I exclaimed, and swiped the food off the table. The plate shattered against the wall, and the meat plopped to the floor.

"A cancer patient refusing treatment won't make their illness vanish. It festers. Your virus doesn't have a cure, but it's something you can learn to function with and thrive like any other person. Hundreds of thousands of people are just fine," she elaborated, stretching open palms to her sides.

"That's *not* true," I bantered with a sharp laugh. "I can't go in the sunlight, I have to drink from humans, and it's illegal to see my younger sister now. Why can't you just respect my choice?" My lip curled in disgust.

"Because, regardless of your decision, I can't release you into the world until I know you aren't a danger to society." Dr. Nolan stepped deeper into the holding room and took a seat across from me, far enough away that I couldn't reach her.

I turned my attention to my tender wrists.

"I have a proposition," she began after a beat of silence. "If you comply, and pass your tests three times, I'll release you two weeks early."

My eyebrow arched, and I lifted my chin. "And if I say no?"

"I'll add a week," she said. I sucked my teeth and slid my gaze to the mess of uncooked food on the floor. Part of me wanted to believe she was telling the truth, but deep down I knew she was lying.

I decided to play her little game. I picked up the glass of blood, and held on to the thought of tearing Briar apart while I drank.

✳

I didn't remember much after that session. I regained consciousness in my assigned padded room. My guess was that I in fact *did not* cling to reality as I'd hoped and had been sedated.

When I faced the display window covering the entire front wall, I expected to see Dr. Nolan gloating on the other side.

To my surprise, I saw Lyra Hart in a flowing cobalt blue sundress, her raven hair tied into two braids that snaked over her delicately sloped shoulders. I blinked and rubbed my eyes, questioning if she was real. I couldn't recall seeing her wear anything other than button-down blouses and jeans aside from the one time I ran into her at The Nightshade bar. Her crimson lips were stark against her ivory skin—a fabled princess in reality.

"How are you doing?" she asked, stretching her arms behind her back. I propped myself on my elbows on the creaky, thin mattress.

"Me? Oh, I... u-uh..." My tongue tangled with my teeth while I searched for words. It wasn't until I caught her eyes, the scarlet discs contrasting with her dress and creamy skin, that the bitter taste consumed my mouth. "I'm alright. I thought I couldn't have visitors until stage two."

"You aren't, but being a cop kinda gives me a pass." Lyra shrugged, lips tugging coyly.

"Last time you came... you laughed in my face," I said, narrowing my eyes.

"Can you blame me?" She frowned. "How long will it take for you to get it through your head? There are good and bad people, and Vampyres are no different. Your sister was wrong, but... I can't completely disagree with what she did."

"Oh, well, now you two can be best friends. You'll be the first one she's ever had." I flopped on my back once more and stared at the paneled ceiling. I had yet to jump high enough to see if I could climb through one of the panels.

"Boy, you're something else," Lyra muttered under her breath. My stomach twisted at the fact that I could hear her.

"Is there something you came here for specifically?" I raised my arm idly in the air, staring at the skin that wasn't banded in angry red stripes.

"Chief Duncan or someone else from the precinct might stop

by to get a statement from you. I wanted to see how you were doing, and remind you I told them White Fang Turned you at their lab."

"Yeah, yeah, how could I forget that you didn't report Briar?" I flicked my wrist to shoo her away, then snapped upright when I heard a familiar voice in the hallway. I ran across the room until the chain at my ankles snapped taut and held me back a foot away from the window.

"What?" Lyra stepped backward.

"You don't hear her?" I dropped to the floor and stretched my body the rest of the way, lying on my stomach. I pressed my face against the glass to peer down the corridor. Lyra turned to the women at the end of the hall. Both wore lab coats and carried themselves with rigid spines and upturned noses.

"Dr. Nolan?" Lyra raised an eyebrow. I gave her an exasperated sigh.

"No, *obviously*. The other one," I whispered. "The woman with the thick Slavic accent."

The beast with the carmine irises, wavy black hair, and olive skin—who had run for her life as Draven set the place on fire.

I dropped my voice another octave. "She was at the lab."

Lyra squinted, then turned back to me. "Are you sure? Why would she be here?" Her brows twitched inward.

"She might still want to use me, even after Turning—or she works here as a cover. Maybe the hospital is in on it, I don't know!" My breaths grew heavier with every racing thought. "You gotta break me out!"

I pressed my palms desperately against the glass. Lyra placed her palm over mine on the other side and shook her head.

"Calm down, Sterling. *Breathe,*" she muttered. "I'll think of something, but breaking you out of here isn't the move. You of all people should know that."

Maybe I was being irrational. The Transition Wing was the most secure unit in the hospital. But that woman... she had some kind of sinister motive. *That* wasn't irrational.

The chains rattled as I shuffled back to my mattress before the doctors stopped by my room. Lyra gave them a saccharine smile, then took a step back. She passed me a wary look before disappearing down the hall.

Dr. Ivanov tore her attention from Dr. Nolan, and pushed her glasses up. My blood boiled at her wicked grin.

"It's amazing how everything comes full circle, isn't it?" Dr. Ivanov clasped her hands behind her back.

Dr. Nolan tilted her head. "What do you mean?"

"Well, Mr. Shaw here had both a glowing and dimming reputation. An amazing detective with a successful track record, but known among his nocturnal peers as a—well—*speciesist,*" Dr. Ivanov sneered.

Dr. Nolan nodded, folding her thin hands in front of her. "I can see that. He refuses to accept any of our treatments. He believes the Vampyre lifestyle is a choice."

"That's okay, if he continues... you know what to do." Dr. Ivanov patted her shoulder before slithering away in the direction they'd come from. From their exchange, I couldn't tell if it was a sign of partnership or if Dr. Nolan was an oblivious pawn.

2
BRIAR

THE DETONATION RIPPED DRAVEN'S HAND FROM MINE. MY spine cracked against concrete and a chalky substance launched into my mouth. I convulsed with dry coughs. While my ears rang, alarms blared throughout Black Bay Prison, strobe lights flashing, people screaming, running, and—gunfire.

The muffled tinnitus faded as the chaos shifted into sharp clarity.

As droves of Nightshades poured through the wall, I searched for any sign of Draven and Astoria among the smoke. I wanted to shout their names, but I didn't want to draw attention to myself.

Bodies dropped left and right. I tried to stand, but something anchored me to the floor. I peered over my shoulder to see a pile of broken concrete and debris.

"Ha, ha, ha! Guys, I got one!" someone yelled. Chilled hands wrapped around my neck and squeezed.

My chest quivered with urgency as I descended into madness like an animal caught in a trap. I clawed at the floor, wheezing while my face prickled and my lungs screamed. Darkness crept into my peripheral vision, peppered by teal and red bokeh circles. I tried to crawl away, but between the concrete pile and whoever was behind me, I couldn't move an inch. My fingertips brushed against a rusted piece of rebar protruding from a cinder block. I gasped, eyes rolling back as the thread of consciousness grew closer to snapping. With the last ounce of my strength, I yanked the loose rod free and swung it over my head. My attacker released a loud groan, and the concrete attached crumbled. More dust swirled, catching in my throat. I continued hacking with watery eyes, feeling as though I were breathing glass.

The concrete pile imploded, and the man's severed head thudded next to me. I crawled to avoid the blood spurting from his mangled neck. I could only determine who killed the Nightshade through the vanilla, leather, and tobacco scent mixing with the gunpowder.

He knew better than to yell for my name too.

"Draven," I whispered, and took his bloodied hand. I shook my legs and rolled my ankles as the pins and needles faded. Draven's cherry eyes flashed orange as he scanned me from head to toe before he switched his focus to the pandemonium around us.

"There they are!" someone hollered, and Draven and I snapped our heads in their direction. The Nightshade caught ten others' attention. I dove behind a flipped table, but Draven stayed in place.

Just as they raised their guns, he lifted his palms and shot pillars of flames at them.

"Briar? Briar, help me!"

I looked around. The divided plexiglass cubicles for visitors were rubble now. Vivian—my mother—was pinned underneath it. Blood trickled down her face, which twisted in both anguish and horror.

The Nightshades passed weapons to the Vampyre inmates nearby.

Which likely meant the dead bodies were the humans and other inmates who'd refused to participate.

I wanted to leave her there as she'd once left me and my family to fend for ourselves. But I knew Astoria would never forgive me for it. I was already on thin ice after Turning Sterling, our brother, into the very thing he despised.

So I vaulted over the mound of rubble, grabbed Vivian under her arms, and yanked her from the debris. I ignored her cries of agony.

A clawed hand seized my arm. I swung my fist into their face. This time when my knuckles crunched against bone, it didn't hurt. I hissed, baring my fangs viciously at the Vampyre who now crumpled at my feet. I jerked his gun from the ground. I had no clue how to operate it, but it was one less weapon the Nightshades had at their disposal.

"Draven!" I screamed, and tossed the gun across the visiting room. He caught it with eyes of pure flame, and immediately fired. He wielded the weapon like it was another appendage. He didn't miss a single target.

"Get out of here! I'll catch up!" he roared, tossing the pistol once the ammo ran out. Blazes crawled from his palms up his forearms.

"Can you walk?" I shouted over the chaos, and Vivian shook her head with a whimper. I rolled my eyes and scooped her up in my arms, then darted for the hole in the wall.

Until it hit me.

"Ria?" I squealed, looking around frantically.

"*Go!* I'll find her!" Draven bellowed. A silver bullet pierced through his chest and he staggered back before raining hellfire. I fought the urge to cry and focused on getting Vivian to safety.

Those bullets can't hurt him. But Astoria and Caspian aren't immune.

I skidded to a stop near the gatehouse and noticed more Nightshades standing shoulder to shoulder, holding automatic rifles.

My heart jumped in my throat, and I changed course, veering to the back of the giant ivory tower. It was once the most secure construction in the country aside from Mundus Novus.

A wide, empty field separated the prison from the thick woods behind it. I pushed my enhanced speed to its limits, bolting for the fried holographic fences.

Vivian wailed in my ear, never taking her eyes off of the destruction behind us. Her tears soaked through my t-shirt while her cries overpowered the gunfire in the distance.

I tightened my grip as I sank into a crouch, then leaped across the field and landed at the demarcation of the woods. I didn't look back—no matter how much I wanted to.

I stopped at a small creek, and set Vivian down near the water. I panted—not from the exertion, but from avoiding a panic attack.

I doubled over, bracing my hands on my knees. My lips trembled, and I swallowed when saliva pooled in my mouth with the threat of vomit.

Deep breath in... out... in...

I observed my unfortunate parent, whose right ankle was twisted at the wrong angle with bone attempting to break free from beneath her skin. Vivian's breaths rattled as if she were the one who'd run a marathon.

"Stay here. I'm going to find Ria." I pivoted on my heel, but froze at Vivian's shrill cry.

"Wait, wait! Don't leave me alone here! They could find me!" she begged. I rolled my eyes.

"Trust me, they don't care about you. They're busy looking for me and Draven, and freeing the inmates," I said coldly. I ignored her desperate pleas and took off in another sprint. I lacked a sense of direction, and followed my own scent as a guide. I halted at the edge of the woods.

Draven carried Astoria, while Caspian followed with the duffel bag of weapons and clothes slung around his back. Claw marks and bullet holes tattered Draven's shirt. With his skin covered in soot, I couldn't tell if the smudges were from their fire or his own.

Caspian's bright red face blistered in the late afternoon sun.

As a human, their speeds seemed so great that they were blurs of light and shadow to the naked eye. As a Vampyre—they ran in slow motion.

I could see every shred of terror on their faces.

The Black Bay Prison skyscraper was illuminated with clouds of red and orange. The explosions shook the ground. Screams of the remaining human wardens and inmates still pierced the air—until they shut off completely.

"Go back! Run before they see us!" Draven exclaimed. He triggered a yelp from Astoria as he tossed her into Caspian's arms, neither of them missing a beat. I didn't move until they reached the tree line, and fell in stride with them. We bounded over fallen trees, blasted through thickets, and sprang over small streams. I led them to Vivian, scooped her up without warning, and kept running until the island ran out.

✳

The stench of gunpowder mellowed into the smell of salt and citrus. The screams were replaced by the squalls of seagulls. Our rapid, desperate footsteps kicking up grass and dirt were now planted in sand, and we took in the graceful waves rolling onto a private beach. We were far enough away that the sporadic gunfire were distant pops, like champagne bottle corks.

I didn't realize how badly I was trembling until we stood shoulder to shoulder in silence, Vivian sitting in the sand. Even Astoria wasn't at her side to comfort her, but instead clinging to Caspian's arm with puffy eyelids and constant sniveling.

"What happened back there?" Vivian whimpered. My face hardened at her voice disrupting the serenity the ocean provided.

Caspian slowly turned to face her with subtle annoyance. "It appeared to be a prison break. Uriah never mentioned it in his plans, but I suppose he lost his trust in me long before I broke it." Caspian eyed Draven warily, who exhaled and angled his head to the sky.

"Uriah is growing the Vampyres' forces as much as he can. Even if it means using the most dangerous, unhinged prisoners," Caspian added.

"He probably offered them freedom if they fought for his cause," Draven said. "And with inmates being mistreated by officers, it don't take much convincing."

I threw my arms up with an incredulous laugh. "How would he get that information to them?"

"It's not hard to pretend you're some other Vampyre's relative. It was probably an idea Wraith and Larkin spread through the prison when they visited a Nightshade inmate," Caspian said, and winced as his blisters grew larger in the sunlight. "I'm... gonna go sit under the shade for a bit."

Caspian flashed to the edge of the woods and stood directly beneath a large oak tree.

If Uriah promised them something like that, then he was confident he could overthrow not only Neoterra, but Mundus Novus.

"Um, hello? My ankle is killing me and you're all talking nonsense," Vivian interjected. I stomped to her and hissed like a feline.

"Nobody cares about your stupid ankle right now!" I yelled, bass in my tone. My claws were out, teeth sharpened to razors. I resisted the feral urge to paint the shore in scarlet. Sterling and the stained concrete he'd left behind flitted through my mind.

An uncomfortable silence blanketed the beach. I shrunk within myself, and when I noticed the judgment in Astoria's face, my gut twisted. Draven held a blank expression, either because he now saw how Vivian behaved firsthand or was also remembering Sterling.

"We should get back to the hotel," Astoria mumbled. "I can take Mom to the hospital and—"

"Dogwood is too deep in the city. We need to get off this island before Mundus Novus sends the Onyx Sentries here," Draven warned. "An attack at that scale is bound to trigger their presence."

I ran a hand through my hair and began to pace across the sand. I screamed internally, hating the fact that Astoria had guilt-tripped me into agreeing to see that woman. We almost died over it, and now we had to find safety *with* her.

A cramp wavered in my stomach and I crossed my arms over it.

"This is too much all at once," I grumbled as I bent over my knees.

Draven bit his lip pensively as he peered at the ocean. "I hate to say this… but we might need to find your friends again," he said. "Malachi's got the medical knowledge, and they're secluded."

My back snapped straight. "What? No, absolutely not."

"Hey, this is my ankle we're talking about!" Vivian scowled. I glowered at her.

"Draven, they already didn't want us there the first time. You threatened their lives too, remember? What makes you think they'd help us again?" My heart wrenched at how distant Malachi had behaved. He hadn't even been relieved when I woke up before they could bury me.

On top of that, what if the Nightshades or White Fang found us there, and killed my friends—or even recaptured Azha and Malachi to finish their sick experiments?

"We'd bring death right to their doorstep," I mumbled.

Draven shrugged nonchalantly. "What other choice do we have? Vivian isn't supposed to be released. We can't take her to a hospital."

"I only had a month left," Vivian cut in.

"Maybe sending you to the hospital is the perfect way to help you finish it off," I threatened.

"Bri, stop," Astoria hissed. "Haven't you done enough damage to our family?"

I scoffed and stormed along the shore, waving my hand dismissively at them. Soft footsteps padded in a quick jog through the sand behind me.

"Briar, wait." Draven reached for my arm once we were fifty feet away from the others. "I need ya to slow down." He held both of my arms firmly and gazed deep into my eyes. I peered at our shoes, the skin around my neck tightening as I braced for another disaster to interrupt our moment like the explosion at Black Bay.

"I get your Ma is unbearable, but... what's wrong?" Draven tilted my chin up tenderly.

"She's holding us up with her ankle and she's gonna get everyone killed," I whispered, despite the distance from the others.

"Ya might wanna tone it down a bit, don't ya think? Your sister's gettin' worked up and we can't come up with a plan when everybody's emotions are at a hundred." Draven scanned my face. "You look like you need some blood."

I glanced at Astoria and my mother at the mention of blood. The ocean breeze carried their human scents toward me, and for a second—they weren't family.

"I don't want to go back to Azha and Malachi's house. They're gonna turn us away!"

"That's literally the worst thing that can happen. Then we'll figure it out from there, alright?" He grinned, the dimples barely surfacing. I closed my eyes with an exasperated sigh, but my shoulders relaxed as he pressed his soft lips to my forehead.

"I trust you," I mumbled, and followed him back to the group with our fingers intertwined. I squeezed when we approached closer, and he did the same.

Caspian returned, the blisters hardly any smaller. "So... have we decided what we're going to do?" He spoke through a stifled wince.

"We're gonna try to find Samara and ask for shelter. If not for that, then at least for Briar's Ma to get her ankle straight," Draven explained. Caspian nodded and immediately trudged back to the shade. Astoria said nothing. To my surprise, Vivian didn't either.

Draven lifted my mother from the sand and carried her as we traversed the woods once again.

3

DRAVEN

It was *always* me and Caspian on our missions as Nightshades. There were two bodies accounted for, and he was more than capable of taking care of himself.

Now?

I had Briar as a fledgling at my side, her insufferable mother in my arms, and her frail sister trailing closely behind Caspian, who was trapped in a vicious cycle of healing, burning, and fighting to keep consciousness. Five people stuck out a lot more than two. The weight on my shoulders crushed me.

To have so many lives in the palms of my hands—lives I *cared* about—distressed me to levels beyond comprehension.

Only the sound of birds chirping and the occasional whimper from Vivian circulated the woods.

Until a quiet thud prompted us all to turn and see Caspian sprawled on his back. Icing on the friggin' cake.

"Cass!" Astoria gasped and dropped to her knees, placing her palms on either side of his face. "What's wrong with him?" she whimpered, and drew another sharp inhale at sight of the burns across his formerly immaculate skin.

"He can't be out here like us," Briar explained with a subtle tremble in her voice, chewing on her thumbnail. Her forehead wrinkled before she snapped a bunch of leaves and laid them over Caspian's face and hands.

"I don't think we can find Samara before our time runs out," she said.

All good points, and all points that added more stress. The scenarios kept getting worse.

Onyx Sentries could arrive at Helios at any moment and make it impossible to leave the island, and Samara and her family could refuse to help us, leaving Caspian to risk potential death and Briar's mother still helpless.

In the thirteen years I'd known Caspian, I never once saw him in such a weakened state. I kept quiet while the others panicked, despite every alarm blaring in my mind as my thoughts ran a hundred miles a minute.

With a deep inhale, I lowered Vivian to the ground, and rubbed the back of my neck before shifting my focus to Caspian. I crouched next to him and lifted one leaf to see if it had helped. Only a quarter returned to normal, the rest still riddled with second- and third-degree burns and blisters. It was a slow rate, but at least he was healing. That was a good sign.

"We need to help him! Why are we still standing around?" Astoria exclaimed, and Briar shushed her with an index finger over her lips.

"Let us think, Ria!" she snapped.

Astoria hardly blinked as she watched Caspian's chest rise and fall with ragged, shallow breaths. Tears glittered along her waterline until she briefly closed her eyes and let them fall. I lifted my chin, squinting at the sky between the intertwining branches and leaves. The sun was still strong.

"We could look for shade until sunset and hope for the best. The best-case scenario... he gets better before the morning and we find Samara while it's still dark." I didn't trust myself to make the right decision. Had the roles been reversed, Caspian would've had the most efficient plan to solve our problem. But these were the cards I was dealt, and the best way I knew how to play the hand.

I wasn't comfortable with how heavily we depended on Samara, Malachi, and Azha agreeing to help us.

I turned in small circles, observing the surrounding woods. The sparse canopy grew denser going west. I passed over Vivian and hoisted Caspian over my shoulder, then began a brisk walk in that direction with Astoria hot on my trail. Vivian was smart—she kept her mouth shut long enough for Briar to decide to help her before changing her mind.

As the air went from humid heat to a damp chill, the woods transitioned to a misty maple and sweetgum forest. I followed the winding estuary cutting through the trees until we reached a cave. There, I eased Caspian over a bed of dead leaves and twigs, completely out of contact with the light beams cracking through. Briar did the same with Vivian, but with a lot less grace. She let her flop on the ground like she was too heavy, which was impossible. Fledgling or not, supernatural strength always manifested early.

But again, I stayed silent. Their beef was not my own, although her crass mother did say my tattoos made me look like an inmate.

Vivian hadn't even seen the Nightshades' clan insignia on my chest yet.

"So this is how you kids handle these things? Live on the run and hide in strange caves that might have bats in them?" Vivian said scornfully as she rubbed her tailbone. Briar squatted in front of her with the same wild spark in her eyes before she attacked Sterling. I bent my knees and inched forward, poised to separate them.

"Like you? Selling yourself on the streets for a thirty-minute high? Running off in the middle of the night, breaking curfew, and getting our dad killed looking for you?" Briar's tone was light, but lethal. "If you don't like how we're handling things, I'm happy to take you back to Black Bay."

"Black Bay is in ashes," Vivian responded without an ounce of fear in her voice, but her skin blanched. She didn't defend herself against Briar's allegations, and my heart sank at the thought of it being true. It wasn't Vivian's nature to stay silent otherwise.

"It's not the only prison that exists in the country." Briar's gaze locked on hers, as if she'd pounce at the slightest movement.

"Drop it, Bri," Astoria demanded, placing her hands on her hips. Briar cut her eyes at her sister, then at me. Maybe she expected me to say something in her defense, but my lips only parted without sound. She stalked to the edge of the cave, leaning against its vine-covered threshold. My shoulders relaxed when she moved away from Vivian, but the tension in my neck remained.

I sank next to Caspian to monitor his condition. He needed blood, but we were far from civilization, and I doubted Vivian or Astoria would donate. I didn't know how deep Astoria's attachment went with him.

"Why isn't he healing?" Briar frowned.

"He is, just at a slow rate. Vampyres don't do well with sunlight or fire. That's why Uriah always used it against his rivals. It's actually ironic that I can control it." I loosed a wry chuckle, and looked down at Caspian somberly. At this rate, he wouldn't be functional until tomorrow night—time we didn't have.

"Is there any way to make it faster?" Astoria asked, zipping her opal pendant across her gold chain necklace.

"Sorta..." I pressed my lips in a thin line and eyed Briar warily. "Blood helps us heal faster..."

"There's no shot in hell we're Turning Astoria," Briar spat.

Astoria didn't let me respond to her sister or take a breath before asking, "Can I give some to him without getting Turned?"

I blinked, taken aback by the blitzed responses from both siblings.

"Uh, well, hold on—"

"I'll step outside," Briar said, as if she foresaw the alternative. "I want him to be okay too. But I don't wanna risk attacking Astoria if she can help him."

"*How?*" Astoria demanded with more irritation.

Briar shrugged. "Cut your hand, let him drink that way."

"Oh, no, Ria don't do that for some boy that could be dead," Vivian condemned. "You'll scar up your pretty little hands!"

Briar growled and jerked forward before I flashed at her side and caught her arm.

"Ignore her!" I shouted.

I shot a dark look toward Vivian.

"Not another word," I added through clenched teeth.

God, my head hurt.

I squeezed Caspian's shoulder when I didn't see his chest move. He wheezed quietly. Good enough.

"Are ya willing to do it? He needs blood regardless." I narrowed my eyes at Vivian. I didn't mind *taking* it from her instead. I was sure the only one here that'd have a problem with it was Astoria.

"Yeah, you'd think a concerned mother would do it in place of her daughter," Briar mumbled under her breath.

"I'll do it, I don't care." Astoria held out her slender, pale palm. Vivian rolled her eyes with an exasperated sigh.

"Thanks," I muttered, and ignored the bitter taste in my mouth as I elongated the claw of my index finger and dragged it across Astoria's palm. She sucked her teeth with a grimace, and clamped her fist to keep the blood in place until she returned to Caspian. Her breath tremored before she held her fist an inch above his lips and allowed the blood to drip.

A gust whistled past the threshold of the cave, and Briar was gone.

"Yell out if he wakes up," I said, and hurried after her. "Briar!"

Stepping outside didn't mean leave, *right?*

I tracked the small frame already a half mile away, trudging through the bushes. I broke into a dash, catching up in seconds.

"Hey, why'd ya go so far?" I reached for Briar's shoulder. "Where are ya even going?"

"I don't know, I was gonna keep going until I couldn't smell Astoria anymore." Briar rubbed her nose with a sniff. Her fangs extended, peeking past her lips with every word.

"Ya don't think you could hold back?" I raised my eyebrows.

Briar laughed dryly. "Do *you?*"

I had to calculate my response.

"I... I ain't expecting it yet."

"Well... you didn't have to follow me. Aren't you worried Caspian can wake up in a frenzy too?" Briar peered over shoulder, toward the cave. I shook my head with a shrug.

"Vampyre-borns ain't typically prone to frenzies."

"But the Turned are? You mean I'm still a risk after I'm out of the fledgling phase?" Briar's tone rose in a crescendo, and I gripped her shoulders with a gentle squeeze.

"No, that ain't what I'm sayin'," I countered. "It depends on the person. Some of us have less resistance than others even after maturing. For example... your Ma... if she was an addict before, somebody like her could be prone to frenzies well into Vampyrehood. A disciplined athlete or a soldier might not be. It just... depends."

Briar was silent. She stared bleakly at a lost twig, then her face returned to the pensive frown she'd been keeping since her brother's attack.

I guessed she'd have chosen differently at White Fang if she'd known.

Astoria called for me. At the very least, her tone didn't sound panicked.

"Let's head back." I held out my hand, but Briar didn't take it, instead shooting off in a blurred sprint. I waited a couple seconds before I followed, feeling the sting of her rejection.

4

BRIAR

E LIVED IN THE CAVE FOR A WEEK. CASPIAN STAYED ISOLATED in its shade, still healing from the severe burns he'd sustained from the sun. Even with the few drops of blood Astoria fed him, it took a lot longer than we expected.

Draven would leave to hunt for deer, squirrel, or firewood during the cold nights. I lingered nearby to watch Vivian and Astoria, but never went within a thirty foot radius without Draven present. The animal blood offered zero satiety—and if I went crazy, Caspian was too weak to stop me from hurting my own family. Of course, I wasn't nearly as concerned about Vivian's safety as I was for Astoria's.

Crooked tree branches spliced the full moon. The limpid sky twinkled, and I couldn't help but wonder how many of the stars were actually satellites instead.

How many were Mundus Novus satellites, tracking our every move?

I disregarded the irrational thought. Mundus Novus didn't know we existed. If anything, their focus was on the Nightshades and White Fang pillaging Helios.

I brushed my hands against the goosebumps prickling along my arms, another nod to autumn's approach. I remained at the mouth of the cave while Caspian rested his head on Astoria's lap. She slept a foot away from our mother, who was curled against the dirt and leaves in fetal position. Draven sat with his eyes closed and his back against the wall, but like all other Vampyres, I knew he wasn't sleeping. He was more likely listening to the owls, coyotes, and crickets. Either to relax, or to make sure unwanted guests didn't disrupt us.

Sleep hadn't visited me since my coma. The last dream I had was a nightmare where Draven was dead in the street, and war had broken out between the Vampyres and the human Onyx Sentries. I hoped I had one more dream in me—a pleasant one—before the Vampyrism completely took hold.

Then again... I didn't deserve it.

For the first time, I contemplated leaving everyone behind and spending the rest of my days alone. It was probably for the best. Even with the war, the nightmare warned that I'd get in the way. Draven would die trying to save me.

I hugged my knees to my chest and buried my frigid nose. The scent of Astoria's blood still clung to the cave from those first few drops. When Caspian regained consciousness, he wasn't hysterical from the blood. Draven was unbothered by it too. For me, her open wound created a deep itch I couldn't scratch, and I wanted to rip my skin open to get to it.

I envied them for their restraint.

"Hey," Draven whispered. I raised my head, but didn't look at him. Every time I did, I remembered my sins. He added, "Are we okay?"

I shrugged. I really wanted us to be. But how could we be okay if *I* wasn't?

His body shifted as he pushed himself upright, his feet planting on the dirt and stone.

"Come on," he mumbled, and strolled out of the cave. I hesitated, peering back at my family. My mouth instantly watered, so I scrambled to my feet and jogged to Draven's side. I didn't comment on the growing distance from the others. I assumed he wanted to be out of earshot of Caspian.

"What's goin' on, Sunny?" He leaned against a tree once we were far enough. The shallow creek we often visited flowed behind him, babbling in harmony with the croaking of bullfrogs. The human version of me would've loved sleeping with the window illegally cracked open to listen to those sounds in the comfort of my bedroom.

"I... I honestly don't know anymore," I mumbled, and kicked a nearby rock. Draven cupped his hands around mine.

"You ain't still blamin' yourself for everything, are ya?" He hooked a hand behind my neck, brushing his thumb over my jawline.

"Of course I am." I unfettered a dull laugh. "From day one, I started it all."

A part of me expected him to contradict me, to say I was being too hard on myself. But I watched his lips press tighter and his eyes search mine for an answer to steal. I stepped away.

"Pretend all you want, but you agree with me, and you probably…" My throat tightened, clamping down on the words before I risked making them a reality.

You can't stand me.

"That's not true!" he rebutted in a rattled, harsh whisper. "Do ya have any idea how far out of my mind I went when I thought you were dead?"

I blinked at him.

"Or how many people *I've* killed? I lost count!" He scoffed at the absurdity.

I shrugged and folded my arms, shifting my weight to one hip and ignoring the burning in my eyes. "I bet none of them were close friends or good Samaritans."

"Try women and children, when their husbands couldn't pay their debts to Uriah. Try to guess how many I've orphaned when I murdered their Ma and Pa, then kidnapped them to work off their parents' debts as Nightshades, where the only way out is through death." Draven's voice went brittle, eyes gleaming under the moonlight. He pushed himself off the tree trunk and turned his back on me, facing the creek.

My soul wept for his.

I didn't mean to belittle his pain or compare, but Moses was inscribed in my memory. I thought about what he said, how Draven's father had supplied the Nightshades but died in a mysterious car wreck with his wife after the crop's yield wasn't enough.

Did Draven know the same thing had happened to him, and was it killing him slowly, knowing he'd once continued the cycle?

"I-I'm sorry," I rasped, then cleared my throat. "But... you can't possibly expect me to believe that you're handling Moses' death this easily."

"I love ya, Briar. A ton. But... sometimes I hate you too, for what ya did even though it was beyond your control," Draven responded in a low, gravelly tone.

I didn't quite hear him at first. Or rather... my brain processed his words before my ears did, because his figure distorted in the wash of my tears before it actually hit me.

"But that's somethin' I gotta work on. It ain't easy, but I ain't tryin' to be a hypocrite. Whether we met or not, it wasn't gonna change Uriah's plans," he added in a clearer voice.

I sank into a crouch, placing my hands over my head. *This conversation isn't happening.*

"Everybody's got some darkness in them. It's just a matter of what shade of black it is," he added, and faced me once again. "I've seen people with much darker souls than yours." He crouched in front of me, cradled my face, and planted a tender kiss.

I watched him amble away in silence. Instead of following, I moved to the edge of the creek, my thoughts drowning out its serenity until morning.

✳

Caspian was speaking to the others with clarity when I returned. His hands and face were free of burns.

If only there were smiles, relief, or laughter among them.

"What do you mean 'wait until nightfall'? It's been a week!

Mundus Novus is probably already here now," Caspian exclaimed. "We need to get off this island before everything hits the fan with them, *and* the Nightshades."

I raised my eyebrows, surprised to hear his voice at a volume above mumbling.

"And goin' out there on a bright and sunny day lookin' for Samara would just land ya right back here for *another* week of healin', man." Draven flicked Caspian's forehead. "Did your brain cells get fried too?"

Caspian fell silent, tilting his head with a restrained, simmering exhale.

"We don't have *time*."

"What good is killing yourself if they're already here?" I cut in, leaning against the wall. "Honestly, White Fang and the Nightshades are bigger problems than Mundus Novus right now." I crossed my arms and ankles, and Caspian's shoulders sank. He ran his hand through his iridescent hair, littered with dirt and leaves, and sighed.

"Who knows, it was probably gonna take us a week to find them anyway," Draven said in a gentler tone.

"I vote we go now, because my ankle is killing me," Vivian said, disregarding everything that unfolded. She sat up, smacking her dry lips and rubbing her head.

"You really don't care about anyone but yourself, huh?" I sneered.

"Maybe, but the apple doesn't fall far from the tree, now does it, sweetheart?" she spat.

"Shut up! Jesus," Draven barked, pinching the bridge of his nose. I wished I could just be quiet whenever Vivian opened her mouth. I was a giant red button she kept slamming her fist on and I had no choice but to react.

"Um... I-I think we should wait," Astoria's voice squeaked, as if she were afraid to trigger another squabble. She raised her eyebrows and stretched her lips in an apologetic grimace as she looked to Caspian. "I don't want you to get hurt again."

Caspian whipped his head in her direction, but his face softened. His shoulders rounded forward with dejection, and he sank back to the ground with a sigh. The corner of my mouth subtly tugged upward.

*

The stars didn't come back that night. Only a small break in the clouds exposed a sliver of the moon, but it provided virtually no light in the forest. Astoria clung to Caspian's arm for guidance while Draven carried my mother. To my family, it was a void of disembodied sounds, but for us Vampyres... it was no different from what it looked like during the day.

No one spoke—not even Vivian, who occasionally grunted when her ankle smacked a bush or a tree trunk. I walked with a frigid hand tucked under my armpit and the other pinching my nose. I tried to hold my breath for as much as I could. I knew it was an unrealistic attempt to suppress the cravings, but after living off animal blood for a week, I went from worrying about the current situation to obsessing over how my human family would taste. The same voice that told me to drink from Moses rang in my ears. I slowed my pace, lingering behind the group while my stomach folded in on itself. They'd only taken three more steps before Draven instantly turned to check on me.

"What's wrong?" he called.

"Nothing…" I didn't want to say it in front of Astoria and Vivian. I especially didn't want my sister to start fearing me any more than she probably did. Draven paused, once again scanning me from head to toe. He gave a subtle nod.

"Don't hang back too far," he said, then continued leading the group forward. I sighed, relieved that I didn't have to explain.

My fangs pricked my inner lip as they lengthened, and despite half of me resisting, the other half picked up the pace and stretched a hand toward Astoria's arm—

"This is it, this has to be," Draven said with conviction, sniffing the air. My hand flinched back, and I clutched my wrist with a curse under my breath.

"What is it?" I asked. The thick, untamed grass and thickets in the forest had thinned out. A dirt path with old tire marks carved into it had appeared. Draven turned to us with a rare, dimpled smile.

"This is the road that takes us to Samara's."

5

BRIAR

The dirt path wove through the trees and every time I thought the cabin would appear around the bend, there were more trees. I consistently tripped over rocks, and the faint aroma of my human counterparts magnified as if I walked into a restaurant. It was all I could focus on.

Just keep staying back, Briar. If you get too close, you'll kill them. Control. You can control yourself.

You need to eat to be able to do that.

No, I don't!

Yes, you do! Go for your mother first, you'd be doing your sister and everyone else a favor.

A sharp pain sliced through my forehead and I fell to my knees. I gripped my head tightly, groaning as I doubled over.

"Briar!" Draven shouted.

"What's that girl's problem *now*?" Vivian grumbled.

"Bri?" Astoria's light footsteps pattered in my direction beside Draven's heavy ones.

"*STAY BACK!*" I roared, and the crows flew out of the trees.

"Briar..." Draven whispered, and his voice sounded closer. With my palms still crushing my temples, I sat up to see him kneeling in front of me. A girl with ivory skin and waist-length sable hair stood behind him, and Caspian eyed me with lethal calm near Vivian.

"Look at me, and *breathe*," Draven demanded. I kept staring at the girl behind him.

"Bri?" The girl squeaked, reaching for her necklace. I bared my fangs, drool running down my chin as I snarled.

"Briar!" Draven shook me violently as he growled, "*Look at me!*"

I jerked my attention to him and observed his blood-moon eyes, the bold, furrowed eyebrows, and the curves of his sharp cheekbones and lips. This was the face of the man who'd introduced me to his world, who protected me, who became my only friend, and now...

I blinked, realizing the girl standing behind him was my own sister, and I hadn't recognized her. Astoria ran back to Caspian's side, eyes wide with horror.

"Breathe," Draven pleaded, and cradled my face. I inhaled deeply through my nose, and exhaled quivering breaths through parted lips. Tears welled as he pulled me against his chest, and I broke down. The headache dulled, but never left.

"Guys, someone is here," Caspian warned. He kept his tone low—muffled for Vivian and Astoria, but coherent for us. I wiped my face while Draven jumped to his feet and scanned our surroundings. Whoever it was must've been a Vampyre, able to roam without a flashlight.

Draven and Caspian elongated their claws and bent their knees in unison, ready to battle whoever dared cross our path. The mysterious footsteps padded gracefully, then stopped fifty feet from us.

"I thought I recognized the yelling," Samara droned with a tilted head and a hand on her hip. "I didn't think you'd need more help *this* soon and with... *more* people."

"Please... please help us!" Vivian cried out. I rolled my eyes at her dramatic tone, then stood from the ground and dusted off my jeans.

"Shh! If I help you guys, you need to be quiet. I don't want to have to deal with Malachi and Azha yet. They're sleeping," Samara warned. She jerked her chin, gesturing us to follow. Draven hoisted Vivian in his arms, and I continued to linger behind the group for fear of another incident.

I wasn't sure how much longer I could last without real blood. I really hoped Samara had some pouches to spare.

The clearing was serene, illuminated only by a single sconce at the front door. Their ivory driveway connected to our path, leading to a three-car garage. The windows were grey with slumber. Trimmed boxwood hedges lined the wraparound porch. While the forest prepared for oncoming autumn, evergreen trees surrounded the property, freezing it in time.

The last time we were here, I was in a coma, and when we left I never bothered to observe how beautiful and cozy the cabin was.

As we entered the foyer, I took in the interior. An antler chandelier hovered over a mahogany dining table bedecked in maple garlands. There wasn't a single dish in the kitchen sink. Once my eyes landed on the stainless steel refrigerator, I ignored everything else. I crossed my arms over my stomach when it contracted at the thought of the blood bags inside.

"For the time being, you guys need to share one bedroom," Samara whispered once she stopped at the bottom of a sweeping staircase.

"Can you help her?" Astoria muttered, pointing at Vivian's leg.

Samara checked her ankle, now black and purple. The swelling had grown until the bulging bone was barely noticeable. Her nose crinkled at the ghastly sight.

"No, but my brother can. I-I'll see if I can wake him up without disturbing Azha." Samara sighed before she ascended the stairs. We followed her, taking each step as carefully as possible. The stairs were sound enough not to creak. Samara pointed at a door down the hall before splitting off in the opposite direction. Draven led the rest of the way and eased Vivian onto the bed while the rest of us stood around the bedroom in a circle.

"I don't think they're gonna help us," he murmured. "Samara offered help, sure, but…"

"You threatened them." I finished his sentence matter-of-factly.

He groaned and sat at the edge of the bed, pinching the bridge of his nose. Caspian observed his friend and swayed his head with dissatisfaction. Astoria's lips parted, an inaudible question hanging from her mouth. I held my palm up and briefly shuttered my eyes.

"I'll tell you some other time," I said, and sank to the floor. The carpet was rough and thin, yet somehow still more comfortable than the cave. It was nice to feel heat instead of the brisk bite of the wind.

I might've been naturally cold as a Vampyre, but that didn't mean I enjoyed it. My frozen cheeks and fingertips tingled as they thawed.

"How long is it going to take?" Vivian griped.

"I wouldn't rush it. He might have to cut it off," I gibed.

"Let's keep the family drama out of it while we're here, yeah?" Caspian finally said, with a tone of steel. I scoffed at his judgmental squinting. Was I the only one who saw Vivian as a problem?

Honestly, it benefited us that she couldn't walk. She couldn't be trusted otherwise.

Samara returned with Malachi, who yawned and rubbed his dark brown eyes as he entered. He flicked the light switch, and we collectively hissed at the drastic change. He shut the door, scanning the room of five guests with his hands braced on his hips.

"Nice seeing you again Briar. Is—um—everything okay?" His forehead creased with an uncomfortable smile. I could sense that he was trying to be kind, but he probably wanted to send us right back to the woods.

"Our mom got hurt. Do you think you could help her?" Astoria cut in. She watched me warily, as if she worried I'd say the wrong thing. I rolled my eyes and leaned against the desk leg. Malachi drifted to the bed and barely touched Vivian's ankle before she yelped.

"*Shh!*" we hissed in unison.

"It's definitely broken. And bad." Malachi rubbed the back of his neck. "I need supplies to do surgery."

"I'm sorry, *what*?" Vivian held out her hand to keep Malachi from getting any closer.

We would be better off leaving her at the hospital and letting them report her to the police.

"I need a splint, scalpel, sutures..." Malachi's list kept growing and Draven flopped his head backward, his Adam's apple threatening to escape as he quietly sighed.

The circumstances consumed him, but he'd never admit it.

"Alright, so... I'm gonna need that in writing." Draven scratched his head with a slight tremble woven in his chuckle.

"Don't worry about it. I'll go." Astoria went for the door and I gripped her wrist mid-stride.

"You're not going anywhere by yourself, okay." I commanded firmly.

"Then come with me," she said. I let her go and she withdrew her hands to her back pockets. "I'm the only one who knows what to look for. Nursing school, remember?"

"I don't think that's a good idea," Caspian warned, and shot yet another wary look in my direction. I wanted to be offended, but he was right.

"I shouldn't..."

"I *want* you to. There's stuff I wanna to talk to you about alone. I trust you enough that you won't hurt me." Astoria's hand stopped halfway toward her gold chain, and instead she tilted her chin upward with conviction.

"I could tag along," Caspian said. "You two wouldn't even notice me."

"Not this time, Cass. I know my sister," Astoria insisted, and gave him a reassuring grin, but his rigid stance didn't loosen. I waited for Draven's reaction. He opened his mouth to speak at first, but not a sound escaped.

Was he deciding if he could trust me?

Was he deciding how to insist coming along, which would also show he *didn't* trust me?

Did I even trust *myself*?

"Actually, Ria... maybe next time. I really think you and Caspian should go instead," I said, twirling a finger around my boot laces. I didn't want to hear Draven's decision, even as he drew a breath to finally speak. I already knew he wouldn't stand for it.

I lowered my gaze when the light in Astoria's eyes dimmed.

Caspian turned to Malachi. "Do you have a car we can use? I'll go with her."

"Yeah, the keys are downstairs," Malachi said. "There's a medical supply store not far from here."

Astoria vanished beyond the doorway, head hanging low. "You're stronger than you think, Bri..." she mumbled under her breath in the hallway.

I almost confused her naivety for optimism.

6

STERLING

DR. NOLAN WAS ON VACATION THROUGH THE WEEKEND, BUT that didn't stop the nurses from continuing the relentless cycle of suppression pills and blood, or my regurgitating behind their backs.

I desperately needed a change of scenery from this bland white room. I sat across the room with my back toward the window, carving stick figures into the vinyl tile with my claws.

I thought about Briar, what she was doing, and if Draven had her under control. Had it been the fledgling side of her acting out, or a result of the animosity she harbored from all our arguing? A part of me wanted to deliver pain back to her tenfold, but another part wanted to believe she wasn't in her right mind when she destroyed my life.

"Mr. Shaw, you have a visitor," one of the nurses announced on the intercom. The sudden voice startled me and something twisted—no, *fluttered*—in my chest. I peeped over my shoulder and groaned under my breath. A human officer stood with the stature of a linebacker next to the nurse. His presence overshadowed the woman beside him. From where I sat, I could see his tiny badge numbers. I sighed at the abnormality of my capabilities and pushed myself from the floor.

"You're here for a statement?" I asked, raising my voice over the rattling chains that followed me as I approached the window.

"Yes. I'm Officer Adam Odaire," he said, and although at first glance it seemed we were holding eye contact, I noticed the microscopic movements of his irises as he determined my threat level, as we were trained to do in the Academy.

"We'll be taking you back to the Resilience Room," the nurse announced, and came into the cell with her key to unlock the shackles at my ankle. I watched her crouch at my feet and thought about how I could've easily snapped her neck and bolted through the door. I could've taken that cop, because we shared the same knowledge—plus I had my newfound strength.

I shook my head, suppressing the impulsive thoughts. The nurse straightened, placing silver handcuffs over my wrists. I bit my inner cheek with a wince and followed her down the hall. Officer Odaire trailed closely behind the two of us. I turned my head slightly, sneaking a sidelong glimpse at him. My skin crawled.

We returned to the room I was in before, where I'd stared at myself in the two-way mirror, fighting the urge to devour the plate of raw steak in front of me. I'd likened it to an interrogation room, but I didn't realize it had an actual name. They couldn't have come up with something better than that?

"This is official police business, so I'd like for no one to be monitoring our meeting," Officer Odaire said.

"Of course, sir. I'll notify the staff. Take however long you need and press that red button to get one of us." The nurse pointed at a square red button next to the door. I took note of it as she guided me to the table and switched my cuffs to the ones linked to a loop bolted in the table.

I sat, scratching at my burning skin. "Can we hurry this up?"

"Yes, I need to get back to the precinct as well," Officer Odaire said as he sat across from me.

"Let's start with the beginning." He clasped his calloused, hairy hands together, knuckles cracking. I inhaled loudly.

"Well, my sister was missing and I started a personal investigation, which led me to a crime syndicate known as White Fang. I was with Detective Hart meeting with a dealer when..." My voice trailed off when I noticed he wasn't taking notes.

I frowned. "Why aren't you writing anything down?"

"Because your statement is irrelevant." Officer Odaire rose from his seat and crept around the table. I watched him through the mirror before he shoved my head forward. My nose slammed into the stainless steel, sending a shock wave of knives through my skull. He jerked my neck back in a tight headlock.

My hands instinctively shot up, but the handcuffs stopped them from reaching his forearm. I wheezed.

"Dull fangs... not embracing your new species, I take it." Officer Odaire's voice was strained while I continued to resist. "It's a shame. Your downfall, that is. Chief was so proud of you for the longest time."

I tugged at the chain, feeling as if the silver handcuffs would cut right through my bones—until the loop on the table snapped. I jumped, throwing us both back against the wall. He grunted and I pulled at his forearm enough to tuck my chin. I flipped him over my shoulder and flung him into the table. Officer Odaire whipped out his silver pepper spray. I dropped to the floor, swiping my leg at his ankles before he could deploy it.

"Did Chief Duncan send you here?" I shouted breathlessly. "Security!"

Officer Odaire arced to his feet in a kip-up and wiped blood from his nose with a maniacal grin. He cracked his knuckles before raising his fists in a Southpaw stance. I narrowed my eyes and mirrored him. I sent the first strike. He countered with a block and a right hook. I ducked and jabbed him in the stomach. Officer Odaire doubled over, and I ran to the door to slam my palm on the red button.

"*Somebody!*" I screamed, banging on the door. He darted across the Resilience Room and I caught his arm mid-swing, twisting before his knuckles connected with my jaw. He cried out, and I rammed my fist into his temple again and again until he crumpled to the floor unconscious. I slumped against the wall as security guards flooded inside. My bottom lip trembled at the sight of blood smeared on my knuckles. The color was mesmerizing.

"What's going on here?" one of the security officers demanded while the other knocked me against the wall and forced my hands behind my back.

"Whoa, whoa, hey! He attacked *me*!" I shouted, trying to wriggle out of the guard's grasp.

"Yeah, we'll see when we roll the cameras," he growled.

"Yeah, you will." I rolled my eyes, and let him drag me back to my room.

I replayed the fight in my head—how carelessly I'd defended myself. Had it really been that long since I participated in trained combat, or was becoming a Vampyre throwing me off? Did Chief Duncan send him to kill me, or was he one of the corrupted human officers that worked with the syndicates?

We passed my room entirely and stopped in front of a solid metal door with a narrow rectangle big enough for a pair of eyes to peer through. I surveyed the small sliding cover over it, and immediately recognized it as solitary confinement. Something I *never* dreamed a hospital of having.

The guard opened the door, and the room was the exact width of the door itself.

"Are you serious?" I asked with a soft laugh. The guard's blank face didn't twitch a muscle. "You're punishing me after a dirty cop just tried to kill me?"

"Until we view the footage," he replied, and jerked his chin toward the cell.

I tilted my head back with an exasperated sigh, and moved forward.

※

I wasn't quite sure how long I waited in solitary confinement, but I hissed at the harsh white light flooding inside when the door opened again. The isolation didn't bother me as much as I expected, but that could've been because I was too preoccupied with analyzing previous events to notice. Dr. Nolan stood with her hands on her hips, head tilted in disappointment. I could at least deduce that the weekend was over.

"I'm sorry that happened to you," she said softly. "You understand why we had to put you in here, right?"

"Yeah, yeah." I sat on the edge of the bed and rubbed my eyes, then blinked at her silhouette until she came into focus.

"Do you know why he could fight you so easily?" she asked, tilting her chin upward with a smug grin as if she already knew the answer.

"He had an advantage because I was cuffed to the table," I said as I held out my wrists to be cuffed again. I just wanted to go back to my room and be left alone.

"No, it was because you're weak. You're not feeding like you should. Trained police officer or not, he would've needed to use his weapons to control you if you were in optimal condition." She stepped aside and rambled while security adjusted my cuffs and led me down the hall like a cow headed for slaughter.

"If not for sustenance, can't you see the practicality of Vampyre strength in your line of work?" Dr. Nolan's heels clicking along the tile became louder, more incessant.

"I don't have a career anymore." If I wasn't fired, I was going to hand in my badge and gun anyway. The lack of support during this ordeal was sobering.

"Regardless, you were attacked and you could've easily subdued him," Dr. Nolan mumbled, and a low growl rumbled in my throat. I didn't need a speech on what I should've, could've, or would've done. I had enough of that going on in my mind.

I paused when I saw Lyra standing in front of my room. She

turned, her face twisted in a sneer before it softened when she recognized me. Her fists opened and closed at her sides until I approached, and she inhaled deeply, her shoulders raising like she was about to scream.

"Are you okay?" she asked breathily, as if that was what she had to charge up for. I gave her a dry shrug.

"Just another Tuesday," I said with a soft scoff.

"What happened?" she demanded, shifting her attention between me and Dr. Nolan.

"I thought you already knew since you're conveniently here after it happened," I snarked, and allowed the security guard to pull me into my room. The intercom buzzed as Lyra continued speaking.

"How many times am I gonna have to prove myself to you? Why, of all people, do you think *I'm* out to get you?" Lyra jabbed her thumb at her chest. "Was the two of us getting abducted *together* not enough proof for you?"

I eased into the mild comfort of the thin, springy mattress and leaned against the wall with another shrug.

"You told me someone was coming to get my statement," I said. "It turned out that he didn't stop by for that."

Lyra put her hands on her hips with a wry laugh and stared at a blank spot on the floor.

"I didn't... know... it was... an assassination mission." She stretched each word through ground teeth. I paused for a moment, considering whether or not she was genuine.

"Well, it was. Someone doesn't like how much I know. I'd start with Chief Duncan," I said, examining my bloodstained knuckles, which were no longer split open.

"Why?"

"Remember my files disappearing?" I raised an eyebrow and Lyra sighed, her hands falling slack at her sides.

"Okay, I'll see what I can find out," she said begrudgingly.

"Yeah, and can you find out how to get me out of here sooner?" I added.

Lyra released a soft snicker and shook her head.

I didn't want to accept Dr. Nolan's arbitrary proposition. Even if I ate the meals they gave me and passed whatever tests she had, she would never let me out early and I would be forced to accept this cursed lifestyle.

"I'll see you in a couple days," Lyra promised, and walked away. I hoped she was serious about exploring my suspicions, but I wasn't going to hold my breath.

7
LYRA

The Neoterra Police Department buzzed wildly as a result of the recent riots. The destruction of Black Bay Prison in Helios, the liberated criminals, and the increased frequency of protests had strained our manpower. Most of the officers took initiative to get control of a situation that was rapidly slipping through our fingers. Chief Duncan, however, remained in his office.

I couldn't stop thinking about the woman Sterling recognized from White Fang, how she'd caught him in a vulnerable state at the hospital, and how casually Dr. Nolan spoke to her. Maybe the woman lied about working there, or maybe something a lot more sinister was developing.

I sat at my desk, meaningless reports of thefts sprawled across it. I remembered when Sterling once accused me of telling Chief Duncan about our secret search for Briar. All of his files on the missing humans were taken from his cabinet right before he could find a connection. Of course, I had nothing to do with it. No one in the department really took me serious enough to listen, even if I wanted to tell anybody.

Not after my husband, Kiegan, died three years ago.

In a sense, I was used to being ostracized—my colleagues assuming every judgment I made was biased, and Sterling looking at me with pure disgust because of my species. He wasn't the only human to do that, and among Vampyre citizens, being a cop meant double the hatred. The badge was a symbol of betrayal.

It was Kiegan and me against the world.

Blue before red. That was the mantra the departments had developed when Mundus Novus declared integration among essential personnel due to staff shortages. It was well before my time, and to this day no one knew who pulled the strings in that tower. In a country with no name, we were the first in the world to have a "phantom leader." A perfect strategy to avoid assassinations.

Sterling was paranoid about corruption within the department, but I never saw evidence of it. Then again, up until I helped him with Briar, I'd focused on the Nightshades to avenge my husband.

After seeing his attack at the hospital, I considered the possibility that he wasn't too far off.

And the White Fang doctor appearing in the Transition Wing might've hinted at corruption far beyond the precinct.

My chair squeaked as I leaned back and rubbed my eyes. It was too much to look at and process all at once. Just too... much.

The heavy wooden door with Chief Duncan's name etched in the frosted glass opened, and he took long strides toward the elevator with a red manila folder in his hands. I frowned, having never seen that color in our filing system in the seven years I'd worked here. My eyes swept over the room, taking note of the three cops at their desks, either busily typing reports or answering the phones. They were off the hook, but I had long since unplugged mine so I wouldn't be bothered with them. Then I waited until Chief Duncan's stout, square body and glistening head disappeared behind the elevator doors.

I went straight for his office and—to look pretty for the camera in the corner—leaned into his door with my back blocking the view of the door knob. I knocked, called out for him, and tried it. Of course, he had it locked. I didn't expect anything less.

I pushed away from his door and ambled back to my desk, biting my lip. Across the room was where Sterling used to work, and the empty desk next to his was Cyrene's. They never bothered to fill that position after her murder. Something still needed to be done about her case.

I raced to the rooftop.

I propped a foot over the roof's ledge and leaned over my knee, peering down at the precinct's front door. I surveyed the perimeter below, looking for Chief Duncan's outrageously expensive sports car in his reserved parking spot. To my relief, it was still there, and I examined the top of every head that went in and out of the building until I recognized Chief Duncan's scant hair heading for his vehicle. He backed out of the space, and I rushed to the edge of the roof that faced the main street. I took note of his blinker flashing while he waited for clearance to turn left, and jumped to the next roof in that direction. I tucked my braid in my coat so it wouldn't whip around my face while I tracked him.

The tightly packed buildings washed in neon blue and teal transitioned to fuchsia and crimson as Chief Duncan drove further north, toward the Nocturne District. Live pop music playing in the square was replaced with shouting, laughing, and buzzing blown speakers blaring music at a car show lining along the beach.

I panted at the top of a hotel building, watching Chief Duncan's car weave through the metered parking lots behind the boardwalk. I waited for him to find a spot, then jumped from the hotel roof and trekked across the busy street to trail him.

The Nocturne District was condemned. Very few highly trained officers were selected to work these streets, and even then it was mostly during the day to make sure none of the Nocturne Vampyres broke curfew to hurt Sun Dwellers. For Chief Duncan to take the trip out there during work hours was beyond me.

Music bounced, engines revved. Farther down the beach, another crowd was being entertained by drivers burning donuts into the shore while a third hung around a bonfire with empty beer cans strewn across the sand. My eyes darted everywhere, catching details of faces until they all blurred together.

I wove through the crowd until Chief Duncan stopped in front of a distinguished man in a black suit with a peppered beard and a side-part haircut. I pulled my hood over my head and moved closer, near the bonfire. I shifted my gaze to the corner of my eye to note a short cigar in the man's metallic hand, which he lit with a normal, fleshed hand. The chief's face didn't change when he shoved the folder into the man's chest. I crouched, tracing circles in the sand while I eavesdropped.

"Happy?" he demanded.

"Why so moody, Andrew? You're one step closer to seeing her again," the man crooned, and the papers rustled as he opened the file to confirm its contents, his gold watch catching the fire's light.

"I'm putting a lot on the line for this. These are good men and women—" He jabbed his index finger into the folder. "And I hope you uphold your end of the deal."

"Do you realize how much this tips the scale, Andrew? After this blows over, you won't have to worry about your daughter ever again." The man tucked the file under his arm and puffed a ring of smoke. "What I don't understand is… why wouldn't you just let her Turn and then join her?"

"That isn't the kind of life I want for her," Chief Duncan snapped. "How many times do I have to say that?"

"This is the superior life, that's why. Sooner or later, she's going to be on the losing side, and you might not have a choice when she gets caught in the crossfire." He tapped the column of ash into the sand.

I turned to peer at the man in the suit better. He patted Chief Duncan's shoulder before walking toward a limo with purple underlighting, far away from the crowds. I squinted, noticing the nightshade and lion skull tattoo peeking over his collar. I faced the fire again before he caught me staring.

A Nightshade… and by the looks of it, a very high-ranking one.

I tightened my jaw as I glared at the blaze. The group encircling the bonfire passed acid tabs around. I shook my head and stepped away, despite it being my legal obligation to arrest all of them for it. My eyes burned and it became impossible to swallow. The wide open spaces of the beach closed in, as if the air had turned solid.

I didn't feel guilty for looking away, essentially abandoning the oath I took as an officer.

That's all Chief Duncan had done when the Nightshades shot my husband like a dog in the street.

⁕

I called for a cab to take me back to the police department. I leaned against the window, replaying the exchange between Chief Duncan and the mysterious Nightshade. If I was going to test out Sterling's corruption theory... I needed to get up close and personal. I'd considered it for years for my late husband's sake, but never had the real courage to do it. After tonight, it seemed like the only way to find answers.

I twirled my keys around my finger idly, debating on whether or not I should visit Sterling.

I wasn't quite sure why I kept checking on that man. I endured countless ignorant questions, like why would Vampyres bother eating food when only blood provided sustenance. I witnessed him call his own sister a monster when they were reunited, even after he spent weeks worrying about her well-being. In the heat of the moment, I thought Briar was in her own right to turn him into one of us, like some sick poetic justice. I had stood there and watched with only one thought: *Good.*

Maybe it was guilt that drove me.

The parking lot was filled to the brim. When I entered the emergency room lobby, it was occupied with bloodied Vampyric faces, gunshot wounds, broken limbs, and shrill wailing. Doctors and nurses alike were rushing to reset injuries before they healed incorrectly. For once, the usual monotoned receptionist, Charlene, was standing on her feet and tending to the patients frantically attempting to check in.

I flashed my badge at the security guards without looking at them and skipped their screening. My mouth hung open at the chaos.

"What *happened*?" I asked an adolescent who appeared unharmed, potentially there for a different reason. Her leg bounced as she scrolled through her phone, and she flinched when I approached.

"A group of Sun Dwellers… th-they… they started shooting up bars and restaurants all along Diamond Street. My mom's a bartender. They called themselves the Skinwalkers."

My heart ripped in two. I had to observe the room again, seeing each victim anew. The noncritical gunshot wounds weren't healing.

Silver bullets.

The civilians must've armed themselves when the news about Helios got out, and I was willing to bet Mundus Novus didn't plan to deploy Onyx Sentries to Neoterra while the roles were flipped.

"Is she okay?" I raised my eyebrows, sinking in the seat next to her. The girl sniffled with a quivering breath.

"I don't know, she's in surgery," she whimpered. "My dad is on his way." I grabbed a tissue from the end table next to me and handed it to her when she fell into a fit of sobs.

"I'm so sorry…" I placed a tender hand on her shoulder. "Do you want me to stay with you until he gets here?" The girl's eyes slid to my badge and she shook her head.

"No, it's okay. He's almost here, thanks," she said, and balled the tissue in her hands. I rose from the seat with a deep inhale, returning my wallet to my back pocket.

Something needed to be done. *Yesterday.*

I rushed to the Transition Wing, knowing I shouldn't—*couldn't*—tell Sterling the state of the world... but I could at least tell him my plans.

Sterling wasn't allowed human visitors. In all honesty, he wasn't allowed *any*. My badge granted a lot of privileges. Dr. Nolan wasn't at work today, so a nurse escorted me to Sterling's room. The wide window displayed him like a zoo exhibit. He slouched against the wall, his shackled legs dangling over the side of his bed and eyes fixed on the tray of blood in the middle of the room. I sighed, knowing it was probably hollowing him out to resist it. As a Vampyre-born, I couldn't imagine how exhausting it must be.

"How are you? I know it's only been a week, but—"

"What do you think? Why are you even here?" Sterling's response was brash, but at this point, my feathers couldn't get ruffled. I didn't expect anything more from him.

"I came to tell you I'm going to investigate your suspicions with the department." I spoke in a bland tone, now regretting my visit. His knitted eyebrows separated and raised. He finally tore his attention from the tray and moved closer to the window, the chain clinking as it trailed behind him.

"What are you talking about?" Sterling scratched his head, as if he couldn't remember what he was suspicious about in the first place. I got as close to the window as possible without leaving any marks and dropped my voice to a whisper.

"I think you might be right about something going on within the department. Between my husband's death and... other things... I'm going undercover and joining the Nightshades clan."

8
CASPIAN

Astoria kept her focus glued outside the passenger window while I carefully drove over the dirt path to avoid branches and boulders. The radio was off, and I initially cracked the windows for white noise to fill the silence. I imagined she didn't have much to say to me, seeing as how I'd thwarted her chance to bond with her sister. I occasionally stole a glance whenever the guilt weighed heavily in my gut, and noticed the hair on her arms standing. I rolled the windows up and she rubbed her arms with a sigh of relief. All she had to do was say something.

"I'm sorry," I mumbled. "I had to."

Was I being too hard on Briar?

"It's fine, I understand," Astoria said, balling her hands inside the hem of her shirt. "I just wish you guys gave Briar the chance to actually try to get stronger."

"Did you forget what she almost did to you before Samara found us?" I tilted my head with a frown.

"Keyword—*almost*."

I rolled my eyes and tightened my grip on the steering wheel, heaving hot air through my nostrils.

"Briar didn't recognize you. What if Draven wasn't there to snap her out of it? What if I didn't get to you in time, because I was a foot too far? What if she was here driving, and she veered off the road and attacked you because she couldn't take it anymore?" All the possible scenarios of what could happen flashed through my mind like strobe lights.

She shrugged. "Okay, then I'd have to learn to live with it. I'm the only human left in my family other than Mom anyways."

I chortled, leaning my head back. She still hoped for her sister. There was a reason why Mundus Novus kept us separated, and Briar proved them right.

"Your chance of surviving a fledgling's attack is next to impossible," I said. Astoria grew silent for a moment, and I wasn't sure if she wanted to end the conversation or if she was thinking of a snide response.

"How do you guys expect Briar to show more restraint if you're always smothering her?" she asked. "She doesn't have a choice, she's not in a controlled environment like Sterling. She doesn't get pills for her cravings or blood handed to her."

"I'm Vampyre-born," I said with a soft sigh. I didn't even know what went on during the Transition or Restraint or whatever program it was called these days.

"Yeah, it shows," Astoria grumbled, and propped her elbow on the door with her lips buried in her palm, as if she were holding back more venom.

"If it was that effective, why doesn't she just go check herself into a program?" One thing I knew for sure—the medical bill was always waived, regardless of whether the patient had insurance. Money couldn't have been a factor, and if it was... Draven could've covered it. *I* could've.

"Gee, I don't know, maybe she didn't want to be held in captivity by the hospital after she just spent weeks as a prisoner of Vampyre gangs?" Astoria snarked.

I couldn't respond.

The woods yawned into a paved two-lane street lined with untamed strips of grass and pine trees. It sloped into a graceful hill, and at its peak, the coastal city of Helios came into full view. Smoke pillars trailed to the heavens across the city, primarily in the downtown area. The largest pillar came from the leveled Black Bay Prison site, where the building still smoldered. Helicopters passed the city with spotlights sweeping over the island below, perhaps searching for the inmates that were now roaming free.

I pulled over at the hill's downward slope, and stepped out of the car to gape at the effects of the earlier mayhem.

"I think we need to turn back." I'd barely finished my sentence before Astoria stood from the passenger seat and pointed below the hill.

"Look, the pharmacy is *right there*." She jabbed her finger at the half-lit sign barely hanging on a thread. "My mom still needs that stuff and it looks calm and empty on this side anyways."

"Yeah, empty because they already pillaged it. We could go there, risk our lives with the Nightshades, White Fang, or Mundus Novus just for nothing to be in there." I pinched the bridge of my nose. I was beginning to think Briar wasn't wrong about their mother's presence bringing us closer to danger.

"That's my Mom, Cass." She tore her attention from the pharmacy, eyes gleaming while her brows furrowed. I drummed my fingertips over the car's hood, contemplating. My mother died during childbirth. I didn't have an attachment to my father. Whatever bond Astoria had with her mom was yet another thing I could never understand.

"Fine," I grumbled, and sank back in the driver's seat. I spent the rest of the short trip trying to swallow the knot in my throat.

"We get in and get out," I said firmly, and left the car running while Astoria dashed inside. I followed behind her, checking every angle outside the store to make sure no one was around. The windows were completely shattered, and neither of us bothered to take the door inside. We stepped over the windowsill, glass crunching beneath our shoes. I pulled one of the pistols I'd brought from Neoterra out of my inner waistband holster and crouched behind one of the shelves in the front while Astoria scrambled to find the supplies. The rustling of cardboard boxes and bags and the rattling of pill bottles made my skin crawl.

"*Shh!*" I snapped, and Astoria scoffed, slowing down the rate at which she tore through what little the pharmacy had. The noise only died a little, and I knew it was impossible to completely silence it. I continued to keep my eyes on the gravel parking lot across the vandalized street, and squinted as I tried to filter her shuffling from the outside noises.

A rumbling engine came to a squealing stop next to the building, and without warning, I flashed to Astoria's side and covered her mouth, then pulled her to the floor behind the front counter. She hugged a bright red, first-aid duffel bag close to her chest, violently trembling against me.

I worried they could smell her fear as easily as I could.

"Today's been wild, man. Those Nightshades are unhinged. I could've sworn their Alpha wasn't gonna sanction that Black Bay raid," a nasally voice drawled.

"No, Uriah's been going rogue lately... ever since those two subjects escaped," a woman responded in a deadpan tone. "Doc told him to hold off until she made more serums but... obviously that didn't get through to him."

"True. Hey, didn't Cyrus say to meet here since the Sentries already checked this area?"

"Yeah he did, he probably got caught up."

Neither voice sounded familiar, but the mention of Cyrus clanged through my skull and jolted my bones.

Their footsteps rounded the building, kicking a few glass shards across the concrete.

"Oooh, what do we have here? A running car..."

The lights were dead toward the back of the pharmacy. The exit sign was greyed out, and I wondered if the alarm would still blare if the door opened. Draven and I had had some run-ins with backup systems, during quick getaways.

"You don't smell that?" a third baritone voice cut in after taking a deep, euphoric inhale. "There's a Sun Dweller and another Vampyre around here."

"We all smell like Sun Dwellers and Vampyres after the mess we been in today," the woman droned.

"Nuh-uh—not like this…" the third voice insisted, and then the glass shifted again. I lowered my hand from Astoria's mouth and pointed at the door.

"*No,*" she mouthed, eyes bulging.

"Come on out, you slippery little snakes," the third voice crooned, followed by the *shink* of his claws opening.

"*Go,*" I mouthed back at her, fangs growing. There were three of them. I could easily keep them occupied while she got away. I raised the pistol, my finger resting over the trigger guard.

Before Astoria could launch from the floor, the man rounded the corner and snarled in my direction.

"You ain't gonna believe this, guys. It's Caspian Bishop and that Shaw girl's sister!"

I swung my arm in front of Astoria and growled at him. The other man flanked the other side of the counter and the woman jumped on top of it, directly above us.

"Rumor has it you killed Wraith's brother," she said. "Is it true?"

I shoved Astoria forward with my forearm and pulled the trigger. The woman jolted off the counter, smoke radiating from her unrecognizable face. The two men roared, one of them lunging at me. He jerked my wrist and the gun went off. I let the pistol fall from my hand and swiftly caught it with the other, then shot him in his abdomen.

Tires squealed outside and I vaulted over the counter, flashing outside.

I scanned the storefronts, eyes darting for any sign of Astoria hiding.

A vehicle sped down the street, carrying her desperate cries with it.

"Astoria!" I shouted after her muffled screams. I kept running, each step slamming into the concrete harder than the last. I couldn't accept taking out two of the three White Fangs and *still* losing her.

Headlights blinded my peripheral vision. My kneecaps burst, and my temple cracked against a windshield.

9
DRAVEN

Briar paced across the bedroom while Astoria and Caspian were gone. She ignored all of our requests to sit down.

Maybe I should've gone with them.

"Briar... I trust Caspian with my life. He ain't gonna let anything happen to Astoria," I said. "I've seen that guy take out ten Vampyres—alone—when he was *eleven*. Imagine now, after all these years?" I kept my voice low, still remembering that Azha was asleep. If I had to explain everything to another person, I would genuinely lose it.

Briar paused for a moment, staring at a blank spot on the floor. She shook her head, crossing her arms and continuing to pace. I sighed.

"You're making me nauseous," Vivian chided.

"Good," Briar snipped.

I sifted through Caspian's duffel bag from Neoterra until I found a pistol, then checked its chamber and magazine before unloading it.

"Hey." I caught Briar's hand in the middle of her hundredth pace and tugged her toward me. "Let me show ya how to use a gun while we wait for them to get back."

Briar nodded with a sigh, and I urged her to come closer with a jerk of my chin.

"Sterling hasn't taught you girls how to use one?" Vivian cut in behind us.

"He's our brother, not our dad, who got killed looking for you while you were getting high," Briar fumed, without looking back at her mother.

I shushed them curtly, and held up the pistol with the barrel pointed downward. "I need ya to focus. Don't let her keep pushing your buttons. So, always check to see if it's loaded like this..."

I went through the motions to explain safety and show her the basics, explaining how to unload, reload, and shoot. Briar caught on fast—I wished I could help her practice outside. If only it weren't so late.

And if Malachi's wife didn't hate us so much.

Rapid footsteps pounded up the staircase. I braced for Azha, but instead was greeted by Samara extending her phone toward my face. I took a step back and squinted at the text message from an unknown number.

Astoria was taken by White Fang. Tell the others. Here's my location.

"*What?*" Briar gasped and snatched the phone. She held it closer to her face, as if the message would change.

"What is it?" Vivian drawled. "Are they back yet with the stuff for my ankle?"

The phone quietly popped as Briar squeezed it, and Samara yanked it back before she could crush it. Briar huffed through clenched teeth. She grabbed the duffel bag and hurled it at her mother, who cried out when it thumped against her broken ankle.

"THIS IS YOUR FAULT!" Briar snarled, extending her claws. She jerked forward, but I clasped her arm tightly. "SHE'S GONE, ALL BECAUSE OF YOUR STUPID—GOD, YOU SELFISH, MANIPULATIVE PIECE OF SHI—"

"How was I supposed to know they were going to get in trouble during a simple pharmacy run?" Vivian squealed with a pained grimace. Briar tugged away from my grip like a rabid dog, swinging her free arm toward Vivian.

I dug my claws into her shoulder and shoved her farther away from the bed, then stepped between them.

"Briar, calm down!" I bellowed, just as Azha stormed inside. Briar gripped her shoulder, gaping at me as blood soaked through her sleeve. I knew she'd heal, but my gut twisted at the brief pain I'd caused her. But it was the only way to stop her blinding rage.

"You said he'd protect her!" Briar rasped. "You said he wouldn't let anything happen to her!"

"What are y'all doing back in my house, waking me up at this hour?" Azha demanded, snatching the scarf from her head and stuffing it in her robe's pocket.

"Shut the hell up! *Everybody!*" I roared. I shut my eyes with a sharp inhale, then turned to Briar.

"Odds are they were outnumbered. Caspian left us his location. We can track it and help him get your sister back," I said, then turned to Azha and Malachi. "I need y'all to just take this woman to the hospital, and let them deal with her. She's caused too many issues."

"Um, excuse me? I had nothing to do with Astoria getting taken away!" Vivian yelled. "Don't you dare send me back there. They'll ship me off as soon as I get a cast!"

Briar scowled. "That's where you belong."

"And that's where you'll stay. I can't babysit everybody," I grumbled, repacking the duffel bag. I reloaded the gun and passed it to Briar with a holster that could fit in her waistband, and loaded a rifle for myself since Caspian probably had the other pistol.

"Babysit, huh?" Briar sneered. "I'll wait downstairs."

"Who do you think you are, calling shots around here?" Azha demanded.

I gathered the bag and rifle, then charged toward her with my chest puffed. I dropped my voice to a low, threatening growl. "Read the room. Ya want us outta here? Start with Vivian. Tell them she was a fugitive runnin' through the woods and knocked at ya door." I clipped my shoulder against hers as I walked past and ignored the scoff she released after, rushing down the stairs to meet with Briar at the front door.

"Guys, wait." Samara jogged to us, her keys ringing. "Take my car, and here's some blood pouches. If you're going after them, you'll need your strength."

"Are you serious?" Briar's eyes brightened. "Why?"

"Astoria's a sweet girl. I want to help any way I can," she said, then gasped when Briar pulled her into a tight embrace.

"Thank you... thank you so much." Briar's whisper turned to static as her voice cracked. She released Samara, then burst out the front door to wait by the SUV. I nodded, and Samara dipped her head in acknowledgment.

Briar tossed me the keys and we piled into the car. The second her door shut, I floored it and we shot into the dark.

※

I sped over potholes and swerved around boulders until the road transitioned to asphalt, and the wall of trees flanking the sides of the road became buildings. Briar clasped the ceiling's assist grip, leaning at the edge of her seat.

"Jeez, man, you're gonna crash Samara's car driving like this!"

"Do ya wanna save your sister or play it safe and go the speed limit?" I snapped. Briar sank back in her seat and dragged her palms against her cheeks before finally opening a blood pouch.

"We need cellphones. Disposable ones at least, since they have immediate service. Ain't no use having Caspian's location and havin' no idea how to get there," I said more gently, and loosened my grip around the steering wheel. She opened another pouch and passed it to me.

I took the first sip, only to spray out the most bitter, acidic, sour blood I'd ever tasted in my immortal life across the dash.

"Draven!" Briar gasped, flinching against the window. "What's wrong?"

"Oh my god, that's disgusting. What the hell is that? *Expired?*

How'd ya drink yours?" I grimaced, wiping my mouth with my forearm.

"Um, it didn't taste any different..." She reached for mine and tasted it, then shook her head with a shrug. "You're tripping, babe. Try some more," she offered, and held it up. I leaned away.

"Nah, I'm good. I can't trust a fledgling's taste preferences," I said with a light laugh. Briar rolled her eyes and drank the rest.

We finally drove past the pharmacy, where the damage was so extensive I couldn't tell if it was a product of Caspian's combat or the earlier riots. We continued down the road with the headlights off and the windows rolled down. Briny, smoky air mixed with the smell of strawberry shampoo, musk, and sweat flowed through the vehicle's cabin.

"I think I can smell them," Briar said.

"Yeah, me too," I said.

Crying and shouting rang two blocks over. I swerved into a parallel parking space in front of a row of storefronts then held my finger over my lips, and Briar held her breath.

"Come on," I whispered, and quietly got out of the car.

We crept close to the stores. She stayed right at my heels, occasionally bumping into my back when I abruptly stopped walking to duck behind a corner. Onyx Sentries patrolled the block. I waited until their footsteps faded before peeking around the corner again.

A large, white dome tent was posted behind temporary barbed-wire fence panels. Helicopter blades cut through the air above, carefully descending behind the tent. Some of the Sentries marched the perimeter inside their makeshift camp, while another five monitored twenty to thirty Vampyres shackled together in a single file line. Most of those people didn't even belong to a clan, but they could've been swept up with the riots. I turned to Briar.

"The city looks like it's on lockdown… so we need to hurry, *now*." I said, and tugged her across the street toward a dimly lit convenience store. Metal bars protected the doors and windows.

"Watch our backs," I said, placing my palm over the metal. I closed my eyes, trying to focus on the rage within. It slithered beneath my skin, but my palms remained cold.

"Can you hurry up with whatever you're doing?"

"Can ya let me focus?" I retorted, and the heat caressed my shoulders, crawling down my arms and coming to life in my palms. A low hum followed by cracking prompted me to reopen my eyes. The metal bars glowed red, then bright orange and white, dripping on the ground and instantly turning back to black and grey. The plexiglass warped and melted.

A small smile broke through as I took a quivering deep breath to ease the adrenaline and stepped inside the store to gather the disposable phones and—since I was already there—a pack of cigarettes.

Briar gasped, "Draven!"

"Hey! What are you two doing out here?" A heated male voice.

I jumped from behind the counter, stuffing the phones and my cigarettes in a plastic bag. We froze as a masked Sentry secured his grasp on a rifle and immediately pointed it at us.

"Get on your knees with your hands in the air!" he demanded. I peeked at Briar from the corner of my eye, hoping she could keep up with her newfound abilities. I put the bag between my teeth and calmly crouched, with Briar mirroring the motions.

As the Onyx Sentry marched closer, I launched across the street to Samara's car. Bullets sprayed and Briar ran in a blurry zig-zag, then jumped through the back window on the driver's side. The Sentry whistled, reloaded, and continued to shoot as more of his colleagues approached. I burned rubber down the street while she nimbly climbed into the front seat.

Then a flurry of bullets shattered the back windshield. Briar cried out as we both ducked. A bullet darted past my ear and ricocheted off of the dash. She grunted, bumping into the window. A loud pop, a whoosh of air, and a flapping sound resonated moments before the car developed a mind of its own. We swerved and veered over a curb even as I fought against the steering wheel, and came to a screeching stop just before hitting a light pole.

"Get out!" I shouted, and tracked the oncoming helicopter whipping through the sky. Briar held her arm close to her side as she kicked the door open. As much as I wanted to climb to the roof of a nearby shop, I couldn't leave her behind.

"This way!" I led the way as we cut through alleyways and intersections back to where we'd come from. Briar matched my pace, ignoring the silver gunshot wound in her arm.

I didn't want the Sentries to know what I was capable of. Not so they could research my weaknesses before I'd discovered them myself. The heat rose in the soles of my feet and I worried that I was leaving scorched footprints, but I didn't bother to look back. The helicopter's spotlight found us, and the only hope I had left was the thick canopy of the forest ahead. We'd long since lost the Sentries on foot, but the helicopter was right behind us. I kept my fists clamped as I ran, smothering the fire that was begging to ignite.

Branches slapped me in the face when we broke through the

wall of foliage. The bag ripped, the four phones and cigarettes tumbling out of it. Briar's steps faltered.

"Keep going!" I commanded. I doubled down to retrieve everything then continued to sprint, rapidly catching up with Briar. The helicopter paused at the edge of the forest before turning around and flying back in the direction of the camp. With its rhythmic, cleaving blades fading, we were left with only our sharp pants and our rapid footsteps thundering against the forest floor.

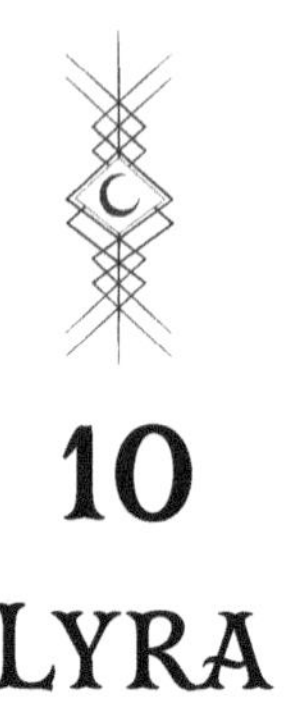

10
LYRA

Sterling's freckled face was blank. He blinked three times before his expression contorted into confusion.

"You're going to... what?" he asked in dismay.

"I'm going to join—"

"No, I *heard* you. Do you have any idea how stupid you sound?" He exclaimed.

"Excuse me?" I scoffed, and narrowed my eyes. Sterling mirrored me, shrugging his shoulders as if expecting a legitimate response.

"How else would I get close enough to get more intel?"

"What do you hope to gain? What would you even do with the information? You realize that you'd have to get a tattoo of their crest, right? And you can't just *leave.*" Sterling dropped his volume, but still spoke briskly as he counted off each point with a finger. I observed him, ignoring the rest of the questions he raised while my lips gradually stretched outward.

"Is somebody... *worried* about me? Do you actually have a heart?" I teased. Sterling rolled his eyes and turned away, shuffling back to another tray with a plate of rare steak and a glass of blood. He held a fixed gaze on it, swallowing. Then he shook his head with his hands stuffed in his scrub pants' pockets.

"Why do you do this to yourself?" I gestured toward him, and let my arms fall limply at my sides.

"The moment I accept it as normal is the moment I'm not human anymore," he said. "There has to be a cure somewhere out there."

"There isn't. You don't think someone would've found it in the eighty-plus years it's been?" I shifted the weight on my feet and added, "You're not human anymore, but that doesn't mean you can't have a moral code. Most of us do, despite what you believe."

The ball of his jaw rolled, a lethal warning to leave the subject alone, even through the thick polycarbonate and acrylic glass between us. Perhaps he could melt it like Draven.

"You're not gonna see me for awhile," I warned, switching back to the initial subject. Sterling shrugged nonchalantly, but his Adam's apple dipped.

"Do whatever you want." He tore his focus away from the tray, shuffling to the bed. He plopped on his back, staring at the ceiling. "You're more than capable of handling yourself."

"How much longer do you have in here?" I asked.

"Who knows. Apparently I keep extending my time here, and there's three tests I'm supposed to pass before they release me." He propped himself up on his elbows, his bushy copper eyebrows seemingly stuck in a deep frown. "I'll be alright. If you go through with that dumb plan—don't forget who the enemy is."

"I've obsessed over the enemy for the past three years," I assured him. "I don't think you have anything to worry about."

"I'm not worried," Sterling said, and lay flat again. "Just update me whenever you can."

I nodded, hesitantly walking away from the display window. I paused and briefly returned.

"Hey... don't stress about Briar either. Remember she's still a fledgling, and won't be in her right mind half the time."

"So? I don't have that problem here. She did that on purpose," Sterling grumbled, then shooed me away. I rolled my eyes, remembering how relieved I'd been to see he was still in here. Maybe the time spent being treated like an animal would shed light on his narrow perspective.

I finally left and reentered the chaotic lobby. The young girl I tried to comfort earlier sobbed in her father's arms, a doctor standing before them.

I had no choice but to keep moving forward.

✳

I spent the rest of the evening reshaping my identity. I went to a salon to have my hair dyed platinum blonde and cut into a chin-length French bob. Granted, my soul ached to see such a big chop surround the chair in a ring, but the more drastic of a change, the better. I was more concerned about running into the Vampyres who'd initially attacked me and Sterling at the club and them remembering my face.

I returned to my townhouse and paused at the fireplace near the front door. Pictures of Kiegan, from the time we dated in high school to the time we got married and joined the Academy together, were lined along the mantle in chronological order. I used to stare at these pictures for hours, hoping they'd erase the image of the five silver bullet wounds pumped into his chest. There weren't many moments he wasn't smiling... except the time he bled out in my arms. With his face twisted in anguish, I watched his soul leave his body.

The photos I had kept the morbid image at bay. I lightly traced my fingertips over his face in a picture from when we were hiking in the mountains. He wasn't looking at the camera, but instead whispering something in my ear that made me laugh. It was one of my favorites, and I had a miniature version in my wallet.

I swept away from the mantle and moved to my bedroom to get ready, starting with the mini photo in my wallet. My throat constricted when I took it out and placed it on my dresser to collect dust for who knew how long.

I dressed in a fitted red halter dress paired with scarlet lipstick and pumps, in hopes of gaining the attention of any Nightshade member lurking in their club. I stared at myself in the mirror, already forgetting what I used to look like.

"Hi, my name is..." I ran through the list of personalities I'd used in previous undercover cases—charming, timid, exuberant, seductive—and chose a name I hadn't used yet. I rehearsed it repeatedly in my mind while I ordered a Ryde and waited for the driver to arrive, up until I approached The Nightshade bar's bouncer.

I'd lost count how many times I'd stood in this line, hoping for my husband's killer to miraculously appear.

The lithe, gaunt Vampyre bouncer examined me from head to toe as if for the first time. He grunted and unclipped the rope to allow me inside. I hesitantly drifted through, stepping through a whole new dimension of inebriated individuals controlled by the dark frequencies of electronic music. I scanned the dancing bodies, surveying any exposed skin for the clan's crest, only to be met with miscellaneous tattoos and blank canvases.

Just a bunch of Vampyres willingly getting intoxicated for the sake of feeling human again.

A mindless DJ played on stage, bobbing his head and throwing his hands up to anyone in the crowd who paid attention to him. I was surprised to see a live band wasn't performing.

I hated to admit how familiar I was with this place, from the bartender to the different performers. The only place I could never broach was the VIP lounge, where the Nightshade clan members mingled exclusively. That was where I needed to be.

I took my place on a stool sandwiched between several other patrons desperately reaching for the bartender's attention. I clasped my hands together, patiently waiting until she met my eye. I recalled her name to be Stella, but I had to avoid acting familiar with her. The last time I was here, she'd detected my law enforcement status by my body language. I let my shoulders sink and rounded my spine.

"What can I get ya?" Stella leaned her ear in my direction, and I shouted a random drink in return. Beyond my shoulder stalked a Vampyre whose aura turned my bones to stone. The whites of his eyes were obsidian, and his bald head and neck were covered in grisly tattoos of skulls, flowers, and obscene language. His claws were painted black, and when he licked his lips, I noted his pierced tongue was split like an asp. If there was anyone I recognized from the night Sterling and I were attacked in the parking lot, it was him.

"Stella," he intoned. She rolled her eyes and turned her back on him while she made my drink. He leaned over the counter, clasping his hands together. I noticed the Nightshade crest tattooed on the back of his left hand.

"What do you want, Wraith?" Stella grumbled.

"When are you gonna go out—" He paused, shifting his black-and-red eyes in my direction. He released a simpering whistle. "On second thought..."

"Are you seriously preparing to hit on me two seconds after you were about to ask the bartender out?" I laughed at the audacity. Stella served my drink, shifting skittish eyes between us. Uncomfortable goosebumps prickled along my skin as he leered me. I raised the glass to my lips, ignoring the shudders trickling down my spine.

He tilted his head. "Would that affect my chances?"

I laughed, hooking a piece of silver hair behind my ear. On one hand, getting his attention could raise my chances of entering the VIP lounge. On the other hand... he was dangerous, and had no respect for Stella's constant rejections.

"I don't exactly like being plan B." I crossed a leg over my knee, the silky split-leg fabric of my dress shifting over it.

"You're not, I just never saw you until now." Wraith scrunched his nose and scoffed. "Is this your first time?"

"Actually, yes... and I'm not impressed," I said, delicately lifting my pinky as I took another sip. The back of my neck perspired, and I scanned the clubroom until my eyes landed on a familiar man in a maroon pin-striped suit with gelled salt-and-pepper hair. The thick gold ruby ring on his finger glinted under the spotlight at the VIP entrance. I shifted at the edge of the barstool slightly, watching him disappear behind the charcoal silk curtains.

Wraith followed my gaze and flashed his teeth.

"I can show you something impressive," he said with a sly grin.

I shrugged and glanced at his hand, the one with the crest on it.

From the corner of my eye, despite being surrounded by other patrons, I could see Stella shaking her head.

"I'm not easy to impress," I said.

"We'll see about that," Wraith challenged, biting his lip while he once again scanned my body from the neck down. It took every fiber of my being not to smash his face into the counter. I hated how his presence made me hyperaware of every shift of fabric across my skin.

"Follow me then," he said. "What's your name?"

I slid off the barstool, regaining my footing in the red pointed-toe heels I hadn't worn in months.

"Dawn," I replied, and held my composure while he slid his arm around my waist. I glanced back at Stella, whose shoulders sank with defeat. Her mouth moved without sound, and if I was reading her lips correctly, they said "*Run.*"

11
CASPIAN

My brain jostled when I crashed into the pavement. I sat up, cracking my neck and snapping my twisted knees back into place. I held my hand up with a squint as the headlights seared through my vision. The driver continued to sit in their car, either disturbed that they hit me or waiting to see if I rose again so they could run me over twice.

My bones continued to crack and fuse back together as I stood and wiped the blood from the corner of my mouth. I moved around to the front driver's window. A human woman in a janitorial uniform trembled, both hands clasping the steering wheel. Her mouth hung open, tears streaming down her face as she mouthed, "*I'm sorry!*" repeatedly.

"Out," I rasped, and grabbed the handle. It was locked, so I ripped the door clean off. I didn't care if she worked the night shift and was running late.

Surely, a Sentry would be her knight in shining armor. The woman screamed, swatting at me with weak force as I pulled her out of the vehicle. She staggered to the ground and I replaced her behind the wheel.

*

Astoria's scent was still fresh enough to follow the road. I swerved around a pothole, decelerated over a small bridge arcing over a garden of lily pads, and continued on a winding road cutting between sand dunes, beach grass, and sea oats. I pulled over in a small cul-de-sac surrounded by more dunes, leaving the gun in the car. I ran a hand through my hair with a deep inhale and rubbed the back of my neck.

Where did they take you?

I couldn't smell her anymore—not past the intense stench of sea salt, fish, and seaweed. I plodded to the dunes and pulled myself up until I crested the sandy hill, where I was greeted by a six-story white building sprawled across the shore on stilts. Various vehicles were parked underneath it, and two Keepers were posted at the door above the sweeping staircase.

I slid down the hill and filled my pockets with sand, then trudged toward the front door with my hands already in the air. The Keepers whipped their guns in my direction when the wind carried my foreign scent to them.

"Stay back!" one of them demanded.

"State your business!" the other said.

"I'm looking for my father, Cyrus!" I called out, and continued to climb the stairs. Their hardened scowls softened to shock and confusion. They exchanged a glance before lowering their rifles.

"You're Cyrus' boy?"

"I mean, look at him, Jeeves. He's the spittin' image."

"Yeah, but..." The first Keeper raised his gun again. "Ain't you the one that killed that guy's brother?"

"They never tell the full story, do they? He tried to kill me first," I said with a shrug. "I want to talk to my father about joining White Fang."

They shared a dubious expression with each other, then looked back at me. One of them reached for his radio, triggering initial static.

"Cyrus, do you copy?" he called.

"Go ahead," Cyrus said, his voice sending a frigid tightness through my chest.

"Your son's here, claiming he wanna join us," the Keeper said. A long beat of silence.

"Copy, I'll be down."

One of the Keepers leaned against the wall while the other kept his gun on me. I folded my arms while I searched the beach, the horizon disappearing into a void. Despite the humid air, I felt a chill roll along my exposed skin.

Cyrus had tried to force me to join White Fang when I was nearing adolescence. We were poor, living off blood from homeless Sun Dwellers when we couldn't afford to buy bags at the grocery store. White Fang offered him a way out of the hole, but I'd refused to be under more control than I already was. He lashed out at my resistance, and I sliced his face with a porcelain shard from a silver plated vase he'd shoved me into, blinding him in his eye. I ran away and crossed Uriah's path, thus becoming a Nightshade solely for protection.

And here I was, knocking at White Fang's doorstep in my mid-twenties, after rejecting Cyrus' final offer at the diner.

My knees turned to water when he appeared in the lobby through the large windows. I took a deep breath, forcing my shoulders to relax. I couldn't afford him to say no, but he'd likely do so out of spite.

A lopsided grin played across his lips before he strolled outside.

He's going to make me beg. My mouth tasted like bile at the thought.

"I never thought I'd see my son coming in peace, let alone to join the very clan he'd denounced," Cyrus quipped.

"Me either…" I checked over my shoulder, ensuring more Keepers hadn't appeared from the dunes.

He tilted his head and narrowed his eyes. "How did you find us?"

"Oh, I have my ways. I wasn't one of Uriah's favorites for nothing," I said.

"And why the sudden change of heart?" Cyrus gave one of the Keepers a nod, and he immediately lowered his gun to start patting me down.

"I have nothing else to lose," I rasped, lowering my gaze to my shoes. Astoria had a bright future, and every second she was in our world, it grew dimmer.

The truth was… Astoria dying at their hands was the epitome of losing everything.

"I'm not convinced," Cyrus sneered.

There it is.

I glared at him from under my brows, and swallowed the knot in my throat as I inched to my knees.

"Please," I croaked.

"I can't hear y—"

"*Please!*" I shouted, and reached into the depths of my core for the sorrow I kept buried. "Let me prove myself! I can't live like this anymore."

"Very well then." Cyrus' gloating grin widened.

I avoided eye contact, my jaw tensing as the pride in his tone shattered my own.

I guess to an extent, I now understood Draven's obligation to preserve Briar's safety, even when it meant taking her humanity and living with the guilt. The satisfaction my father got from humiliating me in front of his two Keepers sent a splitting migraine shooting behind my eyes, but if it brought me one step closer to Astoria, then it'd be worth it.

"Get up and follow me." Cyrus strode back inside and I followed closely behind him. The Keepers at the front door remained at their post, mumbling to themselves.

"Beautiful, isn't it?" Cyrus beamed as we entered the lobby. The walls were lined in skinny, vertical blue neon lights at every corner. A desk, receptionist, and security guard were nonexistent. Only a metal door flush with the wall, complete with a handprint scanner, decorated the lobby.

"How is it the Onyx Sentries haven't seen this place yet?" I asked.

"Because there's an invisible dome over this place that reflects the beach. In their helicopters and drones, it's an empty space. On paper, it's a private beach owned by a Sun Dweller who Mundus Novus has yet to find out is dead. They have no reason to come here." Cyrus pressed his palm over the scanner and opened the door. "Not to mention that we don't have that much staff to begin with. Why do you think we're working with the Nightshades? Uriah's got the numbers."

When I crossed the threshold behind him, a klaxon blared throughout the building until Cyrus put his palm on another scanner to cancel it.

"No worries, once we get you in the system it won't do that anymore." He patted my shoulder and kept his hand there, guiding me through a lofty space held up by smooth, thick columns. This time, horizontal neon lights ran along the walls, flanking the path to various smaller corridors. There were different lounge areas scattered around, with a bar, a coffee cart, and another counter displaying a lunch and dinner menu.

"Welcome to the *real* White Fang headquarters." Cyrus presented the space with his arms spread at each side and a smug grin.

"White Fang is a lot bigger than I thought," I muttered, scanning everything we passed. We crossed to the other end of the room, where I continued to ogle the comforts White Fang provided for their members while Cyrus scanned his palm at the next set of double doors. The blue lighting shifted to white, and I immediately began to sniff the air for Astoria's scent. So far, I hadn't gotten a hint of her presence—or much of anybody else's.

It appeared they were working with a skeleton crew.

Cyrus's watch vibrated and beeped. The lines in his cheeks deepened and he said, "I'm going to give you a tour of the north hall. I think we got your first assignment ready, son." I followed him, carefully observing every room we passed. I caught a glimpse of a laboratory filled with stainless steel tables, microscopes, test tubes, and other equipment.

"I'm proud of you, son. It took you a while, but I'm glad you finally came around," Cyrus said. I faltered a step and blinked at his words, but let them roll off of my back. He was capable of telling me how useless I was in the same breath.

Don't get your hopes up, because I don't plan on staying longer than tonight.

12

ASTORIA

The metal walls in the van shivered while the Vampyre sped through the streets. A crowbar and box of zip ties slid across the floor with each turn, only narrowly missing my face. My wrists were bound behind my back with one of the zip ties. I rolled to my stomach to get on my knees and used the wall to help myself stand. I peered through the window. Caspian was in view as he sprinted after us with his fangs bared.

Then a car emerged into an intersection. I flinched and fell back as its bumpers collided with Caspian's legs and sent him flying over its hood. My breaths became sharper as I scrambled back to my feet. I looked out the window and couldn't see him running anymore.

The van trembled when it bounced off of a pothole. I stumbled and cracked the back of my head against the floor, but regained my stance.

I pressed my knuckles together before doubling forward. I pulled my arms upward behind my back as far as I could, and tried to break the zip ties against my lower back. Even after hitting myself multiple times, they wouldn't snap.

I kicked one of my sneakers off and unlaced it, and just as I was about to run the shoe string through the center of my binds, the van jolted me to the floor again. My face slapped against the wall. I tucked my knees under my stomach again and crawled backwards to the shoelace. I blindly felt for the end of it and managed to loop it through the binds, then tied one dangling end to the other shoe's lace to lengthen it. I kicked off the other shoe and fastened the remaining end to the eyelet of the unlaced sneaker.

The van slowed.

I put the shoes back on and fell on my back, immediately bicycle-kicking and praying my physics class in college would pay off.

I pulled my wrists outward—breathing sharply through tight teeth as the zip ties dug into my skin—until the friction weakened them enough to snap my arms to the side. Right on time for the van to stop completely.

I can't always expect to be rescued.

I grabbed the crowbar with the hook facing toward whoever I'd swing at first.

I can't expect Caspian to kill himself for my sake.

The front doors slammed shut, followed by firm footsteps.

Briar would fight, even if it meant dying to the unnatural.

A rush of cool night air brushed against my slick skin as the back doors opened. I swung at the Vampyre with a loud grunt, and the end of the crowbar embedded into his temple. He howled, stumbling backward as he yanked it out of his skull. He struck my cheekbone with his ringed fist. My head whipped to the side. Stars sparkled in my vision as he kicked my side. I rolled over, balling up with my arms crossed over my ribs while I struggled to catch my breath.

He dragged me out of the back and I flopped onto the ground, a cloud of sand rushing into my mouth and coating my tongue. My chest heaved in a fit of dry coughs and my ribs betrayed me with each shallow breath. The Vampyre forced me to stand and pulled me toward a sterile, contemporary building on stilts. I left a trail of spit as I tried to expel the sand. I blinked rapidly, the grains scraping against my eyes, while the pain in my face sang.

✳

I staggered over my laces until the Vampyre cut them with a pocket knife, cursing under his breath.

The deeper we advanced in the building, the fewer windows there were. Skinny blue lights lined the walls, staining everything sapphire. I tried to keep track of the doors that had fingerprint scanners and the ones that didn't. When the fingerprints outnumbered the doors I could access, I grew discouraged.

I kept replaying the scene of Caspian getting hit by that vehicle. Granted, he could heal, but what if the driver was another White Fang or an Onyx Sentry? How could he track me down? How could Briar or Draven find me once they realized we never came back?

For a brief moment, I thought I could slip away somehow, but White Fang's sophisticated security systems made that impossible, especially as a human.

What was the point of fighting if I already knew how this would end?

I refused to make the same sacrifice as Briar. If I were to Turn into a Vampyre, I didn't want it to be under duress—to resort to a permanent solution for a temporary problem. I'd rather accept my fate, but if a miraculous opportunity to escape as a human presented itself, then I'd take it.

We reached a four-way intersection of corridors, where the lights returned to standard white. Each hall was labeled as an east, west, north, or south wing. A pair of guards dressed in black tactical gear with half-masks similar to police officers marched down the north hall, meeting us at the center.

"Thank you," one of them said with a grunt, and extended a gloved palm for the man to hand me over. He shoved, and I stumbled right into their arms. He left cursing under his breath.

"You come from quite a slippery family, Astoria Shaw." A man with a voice of sharp steel emerged from between the guards. I blinked, surveying the diagonal scar slashing from his chin to the top of his forehead, and the familiar pearled skin and silvery hair with a black patch in the front. He bore a striking resemblance to Caspian, only older. "No worries, though. Third time's a charm."

The man stepped to the side, jerking his chin toward the other end of the hall. The guards immediately marched in unison, pulling me with them. I lowered my gaze, my stomach wringing itself out and the threat of bile crawling up my throat. I vaguely remembered Caspian saying his father had once attempted to drown him in a bathtub. The horrifying image flashed in my mind with this sociopath taking the role. There weren't many people in Neoterra or Helios that possessed Caspian's albinism.

"You're awfully quiet. Not nearly as unruly as your sister," the man continued in a light, snide tone. "I'm Cyrus, head of the Keepers. Has she told you about me? We were best friends when she was with us in Neoterra."

I highly doubt that.

"No," I mumbled.

Cyrus clicked his tongue with a sigh. "A shame. You'll learn about me soon enough."

✳

Cyrus led me to a white room without furniture, the only window being a narrow strip covering the top half of the wall and a glass door, which provided a view of the hallway.

"We'll start your admission process in a few hours. There's some things I have to do," he said.

The only forms of visual interest were the grey speckles in the tiled floor and the occasional Keeper that walked by. I stared at the room's emptiness while he shut the door behind me. I turned to ask him what admission entailed, just to be given a condescending wave as he disappeared before I could speak. My sense of dread only grew heavier in my gut.

The room became a blur behind my tears. I covered my mouth to stifle the whimpers when it finally dawned on me that shoe laces couldn't get me out of this one.

I paced around the room, tracing my fingers along the walls. Maybe Briar was right, our mother would've been our downfall. She'd sure become mine.

I had been alone with my thoughts for what felt like an hour when Cyrus walked past my prison, trailed by a shadow. A younger, familiar shadow, whose presence triggered my heart to jump in my throat and my hand shoot to my necklace.

Caspian locked his cold, cardinal eyes on mine, smoldering with a tight jaw. He raised his slender index finger to his lips, and turned his focus to the back of Cyrus's head. I scurried to the front wall and pressed my hands and cheek against the window. He continued to walk behind the Keeper, but peered back at me with a subtle grin, as if he'd heard me pad across the room. No matter how minuscule the crack in his facade was, it made the dread feel lighter.

13
CASPIAN

I DIDN'T KNOW WHY MY CHEST BURNED WHITE-HOT WHEN I saw the black eye staining Astoria's face, or why I didn't immediately reach for Cyrus' neck to separate his head from his shoulders.

Cyrus gave me a tour of the north wing, explaining the admission process. New subjects were sent to shower and change into scrubs, then taken to a barber to get their heads either shaved or their hair cut to two inches maximum. Then came a grueling full medical examination to determine if they were fit for the experiments. If they weren't, they were shot in the back of their heads.

It was a one-way street regardless.

Once Cyrus showed me the entirety of the north wing—including more laboratories, test rooms, and storage rooms—he stalked back in Astoria's direction.

"So what's the assignment you needed me to do?" I finally asked after two hours of letting him do all the talking. The more I thought about my human friend getting pummeled by Vampyres, the harder it was to keep the sharp edge in my voice from surfacing.

"You probably saw a Sun Dweller girl in room 113A. She's our newest subject, one of the Shaws actually. She'll be your first admission," Cyrus said.

"Briar Shaw? I thought she escaped," I said with underlying humor.

"Ah, no. She's still at large. Dr. Ivanov was able to make five serums from the sampled blood she got from Briar. We only have three left, so we're hoping her sister can finish the job. We're trying to be selective on who we give the last ones to until we make more."

I raised my chin with a squint. "How many do you guys plan on making?"

"How many Vampyres populate the entire Neoterran continent?" Cyrus quipped with a chuckle. Suddenly my skin felt coated in an oily, salty sheen. I tugged at my turtleneck.

We stopped in front of Astoria's room, where she sat in a corner with her arms wrapped around her legs.

"Samuel, come to room 113A," Cyrus ordered over his radio. To me, he said, "He'll accompany you during your first admission."

"Where are you going?" I frowned as he began walking away.

"I got a laundry list of things to do, Cass. Just keep an eye on her at all times, okay? That family has an obnoxious knack for escaping." His voice echoed down the hall before the elevators shut him off for good.

"Cass..." Astoria whimpered under her breath. Despite the three-inch glass between us, I could hear her clear as day. I tilted my head to acknowledge her, but with the camera staring right at my face above the door, I didn't want to speak.

"Thank you for coming back for me," she mumbled. I blinked slowly, wishing I could tell her there was nothing in the world that could keep me from doing so. I was still trying to figure out why I felt so protective of her, even against her own sister. Perhaps it was because I knew she had such promise in her life, and it had been ripped away because of us. That black eye—though it'd heal over time—would permanently blemish my heart.

I peered at my shoes with a swallow as my eyes burned for the first time in years.

✳

The elevator doors sighed open, and a masked Keeper traipsed in our direction. I assumed it was Samuel.

"Are you ready?" He asked. I gave him a short nod and stepped aside so he could unlock the door. Astoria rose to her feet with her gaze bouncing between us. With his back to me, I said inaudibly, "*It's okay,*" and reached for one of the daggers in his belt.

Her shoulders eased and her scrunched forehead smoothed.

"I got her." I pulled Astoria from the doorway by her upper arm, the dagger now tucked in my sleeve. "Can you lead the way to the showers? I think I got a bit turned around back there."

Samuel groaned and shook his head, but agreed to do so. I knew where they were, but playing dumb allowed me to keep him in my sight. I let my hand fall from Astoria's arm, gluing my eyes to the back of the Keeper's head.

Once we reached a metal door labeled "Communal Shower"

with a large square window in it, Astoria's breath hitched. I gave her a reassuring nod.

"There should be fresh clothes inside already," I told her, and nudged her inside. I surveyed the hall for cameras while Samuel leered at her as she shuffled by.

"Always my favorite part about admissions." Samuel released a mischievous chuckle as he elbowed my arm. I flashed him a small grin.

The door snicked shut and I let the dagger drop from my sleeve into my palm. I struck his throat with the side of my rigid hand and I swiped the dagger over his wrist. His hand flopped to the floor. Blood sprayed from his wrist as he collapsed to his knees and wheezed, holding his neck. I grabbed his hair and crushed his face into my knee before squatting to his level.

"Where do they keep the serum?" I asked quietly. I kept one fist over his hair, and reached for his radio with the other, putting it in my back pocket. I caught Astoria staring in horror through the window in my periphery, but I didn't take my focus off the Keeper. Blood streamed from his nostrils and gums before they healed, cutting off the flow. I watched his collapsed throat shift back to normal, his guttural wheezes returning to pants.

"Go to Hell," he growled. I instantly pressed the blade against his neck.

"I'll kill you and find a more compliant Keeper to answer, then kill them anyways," I responded coolly, my fangs lengthening.

"Go find him then," Samuel rasped with a wince. "We'd all rather die."

I pulled the blade from his skin and noted a burn mark, indicating pure silver. The pain from his spontaneous amputation proba-bly still lingered because of it. I released a weary sigh.

"Okay," I whispered, and drove the dagger through his sternum. I picked up his detached hand, grabbed a gun and a second dagger from his belt, and wrenched the communal shower door open. Astoria stood there, still gaping at his dead body. I pulled her over the threshold. She yelped and out of reflex, I pressed my bloodied palm over her lips.

"Shh, take this." I shoved the hand into hers and she gagged, pushing it back toward me.

"Get that away from me!"

"No, Astoria, *take it*!" I whispered harshly. "Use his palm print to get out of here. Take this gun, you have seconds to leave. I'll meet you outside."

"Cass, I can't!" Astoria whimpered, her entire body trembling. The radio buzzed, shortly followed by Cyrus's voice.

"Samuel, do you copy?"

"You can, just pull the trigger." I racked the slide and smeared some of the Keeper's blood over her face and arms to mask her human scent. Astoria gagged again and covered her mouth. I pulled her closer, wrapping an arm around her waist.

"Samuel, *do you copy*?" Cyrus's words slowed, gaining a sharper bite.

"Hold on," I whispered, and took her to the elevator in a blur. I smashed the call button, and while we waited for the elevator to reach us, I held her face. I took a final look at the freckles and to-paz doe eyes, blanketed with dew drops that weighed down her long eyelashes. She tremored so violently that even her necklace couldn't bring her comfort.

Astoria was the last person that needed to experience my world—to hold a dead man's hand in order to reach safety.

It wasn't the first time she'd observed my violent side, but... I feared this was different.

"I'm sorry," I whispered, and planted my lips on her forehead for the first—and potentially the last—time.

I'm sorry you met me, was what I really wanted to say.

"Why can't you come with me? No one's here yet." Astoria's voice quivered so severely that some of her syllables were lost. "I can't outrun *Vampyres!*"

"There's something I still need," I said, and pushed her inside when the elevator doors slid open. "You don't need speed. The blood should cloak you enough to hide, if you need to. Use your head. Now go."

"Please don't die," she muttered, her cheeks damp and flushed. The doors began to slide together, and I angled my head with a subtle, cocky grin before they shut completely.

If anyone had nine lives, it was me.

14
CASPIAN

Once Astoria disappeared behind the elevator doors, I snapped my head forward to see Cyrus and five other Keepers behind him at the opposite end of the corridor. Samuel's dead body was just a speed bump to my father, but to the others—with the rage in their eyes behind those masks—he was a lifeline I'd severed.

Despite that, they were holding batons rather than guns... so my guess was they were going to take me alive as an unwilling experimental subject or a torture victim.

"I should've known you weren't serious," Cyrus growled, looking down at the amputated wrist and back at me. "I guess I let my hopes cloud my judgment."

"Or maybe you thought you knew your son more than you ever could." I let both daggers slide from my sleeves into my palms.

"You can't possibly think that girl is gonna get far with a *hand*, do you? She's not like her sister." Cyrus reached around his back and removed a short black pole. He whipped it out to his side and it snapped into a longer, electrified baton.

"You're right. She's not." I leaned forward in a lunge, tightening my grip on the daggers' hilts. "She's smarter."

A low, guttural growl rumbled in his throat as he sprinted forward, the Keepers following behind him. I waited for them to prepare to strike before I cut to the side. I ran up the wall, backflipped over their heads, and dashed around the corner to the stairwell. I could hear their boots screech against the tile as they raced to catch me.

I skimmed each window and sign as I sped past rooms, hoping a lab would appear on this floor. I couldn't hold a Keeper as a hostage. They were expendable, and comfortable with dying in the name of protecting White Fang's secrets.

I stopped at the end of the hall, where the door leading to the stairwell was also protected behind a scanner. I cursed under my breath, and began kicking the door with brute force. A high-pitched alarm triggered, but I didn't flinch. My footprint was imprinted on the door, the metal caving in further, and further, until—

"Hey!" A rush of wind whizzed past my head as I ducked to avoid the clenched fist of a Keeper who seemed to spawn from the adjacent hallway. He was alone, working separately from Cyrus' group, and released a frustrated roar when he couldn't land the hit. My lips stretched into a slanted, smug grin.

I spiraled like a vortex, and the dagger's blade passed through bone like butter with the momentum. The Keeper screamed, falling to his knees as his hand dropped on the floor, just like his fallen colleague.

"Thank you," I said, and immediately smashed his palm over the scanner as Cyrus' group rounded the corner. "Where's the serum?"

"Screw you, man!"

"Do you want to keep your other hand?" I stomped on his shin and snatched his other arm, pressing the curved blade right at the base of his palm.

"Second floor! Second floor! Room twenty-nine—"

A loud pop, and his body jerked back lifelessly. I snapped my head to the left to see smoke swirling from the barrel of a rifle.

"I'd really hoped you were the only traitor here, Caspian," Cyrus said, lowering the gun with a dejected sigh. "Look for the girl, I'll handle my son!" He barked his orders at the Keepers, who immediately took off in the direction they'd come from.

I gritted my teeth with despair. I'd wanted to hold them off longer than this.

"Finally get to have some much needed father-son bonding time, yeah?" Cyrus snarked, raising the rifle again. He prowled in my direction, keeping me locked in his sights.

"I think you'll be pretty disappointed," I mumbled, and smashed the Keeper's palm into the scanner. I darted through the door, dodging Cyrus' spray of bullets.

I fell down the center of the stairwell and caught the bar wrapping the third floor, swinging onto the second floor. Cyrus was a blur as he dashed down the stairs in a downward spiral to catch up. Whatever the third number was after twenty-nine for the lab, I needed to figure it out in the next five seconds.

I didn't even know what the serums looked like, only that there were three left. The beginning of the unit started in the 2100s, so I ran until the numbers climbed to the 2900s.

"If you think you can find the serum, good luck!" Cyrus shouted, closing the gap between us at a rapid rate.

I caught a glimpse of a microscope among test tubes and machinery and screeched to a stop.

"No!" Cyrus leapt across the hall, extending his hands in front of him as I used the Keeper's hand to gain entry in the lab. A powerful sanitizing fan blew at the threshold while I scanned the room for storage. Halfway from a freezer, a warning sign for corrosive materials labeled one of the tables. I snatched one of the vials, wincing at a drop landing on the back of my hand, and threw it at Cyrus's face. He blocked most of it with his palms, but some melted into his face, exposing the skull underneath. He screeched, thrashing around the lab and knocking glass and chemicals onto the floor.

My heart raced and my body locked in place as I flashed back to the moment I'd sliced his face as a child. I remembered ducking flying furniture and vases, with my heart threatening to break out of my chest.

I returned to the present when the burn in Cyrus' skin began to smooth out.

I yanked the freezer open. Icy smoke swirled around three sealed vials filled with an opaque black liquid. I grasped all three, immediately twisting the cap off of one and downing it like water.

And I thought it'd burn a hole through my throat.

Before I could process the pain, my airflow was shut off as Cyrus grasped my neck and hurled me across the room. My back cracked at every impact as I blasted through wall after wall, finally landing on my back with a thud. Salty wind washed over me and I gasped without sound while my lungs seized, like a fish out of water. I couldn't blink the sand out of my eyes while I tried to catch a taste of air. My head felt like it was squeezing tighter and tighter around my brain. I balled my fist in the sand and turned to my side. The remaining two serums were still in one piece. I couldn't stop panting as I forced myself to sit up, rubbing my face and scanning the beach for Astoria. If she was as smart as I hoped, she hadn't waited around for me. If she made it outside, I hoped she'd kept going without looking back.

Cyrus hurtled from the second floor, spraying more sand in my face before I could get oriented. I fell into a fit of coughs and released a hoarse yelp when my father grabbed me by the hair and started to drag me toward the water, where the malevolent waves attempted to crawl onto the land.

This time, my heart felt like it was going to give.

Whatever reins I'd kept on myself all these years to control my emotions, I lost hold of them.

This time—I screamed.

"No! Dad, please no! No, don't do this! I can't swim! *I can't swim!*" Every syllable my vocal chords formed felt like they were made of nails and shattered glass rubbing together, but it didn't matter while I thrashed against my father's iron grip. The sand had turned into carpet, and the cold water that instantly soaked my clothes poured from the bathtub's faucet.

"Not so tough now, are you, huh? I knew that cold exterior was just a front." He threw me on my back and pinned me with both hands wrapped around my neck. I snapped my fangs, coughing and gasping for air as a wave crashed over my face. I flailed with the strength of a seven-year-old human boy, and I couldn't tell if I'd fallen victim to my mind or if the serum was at work.

"You've given me hell from the moment you were born!" Cyrus shouted, yanking me upright just to plunge me right back under. My nose burned as water shot up my nostrils, as if the ocean were made of fire.

"And after all I've done to raise you, this is how you repay me? If you were never born, at least my wife would still be here!"

Cyrus pulled me up again. My head hung backwards, and all I could do was stare at the sky gradually brightening to mauve. The stars that would bring me comfort were fading into the light of oncoming day. As the sunlight breached the horizon, I felt the subtle sting on my skin. I worried perhaps that the serum was meant to be injected instead of consumed, but at least I'd deprived them of one more. It was now a race to see what would kill me first—the serum, or my own father.

My chest felt swollen with the entire ocean, and when I tried to look at Cyrus, I saw four scarred faces instead of one.

"I wish you were more like me," he said breathlessly. He drew a knife from his belt with a subtle *shing*. I widened my eyes, attempting to focus on the distorted blade that inched closer to my face. He pressed it against my cheekbone.

"Let's see if we can still make that happen," Cyrus said with a sardonic smile, and dragged the blade over my forehead, right eye, and cheek in one slow, agonizing motion. I unleashed a bloodcurdling cry before Cyrus shoved me back into the oncoming wave, my fresh blood mingling with the water.

15

ASTORIA

The elevator began to fall, leaving the pit of my stomach at the floor I'd left Caspian on. The walls were made of mirrors, and my reflection gaped back at me in horror, as if she were pleading for my help.

I shut my eyes tightly, breathing in deep so I could think. I examined Samuel's hand in mine. It was like giving his corpse a distant handshake. I leaned against the mirrored wall, watched the numbers tick down, and pretended the ice in my palm was my own and not the Keeper's. The gunmetal was warm in my other hand, as if the firearm were alive.

I wasn't built for this.

What if I dropped it? What if I shot too soon or too late or missed my target entirely?

I darted through the doors as soon as they opened wide enough for me to fit. The Keepers' distant boots echoed down the hall in a growing crescendo, and my heart pounded to their rhythm. I mashed the Keeper's hand on a scanner without looking where the door led and continued running down the hall.

I didn't get very far. One of the Keepers flew past the threshold before it locked shut, then he blocked my path to the next set of double doors. I gasped and my finger flinched over the trigger. High pitched ringing pierced my ears. He crumpled at my feet with, a blood stain blooming across his uniform like a red spider lily. The silver bullet poisoned his veins instantly.

"Oh my God... I-I'm so sorry," I whispered, and barely jumped over his body, skirting to a stop in front of a fire extinguisher and a crowbar. I jammed my elbow through the glass with a wince and grabbed both, tucking the crowbar under my arm before scurrying through the door. Between the relentless crying and the sharp pain in my ribs, I could barely breathe.

My heart sank when I couldn't feel the natural wind, and instead more air conditioning. But my dying hope instantly revived itself when I saw the entire front wall of the lobby covered in windows, exposing the stars, sand, and frothing ocean.

Indistinct shouting sounded from the other side of the door. I tossed the Keeper's hand across the room before crashing against the push bar leading outside. I slid the crowbar through the handles behind me and bolted down the sweeping steps.

Water splashed amid coughing and hollering. I ducked behind a concrete half-wall, barely peeking over the edge to see Cyrus fighting with someone in the beach's swash zone. The waves crashed over them, but he was like a boulder sitting on whoever was beneath him.

I scanned the beach for Caspian. The Keepers weren't here yet, probably still sweeping the room where I accidentally killed their colleague.

And then my world froze. Cyrus pulled Caspian up from the water. A line of red slashed diagonally across Caspian's face. Water bubbled and sprayed past his lips with violent coughs.

I held up the pistol, unsteady, and closed one eye to aim. Cyrus' head swayed over the barrel's notch, and I didn't know if the sights were supposed to be above or below my target. I rested my hands on the wall for stability and held my breath, terrified to accidentally shoot Caspian. His screams intensified—a soul-crushing sound I never thought I'd hear from him.

All I kept thinking about was his tragic story of being drowned in a bathtub that night on the shores of the Nocturne District, and how it was happening to him again at a worse scale.

I dashed across the shore. Even with a closer target, he kept moving while his son thrashed. What if the bullet went right through Cyrus and still hit Caspian?

I cracked the pistol against Cyrus' temple, throwing him off balance. He snarled and twisted around. I deployed the fire extinguisher and stumbled back, until his clawed hand emerged through the cloud of chalk and ice and caught my wrist. I gasped, tugging away, but froze when he twisted my wrist until it snapped. Fire and lightning ripped through my arm. I shrieked, and he shoved me to the ground.

"Smart, covering up your scent like that... I thought you were a Keeper coming to my aid." Cyrus rolled his neck and cracked his knuckles, prowling toward me with fangs bared. I frantically crawled backwards on one elbow, holding on to my throbbing wrist. Snot ran down my upper lip. "But smarts aren't enough for a puny human like you to overcome the likes of—"

A gunshot rang in tandem with a raspy wail. Cyrus' breath hitched, then went ragged. He pressed his abdomen and pulled his fingertips back to see blood. Before he could process the first one, seven more shots wrenched his body back and forth. He collapsed.

Caspian held the smoking pistol sideways, breathing sharply between mashed teeth. Tears streamed down his mangled face. The trigger repeatedly clicked without fire. I shuddered at the horror of what his family had done to him, and what he'd had to do to his father to save me.

His right eye was sliced, nowhere near healed like the long, puffy vertical scar above and below it.

Caspian released a gravelly whimper, the gun landing in the sand as he fell to his knees.

"Cass..." I whimpered, and pushed myself to my knees. Not once did he look at me, only the blood caking the sand and his father's lifeless body. He shifted his gaze to White Fang's building behind us, revealing tiny black veins around his eyes and cascading down his cheeks. The front doors blew off their hinges like the crowbar was a toothpick.

"I'm sorry," Caspian whispered before his eyes rolled to the back of his head. He fell limply on his side as the Keepers came barreling onto the beach.

16
STERLING

Isolation was a funny concept. It gave my mind a lot of time to think. Too much, because the main thought that occupied it was Lyra's ridiculous plan to go undercover with the Nightshades and Astoria being at risk of getting hurt by Briar or one of the clans.

There were probably ten Vampyres who'd abducted me and Lyra from the warehouse when we met with that drug dealer. The likelihood of her being instantly recognized was high.

And if Briar was capable of taking my humanity, she was capable of anything.

Too much needed to be done, and I was no good being trapped in the Transition Wing to fix it. There had to be a way to accelerate the program.

I got up from the springy mattress and shuffled to the red button across the room to call for a nurse. Dr. Nolan showed up ten minutes later instead.

"Everything alright, Mr. Shaw?" She asked, unclicking a pen before putting it in her lab coat's breast pocket.

"Yeah, I just want to take that test you told me about," I said.

Dr. Nolan chuckled and shook her head. "I'm afraid you're not ready for that yet."

"Why not?"

"You've been starving yourself. Your willpower is going to be at its lowest," she said. "You're guaranteed to fail."

I scoffed and waved my hand dismissively. "I don't care, I want to try it. You don't know me." I folded my arms.

"It's not a process you can rush, but if you insist… very well." Dr. Nolan stepped away from the window, her footsteps fading down the hall.

The faster I could get discharged, the faster I could help Lyra before she got herself killed. If there was indeed a conspiracy, it was too big to uncover alone.

I paced back and forth, running through countless scenarios of what the tests could be. There were rumors that they changed for every patient, to prevent Turned Vampyres from avoiding admission and trying to teach themselves.

Two nurses and a tall, brawny security guard brought me to the same Resistance Room. I observed the nurses warily, expecting one of them to be like Officer Adam Odaire.

"Don't worry, no one is here to get you," Dr. Nolan said through a speaker. I stared at the two-way mirror with a low growl.

"Are we doing this or not?" I grumbled, and took a seat at the table.

"The test consists of four stages," she said, and the security guard approached the table with a donated blood bag and a glass. He set both on the table, then took a step back. I stared at it with a frown.

"Okay...?" I scoffed at the simplicity of it. "What am I supposed to do, *not* pick it up?"

"Yes. Wait thirty seconds."

The quiet was deafening, and I homed in on the quiet tick of the guard's watch, counting the seconds.

"Stage two for sixty seconds," Dr. Nolan announced, and the man twisted the cap. He waved it in front of my face, closer to my nostrils. My mouth watered, my fangs growing, as I clutched a fistful of fabric over my thighs. My thoughts blurred and sharpened like a camera lens. I jerked to the edge of my seat when he pulled it away. I blinked and swallowed, shaking my head with a soft sigh.

"Stage three, one minute and thirty seconds." The security guard poured half of the bag into the glass and slid it across the table. The sweet but metallic tang wafted toward me, stronger, and I stood from the chair.

"You have to stay seated, Mr. Shaw," Dr. Nolan chided. "Only one more stage, and you'll have passed the test for the first time."

This isn't anything different than you refusing to touch your plate.

My stomach wrenched and folded in on itself. My eye twitched.

"That's time. Stage four," she announced. The security guard splashed the glass in my face. I licked my lips, and lurched forward at the human with a ferocious snarl.

Electricity shot through my veins, throwing me to the floor. I gasped at a wire pulling taut around my neck as the guard forced me to my knees with a snare pole. I huffed through my nostrils, snapping my fangs at the guard despite the distance.

"I told you, Mr. Shaw. You're not ready," Dr. Nolan droned, appearing at the door.

"What Vampyre can resist when human blood is dumped on them?" I snapped. "This isn't fair!"

"There's plenty who do. We'll try again next week if you actually consume what we give you." She turned away and swaggered down the hall. I snapped and growled, swinging my arms at the guard, my claws to barely catching his vest. He tightened the wire and I gagged.

"You'll get more to drink if you calm down. Don't make me tase you again," he threatened. I rubbed my nose with the back of my hand, taking a deep breath.

Find a thought, and hold onto it.

Dr. Nolan's words echoed through my mind. I closed my eyes, following the security guard blindly.

The first thought that came to me was Lyra waiting outside of my room in her cobalt sundress.

"Ugh," I groaned audibly, eyes flinging open with my lip curling in disgust. I had to get out of here fast, because the delusions were worsening.

The usual tray of food and glass of blood waited for me on the floor of my room. The security guard shoved me inside and raised the loop over my head to release me. I growled at him, rubbing my neck for the two seconds of throbbing pain. I shuffled to the tray and sank to my knees.

I suppressed a scream, eyes burning. The test was supposed to be easy, like defending myself against Officer Odaire should've been. The countless hours I'd spent staring at the food they gave me, accepting the frailty I'd felt for the past couple weeks—all for the sake of staying as human as possible, because I foolishly thought defiance against my own body was true strength...

Ironically, I felt stronger as a human, going to the gym relentlessly after long work hours. I hardly felt exhaustion. Then Briar took that away from me.

She had single-handedly put me in here.

I balled my fists over my knees. A raspy wail erupted from my lungs, and I punched the floor until my knuckles bled and healed. I doubled over, my forehead pressed against the stained tile, sniveling until the hiccups faded into lethal calm.

I didn't leave a single drop or crumb, and I didn't run to the toilet to erase it.

You wanted to create a monster... now you've got one.

17
DRAVEN

BRIAR AND I FOLLOWED THE SOUNDS OF BULLFROGS UNTIL WE reached a creek. She stumbled down the slope, staggering into the shallow water. I stood there with the smashed box of cigarettes and sifted through it until I found at least one that was intact. I snapped my fingers until my thumb ignited with a soft flame, like the time I burned down White Fang's headquarters in Neoterra. At least I was consistent with that trick.

"How are we supposed to get Astoria and Caspian back with the Onyx Sentries everywhere?" She leaned down to splash her face with water and pushed her hair back.

I took one long draw, leaned against a tree trunk, and slid to the ground with a smoky sigh. I unboxed two of the phones and tossed one to Briar.

"We take the back roads," I said, the cigarette bouncing with every word. I followed the prompts of the first phone until I was able to access the GPS.

"How are you so calm?" Briar asked as she clicked and swiped through her phone.

"It ain't the first time people tried to kill me," I droned. "And I ain't necessarily *calm*, I just can't afford to seize up."

"Fair enough," she mumbled, and plopped next to me. She grimaced as she waved the smoke away from her face. "Samara's car is done for."

"I got enough to replace it for her. Ain't like she was all that attached to it anyway," I shrugged. "Besides, it's better for us to get there on foot."

I inputted Caspian's last known location into my phone once it finished updating, then rose to my feet. Briar scrambled to stand on her toes, peeking at my screen.

"You got it!" she exclaimed.

"Yeah." I immediately began trailing the GPS's route, leaving everything behind in a blur. "Try to keep up, will ya?"

Briar rolled her eyes, her hair whipping around from the wind I left behind.

She caught up to me in seconds, and didn't lag behind the rest of the way. Her Vampyric stamina could've been kicking in, or maybe she was fueled by the sheer desperate adrenaline to save her sister. Either way, I hoped she would be more of an asset than a liability as we tried to get them back.

✳

We ran on foot until the forest ended at a road flanked by sand dunes. The sky was brightening to lilac, and I hoped Caspian at least made it inside the building before he burned again. The GPS led us down the narrow road, where the seagulls' squawks were the only sounds, ushering in the brisk morning.

A vehicle sat on the shoulder with the driver's door ripped off. I leaned over the driver's seat, examining the passenger side and backseat for any hints of Caspian's presence. The damage could've been an act of Keepers or Sentries, or Caspian himself. Briar wandered toward the sand dunes, her nostrils fluttering while she climbed the hill.

"Hey, what are you doing?" I whispered harshly, and rounded the hood of the car to catch up. Briar ignored me, pausing at the top of the dune and staring at whatever was on the other side.

I ain't got time for her crazy right now.

Coming up behind her, I observed the long white building on stilts. It towered over the ocean. A massive hole blemished the second floor, where loose wires arced, lights flickered, and a ring of shattered glass mixed in the sand.

"That's gotta be it," Briar mumbled shakily. "My sister's in there."

I nodded, recognizing the same heavily tinted black luxury SUVs and trucks White Fang had at their headquarters in Neoterra.

"Caspian's in there too," I whispered, and Briar closed her fists.

"What are we gonna do?"

"We're gonna do what we do best," I said, and climbed the rest of the way over the dune's crest.

"What's that?"

We crept across the shore. Each step closer reminded me of the Keepers using their electric batons on me, draining Briar of blood, whipping her back to ribbons, and all the other horrors we'd endured. I had been weak and powerless my entire life—turned into a killing machine by Uriah only to lack the strength to use those skills against him when I'd finally had the chance.

The tiny sparks flashed at my fingertips as my palms tingled with heat.

"We're gonna burn it down," I replied with a lopsided grin.

✳

We broke into a blur of speed toward the crumbling hole in the wall. With Briar at my side, I grabbed her hand and launched onto the second floor. We ducked to avoid the dangling wires and stepped further into the lab.

My ears twitched at the sound of Astoria screaming and pleading.

"No..." Briar breathed, and blindly burst into the corridor. I sucked my teeth and went after her, the sweat in my palms evaporating in a feverish haze.

Briar bared her fangs, fists readied. Her eyes flared bright vermillion, and black veins splayed along her neck, eyes, and cheeks like tectonic plates. Charcoal smoke emitted from her back like a cape. Black footprints burned in the tile in her wake, and I could've sworn the cracks in the floor began to spread and glow like lava—

We veered around the bend, and I snatched her by the shirt to duck behind the corner as a group of Keepers appeared in the corridor through a set of double doors. They spoke among themselves, loud enough to conceal Briar's low, guttural breaths. I caressed her back, watching the smoke, veins, and fangs vanish like a nightmare.

"I can't believe Cyrus is dead, man."

"I mean… he did go out there by himself."

"You're saying it's *his* fault his own son killed him?"

"Isn't it?"

"You're unbelievable, bro."

"What are we going to do about the Shaw girl?"

"Dr. Ivanov is busy at the hospital, but she gave word to start extracting."

"Well the one lab is busted, where else are we taking her?"

"A couple other docs cleared room one forty-five for it. Weren't you listening to the radio?"

I scanned the door signs on our hall and cursed under my breath. The numbers ascended in the Keepers' direction. I couldn't risk burning the building with Astoria still in captivity. I didn't want to be the reason she bore scars like Azha's.

No more running and hiding. Just do what you were made to do.

I put my finger over my lips. Briar nodded, and I stepped into the hall.

"Hey, guys." I held my hands up, still clinging to the thread that held me and the fire within together.

"Hawthorne!" one of the Keepers alerted, and they all pointed their guns. I laughed.

My smile faded as I slanted my head in feral tilt. "Don't y'all ever learn?"

I lunged. Their bullets spattered, and I let them hit me as I landed right in the middle of them. Briar sped by in a streak while I wrested one of the Keeper's guns and bent the barrel toward his face. One of his colleagues struck the back of my knee. It buckled and I twisted around with a jab to his stomach. A third Keeper pushed between them and curled his arm around my neck, and I sank my fangs into his forearm before he could lock me in a choke hold.

And then the thread snapped.

Everything went red. I expected his blood to taste bitter, but it was sweeter than Briar's when she was a Sun Dweller. My stomach wrenched, the starvation rising like a sleeping dragon.

I forgot why I was even there.

All I wanted was more.

18
BRIAR

I TOOK THE NARROW WINDOW OF OPPORTUNITY WHILE Draven flung the Keepers around like rag dolls. The bullets didn't slow him down—they only fueled his undiluted fury. He bit one of their forearms when they tried to choke him, and his growls went feral.

I sprinted until I reached room 145 and burst through the door the second I saw an arm fly without a body attached to it.

Astoria was strapped to a leather chair and hyperventilating—as I once was back in Neoterra. Tears streamed down her flushed face. Her wrist was twisted, purple and swollen while the other one was tied down to the armrest.

"Briar!" she squealed, and tugged at her binds as I rushed to her side.

"Ria! Oh my god." I ripped the leather straps with my bare hands. "What did they do to you?"

"Cyrus—" Her eyes darted to the corner of the room, where Caspian lay unconscious on a stainless steel table under a thin white sheet.

"Cass!" She ran up to him and checked his pulse, then choked as she covered her mouth. I approached and took note of the black veins creeping all over his face and neck. I remembered seeing that on myself after I bit Sterling, and placed a gentle hand on Astoria's shoulder.

"If you didn't feel a pulse, that doesn't mean he's dead," I promised, and pulled him off the table. I slung him over my shoulder with a light grunt.

Still in the hall, Draven unleashed a bellowing roar. The walls rumbled, followed by a blaring klaxon and splashing sprinklers.

"We need to go, *now*!" I held Caspian in place with one hand and grabbed Astoria with the other, tugging her to the hallway. I jogged, because going any faster would've left her behind.

My heart jumped in my throat. Draven crouched on all fours in the middle of the hallway, hovering over mutilated flesh and devouring what remained. The skin on his arms had shed, revealing fire underneath.

I pushed Astoria toward the stairwell behind me, and crept backwards.

Draven jerked his head up, sniffing the air with a quiet snarl. The flames on his arms had vanished, but the crazed savagery remained.

I froze in place as Astoria carefully twisted the knob completely. She pushed the door open, and Draven snapped his head in our direction.

"*Run!*" I screamed. I tossed Caspian through the door, then slammed it shut.

The air was knocked out of my lungs when I hit the floor. I tried to crawl away and cried out when something sharp plunged into my calf, dragging me back across the tile. I rolled onto my back and Draven pinned my shoulders with *all* of his teeth turned to fangs, drool cascading down them.

"Draven! It's me! *It's me!*" I shrieked, and pushed my palms against his chest to hold him back. He snapped his teeth and I jerked my head to the side, shutting my eyes so tight that tears squeezed out of them. Whoever this was, it wasn't the man I knew and loved. I didn't recognize him any more than he recognized me.

"Stop! It's Briar! It's *Sunny!*" I pleaded, and for a split second, Draven's face softened. He squinted, reaching for my face, and stopped midway before he touched my cheek, nose scrunching in despair.

More gunshots spewed from down the hall. Draven lurched upright, arms reigniting. He roared at the Keepers who flooded in. The bullets grazed and pierced his fiery skin, and one seared through my calf as I crawled away. I didn't feel the pain until I put weight on my leg, and a jolt shot up my thigh. While Draven turned his ferocity on the drove of Keepers, I burst through the stairwell and scooped up Caspian. I winced at the skin and muscles expanding and contracting around the bullet as my body attempted to heal around it.

"Bri!" Astoria called from the bottom.

"I'm fine! Just hurry outside!" I shouted shakily, and adjusted Caspian's deadweight across my shoulders. Taking one leg at a time, I swung over the railing and fell down the center of the steps. I yowled at the impact despite it only being two flights, and tumbled on my side. Caspian was flung off my shoulders and I breathed sharply through tight teeth until the pain faded.

Keep going. I pushed myself and gathered Caspian up again, then limped out the door. I froze, staring at the SUV idling at the bottom of the staircase outside. Its headlights blinked shortly before Astoria poked her head from the driver's window.

"Come on!" She whispered harshly before jumping out and throwing junk out of the backseat so I could lay Caspian there.

"How did you start the car?" I asked.

"Cass taught me how to hotwire back in Neoterra," she replied with a nonchalant shrug. I suppressed an amused laugh and shook my head, snapping back to the present moment.

"I need you to get as far away from this place as fast as possible. I'll track you down, but right now I need to snap Draven out of whatever kind of frenzy he's in." I spoke promptly, my sister's eyes darting as if trying to keep up with subtitles on a TV screen.

"O-okay! Please be careful!" she exclaimed, and scrambled to get behind the wheel. She swerved through the sand and sped off in a tan cloud.

With a wince, I hobbled toward the stairs, and released my claws. I ripped my jeans to expose the wound in my calf, and pulled my shirt collar up and bit down on it. I shut my eyes tightly, then dug my index and thumb claws through my calf. I removed the compressed, rounded metal piece and jumped through the hole on the second floor. Just like that, the wound mended, and a rush of heated energy ran through my veins like nothing had happened.

The sprinklers burned, the water searing like hot grease. I followed the sounds of Keepers ordering each other to fall back. They stampeded down the corridor, running around me like a boulder in a river. I advanced toward the danger they fled from with my heart thundering in trepidation.

Draven's fire flickered like a dying star, and he stared at the blood staining his clothes and palms. Steam rose from his pores.

"Draven!" I shouted, cupping my hands around my mouth. He didn't react.

"*Draven, come on!*" I screamed louder, and he finally lifted his gaze.

"Briar?" he rasped. I sighed with relief, and ran to grab his forearm. He hesitated, but followed closely behind me while I led him back to the lab so we could jump from the second floor directly onto the beach. With morning growing in strength, I knew we had a good chance of getting away. Hopefully Astoria found a safe place for Caspian in the shade.

The ocean breeze drifted through the hole in the wall as if to push us back inside. Red and white lights flashed on the other side of the dunes as sirens neared.

"We need to go," I urged. Draven nodded, and I counted to three before we jumped together. The Keepers had all vanished except two, who flagged down the fire truck barreling across the shore. Smoke engulfed the White Fang headquarters, but its sprinkler systems were more advanced than the one in Neoterra.

As we bolted away from the beach and followed Astoria's trail, I felt our failures manifest as a rock in my gut.

* * *

Astoria's trail led to an underpass beneath a railroad track, outside a grid of abandoned silos and factories. The SUV's engine was shut off, and she was humming a soft lullaby to Caspian. The soles of my shoes scraped against the concrete and her voice abruptly shut off.

"It's just us, Ria," I announced, entering the dark tunnel. It was a great spot, assuming it wasn't near a Nocturnal Zone for Onyx Sentries to patrol. Astoria jumped out of the backseat, running into my hug. She hugged me with her non-injured arm, squeezing as tight as she could. As much as I wanted to do the same, I wasn't familiar with my own strength yet. I didn't want to risk breaking her spine.

"I'm so glad you guys made it. Th-that was... horrible." Her breath hitched and she reached for the base of her bare neck. Her shoulders slumped with defeat.

"We'll get you a new necklace..." I said.

"That was from Dad," she said, and sank to the ground, leaning against the SUV's tire. I kneeled next to her, and we both glanced at Draven, who appeared as though he waded through a sea of death.

"Are you okay?" I asked, eyebrows pinching with concern. Of course, I already knew the answer. I watched him do the unthinkable, like the Vampyre who killed Cyrene. He would now be considered one of White Fang's failed experiments, unleashed unto the public.

My main concern—was this manifestation only delayed? Were we all potential failures?

"Yeah," Draven said, and stepped beyond the underpass. I

cringed at the sound of vomit hitting the grass. I thinned my lips with a short nod, deciding to table it for later.

"We need to get back to Neoterra," Astoria announced. "Caspian needs *real* help. He... h-he's not waking up and his skin has these weird—"

"Briar had the same thing happen. Ya gotta let it happen." Draven said as he returned, brushing the back of his hand against his lips with a grimace.

"Nobody move," demanded a woman with a voice made of smoke and ice. She came from the opposite end of the underpass, and I instinctively put my arm over Astoria so we could stay hidden behind the vehicle. Draven sighed, gravity tugging his face in the most defeated, exhausted demeanor I'd ever seen.

"Just do what you gotta do. I ain't got no cash," Draven droned.

"We're not here for your money, we're here to see why *you're* covered in so much blood but the Sun Dweller you're harboring is in one piece." The woman's footsteps were joined by eight others.

I frowned, and stood. Astoria hesitantly followed suit, slouching to hide behind me. The woman, surrounded by five other men and women carrying various weapons, gawked at me like I had two heads.

But the *real* anomaly was the sight of scarlet, blue, hazel, and brown eyes in their group.

"The person we're 'harboring' is my sister..." I spoke slowly, because I was only going to say it once. "If this is your territory, we'll leave right now."

"Are you... you must be Briar Shaw," the woman gasped, saying my name like I was an urban legend. I took uneasy steps backward until Draven was between us and the group.

"Who are you?" he demanded.

"Ada. We can take you somewhere to help take care of your sister's wrist, you know." The woman and her friends were bedecked in tactical uniforms. Some had scars on their faces and arms, but the only flaw in Ada's ebony skin were deep smile lines. The group stepped further into the tunnel, but still kept considerable distance.

"What makes you think we'll just *follow* you? What clan are you?" Draven challenged. I shifted my gaze to the vehicle, already calculating how we could get Caspian out before these people could hurt him.

"No clan you've ever heard of, or anyone else for the matter, pretty boy," Ada chortled with a proud grin. She lowered her gun, allowing it to dangle on its sling. "Don't worry… we've heard about you too, Draven."

"What do you want from us?" Draven put his hand behind his back, and I grabbed it. I couldn't tell if it was his palm or my own that sweltered, or if he was trying to comfort me or needed comfort himself. Either way, I remained tense, waiting for the signal to run. The lines deepened around Ada's face—the kind of smile that lights your face after seeing the sun for the first time after a hurricane.

"A revolution."

Part 2

Depression

19
STERLING

Group therapy sessions were the bane of my existence. As a human police officer, I always declined sessions when we were forced to get mental help after a major incident. I preferred one person to know my business, and no more than that.

At the hospital, I didn't have a choice. Any human Turned without their consent was required to sit in on those sessions every week. Today was my first one.

Another thing to add to the laundry list of reasons to hate Mondays.

The room designated for group therapy was painted pastel pink, supposedly to keep us relaxed and calm. Posters with words of affirmation and hope hung around the room, but one stuck out the most to me. It depicted a woman in a meadow, basking in the sun, with the quote "They can take your humanity, but they can't take your soul."

I tried to get the chair facing it, but someone else beat me to it.

I shifted uncomfortably in the rough plastic seat with my back to the poster. There were only five of us, with one empty chair reserved for the therapist. I crossed my arms, observing the boredom, melancholy, and anger plastered across everyone's faces. They didn't react when the door opened.

"Good morning, friends." Dr. Reagan pushed his round glasses up his hooked nose. He smiled brightly, revealing a wide gap at the center of his fanged teeth. He had naturally rounded shoulders from slouching, and always wore khakis and a shirt buttoned to the very top even though the collar appeared to dig into his wide neck. His cheeks were always rosy, the epitome of how I imagined a modern-day Santa without a beard would look like. It was annoying to witness how happy and optimistic he was while the rest of us remained dead inside.

"We have a new face today." Dr. Reagan gestured his hand in my direction. "Please stand and tell the group your name, where you're from, and your species. There's no judgment here. We're all family."

Family. I don't even know what that word means anymore.

Astoria's whereabouts were unknown, and Briar was on the loose, probably trying to ruin her sister's life like she ruined mine.

I surveyed the circle once again, everyone's carmine eyes staring back at me expectantly. One rigid, sinewy man sat in his chair with his russet hair closely cropped. I assumed he was military. The girl next to him—with eyes so light they almost appeared orange— had patchy red hair and minimal eyelashes, probably from plucking them. Another woman next to her, with dyed blonde coiled hair framing her face like a lion's mane, wore an eye patch. Finally, the man next to me, maybe around Briar's age of twenty-three, was missing a leg. From the knee below, it was replaced with an intricate metal prosthetic operated by hydraulics, gears, and cogs. It was hard to tell whether their ailments were self-inflicted or not.

My heart sank. Beyond the Vampyre eyes I despised so much… there were stories of pain and suffering.

I peered over my shoulder at the poster again before standing up with a quiet sigh.

"Sterling. I'm from here," I announced in a terse tone, and sat back down.

"You forgot one more thing, son," the doctor lilted, jerking his chin to urge me to stand again. I chewed my inner cheek before doing so.

"My name is Sterling and…" I sucked in a breath, staring at my feet as freezing shame rained on me. "I'm a Vampyre."

"It's okay, we all have to say it." Dr. Reagan shared eye contact with everyone as he spoke. "That is how we start our sessions every week."

"Cool," I grumbled.

"That don't mean you gotta be okay with it," the girl with the eyepatch droned.

"Yes it does, Cassidy," the doctor countered. "We all aim to be okay with the changes we face. We feel as though something was taken from us, but we should embrace entering a new chapter in our lives instead and treat it as a gift."

I snickered under my breath.

"Do you have a different perspective, Sterling?" Dr. Reagan subtly cocked his head.

I cleared my throat. "Yeah, um… it kinda sounds like something a priest would say at a funeral. This is actually worse than death," I said. "And most certainly a curse."

"Oh, is that so?" He leaned forward in the seat. "Elaborate."

I shook my head. I knew exactly what he was doing. He clicked his tongue and examined his clipboard, then jotted something down. The other patients stared at me.

The guy directly next to me in the circle broke the stillness. "What happened to you? You don't seem like the type that'd go anywhere near a Vampyre."

I scoffed, caught off guard by both the question and the assumption. Sure, I wouldn't have gone out of my way to do so, but my line of work made it impossible. Usually people could sense I was a cop from a mile away.

"Let's introduce ourselves if we speak, okay?" Dr. Reagan cut in. The guy rolled his eyes and leaned back in his chair.

"Sean," he spat with an exasperated sigh, then repeated, "What happened to you?"

"I was abducted, then Turned at a lab."

It wasn't my story. The rage bore into my bones and melted my core.

Briar did this to me. My own sister. And the worst part? She spit on me and laughed in my face while I was bleeding out.

Sean scrunched his nose. "What kind of lab?"

"Let's not push him to get into details on the first day, okay?"

Dr. Reagan clicked his pen a couple times before pressing the tip to the paper. "We still need to go over some rules."

"Great," I whispered, and braced myself for even more restrictions.

"First—keep things confidential outside this room. Second—no one here is obligated to answer questions or reveal anything about themselves. We're all here to support each other emotionally. Third—we don't judge, harass, verbally abuse, or physically harm anyone. Fourth—no relationships with other group members. And finally, only use 'I' statements, and no accusatory 'you' statements. We like to express our emotions through concise communication."

I nodded, and checked the clock above the door to the hallway.

"Can I go back to my room now?" I asked. The copper taste was trying to come back in my mouth, and I knew that in a few moments, hunger would overwhelm me.

"We don't bite," Cassidy promised, her voice honeyed. "Come on. Will it make you feel better if we share some of our woes?"

I shrugged. It sucked that they were all in the same boat as me, but frankly it didn't make me feel any better. Hearing their burdens would only make it worse. Cassidy shrugged and stood anyway.

"So I went on a date with this guy." She shifted her weight on her feet while she stared at an empty spot on the ceiling. "We had brunch, everything was okay, kinda boring. He asked me for a second date when he dropped me off at my house and I said we weren't vibing so... he stabbed me in the eye and bit my neck. How was he able to stay in the sun without getting burned for so long? I don't know. But he had brown contacts on the entire time too, so..."

"And what do we tell ourselves?" Dr. Reagan interjected.

She shifted her gaze from the ceiling to the floor.

"I can't be at fault for something that was beyond my control. The shame belongs to the monster who did this to me." She sped through the words like she repeated them ten times a day.

"Cassidy... remember we don't use the term *monster* in here," he chided in a calm tone.

"Right. Sorry, whatever," she grumbled before plopping back in her seat.

The session continued, with Dr. Reagan mostly teaching breathing techniques and everyone going around the room to say something positive about the Vampyre species. I requested to skip a turn twice before I had no choice but to give an answer so we could be dismissed.

All I could say was Vampyres had astounding strength, speed, and tracking.

The skills I needed to help Lyra with her case, rescue Astoria, and kill Briar.

20
LYRA

I OPENED AND CLOSED MY FISTS REPEATEDLY AT MY SIDES AS Wraith ushered me toward the VIP lounge entrance. His hand slid below my lower back, and I glared at him from the corner of my eye.

"Bringing a guest, sir?" the security guard asked. Wraith nodded, and the man stepped aside to allow us through the black silk curtain. We descended a flight of stairs, where the basement opened into a much larger space than the club upstairs. Human and animal skulls were plastered to the ceiling with nightshade flowers woven through them and around the spherical pendant poles. Liquid light churned like golden lava lamps in the pendants, casting a glow throughout the lounge. Tufted, half-circle sectionals and mahogany tables created intimate spaces for the clan members and their exclusive patrons. A hexagonal bar, bedecked in warm amber underlighting with pennies cast in resin on the countertops, was the central focal point.

As much as I hated to admit it, it was impressive. But something told me those skulls weren't synthetic.

"What do you think?" Wraith asked. I wished he'd stop smiling with those teeth. I slid away from him, rubbing the goosebumps on my arms.

"It's cool." I hooked a piece of my hair behind my ear, sweeping my eyes back and forth over the lounge, and focused on the woman with black-and-white locs in a champagne-colored mermaid dress strutting in our direction. Her chin was tilted up. She was already sizing me up, as if I were a peasant who'd wandered into the throne room.

"What stray did you bring in this time, Wraith?" she asked with a bored sigh.

"Excuse me?" I scoffed.

"Dawn here said she wasn't impressed with the club so I wanted to show her around." When I thought I'd escaped the invasion of my personal space, Wraith threw his arm around my waist again.

"You're only supposed to do that for people interested in joining our clan." The woman frowned, and folded her arms. Wraith drew in a breath.

"Oh, come on, Delilah—"

"I am," I cut in. Wraith blinked, pulling away from me.

"Why?" Delilah asked defensively.

"Why not? I don't have friends, a family, or a job. My only purpose is to exist," I said.

"We don't take just anybody," she laughed. "This isn't some orphanage."

I rolled my eyes.

"I'm sorry, is my presence bothering you? Let me get out of your way then." I clipped my shoulder against hers as I sauntered toward the bar. My feet were barking in these heels, stuck in a vicious cycle of healing for two seconds and returning back to soreness.

"Oh, I know she—"

"Calm down, Dee." Wraith patted her back and trailed behind me. I took a spot at the counter, climbing onto the barstool while I scanned the lounge for the man in the maroon pin-striped suit and ruby gold ring.

"Sorry about Delilah," Wraith said. "She doesn't like meeting new people."

"Yeah, well, I didn't come down here to meet your girlfriend," I said, examining the liquor bottles on the shelf. The bartender was dressed much more sophisticated than Stella, clad in a white blouse and black bow tie. He approached, and I ordered a glass of brandy on the rocks, mainly for appearances.

"She's not my girlfriend. She was developing a thing with my brother though." The wild, inebriated cloud in his eyes cleared, replaced by a lethal darkness.

"Where is he?" I asked. Wraith grabbed an abandoned drink on the bar and downed it.

"Up there." He pointed at one of the skulls above us. It was fresh, judging by the whiter bone compared to the rest and the gold grill on one fang.

"Oh my god..." I gasped. "W-what happened?"

"He was killed." Wraith squeezed the drink in his hand. I flinched at the melting ice cubes and glass scattering across the counter. I gnawed on my lip, holding back the string of questions

I wanted to ask. I couldn't risk him detecting my background as a police officer.

Dawn held the spotlight, and Lyra was back home on my dresser with Kiegan.

The man in the suit with the mechanical arm approached.

"What's wrong, Wraith?" His voice was as smooth as the whiskey I'd had earlier. "I couldn't help but hear glass breaking."

"Nothin', boss," Wraith grumbled. He shoved away from the counter. "I'm gonna get some air."

The man took his place on the barstool next to me.

"Sorry, about that. He's grieving," he said, and propped an elbow on the edge.

"I understand," I said, swirling the ice cubes in my drink with a stirrer.

He tilted his head. "You've lost someone?"

"Haven't we all?" I laughed numbly. If it wasn't death, it was the law that kept families apart.

He eyed me for a moment with an unreadable expression, twirling the ring around his finger with his thumb.

"What's your name?" he asked.

"Dawn," I said curtly, still replaying his conversation with Chief Duncan in the Nocturne District. I tensed when his chilled fingers brushed over my forearm. He scooped my hand in his and brought the back of it to his lips.

"Uriah King," he said, and released my hand with a charming grin. "It's a pleasure to meet such a stunning woman."

"The pleasure is mine," I said, ignoring the heat in my cheeks.

I hadn't received a compliment in years—not since Kiegan was breathing.

Focus, Lyra.

"So... who did you lose?" Uriah asked. I brought the drink to my lips, taking a minuscule sip to wash down the knot forming in my throat.

"A boyfriend," I said. "He, uh, got shot."

Actually a husband. Soulmate. Best friend. Someone your men snuffed out like nothing, all over a bank robbery.

"That's unfortunate. If you need anyone to talk to, you can talk to any of us," Uriah offered.

"Wouldn't that mean I need to be a Nightshade?" I slid a glare in Delilah's direction. She was in one of the sectionals, running her mouth a mile a minute with two other women. An itch in the back of my mind wanted to say she was talking about me, but I brushed it off. I couldn't have possibly made that much of an impact.

"Who told you that?" He frowned.

"One of your people, I don't know. She said I don't belong here."

Uriah closed his eyes briefly with a wry chuckle. It seemed he already knew who I was referring to.

"Well, that's not true. We would be happy to have you."

"What exactly are the Nightshades?" I leaned back on the barstool expectantly. Uriah released a hearty laugh that shifted near to mania.

"We are the future, love."

*

Sunrise was approaching. I'd lost track of time in the VIP lounge and found myself racing to catch the subway and meet with the only Ryde driver working at this hour. I had taken my heels off, now running barefoot across intersections to get to the station.

"Better fly home, bat!" a Sun Dweller officer crooned from the crosswalk. I didn't stop to entertain his slur.

I caught a glimpse of the road block where the Skinwalker shootings had occurred. A small group of the victims' friends and families handed out flyers nearby for a vigil later that night in honor of the fallen.

I hadn't been there to stop it, and I wished I had the time to support them now.

I boarded the train, leaning my head against the window as I flipped the black metal business card Uriah gave me in my hand. It appeared blank to the naked eye, but a phone number appeared under black light. He told me if I wanted a better life and a sense of belonging, I could call this number.

After three years of circling their bar, trailing bank robberies, and monitoring drug deals, I was finally one phone call away from infiltrating the Nightshades. Yet... instead of excitement, I felt dread, and all I could hear was Sterling's voice protesting in the back of my mind.

I flipped the card back and forth between my fingers until the subway reached my stop. I tucked it in my pocket, and met up with the Ryde driver waiting above ground. I ordered him to take me to my townhome, where I discarded Dawn and put my Lyra suit back on.

Uriah seemed to have taken a liking to me, perhaps even to let me get close enough to find the red file Chief Duncan had given him. I shuffled around my living room, then the kitchen and my dining room, chewing my nails while I watched the clock for Gloaming to return. Frazzled, I decided to dig through a box of old wigs upstairs to find one that matched my natural black hair. I didn't want to risk any of the Nightshade members recognizing my new identity in public.

I slathered copious amounts of sunscreen over my neck, face, ears, and hands before stepping into the sun. What had once felt like thumbtacks prickling along my skin with intense pressure now felt like hot wax with a slower, more gentle burn. The sunscreen would buy me thirty extra minutes, which was usually not enough to warrant using it. But today it was enough to get me through driving to the hospital.

✳

Traffic dragged between my neighborhood and the medical district. One of the streets was blocked off for an organized protest of Sun Dwellers demanding Mundus Novus to do away with Vampyres entirely. Only one officer was supervising. They were confident no escalation would occur since Vampyres couldn't be in the daylight without burning to death after too long. I scoffed, reaching in my glove box for a pair of sunglasses.

Why not do it at night, where we could at least protest our side? Cowards.

It was a shame. Sun Dwellers brazenly shot and killed Vampyres out of hatred, yet they were the ones hosting protests in Neoterra. A bitter taste entered my mouth when I imagined Sterling standing with them. I almost turned my car around, until I remembered he couldn't stand with them even if he wanted to anymore.

I sat in my car for a moment, adjusting the wig in the rearview mirror to make sure I didn't have any blonde hair poking underneath, then made my rounds through the lobby to visit Sterling.

I didn't realize how often I visited him until the nurse greeted me by name and the receptionist waved me to go on without signing in on the clipboard.

Stale lunch for human patients filled the hallways. No flatlines or weeping weighed down the air like the night of the shooting. Yet I still expected to see another motherless child.

I held my breath until I reached the Transition Wing, the only place in the hospital isolated from the horrors of the outside world.

I waited outside the unit until Dr. Nolan came to let me through the back. I somewhat hoped one of her nurses would get me instead, because after Sterling saw her with that White Fang woman, I didn't trust her.

"So... you and Sterling Shaw are pretty close?" she asked, her clogs clomping loudly against the tile.

"Not really, we just worked together," I said, scratching my head. The wig was definitely going to be problematic.

"Hm. Well, you visit him often," she asserted with a short shrug.

"He doesn't have a support system," I replied flatly.

"I was hoping you could talk to him about life as a Vampyre. This has been very hard on him."

I remained silent, considering. Sterling had to be the most stubborn guy I had ever met, so I doubted anything I said to him would hold merit. It didn't hurt to try, though.

We paused in front of his window and my eyes widened.

For the first time since before he Turned, color had returned to Sterling's skin. His freckles were more vibrant, the sharp emaciated edge to his jawline had softened, and his hair shined like pennies. He was himself—healthy and brutal. The only thing missing was the angry scowl glued to his face, instead replaced by a vacant countenance while he performed crunches on the floor. He paused when our gazes met, and rose to his feet.

"I'll leave you to it," Dr. Nolan said, and plodded off to tend to other patients. I scanned Sterling, taking note of the weight he'd gained back. The broad shoulders and chest, outlined in his scrubs that almost fit too snugly. I wondered if the hospital cared enough to get him new ones.

"You look better," I said, clasping my hands behind my back. "Finally eating?"

Sterling shrugged.

"Might as well if I'm ever going to get out of here," he grumbled, and sank into a cross-legged seating position. Only then did I notice he didn't have shackles around his feet anymore.

"You look like you're moving along the program pretty well," I said.

"Thanks... any reason you're here today?" He leaned back on his palms. My eyebrow twitched, threatening to form into a frown.

"I just wanted to see how you were doing... and to let you know that I have a way in."

"Into what?"

"The clan," I mumbled.

Sterling sucked his teeth. "Why can't you wait until I get out? We could work on it together."

"Because Vampyre or not, they'd recognize you and you'd blow my cover. Then we're both screwed and right back where we started—or worse—and Draven wouldn't be around this time to lend a hand."

"How is it that you can't see how dumb of a plan it is? Their Alpha going undiscovered by humans for so long indicates a dangerous level of intelligence, don't you think?"

"Why do you care what happens to me there?" I snapped. "I'm not some damsel in distress."

His scowl shifted to something weary and sullen.

"Because whether I want to admit it or not, you're the only friend I have left," Sterling said with a sigh. My face softened, and for a moment the world stopped.

A friend? He barely wanted to admit we were partners when we were searching for Briar.

Hearing his words somehow made me feel lighter.

21
BRIAR

WE ALL PILED IN THE BACK OF ONE OF THEIR PICKUP TRUCKS, lying flat among diesel drums and propane tanks with a tarp covering us. Astoria had her arms wrapped around Caspian like he was a security blanket, despite his coma. I curled against Draven with my face buried in his chest while I trembled in the afternoon heat. His heartbeat was slower than the average human's, I suppose because we were closer to the walking dead than the living. I couldn't breathe at the thought of being someone's prisoner again. I flinched at every bump the truck hit.

As much as helping them start a revolution sounded like a dream, I had already learned that nothing anyone says or does is ever what it seems, no matter how noble it sounds.

"Draven... what if they're part of White Fang or the Nightshades, and they're taking us right to them?" I whispered. He squeezed his arm around me, staring at a blank space on the tarp.

"I don't think they are... as much as Uriah had different sectors in his pockets, he'd never work side by side with Sun Dwellers, let alone his members." Draven lifted a corner of the tarp, peeking through. I rolled over to peek as well, and the sky was blocked by a thick canopy of leaves. My heart jumped at the disembodied echoes of robins.

"Are we... back in the forest?" I asked in a strained whisper.

"Look's it," Draven grunted. He sensed my anxiety and stroked my hair. I balled my fist in his shirt, fighting the tears that threatened to come.

"I can't be locked up again," I muttered. I would've felt better about the whole situation if I had any skills to defend myself, or knew how to control whatever abilities I had. After the White Fang visit, I noticed the rise in my temperature and the pain from the cold sprinklers... so I knew I had *something*.

"You won't," he promised, though I couldn't entirely trust his authority on that.

Astoria hummed, tracing the black veins spidering through Caspian's marble skin. Her lip was stuck in a small pout, as if she were cradling a broken porcelain doll.

I tugged away from Draven, poking my head above the tarp. We were far from civilization, deep in a pine forest that ebbed and flowed along inclines of varying degrees. Fireflies illuminated the winding path, and suddenly I wasn't so afraid anymore.

"Bri, get down!" Astoria muttered harshly.

"We're not in town anymore, we don't have to hide," I whispered back. Draven hesitantly sat up, his eyes darting in every direction before pulling the tarp off entirely. I rose to my knees, peeking over the hood of the truck. We were last in the short convoy, with Ada's vehicle first in line. We could technically jump off the tailgate and run, but we'd be leaving Astoria and Caspian behind. I balled my fists tightly, returning to a seated position with my back against a drum.

I hated it—I hated how fearful I'd become, despite gaining lethal strength and speed. I couldn't understand where that part of myself went, but I knew I had to push through it. I wasn't going to keep letting Draven bear the brunt of our circumstances all on his own because of my fear.

So I sat there, watching the forest open into a cave. When the shadows swallowed us, Astoria gasped, frantically looking around with eyes wide. I still saw with precision, and Draven's eyes glowed like a feline's. I guess mine did the same too now.

The narrow tunnel yawned into a vast cavern, with chambers, levels, and houses carved into the mountainsides. The houses appeared stacked and layered from the floor to the ceiling, lined with lanterns illuminating deep inside. Whatever cave we'd entered was actually a gateway to a full-fledged city.

I perked up, gripping the edge of the tailgate while I surveyed the Tuscan magnificence. People—humans and Vampyres alike—milled about *simultaneously*. No one was attacked, no one was uncomfortable, and police officers weren't present to arrest anyone for breaking curfews.

Because whatever this place was... it didn't *have* curfews.

"Are you seeing this?" I exclaimed. The cavern's ceiling had two giant words seared into it: *Until Equinox.*

"Yeah…" Draven trailed, still craning his neck to see everything. The convoy took us down a street filled with market stalls. Several people stopped their shopping to look at us, some with curious raised eyebrows and others with wariness. A child waved at me, and I hesitantly waved back with an awkward grin before her mother pulled her to the side.

The street widened, and instead of carved structures, there were peaceful fields of barley, and various vegetables and legumes bathing in the shaft of sunlight pouring through the cavern's vast skylight. Ten people were scattered throughout, tending to the fields. A woman recorded them working with a professional camera on a tripod.

"What is this place?" Astoria asked.

"No idea… I don't think we're supposed to know," Draven said.

The trucks decelerated, barely fitting through a narrow tunnel as we drew near another chamber. The second our truck stopped, I hopped out of the back. I helped Astoria get out while Draven scooped up Caspian's limp body. Several doors slammed shut as everyone else got out of their vehicles.

Ada shuffled toward us with a proud grin, but with how much Uriah and Dr. Ivanov smiled, it was difficult to determine whether it was simple pride or a red flag for danger. My shoulders hiked up to my neck.

"Welcome to Avant Garde," she said, arcing a hand above her head.

"What is this place?" Draven asked with a frown. "What's with the lady and the camera?"

Ada's eyes shifted to Caspian and she held up a finger.

"I'll explain. First we'll take this fella to one of our doctors."

"W-wait, let me go with him," Astoria offered.

"No worries, honey. We'll take good care of him, I promise. They'll get him cleaned up, give him an eye patch, the works," Ada explained. The three of us exchanged wary glances, and Draven's jaw feathered. I expected another threat like the one he'd delivered to Azha and Malachi, and braced for us getting kicked out before we learned what the place was.

But he said nothing—just gave a comforting pat on my sister's shoulder, and two men with a gurney came to take Caspian away. Astoria reached up to her bare neck, still clinging to that nervous tic despite the necklace being gone.

Ada laced her fingers together and cracked her knuckles before putting her hands behind her back.

"You three... follow me," she said, and strode back toward the fields. Draven widened his fingers, and I grabbed his hand in response. Astoria's shoulders rounded as she folded her arms and trailed closely behind me.

"So... you're probably wondering what this place is, and what's gonna happen to you," Ada began. "The lady with the camera is just recording so we can show the public the truth when the time comes. As far as this city we've built—well, it's a place of hope and healing, and it can be that for you too."

"Hope for what?" Draven asked.

"Freedom, peace, safety... for all of us. The majority of the people you see here?" She gestured to the people tending to the fields. A couple of them straightened and waved, and she returned the gesture with a warm smile. "They're half-breeds. Lightstalkers."

"Lightstalkers?" Astoria echoed.

"How?" I cut in. "What does Until Equinox mean?"

"Not every Vampyre sees humans as cattle, and not every human sees Vampyres as monsters. It's simple as that," Ada said.

I extended my hand with a soft smile, letting the barley brush against my palm.

"How long has Avant Garde existed?" Draven asked.

"Since the Crimson War. Those who survived fled here, and brought their human family members with them, and vice versa. Those families blended together over the years, and we've since brought victims of Mundus Novus here on scouting missions." Ada pointed above us, at the words I'd previously addressed and added, "That serves as a reminder to all of us that one day, we will live on the surface again. Where day and night meets at equal length. Until equality and equity is given to Vampyres *and* humans, we won't give up."

The vendors seemed a lot further away on foot than when we were in the trucks. The warm glow of the cavern's skylight caressed my skin, and for once... my neck wasn't taut from the trepidation of impending doom.

"There's a lot more Lightstalkers among you on the surface than you think," Ada continued. "They often don't inherit the Vampyre parent's red eyes, and they almost always have sun immunity. We tend to send them out to scout or gather supplies."

My heart sank. If White Fang or the Nightshades ever found out about this place...

"There's rumors of a scientist who used to work at the Mundus Novus tower and had to flee when they discovered a cure for the

Vampyres' sun blight and blood dependency through a half-breed's DNA. No one knows if it's a man or woman, if they're dead or alive."

Draven grunted and mumbled, "Convenient."

Just as we approached the markets, Ada took a sharp left turn to another tunnel, leading us to a wide chamber that sloped downward. Deep in the cavern, where it cleaved into a gorge of rushing, crystal-clear water. We stared at it over the jagged edge, where small pebbles from our shoes dropped to their fates.

"It's true. We have their notebook with their formulas, observations, tests, trials, and notes. Only half of it was ripped out. The answer lies in those last pages."

Draven's eyes lingered over the chasm, his body swaying as if contemplating the jump. I tugged at his hand, pulling him away from the edge. He blinked, tearing his gaze away from it.

"Ain't doin' no good for anybody now. Y'all got a nice life here anyway... what do you want a revolution for?"

"We're *surviving*, not living. Generators, hydroelectricity, farming. We can't thrive in hiding. We have to be extra careful of being followed, to avoid Mundus Novus sending their Sentries here. These people... they have dreams. Doctors, teachers, engineers..." Ada placed her hands on her hips. "Don't you have dreams?"

Draven's lips parted slightly, his eyebrows sinking into a deep, pensive frown. "I used to."

"And they were snuffed out, weren't they? See, Mundus Novus took that from everyone. If we could show the world that we can live as one, they would lose their credibility and validity as a government."

I clung to every word she said. Something swelled in my chest, heat charged at my fingertips. I was ready to go after Mundus Novus that second.

"It was snuffed out when I became a Nightshade. Their curfews ain't bother me much, because up until I became a lab rat, I went out during the day when I needed to. Even when it hurt."

"Well... whether you acknowledge it or not, Draven, the system they created affected every aspect of your life. Anyways... we'll talk more about it." Ada resumed her stroll, leading us to a chamber that had beds carved out of its circular walls like an open bay.

"I want you kids to take a moment to breathe. You all look like you've been through Hell. This room sleeps six, so pick your beds. My son will take you guys to the market for fresh clothes."

"Um... where do we bathe?" Astoria scratched the side of her cheek with a sheepish smile.

"Ah! Of course!" Ada popped herself on the forehead before pivoting on her heel. "Follow me, loves."

Ada led us back to the gorge, over a narrow simple suspension bridge. A subtle breeze borne from the depths sent us swaying, and the swinging became more prominent as we walked across. Astoria had practically chewed her thumbnail off by the time we reached the other side.

Stairs carved into the bedrock sloped in a half circle. Another cavern skylight spotlighted a natural underground spring with turquoise water. My mouth dropped.

"We have two of these. The other one is reserved for drinking water and irrigation. This one, we bathe in. If you prefer showers, we have some under these stairs," Ada explained. "Similar to the kind at the beach."

I ogled the spring, feeling excitement for the first time since The Hole. After running for our lives, coping with the fledgling phase, and everything else… I convinced myself that nothing could rekindle the light that had died inside me.

"Thank you so much, Ada. For everything." I clasped my hands together in front of my chest, my eyes riddled with tears. "This is… amazing."

"It's no problem, honey. We've been waiting for the day we could fight back, and you two have made that possible." Ada placed a hand on my and Draven's shoulders.

"Yeah, um, that's great and all, but I only have four people I'm interested in killin'. Then I'm off to some peace and quiet. We can get outta ya hair if war is the price to stay here." I frowned at the back of his head.

Speak for yourself, I thought with an audible scoff.

"It's not a price, but you really would be that selfish?" Ada folded her arms.

"This whole mess started with me bein' selfless. I tried to save a guy's life by cuttin' off his finger instead of his head, and then later down the line, I got cast out by my clan as a two-timing lab rat."

Ada sighed and rubbed her temples.

Draven forgot to mention that he'd also spared *my* life, which I thought was the true catalyst to his downfall.

Regardless, I kept my mouth shut.

"There's still some time to think about it. Make yourselves at home." She waved dismissively, then shuffled back through the archway leading to the bridge. I turned to Draven, folding my arms.

"What's wrong with you?"

"Nothin'. How are ya trustin' these people so easily after everything that's happened?"

"Wha—they built an entire city underground to stay hidden from Mundus Novus. If we were prisoners, we would already be locked up somewhere. They have too much to lose to set us off, especially you," I said.

"She's right…" Astoria mumbled, and sat on one of the steps.

"Well, they only care about helpin' us because of what they can get outta us. I'm tired of being used as a tool." Draven stalked off, and I hung back to let him blow off some steam. None of it sounded rational to me, but I wouldn't keep arguing with him. This place was still too unfamiliar.

I peered at the spring. With water so clear it was hard to determine its depth.

"What is it you guys want?" Astoria asked suddenly. It was a loaded question, because for the longest time, I didn't know what I wanted other than a purpose. A life with *meaning*. Helping in a revolution would've been a great start.

Hopefully, if Delilah crossed my path, I could erase her off the planet too. I wanted to fight back, but had lost sight of that with all the running.

Draven was jaded. He wanted to withdraw from the world, never to be seen or heard from again. Which I understood—considering his background—but I also didn't make it any easier. His wants were simple, and sometimes I still wondered if I was a part of them.

I finally shrugged.

"I hated the Check-Ins. I'm technically never supposed to see you again because we're different species. Maybe if we'd grown up in a unified society, and Dad was still alive, Sterling wouldn't harbor so much hate toward us. White Fang and the Nightshades shouldn't be able to get away with all the bull they did to us either. And Cass..." I shook my head. "I guess I want to get stronger, so that we can live. Like *really* live."

Astoria nodded and stared off into space pensively before replying, "Then... show Draven a life that's still worth fighting for."

22
STERLING

THE AIR CONDITIONING UNIT'S LOUD HUM RESOUNDED through the walls. I blocked it out with slow, controlled breaths as I completed single-handed planks. What once brought tremoring, tight pain to my abdomen was now a mild throb, even after holding the position for ten minutes. My heart rate slowed, thrumming in my ears like it sat outside my chest. I went for another ten, and another...

Someone's watch ticked. Another person quietly wept, possibly ten doors down. The staff whispered gossip about their patients in the nursing station two hallways down from my room.

I stopped planking after an hour, still lacking pain.

"Maroon looks good on you." A steely Slavic voice sliced through my thoughts and sent chills to my bones. My eyes flung open. There stood the woman from White Fang on the other side of the plexiglass. She pushed her glasses up her hooked nose and clasped her bony hands in front of her.

"Who are you?" I narrowed my eyes. "I remember you at the lab."

"Dr. Ivanov. It's a shame you were Turned. We could've used your blood to create a cure for your sister," she said, tilting her head with a disappointing sigh.

I scoffed. "You really expect me to believe that's possible? A cure, just like that? After almost a century?"

"There's been many astounding advancements in medicine." Dr. Ivanov carefully scanned me. "Perhaps I could pull a few strings for your early release—if you agree to come with me."

I should've known.

On the one hand, it was a golden opportunity. On the other... it was equally as stupid as Lyra going undercover with the Nightshades.

"Think about it. I'll give you until the end of the day," Dr. Ivanov said, and walked away without sound.

"Wait," I called, and stood with a grunt. Dr. Ivanov ambled back to my window, already gloating with her smug grin.

"I'm not human anymore, so why do you still need me?" I asked.

"The serums we created accelerated Vampyric evolution, and there's a theory that Vampyres pass traits to those they bite. I'm sure you're aware of Draven Hawthorne's fire manipulation, yes?"

I nodded stiffly.

"He bit Briar, and we believe she may have something. There's rumors of her creating a small earthquake at the Nightshade Alpha's residence. With that being said... she could have passed something to you."

How did she know?

"Where's Dr. Nolan?" I asked. "Is she in on this charade you got going on?"

"I wouldn't risk my operation with a Sun Dweller. Not in this climate," she said matter-of-factly. "As far as she knows, I'm assessing her patients for collection while they're unable to go to clinics to fulfill their monthly donation quotas."

"Fine," I said curtly. "What do you need me to do?"

A dumb idea indeed... but even dumber to refuse.

"Pass the test a second time, and I can convince Dr. Nolan to release you. If you can't, well... there's other ways of handling it."

I sucked in a deep breath, then blew a slow stream through tight lips. "Alright, I'll give it a shot."

"Your contribution will be greatly appreciated, Mr. Shaw." Dr. Ivanov grinned, and left with a quiet hum. I let her go that time, flopping on my bed. I rubbed my chest, feeling as though my heart would jump out of it.

I walked with my chin up and shoulders back, and fought the corners of my lips threatening to tug outward as a nurse escorted me to my next test. I was ready for it, relieved to know what to expect. After finally accepting drinking blood, I figured it would be a cakewalk.

Except... we passed the Resistance Room I was so familiar with.

"Where are we going?" I asked with a frown.

"Your next test," the nurse responded.

"We passed the—"

"We don't give the same tests consecutively." She led the way to the elevator, and scanned her badge to access a basement level. I swallowed, keeping the security guard in my peripheral vision in case he reached for his baton.

"Why don't you ever tell us what the test is gonna be?" I asked to fill the silence. The elevator seemed to shrink.

"Life is full of surprises. Vampyres could be triggered at any moment. The tests are to make sure you can adapt and resist, no matter the circumstance you find yourself in," the nurse explained.

I expected a dungeon, but when the elevator doors released us, bright white light reflected off of polished concrete. Secured doors flanked both sides of the hallway. We went straight for the one at the end, where the nurse once again scanned her badge. The heavy metal door creaked as she opened it with a quiet grunt, revealing an inmate in a black jumpsuit. He was strapped to a chair and gagged with a wooden block as if he were getting prepped for electrocution.

"What's this?" I demanded.

"Your test. This man is scheduled for execution. When Black Bay Prison fell, he was one of hundreds who escaped. Mundus Novus pushed his date up for his escape."

"Black Bay—what?" I exclaimed. "Hold on—"

"Your goal is to try *not* to kill him."

The nurse stepped up to the inmate, who squirmed in his chair as he uselessly attempted to get away. She put on a pair of gloves and grabbed a scalpel from a nearby tray of surgical tools. He screamed as she cut deep straight down his forearm, releasing the aroma hiding beneath his skin.

I took a step back, shutting my eyes tightly as my mind turned to static. I pinched my nose and turned away. The security guard shook his head.

"Turn around and lower your hand, sir," he said.

"Are you kidding me? I can't even take measures to—"

I released a snarl, forgetting what I was going to say. I stepped toward the inmate with my nails sharpening. A thought loomed in the distance—a piece of reality to cling to. I tried to grasp it, falling to my knees and biting my lip until it bled. A bitter taste like bile coated my tongue, and the fog faded.

I spat on the floor and gave the nurse a half grin with an arrogant chuckle.

"Congratulations, Mr. Sha—"

A bang stabbed my ears and the nurse crumpled to the floor with a gouging hole in her forehead. I doubled over, covering my ears with grating teeth. The security guard holstered his gun with a blank face.

"Wha—"

The nurse's corpse gaped back at me. For a moment, I expected her to blink—maybe even laugh and reveal it was part of the test. The pit of my stomach hollowed out.

"We can't have any witnesses, now can we? Dr. Ivanov is waiting." He reached for my arm, and as much as I wanted to snatch it away and attack, I allowed him to take me.

At least until we were out of the secured basement.

Our footsteps alternated down the narrow hallway, but soon fell in sync.

"You're not really a security guard, are you?" I asked.

"Excellent observation, *detective*," he sneered, and scanned his badge once we were in the elevator.

"It was my understanding that she was going to tamper with paperwork for my release, not break me out..." I said, my mind flashing back to the unsuspecting nurse. "You didn't have to kill her!"

"Dr. Ivanov did," he said, and led me to the nursing station, where they handed me a clear bag filled with my belongings. "That woman would've reported this to Nolan."

"Feel free to change back into your clothes. They've been washed. Congratulations on reintegrating in society." The salutations were flat, and the nurses and techs spoke in unison like it was a rehearsed farewell for every patient. I twisted my nose at the petite woman holding my stuff, pulling the bag from her grasp.

"Yeah, thanks..." I followed the imposter to a bathroom while he stood outside the door. The first thing I pulled out of the bag was a plain white t-shirt, still stained with faded brown blood when Briar bit me. I sucked my teeth, shoving it back in the bag. I slipped on my sneakers instead, opting to stay in the scrubs. I shoved the bag in the trash and stepped out.

"You have a ride waiting for you outside," the man said, resuming his stride two paces ahead of me. Even though he was affiliated with White Fang, my first thought was Lyra had heard news and came to pick me up.

But what waited for me in the drop-off zone was a blacked-out SUV.

I paused at the curb, gazing at the sky beyond the parking lot that had deepened to marigold, magenta, and violet. The smell of cinnamon and burnt leaves wafted in the crisp breeze. Goosebumps prickled my skin—I hadn't felt fresh air in weeks.

The SUV's windows rolled down with a low hum. A woman drove while two men sat in the passenger and back seats. They all wore sunglasses and had ashen skin. I caught a glimpse of a white cloth in the man's lap in the backseat, and dug my heels further into the concrete when the "security guard" tried to nudge me closer. The back door snicked open.

"What are you doing? Let's go!" he demanded.

"Where's Dr. Ivanov?"

"At the lab. Now *go*," he hissed with rising irritation.

"We don't bite," the woman intoned from the driver's seat.

I jammed my elbow into the guard's gut. He doubled over and I snagged his gun from his holster. The White Fang Vampyre in the passenger seat stretched his arm out the window, metal glinting under the awning's lighting. He spewed bullets, shattering the windows to the lobby. I roared and dove behind a thick concrete column. Distant screams rang.

"We need him *alive*, you idiots!" the woman shrieked. A sharp pain ripped through my side, but I didn't bother to look as I sprinted across the parking lot.

Tires squealed as they swerved into the road, and the White Fang member disguised as security bounded after me on foot. His keys jingled wildly at his belt, and I vaulted over a moving car's hood before it clipped my knees. The Vampyre grunted as he crashed into the car right behind me. I leaped diagonally across the intersection and the pain in my side shot up to my chest. I gasped, leaning against a light pole to regain my bearings. I waved my arms wildly at a taxi, but they all kept driving past.

I finally examined the growing bloodstain on my shirt, blinking at it as my vision went double. I staggered down the wide sidewalk, pressing my hand against the wound, and snaked past Vampyres emerging as the humans' curfew began.

I reached an empty park and opened fire at the guard.

"Hey!" he shouted, and ducked behind a wooden bench. Splinters sprayed as the bullets pierced through, and I stopped with one bullet left. "You promised!"

"I didn't promise to get knocked unconscious!" I yelled breathlessly. "Deal's off, and you can go tell Dr. Ivanov I said that!"

The man raised his hands over the bench before rising with a sneer.

"You really want to do that? Do you have any idea what connections White Fang has? She can ruin your life before she kills you."

"I don't think she plans on killing me any time soon. You're gonna let me go, and you're gonna tell her I'm no longer compliant." I kept the gun pointed at him as I continued to step back, occasionally glancing over my shoulder.

The man scoffed and shook his head. "You just threw away a golden opportunity."

"I think I can live with that." I jerked the barrel in a stiff shooing motion.

"Fine," the man snapped. "Be prepared to keep running."

"Be prepared to lose men," I retorted, and watched him flash back in the direction of the hospital in a blur.

Sirens wailed a couple blocks over.

Sneaking between alleyways and houses to avoid the authorities, I limped the rest of the way to the only place I could think of to hide.

23
LYRA

I stared at the blank business card on my dining table, a small pen-shaped black light lying next to it. I refused to look at the mantle, where I kept memories of Kiegan on display. My leg jumped up and down underneath the table, and I gave myself ten seconds to breathe before I finally picked up the flashlight and my cellphone.

I had to remind myself what I was doing this for.

This was bigger than avenging my husband's death. This was for Helios, the riots and protests, the web of lies Chief Duncan had constructed, and the plans of Mundus Novus as a whole. I might not have considered myself much of a detective anymore, but I still lived by my oath. At the end of the day... this world was wrong.

I waved the black light over the card and dialed the phone number.

It rang for a while, and I thought about hanging up to dial again before a gruff voice answered.

"Name. Intention. Identify who gave you the number."

"My name is Dawn, I wanted to know what I needed to do to join the Nightshades, and Uriah King gave me this number," I said, my spine locking straight in my chair.

Radio silence.

"Hello?" I frowned.

"You will meet someone at the fountain in the town square in precisely twenty minutes."

The line went dead, and I jumped up from the table to get dressed. I grabbed my keys and paused at the mirror near my front door. I plucked the wig off and returned it to its designated bust mannequin, then combed my fingers through my bleached hair. I ignored my heart's relentless attempt to escape my chest as I hustled to beat the time limit.

✳

The town square was sparse. Downtown didn't teem with life like it normally did, and I figured it was due to the hate crime that had recently occurred. Vampyres with all their strengths and might... cowering before humans hiding behind silver bullets.

I scoffed at the notion.

A black pickup truck parallel parked across the street, in front of City Hall. The engine rumbled as the exhaust pipe smoked. I checked my watch.

Twenty minutes on the dot.

The door opened and Wraith dropped out of the driver's seat.

He sauntered to the fountain with his hands in his pockets and his shoulders back in a nonchalant lean.

"I thought Uriah was kidding when he said you decided to join us," Wraith said. "Before that happens, you have to pass a test to prove you ain't a pig."

"What test?" I frowned. He surveyed the square and jerked his chin toward the truck. I hesitantly followed, and got in the back seat despite the passenger side being empty.

"What are you doing back there? I ain't your chauffer." He leaned over and slapped the passenger seat. I sucked my teeth and jumped back out to reposition.

"So what's the test?" I asked again once we started moving again.

"Prove you're willing to fight for the future."

"And that involves...?"

"Well first, you have to be searched for wires and bugs. After that, Uriah will explain." Wraith leered at me, his fangs catching a glint from the neon lights beyond. "I would've preferred that assignment instead of picking you up."

Vomit crept up the back of my throat and I turned to the window.

"Is there an alternative way to prove I'm not wearing a wire?" I clasped my fingers over my lap.

"Nah. Uriah's old-fashioned."

"Who's going to search me?"

"I dunno, probably one of the fledglings. Does it matter?"

"No," I replied curtly, and turned to face the window.

We crossed the forgotten region of downtown, where the streets and storefronts were dilapidated and boarded off. As we drove toward residential neighborhoods, the wild weeds became vibrantly trimmed lawns. The concrete houses framed in chain-link fences grew in size—bigger, bolder two-story homes and two-to-three story mansions. We entered the nicer half of Neoterra, the stomping grounds I rarely entered even as an officer. Wraith turned down the small strip of old money before the road sharply turned downhill and sloped into the infamous Nocturne District.

We passed a partially burned Mediterranean home, charred and ashen from a fire reported weeks ago. The investigation stalled as arson detectives had failed to determine its source. It could have been Draven's doing, but I wasn't the one to tell anyone about it. I'm sure he had valid reasons. He'd proved himself a pretty decent guy, considering what he was involved in.

"So what happens if I don't want to do the test?" I asked as we drew near a 1950s styled mansion nestled in a cul-de-sac.

Wraith laughed, slapping the steering wheel before pulling into the driveway. Solar-powered LED lights lined the path, sprinklers misting over the emerald bermuda grass. He pressed the ignition button to shut the engine off, and the soft mechanical whirs whispered as the vehicle settled.

"This ain't some book club you're trying to get into," he said, and jumped out.

So this is it.

I unbuckled my seat belt, biting my inner cheek as I followed him inside. We were greeted by an arrogant abstract portrait of Uriah King and a console table beneath it with a decanter and glasses. Picture windows lined the front wall, the blinds folded up to let the moonlight in. The floors were pure wood, honeyed herringbone.

Other than the furniture arranged around the living room, the house appeared sparsely decorated. I caught a glimpse of a few boxes stacked in a corner. A gas fireplace glowed with faux flames, a blackened flat screen television mounted above it.

My heart sank when I caught Delilah sitting on the plush white sectional with her legs crossed, sipping blood in a wine glass by the fire. She swirled the glass and rolled her eyes with a quiet groan.

"Where's Uriah?" Wraith asked by way of greeting.

"Putting his new study together. Why?" She scrunched her nose.

I still hung by the front door... just in case.

"I gotta let him know Dawn's here. She's gotta get searched. Which way is the study again? I'm still trying to learn this dumb house."

The red folder Chief Duncan gave Uriah might be in his study.

"Upstairs, on your right. He should have those lions up by now," Delilah droned. Wraith nodded and drifted to the stairs.

"You can come in, you know," Wraith quipped, and disappeared at the top of the staircase. I barely walked deeper into the living room, folding my arms as I waited.

"So what are you up to?" Delilah asked, narrowing her eyes.

"Trying to find something fulfilling to do with my life." I stepped up to the window, switching my focus between the white rock flower beds and the reflections of what went on behind me.

"Yeah. Right." Delilah leaned forward, setting her glass on the raw-edge coffee table. She padded across the white fur rug and put her hands on her hips once she stood in front of me. She never broke eye contact, and neither did I. I raised my chin defiantly.

"What are you here for *really*?" She asked.

"I just told you."

We both turned our attention to the creaking steps as Uriah descended from the darkness upstairs. I blinked, surprised to see him in a white blouse with the sleeves rolled up and jeans with holes in them. Tattoos covered his fleshed arm, and intricate metalwork formed his mechanical one.

"Welcome. Sorry, I didn't think you'd actually show up so I'm not exactly dressed appropriately," he said. Wraith hung behind him, taking a seat on the steps.

"I didn't expect you to," I said, stuffing my hands in my hoodie's pockets. He raised his eyebrows, as if my response came as a shock. He cleared his throat and straightened, back to the proud stance he'd held in the suit he wore at The Nightshade bar.

"Hartley will search you. He's our driver, but also my most impartial member. I trust him." As if his name alone summoned him, a slender but round-faced man with a curled mustache emerged from behind the fireplace. He dipped his head in a shallow bow.

"Let's get this over with," I grumbled. I forced a swallow before following him. Hartley led me through the backyard, past the pool, and into the pool house. He didn't say a single word, and I wasn't sure if that was better or worse for my nerves as I sacrificed my dignity.

For Kiegan, for Neoterra.

I had to keep repeating it to myself after removing each article of clothing. The cold tugged at my skin.

For Kiegan, for Neoterra.

I crossed my legs and slouched with my arms folded over my

chest. I kept my gaze locked on the wall, at a random generic beach painting, imagining I was there instead.

Hartley showed no emotion. His eyes scanned me as he walked in a circle as if surveying a statue. He grunted with a nod, and left me alone to redress, like the privacy suddenly mattered.

✳

I stayed there for a couple minutes, only allowing a couple tears to stream before shutting them off entirely. This was just one of many sacrifices I made for vengeance, and the first I'd made for a city I ignored for far too long. I wiped my eyes with a sniffle, and swaggered out of the pool house. For once, I wished Sterling was here to confide in, or at least here to make me angry enough to forget about the humiliation.

You're more than capable of handling yourself.

Sterling's voice scraped at the back of my mind, and I slid the back door open to step inside with a deep breath.

Delilah was in her usual seat on the couch with her now-empty glass. Wraith still sat on the stairs, grinning like a fox.

"I heard you're clean," he said. "Welcome to the fam."

"Not yet," Delilah intoned, and narrowed her eyes with a sly smirk. "Dawn still has a little piggy to take to the market."

24
LYRA

Delilah's words bounced around my skull. The silence was heavy, filled only by Uriah's footsteps as he returned to the living room.

"Congratulations, Dawn. Now for the next step," he said, waving a small sticky note on his index finger. I frowned, glancing at Delilah while she continued to watch me with a smug grin. "You need to go to this address and eliminate this person."

"I'm sorry, what?" I scoffed. Uriah spoke so casually, as if asking to take the trash out.

"A former member of the clan was supposed to do it, but instead murdered Wraith's brother and is now at large," Uriah explained. "It's imperative she dies."

"Who?"

"Amanda Calloway," Uriah replied. She worked in my unit. Rumors circulated that she took bribes whenever she busted Vampyres breaking curfew. She was a Sun Dweller who cared only about money, not morality or the law. Chief Duncan either never had the evidence to fire her or simply didn't believe in double standards.

"Okay," I said, taking the sticky note. I memorized the address scribbled on it, then handed it back to Uriah so he could potentially shred it.

"*Okay?* That's it?" Delilah frowned

I narrowed my eyes at her with a wry chuckle. "What do you expect? For me to beg you guys to ask me to do something else? I'm here to prove myself whatever it takes. I just have one question, if I'm allowed."

For Kiegan, for Neoterra.

"Go ahead." Uriah hooked his thumbs in his belt loops expectantly.

"You told me the Nightshades were the future. What does she have to do with it, and what future are you building?"

"That's two," Delilah sneered.

Uriah held a hand up. "We're building a future for *us*. Vampyres as a whole, not just Nightshades or White Fang or what have you. Mundus Novus has their Onyx Sentries, but if we take away their auxiliary forces like law enforcement, that's fewer bodies to worry about when it's time for the coup."

I paused, considering. The concept was alluring. A life without judgment, fear, oppression... but at what cost? How far was Uriah willing to go to achieve that power, and how would he overthrow Mundus Novus?

"Their power stretches beyond Neoterra, you know," I said.

"Trust me, I know. You don't need to worry about the logistics," he replied, running a hand through his hair. "Anyways, if you do this, and you're willing to sacrifice yourself for the greater good of our kind, then you'll be a Nightshade. If freedom from the Sun Dwellers' oppression isn't enough motivation, I don't know what is."

I wanted to ask if it had to be tonight, but I worried that would mean either another humiliating search or instant death. Going home with the information they gave me would be too much time for me to tell others.

It didn't feel right. Amanda didn't kill my husband. She had nothing to do with my life, and she'd taken the same oath I did. The extent of my sins stopped at taking Nightshade suspects to the warehouse, with the intent to annihilate them because deep down... I knew they would be free at the end of the day.

And someone else would die at their hands.

I clamped my fists so tight in my hoodie pocket that my nails broke the skin in my palm.

"I need a gun," I finally said.

✳

Uriah stayed behind at the house while Wraith drove Delilah and me across town to a Nocturnal Zone, where Amanda Calloway was only legally authorized to live due to her status as essential personnel. We passed a couple houses with "Beware of Dog" signs hanging on fences. Driveways were cracked, the houses were turning green and black and were in desperate need of power washing, and a pair of sneakers was hanging from a power line. A forgotten zone, not only by the city but by the residents themselves.

Wraith passed the only house with a patrol car parked in front of it, then stopped in front of an abandoned home with a "For Sale" sign in the yard. His knuckles turned white as he gripped the steering wheel, staring at a blank space in the street.

"Are you okay?" I leaned over the middle console, following his gaze.

"This is where his brother died," Delilah uttered.

"*Larkin*," Wraith scowled. "I'm sick of everyone only referring to him as *my brother*."

"Sorry," she grumbled, and lowered her gaze. Her fingers fidgeted in her lap. "I miss him too."

I leaned back, hesitantly getting out of the back seat. I tried to picture the events that had unfolded—the clan member who decided to turn against his own people. I wondered who it was, and what made him throw away his undying loyalty, especially with Uriah's goals being so attractive. It felt too soon to ask.

The gun they gave me felt heavy in my waistband. I threw my hood over my head, looking around for security cameras and nearby electronic doorbells.

Wraith ran in a blur across multiple backyards. I pulled the pistol out and followed with Delilah close behind me, and we stopped around the side of the woman's house. I spotted a narrow awning window halfway up the house, potentially leading to a bedroom or bathroom on the second floor. My body was slender enough to fit through it.

That would've allowed me enough time to warn Amanda.

"It's your time to shine," Wraith whispered, and tossed me an instant camera. I raised an eyebrow with a scrunched nose.

"For proof," Delilah said.

I nodded, pursing my lips tightly before looping the camera's strap around my neck. I put the gun back in my waistband and scaled the house's brick wall. Gripping the windowsill with one hand, I pulled the window's frame until it snapped open. The latch on the other side popped, and I crawled through. I carefully extended my arms downward in a reverse pull-up, landing on the bathroom tile floor with stealth.

The bathroom counter was cluttered with combs, straighteners, and two toothbrushes—a plain white electronic one, and a smaller princess-shaped one.

I shut my eyes tightly in an attempt to erase the image.

I turned the knob completely before creeping inside the hallway, where every door was shut. I followed the sounds of steady breathing and the occasional snore to a door next to the linen closet, carefully cracking it open. The lump in the bed moved up and down in peaceful slumber. I checked behind me to make sure Wraith and Delilah were still outside.

Amanda didn't stir when I approached her bedside. I surveyed the scissors, thread, and decorative patches on her nightstand, then slammed my hand over her mouth. Her eyes flew open with a squeal.

"Shhh!"

I reached for the scissors with my free hand. "I'm supposed to kill you. I won't. There's Nightshades that want you dead. I'm going to stab you and give you time to call for help and survive the wound, but I need to take a picture of you dead," I spoke in a rapid whisper, praying she clung to every word. If there was anything I wanted to achieve tonight, it was to maintain my cover without destroying a life. Although without a mask, it was a risk to let her live.

Tears squeezed out of Amanda's eyes, and for a moment, the spark of fear transitioned into awareness.

"I'm undercover," I whispered, and punctured her side with the scissors without warning. "I'm so sorry."

Amanda screamed, and I shot the gun twice, one in her headboard and one in her bed, then took the blood from her wound and smeared it all over her face, pillow, and pajama shirt. Her breaths became labored.

"Lyra... H-Hart..." she wheezed. I snatched up the two casings and tucked them in my front hoodie pocket. I forced her to look to the side, and snapped a photo while her eyes were open in blank shock. Scissors still in hand, I darted for the bathroom window, leaving a bloody handprint on the sill. I frantically snatched a hand towel from the rack and used cold water to wipe the handprint away, then used the towel to block additional prints as I climbed back through the window. Wraith and Delilah were gone, but the truck screeched to a stop in front of the house. I kept the towel and scrambled to my feet, sprinted across the yard and plunged into the back seat. Wraith accelerated before the door was closed completely, burnt rubber filling the air.

My entire body trembled while I gathered my bearings. Wraith laughed wildly as he drove, and Delilah held her palm out patiently. I passed the picture to her with a red-stained hand, the wind from the windows drying the blood into a sticky film.

"Huh. She really did it," Delilah said as she examined the picture in an incredulous manner. She turned it in multiple angles, and held it up for Wraith. He did a double take, switching his focus between the road and the photo while he wove through traffic.

"Man! Who knew a pretty face like yours could be so deadly, Dawn! Ha, welcome to the family!" he exclaimed joyously.

Why couldn't it be spray painting City Hall?

I rolled onto my back, laying across the back seat. I closed my eyes, praying Amanda's daughter was old enough to call the police for her mother.

I could never show back up to work again.

For Kiegan, for Neoterra.

✳

The incoming dawn was like a rose. Deceptively soft and gentle, but with a subtle burn from the prick of thorns as the sun emerged. The blinds were closed in Uriah's house in preparation for the daylight, but he waited for us in the living room with a wide grin stretched across his shadowed, chiseled face.

"I heard you're full of surprises," he said by way of greeting. I forced a weak smile and looked down at the blood on my hand. My stomach twisted with hunger, but I knew I had bags waiting for me at home. I couldn't live with the thought of drinking Amanda's blood after trying to save her life.

"Whatever it takes," I said quietly, glancing at Delilah. She folded her arms, still sizing me up like that first night at the club. But the smiles on Wraith and Uriah's faces... celebrating what they believed I did... it sickened me.

"Well, hurry on home. We have much to celebrate tonight. You'll be getting your tattoo of the crest so... think about where you want it. It must be in a location that's easy to expose for cautionary purposes."

I understood why Sterling's hatred was so ingrained, even though the Nightshades weren't a representation of our kind. But he must've seen a consistent pattern to draw his conclusions. The events our men and women in blue endured made it easy to feel such passions. I had been too distracted by Kiegan's death to fall into it.

"Thank you, Uriah," I mumbled, laying out the gun, photo, and towel in the middle of the floor. I didn't want to dirty his precious coffee table in the living room, or the console table displaying the decanter and glasses.

"We'll burn the towel and photo for you." Wraith leaned down and picked up the items.

"Hartley will take you back to your car," Uriah said, and once again, the driver manifested from the kitchen. I wiped my clammy palms against my hoodie at the sight of him and forced a smile before averting my gaze.

"I'll see you guys tomorrow," I said, and rushed outside. I kept my head low under the hood, tucking my hands in my pockets when the sky seared my skin. Hartley emerged from the front door with an umbrella, holding it above my head.

"Sorry about earlier," Hartley mumbled. He opened the back door for me, and I hastened to sit. I couldn't get out of there fast enough.

I leaned my head against the window, keeping my head slumped. I rolled the casings between my fingers in my hoodie pocket, replaying the night's events. The sun felt like it intensified every five minutes, and the trip back to the town square dragged on.

I mumbled a thank you to Hartley when we returned to my car, then sped through roads that never got patrolled.

I barely parked straight in front of my townhome, rushing to get inside. I slammed the door shut, wincing at the fire that spread across the backs of my hands and face. The cool darkness of my home caressed my skin, like spreading aloe over angry burns.

Thud.

My body tensed as I pulled a revolver from inside the fireplace I never used. I crept past the living room, kitchen, and dining space.

Another thump, then a shallow groan. The sounds tugged me toward the back door, which I opened with a quick shove. I pointed my gun with my finger on the trigger at the person slumped against my flower pot with his hand resting over a red splotch in his side.

Every muscle loosened, and the air escaped my lungs.

Sterling—so pale that even his freckles lost their pigment—peered at me with his eyes rolling to the back of his skull. His hand flopped from his side, coated in crimson. I pulled him inside without another second wasted.

25
DRAVEN

I TRUDGED THROUGH THE CAVERN FEELING AS THOUGH THERE were anchors strapped to my ankles. I blocked out the gossiping whispers between the Lightstalkers and Vampyres as I wandered, following Caspian's scent. There were too many curious minds, too many mad scientists.

"Where are you off to, love?" Ada's voice sliced through my thoughts.

"Just lookin' for my friend."

"Ah, of course. He's still in a coma but he's stable. Follow me." Ada rested her hand on my back, and I bit my tongue at the unsolicited touch.

We cut through the fields, hopped into one of the trucks, and rode up a narrow slope toward the homes carved out of the cavern walls. The cabin rocked over the uneven bedrock, and I kept the corner of my eye glued to the bottom of the unguarded cliff.

"So... you and Briar, how did you two meet?" Ada asked, not at all bothered by the hazardous road conditions. To be fair, she probably could've driven it blindfolded.

"It's... complicated."

"You two *meeting* is complicated? Jeez, I'd hate to hear about your relationship," Ada quipped with a soft snicker.

"She caught me committin' arson, we ran into each other at a hospital, and then again at a bar. She'd broken curfew twice at that point and I saved her from a couple of lowlifes," I said, then leaned my head back against the headrest with a quiet sigh. "Why?"

"Ah. I suppose that is complicated. I was only curious. No need to be so defensive around me, Draven."

I chuckled dryly. "And I'm just supposed to take ya word for it?"

"No, and I understand why you won't. I want you to know you're not in enemy territory, and we're all on the same team." Her eyes softened, but it didn't melt my heart of stone like she probably hoped.

"We have medicine to help Briar's cravings. It'll help speed her fledgling phase and develop resistance. It's the same medication the hospital uses."

"I just want to see my friend... and silence." I drummed my fingertips against the door's armrest impatiently, but still held on to those words in the back of my mind. I didn't trust the pills or shots or anything else this place had to offer. I didn't want Briar to find out about this until I knew for sure.

I surveyed the homes. Clothes and banners hung on lines

stretched across the road, shared between balconies bedecked in vines thriving in the full shade. The truck slowed to a stop, and we unloaded in front of a two-story home made of mud, clay, and stone like all the others. Honeyed light poured out of its oval windows. Ada approached the door and lightly knocked.

"Doc? It's Ada. I'm here with Draven, he'd like to see his friend's condition."

"Yeah!" Heavy coughing and a thick sniffle sounded behind the door, followed by thudding footsteps descending the stairs. The door swung open, and a scraggly older man in a soiled white tank top and grey shorts appeared. His face glistened with beads of sweat, and various smudges coated the black-rimmed glasses resting on his bulbous nose. Ashen brown eyes sat behind them, glazed over from either the liquor he reeked of or from age. My lips sucked inward, holding back the words bubbling behind my teeth. If anything, I was concerned about Caspian's condition *worsening* around this guy.

"Come in, milady," he drawled, leaving the door ajar as he shuffled across the foyer. The curtains danced against an oscillating fan pointing at whatever lay behind a paper partition. Blankets peeked from behind it.

"Thanks, Vyrn." Ada stepped inside and I followed, instantly observing the home.

"Your friend is over there, he's still unconscious but his vitals are stable." He pointed with a crooked finger toward the partition, and I sauntered behind it. An eye patch rested over Caspian's eye, the glistening, jagged pink scar poking above and below it. The similarity to his father was uncanny, and I dreaded the moment he realized that when he woke up.

"It's quite impressive, actually," Vyrn announced as he plopped into a squeaky desk chair.

"What is?" Ada asked.

I tilted my head at different angles, observing the rise and fall of Caspian's chest with narrowed eyes. His breaths were steady, yet... something seemed off. It was like a dark aura rippled around him, like a mirage in the middle of the street on a hot summer day. I stretched a comforting hand toward his shoulder.

"A Lightstalker living this long on the surface undetected? I got a lot of questions for him when he wakes up," he said.

I frowned, swinging my head around the corner of the partition before I could touch the shadows surrounding Caspian.

"What do ya mean, 'Lightstalker'? Caspian burns faster than the average Vampyre. He was never Turned, and his dad wouldn't be caught dead with a human," I said, throwing my hand up at the audacity of it.

This Doc is a quack.

"I hate to burst your bubble, son, but not all Lightstalkers are blessed with sun immunity, without blood dependencies, or with any other quirks you guys have. Genes choose whatever side they wanna lean on. The only thing that's pretty much certain is that if the mother is a human, her pregnancy is a death sentence. It's an extremely rare case when the mother survives." Vyrn gave a pointed look at Ada before reaching for a flask. He tossed it in his palm, checking the heft of it. He groaned and set it down on the coffee table, which was covered in paper plates with crumbs and grease stains.

Caspian was completely still, and his natural skin of frost made him look like a corpse. The black veins stretching across his neck, jaw, and cheeks were like tree branches. He'd had a secure place with the Nightshades—Uriah's most trusted clan member. Yet... he chose to help me, and destroyed all of it.

And later got mutilated by his own father.

Whatever he had going on may have been similar to Briar, but being a Lightstalker could change how his body reacted to the serum. Dying was now more of a possibility.

"How do you know?" I asked, turning back to Vyrn.

"Oh, I took a sample of his blood," he said with a shrug.

The skin in my face tightened as I snarled. I flashed toward him, snatching him by the neck so hard that his chair toppled over. I reared my hand back with my claws completely sharpened.

"Draven!" Ada shouted, her holster flopping open. I didn't take my eyes off the man while she aimed her gun at me.

"You... did... *what*?" I growled.

"I-I—" Vyrn wheezed, clawing at my hand with sweaty fingers.

"Y'all doin' experiments too?" The skin around my knuckles began to peel like ash and embers. "What's it gonna take for a little *decency* around here?"

For a moment, I didn't see Vyrn.

I saw Cyrus electrocuting me with a baton.

Briar strapped to a chair, her blood being withdrawn against her will.

The firing squad lined up to test my reaction to silver bullets.

Vyrn's eyes began to roll to the back of his head.

"Draven, stop! He needed to know how to treat Caspian! This isn't White Fang!" Ada screamed.

It took every cell in my body not to snap his neck. I let go, and Vyrn fell on his side, overwhelmed by wheezes. I roared and stormed out of the hut, beginning my singeing trail down the rocky slope.

"Draven!" Ada's raspy voice rang out as she jogged after me. I took a deep breath with flared nostrils and bit my inner cheek to smother the fire swirling within. I exhaled, and smoke escaped my nose.

"I'm sorry, I should've warned you. Please wait—" She spoke breathlessly and gripped my shoulder. I gave a warning snarl, stopping in my tracks. Nevermind the few Lightstalkers and Vampyres pointing their guns at me from their balconies, waiting for one wrong move.

"Is everybody armed to the tooth down here?" I asked with a wry chuckle.

"We've been planning to break the surface for decades," she said, and ran a hand over her short, coiled hair. She pressed her palms together. "I know you're still healing from everything you've been through. But you and your friends aren't guinea pigs. We've been keeping an eye on everything for answers, not evolution."

"Ya know something? People like you, Uriah, Dr. Ivanov... y'all got a real gift of sugarcoating poison." I folded my arms and jerked my chin at Vyrn's house behind her. "Cass looked a lot worse in there than before we got here. What did he do to him?"

"I *swear* to you, Vyrn didn't do anything except draw a sample of blood. He discovered genetic mutations, common ones that

Vampyres share from the Red Plague, but also... something else. Something similar to what White Fang achieved, but not quite."

"How do ya know so much about what White Fang is doing?" I barked.

My head felt like it was going to explode with the number of people I couldn't trust. What crests did Ada have on her body? It didn't matter what species she was—nothing was predictable these days.

The gears began turning as I tried to figure out how I could get Caspian out and alert Briar and Astoria.

"My son went there, was one of their successes. A delayed one... he almost died, but—"

"Who?" I narrowed my eyes.

"You're standing a little too close to that guy, Ma. He's got a serious temper." A familiar, young voice—one that struck a chord inside me so violently that it snapped—

I turned to see the person who called himself my biggest fan.

The one who tried to drown us on the ferry. The one *I* should've been able to kill—for Briar's sake.

I lunged for Oren's neck.

26
STERLING

ALL THE ADRENALINE IT TOOK TO RUN AWAY FROM THE WHITE Fang thugs seeped out of my pores the second I fell over Lyra's fence and face-planted against the concrete patio. The pain in my side intensified and vanished repeatedly, like squeezing a stress ball. I crawled up against her oversized flower pot and leaned against it with a wince.

I wasn't sure how long I was out there waiting and fighting to keep conscious, but the sun crept higher in the sky. To my surprise, it didn't make my skin peel like burnt paper. I heard the front door open.

I mustered up the last of my strength to bump my head against the flower pot a couple times.

The door slid open, with a pistol pointing at my face. My blurred vision sharpened on Lyra's face. Her breath caught. She slowly lowered her gun with tense eyes softening and forehead wrinkling with concern. She blinked rapidly before tucking her gun in her pants and carried me inside in silence.

The leather couch was cool, its cushions sighing under my weight as they enveloped my body.

"What happened?" she called out, suddenly sounding farther away than when she first laid me down. I smacked my lips, mumbling incoherently.

Lyra flashed to my side with a first aid kit. She took a small pair of scissors that barely fit over her thumb and index fingertips and cut the side of my shirt, then reached for a bottle of alcohol. She worked deftly with her lips thinned, breathing heavily. I watched her ruby irises switch between my injury and the first aid kit. The sharp and throbbing anguish drowned out all other thoughts. I lurched upward and she used her hand of steel to hold me down.

"What are you doing?" I croaked.

"The bullet is still in there, that's why you're not healing. It doesn't help that it's probably silver." She pulled out a pair of tweezers and pulled my skin taut.

"Find something to bite on," she mumbled. I clutched one of her pillows. My fangs punctured its fibers as the teeth of the tweezers scraped and poked around my side, and an agonized roar ripped through my throat. Lyra held the smashed bullet in her palm with a pleased grin, the silver sizzling against her skin. My pain instantly vanished. If only the puncture marks in her pillow could disappear like that.

I flopped my head against the armrest. Exhaustion plagued me, but sleep had fled my body a long time ago.

"Thank you," I rasped as she cleaned the blood around the area. I was perfectly capable of cleaning myself up, but she continued as if I were still a debilitated human.

"Who were you running from? How are you out so early?" She gathered the soiled cotton balls and gauze, then shuffled to the guest bathroom. Amber light poured into the hallway in the shape of a trapezoid, framing the shape of her curved silhouette.

"White Fang. I, uh... thought I was making a deal with them to get out sooner, and they tried to drug me." I sat up with a grunt, resting my arm across the back of the couch. Lyra sucked her teeth, and the darkness swallowed her shadow when the light shut off. She returned to the living room with her arms folded.

"So it's crazy when I suggest going undercover with the Night-shades, but it's totally logical for you to accept a deal with White Fang?"

Granted, I'd recognized the double standard when I'd considered Dr. Ivanov's offer. But it was a onetime thing.

"You suggested something that would expose you to danger for months. I just needed access to the outside world." I shrugged. "The blonde's not a bad look on you, by the way."

Her eyebrows twitched, threatening to form a frown at my compliment. She could've mirrored Cyrene aside from her angular, Vampyric eyes, and her sharper chin and cheekbones.

"And you decided to come *here*?" Lyra scampered to her windows, gun in hand, and peeked through the blinds.

"I wasn't followed," I promised. "I didn't... have anywhere else to go."

She turned to me, her face softening to pity. She shuffled to the couch and took the spot next to me, her ankle tucked under her knee.

"You know if they sense you in any way, my cover's blown and I'm dead," she said with a scowl.

"You got that deep with the Nightshades already?" Once again, my efforts were pointless.

"The second I called that number it was too late. They still don't trust me, but I'm supposed to get the crest tonight, so maybe more information will come to light."

I folded my arms. "Did you learn anything useful?"

Lyra bit her lip, looking down at the soft shag rug beneath the couches.

"They're targeting law enforcement officers to weaken Mundus Novus' forces. Part of my initiation was to kill Amanda Calloway—"

I gasped, and she held her hand up.

"But I *didn't*. I warned her of what was happening and made it look like a murder. I think it was convincing enough."

I shifted my weight on the couch. My spine turned into a rod.

"We gotta warn everybody if that's the case," I declared.

"With what proof? And with what support? I followed Chief Duncan one night and he met up with Uriah King. He handed him a confidential folder like he was working with just another officer. He's the whole reason I wanted to start infiltrating the Nightshades in the first place."

I blinked, her words hitting me like a delayed echo. Then my brows tugged inward tightly once I finally processed it.

"*Chief* is involved in this mess?" It explained the number of times he'd dismissed me.

"Yeah, I think that's the reason why your files disappeared. I don't know his motive, but I need to find that file he gave away." She examined the tear in my shirt.

"I... may have some clothes that could fit you," she said hesitantly. I cringed, knowing full well that those probably belonged to her dead husband.

"Lyra, it's okay. I don't think I'm comfortable wearing your... uh... husband's clothes."

"Yeah, well, I don't want your nasty scrubs all over my couch all day," she retorted, and once again she disappeared down her murky hallway.

I guess I couldn't complain much. She could've sent me right back onto the street to figure everything out on my own.

The hall light flicked on, and she appeared with a towel and a stack of neatly folded clothes.

"I'm leaving this in the bathroom. Feel free to shower or whatever," she said, disappearing briefly before she went into the kitchen. I stood up and joined her there, leaning over the peninsula countertop.

"Let me go with you tonight," I said, eyeballing her fridge full of blood bags when she opened it. Lyra laughed, shaking her head.

"Absolutely not," she said, plopping one of the pouches on the counter and grabbing another for herself. I opened mine without hesitation. She paused with her bag right at her lips, watching me. Studying me.

"They don't know I'm a Vampyre, I could have a completely different scent now," I insisted.

"I'm not willing to take that risk, and since Dr. Ivanov saw you, they definitely know. They're still coordinating," she said firmly.

The silence was alive and menacing as we stared each other down like a pair of territorial wolves. My jaw twitched as I bit down, reining in the urge to say she didn't have a choice.

"Why didn't you tell me about Black Bay Prison's invasion?" My voice was sharp. Lyra tossed her empty blood bag in a biohazard trash can with a scoff, and folded her arms with her weight shifted to one hip.

"I didn't think I was obligated to tell you *everything*. You were busy enough being a fledgling. Why does it matter anyways?"

"Because that means my mom could be dead."

The irritation in her face melted to sorrow. "I'm sorry..."

I never specified whether she was an inmate or staff, and I didn't plan to until probably... never.

"I need to go to Helios to make sure she's okay, and I need your help to track down my sisters."

"Why? To make sure they're safe too or to get back at Briar?" she asked with an incredulously arched eyebrow.

Judging by her tone, she wasn't going to offer any support regarding Briar.

"Can you just help me get to Helios?" I couldn't bring myself to give her the obvious answer she wanted to hear. But my mother... that was something we could agree on.

"After I meet with the Nightshades tonight," she said, running a hand through her hair with an exhausted sigh. "I think the ferry is back open."

"Thanks," I mumbled. Lyra was stretched thin between her job at the precinct, her undercover work, and now me selfishly asking for favors. I swallowed my guilt, only because I didn't have a car or a home anymore. She checked her watch and stood from the couch.

"Make yourself at home, I guess. I need to get ready," she muttered, and retreated down the hall again. I hated that I was invading her space, but I had no choice. If it wasn't safe at the hospital, it wasn't safe anywhere else. I couldn't trust the Neoterra Police Department either.

I listened to the shower turn on and rose from the couch, shuffling to the fireplace. I scanned the photos of Lyra and her late husband, full of smiles I rarely ever saw. I stopped at two photos where they appeared very young, like high schoolers. He wore a bomber jacket and she was in a spaghetti-strap dress holding a bow and violin, leaning her head against his shoulder. I had no idea she'd played instruments when she was younger.

Then again, I never took the time to learn anything about her.

I moved on to the next set of photos depicting their wedding. I lightly traced the shape of her satin curves and the laced train. Remembering myself, I jerked my hand back with a cursed breath. I shook my head and moved to the last picture on the mantle, where they hiked and he was leaning into her ear. Something in my chest burned at the thought of them having all the time in the world together.

I wrote it off as acid reflux.

But the guilt still scratched there, reminding me of all the despicable things I'd said to her while she grieved.

I made my way back to the couch, turned the television on, and flipped to the news channel.

The news anchor sat at a granite desk, confidently explaining the events unfolding in the clips overlaid on the screen next to him. My brain didn't process his words as I immediately became engulfed in the images of Helios in shambles. Onyx Sentries marched through the streets. A tank crept behind them, leading a string of Vampyres with their ankles and necks shackled.

"... and they will be taken to camps for reconditioning until further notice."

I snapped my focus to the news anchor with a deep frown.

Reconditioning?

"Helios is eighty percent cleared, but still remains in a state of emergency. Governor Elise Donovan and Chief of Police Andrew Duncan will be addressing the matter and how it will affect Neoterra."

The screen switched to City Hall, its front steps saturated with journalists held behind aluminum barricades. Cameras flashed at every angle and microphones floated, supported by long poles.

"In light of the recent violent crimes Neoterra has endured, and the extreme state Helios is currently in, I am enacting stricter curfews." Governor Donovan occasionally looked down at her notes on the podium she stood behind, and swept her human gaze over the crowd after every sentence. Poised and careful.

The crowd clung to every word, and groaned in dissent at her announcement.

"What are the new hours?" someone demanded, jutting their microphone closer.

"Vampyres will only be allowed to be out from midnight to three in the morning. Humans are still required to be sheltered during those hours." She broke her robotic demeanor, swatting a fly from her face. "Effective immediately."

"What? They get three hours? Don't you think that's inhumane?" someone exclaimed. They sounded genuinely shocked.

"Are the Onyx Sentries coming to Neoterra?"

"If we can prevent falling into a state of emergency, then no," Governor Donovan responded flatly, ignoring the previous reporter's question.

"What is Reconditioning?" The same reporter she ignored spoke again, and I began to suspect he was a Vampyre disguised as a human, trying to fit in as many questions before the sunburns gave him away.

"The Vampyres who were involved in the riots are being taken to facilities to retrain them in restraint and civility. They will reintegrate with society once those standards are met." Governor Donovan kept her palms flat on the podium, covering the index cards in front of her.

"Are you suggesting the Vampyres need to be retrained like animals?"

"I would never. I urge everyone to continue with your lives while we get this sorted out. We suspect this is the work of crime lords." Governor Donovan's eyes briefly flitted in Chief Duncan's direction. He held his hands behind his back, looking down at his feet as if in prayer. If anything Lyra said was true, it wasn't God he was praying to.

He raised his head, making his announcement with a booming tone. "There will be heavier patrols throughout the city, and two Check-Ins. One at the usual time, and a second one at midnight. I understand there may be sleep disturbances, but those are measures we have to take to ensure the safety of all humans."

"What about the safety of the Vampyres?" the same reporter shouted, and Governor Donovan jerked her chin in his direction. Almost immediately, an officer knocked the microphone out of his hands and used a baton to strike the back of his knees. The press gasped, backing away. From the angle of the camera, all I could see was the baton rising and falling, the reporter's screams puncturing the air. Once he quieted, Governor Donovan clasped her hands together on the podium with a broad smile like nothing had happened.

"Any more questions?"

*

I shut the television off, suddenly feeling lightheaded. Lyra returned to the living room, adjusting a gold link watch band on her wrist. Strikingly bold winged eyeliner accentuated her sharp, sleek eyes. Her lipstick was dark plum, almost black. Lyra's previous platinum French bob was transformed into a half up, half down style. She wore a black cold-shoulder minidress paired with stockings. She gripped the edge of the countertop to put on a pair of black-and-white pumps, and paused in the middle of her second shoe when she caught me staring.

"What are you looking at, Sterling? You got something you wanna say?" Lyra frowned, straightening. Her weight shifted as she stood lopsided, one foot in a heel and the other flat on the floor.

"N-nothing," I stammered with a small laugh. "I just didn't expect you going all out. You look..."

"What?" Her eyebrows cinched together.

"Pretty," I blurted, and thought I felt bile inch its way up my throat after my big mouth betrayed me.

Lyra's tensed shoulders sloped back and her eyes softened. She stared at me, her rapid blinking louder than the words she lost. Something glimmered in her eyes, and she rushed back to the bathroom.

27
LYRA

I HAD A LOT ON MY PLATE. THINGS A HUMAN WOULD LOSE sleep over. Neoterra's shootings, stricter curfews imposed on Vampyres, Onyx Sentries in Helios, White Fang's experiments, the Nightshades potentially finding out my status as an officer...

Yet none of those things occupied my mind as I drove to the town square. No... it was Sterling's reaction when I emerged from the bathroom in the old dress I hadn't worn since high school, in makeup I hadn't painted on my face since I first ran into him at The Nightshade bar. Hearing the word *"pretty"* come out of Sterling's otherwise hateful mouth was like trying to force lemonade out of limes. It was blunt, it was weird, it was—

Kind.

It was... *lovely.* And it made my eyes burn every time I thought about it.

"Pull yourself together," I mumbled, parallel parking across from the fountain in the center of the town square. I waited in my car and kept an eye out for the truck that had picked me up last night. Instead, Delilah stepped out of a low-riding sports car with opaque black windows, wearing a pencil skirt and a strapless crop top. While my gut roiled at the sight of her, I was relieved I hadn't overdressed.

"I was hoping you forgot," Delilah sneered, and returned to the driver's side when I approached.

"Happy to disappoint," I retorted. I expected her to drive off as I grabbed the door handle, but to my surprise she didn't. I settled in the passenger seat, and purposefully left the seat belt off to appear less uptight.

She slammed the gas, and the car lurched forward and swerved in the roundabout. I gripped the door's interior handle, waiting for the moment we flipped over. Delilah increased the speed as we shot forward.

"Are you crazy? You could kill someone!" I exclaimed.

"And you care, why?" She crossed the double yellow line, driving recklessly in the oncoming lane. "It'd be a useless Sun Dweller anyway."

"Wha—I'm not interested in doing it for fun, you psycho!" I exclaimed.

"There's something about you that's off, and I'm gonna figure it out tonight," Delilah said, the car cutting through the air like wind resistance didn't exist. "I couldn't find you anywhere online, *Dawn*."

"Why would I be online for anything other than shopping?"

I exclaimed. Even under my real name, I didn't have social media. It was more trouble than it was worth in my line of work. The real world was dark enough as it is, and I didn't want to look at it in the comfort of my home.

Qualities—I *thought*—would win me brownie points with a crime syndicate that lived in the shadows.

"Yeah, well, I never saw any criminal records either," Delilah said.

I rolled my eyes. "That just means I'm not dumb enough to get caught."

A box truck's headlights flashed frantically in our direction, its driver laying on the horn. I shut my eyes tightly, praying that the driver was a Vampyre like us.

My head smacked against the window as the car jerked into the other lane at the last second, squeezing between two other evenly spaced vehicles. My whole body relaxed at once, followed by violent tremors. Delilah, on the other hand, only released maniacal laughter, and finally drove at the normal speed limit.

"Do you do this to every new clan member?" I rasped.

"Nope. Only you." She smiled sweetly, and cranked up the radio to max volume.

I thought my ears would bleed.

✳

Ten cars wrapped around the circular driveway of Uriah's house, and three more parked in the cul-de-sac. White and gold light filtered through sheer curtains in the windows like milk and honey. Music blared inside, and people stood in silhouetted clusters. I bit my lip, hoping that Uriah wouldn't turn it into a celebration for my successful initiation.

Delilah pushed past me up the walkway, determined to enter first. I sucked my teeth, but held back my growing temper as she strutted inside. The music increased in volume, then became muffled again as the door shut behind her. I yanked it back open, following her into the lion's den.

If the house was alive, then the music was its beating heart.

The floor, walls, and ceiling all reverberated with the bass. Some Vampyres danced, others mingled, and a group played a game of cards on the coffee table next to lines of white residue. Tendrils of cigarette smoke wafted from somewhere, but I couldn't pinpoint the source. My eyes darted in every direction, and stopped on a younger boy no older than twenty standing alone in a corner. He stared intensely in my direction. His appearance was striking—with patterned skin of night and day, tightly coiled bleached hair styled in a crisp fade and waves, and slate grey eyes. When he flashed his teeth at passing clan members, I expected blunt incisors. But no—he had fangs. I frowned, having never seen a Vampyre without some shade of red eyes before in my life.

He must be special like Draven.

Delilah got lost in the crowd, and I rehearsed how I could approach him without being offensive. As I drew near, he leaned further against the wall as if he wanted to morph into it.

"Hey." I hooked a piece of my hair behind my ear and gave him a gentle smile. "I'm Dawn."

"No you're not, but it's okay." He mirrored my smile, except it didn't reach his eyes. I reeled from his response, as if he physically punched me in the gut.

"Excuse me?"

"They're not here, if that's who you're looking for."

"Who?" I scrunched my nose and folded my arms with a scoff.

"Act like you're having a good time." His placid face contorted into a grin, and he crinkled the corners of his eyes.

"What—" I kept my back turned toward the direction Delilah had disappeared. "Who are you?"

The boy leaned closer to me, and I tipped backward until I realized he was aiming for my ear.

"Draven and Briar are in Helios."

I wasn't there for them, but that was enough to know my cover was blown and I needed to disappear before Uriah showed up.

I peered at the boy from under my brows.

"Who... *are you*?" I repeated slowly through a locked jaw. He took a long swig of the beer in his hand, and I resisted the urge to snatch it from him. If I made a scene, I might as well dig my own grave in Uriah's backyard. The boy leaned forward again.

"Oren. I volunteered at White Fang and saw you and Sterling Shaw get brought in. You've got some nice fighting skills, by the way."

I faltered, my heart speeding even faster than my racing mind. I turned and pushed past a group of inebriated Vampyres, heading for the front door.

"Leaving so soon?" A gust of wind rushed by as Delilah flashed in front of me. She leaned against the door and stuck out her bottom lip in a mocking pout. "Getting cold feet?"

"No, I just needed some air," I said firmly.

"What did the creep say to you?" She jutted her chin in Oren's direction.

"Nothing, I—hey, I don't need to answer to you!" I snapped, and my arm twitched back as Uriah descended the steps.

"What's going on here, ladies?" he demanded. I took a deep breath and loosened my fists, stepping away from Delilah. I smoothed my palms over my hips, wiping the sweat away.

"I think we need to go ahead and get her crest," Delilah said. "She's getting restless."

"Ah, yes, of course," Uriah chuckled. "I forgot to tell you tonight was also my housewarming party."

"We could always do it another night," I said, and forced a laugh.

"No, we need to do it now. Have you decided where it's going to go?" Uriah slid his massive arm over my shoulders and walked toward a door under the staircase. I thought it was a storage closet...

To my horror, it was a basement.

"Forearm," I whispered, my voice lost in the music.

"A popular one, excellent choice." He guided me down the stairs. Wraith sat next to an adjustable tattoo chair with a tattoo machine in his hand.

I didn't have a single tattoo on my body. I never denied the artistry, but I'd never had the desire for one. Kiegan had a couple.

No. Don't start thinking about him now. Not now.

"I promise I won't hurt you... a lot." Wraith's lips stretched into a sickly, sadistic grin as he gestured to the reclined chair.

"Welcome to the family, Dawn," Uriah said, and retreated to the party. Wraith took his seat on a stool next to his supply cart as I eased into the recliner.

I forced a dry swallow.

And prepared to get the crest of my husband's murderers.

218

28
DRAVEN

I swiped the air with my claws, barely missing Oren's neck as he flinched back. All I could see was the cocky grin on his face as he stood on the gunwale, summoning a wave to wipe us off the map.

"Whoa, whoa!" Ada shouted. "Calm down! Everyone, hold your fire!"

"We ain't in the middle of the ocean this time!" I yelled with wild laughter, my palms igniting.

"Draven, what are you doing!" Briar shouted as she wedged herself between Oren and me. Where did she come from? She placed her hands over both of our chests, pushing us apart. Breathing sharply through tight teeth, I took a step back. Briar's voice was the anchor keeping me from ripping his face to shreds.

"He tried to kill us, Briar!" I jabbed a finger at him.

"Yeah, well I also carried you morons to shore!" Oren spat. I seethed, scrunching my nose up with a deep scowl.

"Bull!" I retorted. Briar drew in a breath, snapping her head between us.

"Hey—"

"I made those waves take y'all to Helios, far enough away from Uriah so I could sell my story that I killed you guys," Oren interjected in a slower tone, as if he were talking to a child. It made everything in my body boil, down to the molecular level.

"Draven." Briar waved her hand in front of my face, and I shifted my gaze to hers. "Let's take a walk."

"I'm not leaving Caspian here with a Nightshade," I said, jerking my chin at Oren. He rolled his eyes.

"How do you think Avant Garde is capable of keeping up with what's happening on the surface?" he asked with a scoff.

"Oren..." Ada warned, stepping forward. "I'm sorry for whatever my son did, but he did it for our mission. I think Briar's right. You two need to take a walk. Calm down first so we can have a real discussion because right now, your trauma is speaking for you."

I scoffed. *I ain't got no trauma, I just know we can't trust y'all.*

Briar's nimble, cold fingers wrapped around mine, leading me toward the street's downward slope. I let her lead, but I didn't take my eyes off Oren until he was out of view.

Briar squeezed my hand until the Vampyres and Lightstalkers lowered their weapons and vacated their balconies.

"What happened back there?" Her rough voice softened to a whisper, as if she suspected people could still be listening.

I ran a hand over my face and took a deep breath.

"First of all, the doctor they got here looks like some alcoholic they picked up off the street that's *maybe* read two anatomy books," I began, counting off my fingers. "Second, he admitted to taking a sample of Caspian's blood while he's unconscious. I don't know about you, but I ain't relivin' that scene, and I don't want Caspian to either. So, I kinda lost it 'cause it seems like we went from one mad scientist to another. At least Dr. Ivanov was sanitary though. And don't get me started on Oren, who conveniently turns out to be a Nightshade *and* Ada's son."

Briar's lips compressed into a pensive frown. I walked ahead and turned around when my footsteps were the only ones still moving.

"How did you find out he took blood?" she asked.

"Because he was drooling over the fact that Caspian had survived adulthood for so long. Get this... he's supposedly a Lightstalker and should've been snuffed out by Mundus Novus a long time ago," I said.

Briar's eyes widened and her jaw dropped, then her face scrunched into confusion. "Wait, how? I thought Lightstalkers couldn't burn."

"That's what I thought too, but apparently it's genetics. They might gain more human genes than others. Some have blood dependencies, some don't. Some are already immune to silver bullets and the sun, and others are unfortunate. Cass took on more of his pops." I sat on a small boulder, pondering in the moment of silence between us.

Caspian never talked about his mother. It didn't come up organically and he didn't volunteer information. If Vyrn was right, and few human women survived the ordeal of birthing a Vampyre, then that could explain Cyrus' deep hatred toward his son. I didn't know Caspian's stance on Sun Dwellers now that he'd been involved with Briar and Astoria. He never cared about them before. They were a means to our survival as a species, and he'd been at peace with it.

"What do you want to do?" Briar asked.

"I want to kill them all, but that ain't realistic or right." I scanned my surroundings for eavesdroppers. "At the very least, keep a close eye on them and wait for Caspian to wake up. Then we can get outta here."

"I support you in everything, you know that right?" Briar caressed the side of my face with her index finger. I smiled hesitantly, sensing a but...

"Yeah..."

"But I think we need this place to regroup. Completely learn your powers, discover if I have anything worth using, get out of this fledgling crap, let Astoria *breathe*..." Briar inhaled deeply. "I don't trust them either, but I haven't been getting similar vibes to White Fang from these people. They've also got a pretty nice sized militia to stand against Mundus Novus."

"Do ya think your *vibes* are accurate? I mean... you asked your Vampyre stalker to show ya 'round the city," I teased. Briar laughed, nudging my forehead.

I didn't deny they had a good number of people to fight.

If I cared to fight.

"I guess I never minded taking risks." Briar shrugged, then leaned in to plant a soft peck on my lips. She dropped her voice to a whisper and said, "Which is why I'm asking *you* to take this one."

＊

Briar managed to convince me to return to Vyrn's, and the broken pride I carried manifested itself as a rock in my shoe. Her eyes darted around his house as she observed it for the first time. Vyrn popped from behind the partition, and I had to swallow around the knot in my throat before I said those dreadful words.

"I'm sorry I choked ya," I grumbled. "This is… a lot to process."

Vyrn grunted and waved his hand.

"I know you think I'm like those white-coat-wearing creeps. It's okay, I get it." He opened a closet next to his desk and pulled out a rag, then carried it to a small bucket of ice water, dipping it inside. He wrung it out and vanished behind the partition once again, and I poked my head around to monitor him placing it over Caspian's forehead.

"So…" Briar scratched the top of her head and turned to Vyrn. "What's your medical background?"

"Vyrn used to work for Mundus Novus in their disease control unit," Ada chimed in. "He was on their research team, and they were close to finding a cure to the virus. When they shut them down, he saved a lot of their research on a flash drive and continued the research here."

"Dr. Grace Murphy was leading our team, and she was a lot closer than the rest of us," Vyrn added. "I think she found it."

I tilted my head expectantly.

"She's dead," he continued. "We told the others she could be out there to keep hope alive."

I couldn't decide if the crack in my chest was from despair or rage.

"Why wouldn't Mundus Novus want a cure? That'd put an end to all the segregation laws," Briar said.

I gave her an incredulous look.

"Come on, Sunny..." I nudged her elbow.

She threw her hands up in a shrug. "I don't really see the money in it either. The blood donations are mandatory, but we didn't have to pay to get them done."

"It's more than money, sweetheart." Vyrn sighed heavily. "Power is priceless."

Briar sank in his rickety chair and ran both hands over her head. "Who's in charge? Seriously. Who's behind all this?"

Vyrn simply shook his head. "That was above my pay grade. Dr. Murphy would've known—another reason to do away with her."

"Who cares? Let's just find their building and burn it down," I finally said. Briar rolled her eyes with a groan.

"Our solution to everything can't be arson, Draven." She chuckled drily.

I shrugged and leaned against the wall, hooking my thumbs in my belt loops and crossing my ankles. "It's a lot faster than trying to cut the heads off a hydra," I grumbled under my breath, my eyebrows twitching upwards.

"You two are our only chance to put a dent in the Onyx Sentry army," Ada said. "If it's fighting fire with fire, so be it."

"Why bother? Y'all got a nice setup down here and plenty of Lightstalkers to do your supply runs. Why stir the pot?" I asked once again.

"This ain't living, boy," Vyrn grumbled, and reached for his flask to measure its weight before throwing his head back.

"Y'all ain't missin' out on nothing." I pushed off the wall and left, but I could hear Briar promise to try to get through to me.

I'd spent my life as a Nightshade. A monster of monsters. Fighting in a new war where neither side cared whether I lived or died... it didn't make much sense to me.

✳

I was back in the fields underneath the skylight, out of earshot of their whispers. I ran my hand over the gilded barley, watching the clouds drift. An hour passed, and I peered over my shoulder at the sound of rhythmic footsteps.

"Hey," I grumbled at Briar, and turned my back to get lost in the barley.

"Hey..."

"I don't wanna talk about it anymore," I said, recalling the promise she'd made them. I tensed when her arms wrapped around my waist, then relaxed. She pressed her forehead against my spine.

"I didn't come here to talk about it. I found something I thought you'd like."

I inclined my head, quirking an eyebrow.

Briar giggled, then slipped away from me. "Follow me," she said, and broke out into a playful sprint across the fields toward the tunnels that led to our sleeping quarters.

The amber lights lining the tunnel floors dimmed and brightened, breathing in our presence. The empty beds carved into the walls of our pocket room were now made up with thin foam toppers, blankets, and pillows.

Except one, with an added feature.

A pristine acoustic guitar.

29
CASPIAN

RED WAS EVERYWHERE, GLINTING OVER SHARDS OF BROKEN porcelain like glitter. Cyrus shouted obscenities as he writhed on the floor. I panted, dropping the shard I'd used to slash his face, and bolted for the front door. The navy sky flashed with oncoming lightning, rumbling as the universe mirrored my father's furious roars. I ignored the concrete biting the soles of my bare feet as I ran down the street.

Two boys, maybe three or four years older than me, shared a cigarette at a bus stop around the corner. I stopped in front of them with sharp, heaving breaths and glanced over my shoulder.

"Help," I breathed, bracing my hands over my knees. The one with tousled black hair and inked sclerae jogged into the street.

"What's going on, Wraith?" A gold fang flashed in the other boy's mouth when he spoke. He smothered the cigarette on the bench and followed the other Vampyre—Wraith—into the street. Cyrus sped toward us like a bullet train.

Wraith rolled his hoodie sleeves up, revealing tattoos that I thought you had to be older to get. Cyrus skidded across a puddle, lips pulled taut as his fangs sharpened. A scar covered the gash I'd created on his face, but his eye remained disfigured and bloodied.

My heart sank, because I thought it'd heal like anything else. I didn't know eyes didn't grow back like limbs. I only wanted to buy myself some time to run away.

"Come here," he demanded in a low growl, and crooked a menacing finger. I shuffled backward. I caught the tattoo on the back of the boy's hand, immediately recognizing the lion skull and flowers.

"I'm going to be a Nightshade," I exclaimed, stepping closer to the other boy with the gold tooth. "I'm not going anywhere with you, especially with them!"

"You're gonna be White Fang, whether you like it or not!" Cyrus lunged forward, and the boy whipped a pistol from under his oversized hoodie. He aimed it sideways, cocking his head in a primal tilt.

"Sounds like he made his decision, old man," he threatened.

"Don't worry." The other Vampyre threw an arm around my narrow shoulders with a smirk. "We'll take good care of him. Looks to me you two need some time apart anyway."

"Yeah, wouldn't wanna start a clan war over a kid that clearly doesn't want to be around you, right?"

"You're gonna regret this, Caspian," Cyrus snarled. "You chose the wrong side."

I collapsed to my knees when he took off in a flash, choking as if I were being held underwater again.

＊

I gasped awake. Half the room was black, the other half full of Astoria's wide eyes. My hand was clamped down on her shoulder, my other fist rearing back. Charcoal wisps clawed around my skin like thin smoke. I flinched my away and lowered my fist with a quiet gasp.

"I'm so—God, I'm sorry, I didn't—" My words felt foreign, like my tongue was too big for my mouth. I scooted backwards on a thin twin-sized mattress until my lower back hit the short headboard. Everything to the right side of me was in total darkness. I felt lopsided, as if I stood on one leg while the world spun.

"Cass, wait, breathe!" Astoria exclaimed, grabbing my forearm. "*Vyrn!*"

"Who's Vyrn? Where are we?" I scanned her from head to toe for injuries or binds, pausing at the cast on her wrist and the sling cradling her forearm. "Are you okay?"

"Yeah, I'm fine. I promise. Vyrn's the doctor here, he helped me."

I touched my face, my fingertips greeted by silk fabric and gauze over my right eye. Astoria swatted my hand away.

"Don't mess with that, okay? We're safe," she insisted. I blinked, and only my left side reacted. Suddenly the strength vanished from my fingers, my face went numb, and my chest tightened.

"No," I rasped. "No... no, no, no—" I jumped from the bed, wobbling until I caught myself on the thin paper partition. It fell over with a clamor, knocking over a tower fan and an ice bucket.

"Cass, sit down!" Astoria squealed, and a greasy older man came rushing into what appeared to be a dilapidated living room.

I swayed as the floor shifted. Astoria steadied me, her slim hand barely wrapping around my arm. I would've resisted as she eased me back on the bed, if I didn't almost fall backward in the process.

"You're awake! Finally." The man Astoria called for—Vyrn—waddled to my bedside with a mini flashlight. I caught my reflection in the chrome of the metal bed frame, and examined the eye patch with a blank stare as he waved the light beam over my remaining eye. Cyrus glared back at me.

"Your pupil reacts fine," he muttered. "Do you know who you are? What year it is?"

"Caspian Bishop. 2120." My voice was a lot more robotic than I intended, but I was too busy trying to keep my mind on earth. I squinted, the bandaged eye patch tugging on the skin surrounding it. I could still feel my father dragging his blade across my face, cutting through every sinew.

"Do you know this young lady here?" Vyrn gestured with his palm face up, and I finally tore my focus from my reflection.

I stared at Astoria as if seeing her for the first time. The memories came flooding in all at once. Watching her from the farthest corner of St. Brine's Bibliotheca, waiting for the right moment to approach after my sunburns disappeared. The beach, our embrace while she struggled to cope with her brother's attack...

I watched the jugular notch at the base of her neck rise and fall with steady life, occasionally hitching as she held back tears. She swallowed as crimson suffused her damp cheeks. I could have ten concussions in another life as a Sun Dweller, and still would never forget her face or her name.

I lifted my gaze to her bourbon irises and whispered, "Astoria Shaw."

Vyrn sighed with relief, running a hand through the sparse hair on his head, and sank onto a stool.

"Your friends will be pleased to hear you're awake," he said, and unclipped a handheld radio from his hip. "Ada, do you copy?" A raspy woman's voice answered.

"Where am I?" I turned to Astoria with a small frown. "Who's Ada?"

"We got a lot to catch up on..." Astoria wove her fingers together, her thumbs at war with each other.

"Tell Draven and Briar that Caspian is awake and talking," Vyrn announced over the radio. He clipped the radio back on his side and forced a smile before stepping away. He returned shortly with three bags of blood, passing them to me.

"I'll give you two a moment alone. There's some stuff I wanna talk to you about, but I'm gonna let you get your bearings first." He patted my leg before shuffling back upstairs with a dry cough.

"Where am I?" I repeated, more annoyed. My body felt brittle. I didn't bother twisting the caps on the bags, simply punctured them with my teeth from the bottom and drained all three in seconds. It wasn't long before strength returned to my bones.

Astoria rose from the edge of the bed and held out her hand.

"It's better if I just show you. Do you think you can you walk?"

I stared at her palm for a moment, then took it. My skin drank in its warmth like I was starved for that more than blood. The ground felt more stable as I stood.

"Don't push yourself," she whispered.

"I'm fine, I just... have to get used to seeing with one eye." The words drew the air right out of my lungs. I shook my head—tried to shake the sharp sensation digging under my skin, as if Cyrus were still slicing my face.

Astoria led me outside, where it was drastically more serene than inside of Vyrn's house. Except, the sky was replaced by rocky ripples, waves, and spikes above. Lanterns and makeshift streetlights illuminated what appeared to be a massive cavern.

"Are we—"

"Yes. We're underground." The narrow street swept downward, toward a complex town bathed in warm amber lighting. A city, hidden from the evils above. Children played in the streets two miles below, but it was hard to tell their species with their faces turned downward.

"This place is called Avant Garde, and it's full of humans, Vampyres, and Lightstalkers. There's no curfews either." Astoria gestured all around us, beaming. Her tone was bright and energetic, as if she'd held in this good news for a long time.

I still had my doubts that any of this was good for us.

"What are Lightstalkers?"

"Hybrids, half-breeds, mixes, whatever. I've heard a bunch of other terms at this point. Anyways, they're, um..." Astoria spoke softer than usual, like she was afraid to admit something bad.

I frowned, tilting my head expectantly.

"Most of them can walk among humans undetected in the daylight," she said.

"That's impossible," I said with a small laugh. I stepped away from the guardrail on the street and turned my back against the city below. If that were the case, White Fang would've raided this place first and left the Nightshades alone.

"It's not. Vyrn used to work for Mundus Novus as one of their epidemiologists for the virus."

I recalled Vyrn's disheveled appearance and unsavory house. I arched a dubious brow.

Your naivety is showing, Astoria.

"He…" She bit her lip, eyes darting back and forth as if calculating the world's most complex formula to avoid triggering me.

"Tell me," I demanded quietly.

"Vyrn took a sample of your blood while you were in a coma. He told Draven and Briar that you shouldn't have survived so long out there because Mundus Novus wipes Lightstalkers out whenever they come across one. He actually wanted to talk to you about that."

I chuckled again.

It's a wonder I survived the coma if that guy is this level of insane.

"It's impossible. My father would never have relations with a human. *Ever.* He hated Sun Dwellers, and hated me even more. I would dare to say he'd kill me before Mundus Novus would if he found out. Not to mention it's literally impossible for Vampyres and humans to procreate together." I swatted the air dismissively, heading back to Vyrn's house when I felt a wave of dizziness crash over my head. Not because of whatever effect White Fang's serum had on me or the fact that I only had one eye, but because the idea of humans and Vampyres living in a fully developed underground society took me for a spin.

"Mundus Novus lied about everything," Astoria called after me. "Vyrn explained that virtually all human mothers can't survive giving birth to a Lightstalker."

I stopped in the middle of my stride, nearly toppling over.

"What did you just say?" I demanded in a low growl.

"A-a human woman getting pregnant by a Vampyre is a death sentence," she stammered. "Survivors are rare."

There was no way Cyrus had loved a Sun Dweller. No—he *couldn't*. It was outside of his nature; he was incapable of loving *anyone.*

But then again...

What was to stop him from developing that hatred later, if the very blood he spawned was the sole reason he lost the love of his life? What if his hatred for humans was because of their mortality?

I grew up hearing him tell me, "It should've been you."

The only use I have for you is fetching blood for us. At least it's less dirt on my *hands.*

I should've known you were going to be a thorn in my side the second her heart stopped.

I don't know why I expected anything more from a slut's offspring.

"Cass!" Astoria's voice broke through with a gasp, and I opened my eye to see a murky onyx vapor undulate and curl around me. The string lights wrapped around the balconies above us flickered, as if the darkness drew life from them. When my father's voice quieted in my head, the inky cloud dissipated. Vyrn, Draven, Briar, Astoria, and a woman dressed in tactical gear whose skin was heavily weathered by the sun encircled me.

Vyrn gawked at me like a kid in a toy store, the woman's pearly teeth gleamed, Briar's jaw hung open, Draven held a wary gaze, and Astoria... her face contorted in fear.

30
DRAVEN

I CAREFULLY PICKED UP THE POLISHED MAPLE WOOD GUITAR, the strings subtly humming with the movement. Carved filigree designs curved around its base and stretched along the neck, and I traced my fingertips tenderly over them, then lightly plucked my thumb over the strings. I closed my eyes with a pleased chuckle, reveling in its perfectly tuned, rich timbre.

A knot formed in my throat as I buried the childish excitement that wanted to claw its way into my mind and make me jump around with glee. I lifted my gaze to Briar's, and my mouth moved without a sound before I found one word.

"How?"

"After you left, Ada took me on a walk and asked what could she do to help us feel more comfortable." She gestured toward the guitar with a proud grin. "I mentioned how you can play and sing and she got extremely excited. I guess they don't get much entertainment down here. She's also going to surprise Astoria later."

"Oh, I ain't singin' in front of these people, Sunny." I set the guitar down on the bed and took a step back.

"I didn't tell her you would, but she's definitely gonna ask. And... I think you should consider it." She shrugged. "Imagine a world where you can though. How cool would it be knowing no one is out to kill you, only to listen to you?"

I peered down at the guitar again. Electricity ricocheted through my bones, pleading for me to pick it back up—but it felt wrong.

Uriah was still out there, building his army to destroy the country. Dr. Ivanov was still searching for us. The Onyx Sentries were scrambling to regain control of Helios and—who knows—maybe Neoterra. What did I look like, sitting around singing and strumming?

"Thank you," I said hoarsely, and pulled Briar into an embrace, planting a kiss on her cheek. I figured I was probably being irrational, but I wanted her to know I still appreciated it. "I love you."

"I love you too," she said, and flopped on the bed. "Would you play a song for me, if no one else?" I felt heat reach my cheeks, but remembered that she'd already heard me perform at The Hole.

I picked up the guitar, sitting on the edge of the bed with one leg bent and the other hanging over the edge. I slouched over the guitar with an unstable breath, then strummed my first chord.

Like a defibrillator, the hum of the strings struck me with life. I was a kid again, on Moses' front porch, showing him the songs I'd created. The sound waves reverberated against the cave walls, and Briar leaned back with a serene smile, closing her eyes. If it weren't for the Vampyre curse of dreamlessness, she would've been lulled to sleep.

As much as I wanted to though... I didn't sing. I knew my voice would crack if I did.

Keys clinked together as heavy thumping sounded at the cave's threshold, and every muscle in my body tensed. The music died. Briar lurched to her feet and craned her neck toward the archway.

One of Ada's men strode inside with a rifle slung across his back.

"Your friend is awake," he droned, and promptly walked away. Briar and I exchanged wide glances, and took off in a rapid dash.

⁎

Caspian stood at the center of the sloped pathway between the carved homes. Much like the smoke that often rolled off my shoulders, darkness engulfed him, and a small breeze carried hushed voices, almost like the shadows were whispering.

"Cass," Briar breathed, her voice getting caught in her throat. She took another step forward, but I held her back by the shoulder and shook my head.

"He ain't right," I muttered, and for once I feared I didn't have any answers. Fire, I could handle. Whatever this was...

The temperature dropped drastically around us, and ice puffed past my lips. Briar tucked her hands under her armpits and glued her wide gaze on the flickering string lights above.

"*Caspian!*" Astoria shouted shrilly.

The shadows unfurled from his shoulders and back, twisted around his arms down to his hands, before they suddenly dispelled. Caspian turned around with a wide eye, as if we'd caught him red-handed mid-crime.

"I... I don't know what that was," he mumbled, looking down at his shoes. He pulled back when Astoria reached to comfort him.

"I have an idea." Vyrn scratched his head with an amused grin. "Actually could explain a lot for all of you kids."

"How would ya know anything?" I asked, my voice a lot more terse than I intended.

"From your best friend, Oren. I helped him master his skills in a week because of it. It was pretty simple, actually," Vyrn said proudly, and pulled his flask from his pocket.

I scoffed under my breath. I wanted to doubt it, but Oren wielding the ocean as if he were born from it proved otherwise.

"And you, young lady." He pointed at Briar and reached in his other pocket, pulling out a pill bottle. He rattled the pills before tossing the bottle across the street.

"What's this?" She turned it in her hand, reading the label and instructions.

"Something the hospital would've given you if you were a model citizen who checked yourself into their fledgling program."

"How about more direct answers to our questions, man?" I snapped.

Vyrn chuckled wryly, and began his trek up the hill.

"It's a medication for Briar's cravings. It'll help her transition into a mature Vampyre," Ada explained. She didn't take her wary focus off of Caspian until her radio buzzed.

"You four, follow me. I'd rather show you in my lab," Vyrn called as he tucked the flask back into his cargo shorts' pocket. "If you're gonna help us win this war, then you kids need to be able to win against yourselves first."

❋

I wanted to stay behind, perhaps even leave Avant Garde entirely at the mention of Vyrn's "lab." I was glad I didn't, because it would've been the equivalent of thinking a rustling bush housed a wolf when it was just a rabbit. The laboratory consisted of three stainless steel tables arranged in a U-shape, with microscopes, test tubes, and notebooks strewn everywhere.

I released a long, drawn-out sigh.

There was no firing squad or UV lamp. Dr. Ivanov wasn't standing in the corner with an IV and a saline bag. Briar and I weren't strapped to leather chairs, forced to watch each other's torment.

It was a hodgepodge of a lab thrown together with whatever the Avant Guardians were able to scrounge up.

Vyrn took off his glasses, briefly wiping them with the bottom of his shirt. "So, when White Fang was satisfied with Oren's results, they released him to return to the Nightshades. He came to us and told us about you two."

I growled under my breath when I noticed Oren lingering at the foot of Vyrn's staircase.

"Anyways, when Briar's AB negative blood came into contact with yours, instead of your bodies rejecting it like a failed transfusion, it triggered genetic mutations—due to the Vampyric virus being resistant to, well, everything."

I never really cared about the why or how, I only wanted to be able to control it when I needed it. I didn't want another scare like the shipwreck.

"Now, Draven... we suspect that you and Briar may have similar abilities because you bit her. Your venom can pass traits on to the next person. If Briar bites someone, the likelihood of that happening is diluted."

Vyrn rambled on, flipping through the wrinkled pages of his notebook, riddled with rum and coffee stains. Astoria leaned over his notes, cheeks puckered with a wide, fascinated grin.

"How often am I supposed to take these pills, and for how long?" Briar asked.

"Ordinarily it would be a course of six weeks, but since you've been a fledgling for some time, we'll half it."

Briar threw the pills back without any more questions. I didn't think she was doing too bad with her cravings lately.

Me, on the other hand...

I could still taste the Keepers' flesh and feel their bone fragments between my teeth.

I didn't want to ask about my situation in front of the others. I might've thought Vyrn was a quack, but he was my only option to figure out why I suddenly favored Vampyre blood.

"Most of White Fang's experiments failed because they were using pure Vampyre-borns and Turned Vampyres whose blood types remained consistent when they changed. The key differences among you four—Oren and Caspian being Lightstalkers, Draven's blood type changing after he was Turned, and Briar's blood type triggering it all."

Could my changed DNA be the reason why I felt side effects? Had the same thing happened to the mutated Vampyre who got murdered with a flamethrower?

I suddenly began to get awfully hungry, and Briar's neck was rather tempting with her short hair exposing it clear as day. I moved away from her, holding my breath for as long as I could without forcing an audible exhale.

Caspian hadn't said a word, only stared at one of the metallic tables. Probably at his own reflection as he processed the major loss he'd suffered.

"Mental state, personality traits, genetics... I believe they all played a part in your connections to the elements. Water, fire, darkness... this may mean there's others out there with connections to light, earth—who knows."

"Metal," I blurted. Vyrn's head popped up from his notebook. He arched an eyebrow.

"You know of someone with metal manipulation?"

"Uriah King. I couldn't—" My mouth filled with cotton. "I couldn't kill him." Briar placed a soft hand over my biceps, as if it could erase the dread of my fatal failure.

"Do you know what type of metal?"

"Steel, maybe? I don't know, my fire wasn't hot enough to melt him." I took steps back until a stool hit the back of my knees, then sat on it. Vyrn fell silent, reaching into his pocket. He didn't pull the flask out, as if he had to fight the urge to lean on it after the news.

"While you're with us, we're going to do breathing exercises to control your abilities. You might wield it when you're angry, but true control comes when you're calm in the storm." He gave me a pointed look, then shifted his attention to Caspian. "I have a feeling you'll catch on rather quickly."

"It might take a while," he added with a shrug, and pushed his glasses up his oily, rounded nose. "So let's get to work."

31
ASTORIA

Vyrn announced training would begin first thing in the morning as we dispersed from his home. The cavern was dimmer, solely dependent on lanterns. My pathetic human eyes strained to see the majority of my surroundings, widening to compensate for it.

"Are you going to bed?" Caspian spoke low and gentle, as if speaking a notch higher would wake the entire town. I shrugged. I still felt wired from everything that had happened, and he gave the impression that he wasn't ready to split off yet. I scratched my head until a light bulb went off.

"Let's go swimming," I said with a smile.

"Wait, you can't be s—" I grabbed his wrist before he could protest, dragging him through the town. He didn't pull away, but his skin turned icier than usual. I slid my hand to his palm, interlacing our fingers. I led the way to our cave and grabbed a couple towels. I removed my sling and examined my cast one more time to confirm it was waterproof. Caspian paced at the tunnel's exit until I was ready.

We crossed the bridge to the spring. He let me lead all the way to the edge of the water, where he finally locked his knees in place like a mule.

"Astoria, you know I can't." His voice broke, hands trembling like I never thought they would. I removed my ponytail, adjusting it into a higher bun so my hair wouldn't get wet.

"You need to learn," I said, and grabbed his hands again before stepping backward into the water. He only stepped forward half an inch.

The full moon cast the cavern in silvery blue light. The spring glittered, rippling subtly as I moved back further until the water reached my calves. Caspian's skin of stone cracked as his nose crinkled. He breathed heavily through his nostrils, and something in my heart ruptured. The nervous energy rippled off him, passing through me, and I dreaded the moment he might actually have a mental breakdown.

"You said we fear what we don't know, remember?" I stepped up again, raising a gentle hand to his glacial cheek. He closed his eyes, leaning his head further into my palm and squeezing my other hand. A tear pooled at the corner of his eye, catching the moonlight like a diamond. His quivering breaths slowed.

"Every time I'm submerged, he's drowning me," Caspian uttered, nearly inaudible. The tear finally dropped, his face contorting into the same agonized grimace as when he emptied the magazine into Cyrus.

"He's not here anymore. He can't hurt you *anymore*." I stepped closer—the space between us mere inches. "Let me teach you how to survive the water. If you know how to conquer and respect it... then you can't fear it."

Caspian's nostrils widened as he inhaled deeply, then exhaled slowly through tight lips. He stripped down to his underwear, triggering a rush of heat to my cheeks. The moonlight gilded every muscle, its silvery light turning his skin into shimmering silk.

The bottom half of my pants was submerged, but I refused to do the same as he did. I couldn't... because he would see the scars my mother had left me as a child.

I cleared my throat, keeping my eyes on his as I guided him down the shallow slope. The cold water rose until I stopped when the water reached my waist. The further we went, the tighter his hold on my hands. I winced, and he relaxed his grip before he crushed my bones.

The water stopped at the top of Caspian's hips, but it didn't make him any calmer as he fixed a horrified gaze at the spring's dark center a few feet ahead. Even with Vampyric sight, the water's impeccable transparency made it difficult to judge true depth.

"You're almost there," I said, and tugged him further until the water reached my shoulders and the bottom of his chest. Caspian gasped, glancing over his shoulder at the dry land.

"Do you trust me?" I asked, raising my eyebrows.

"Y-yeah..." His throat shifted with a hard swallow.

"Then lean back," I directed.

"Excuse me?" Caspian released a dry laugh.

"First thing you need to learn is how to float on your back. If you're ever tired from swimming, you can relax and stare at the stars." He blinked at me, dumbfounded.

It had been pointless to put my hair up. I sighed, leaning back and relaxing my body in the water's arms, allowing it to cradle me. After my presentation, Caspian took another deep breath.

"Okay, okay. Let's get this over with."

✳

The moon shifted, indicating two hours had passed. Caspian mastered floating, but refused to go underwater. The extent of our training boiled down to me demonstrating different strokes above and below the surface. I was now lethargic, and dragged my feet through the water to the edge. He didn't hesitate to follow. My clothes weighed me down as I rose from the water. Caspian dried himself off, wrapping a towel around his shoulders. He stared at the spring, the glimmer in his cardinal eyes absent.

Echoing footsteps trailed into the cavern and we both looked to the top of the steps.

Ada jogged down the sweeping steps with a wide smile—I never thought I'd see anyone smile as often as she did—as she approached us.

"Someone said you're a very studious young lady," she said, beaming. I tensed, glancing at Caspian with water still dripping down my cheeks.

"I was in school for nursing, but I never got to—"

"I have something to show you," she said, and waved her arm. "Go ahead and take a few minutes to dry off. Meet me in the fields!"

With that, I wrung out my shirt and patted dry most of my pants, then followed her.

Ada's truck idled in the pathway between the fields, drumming her fingers against the side of the door.

"I'm right here," Caspian promised. I nodded, and climbed in the back seat. But he paused, shifting his gaze from the spot next to me to the front.

"You can sit in the front with me," Ada said with a laugh. "Boy, you kids been through it, huh?"

The grin left her face when she met Caspian's cold gaze. He climbed in the front seat, and I could've sworn he growled under his breath.

We drove away from the fields, down the main street, and closer to the mouth of the cave where we first entered. Here, a two-story building with windows devoid of life was also carved out of the wall. An old bicycle with scratched chrome emerald paint and a moderately rusted chain leaned against the wall. The noise in the town was faint, nearly nonexistent, and one cricket found its way around the area but fell silent as we approached.

"What is this?" Caspian asked in low, lethal calm. Goosebumps prickled along my arms, and my breath hitched in my throat as I feared his tense instincts indicated danger.

"Calm down, son. It ain't a slaughterhouse," Ada said, and promptly jumped out of the truck. We followed behind her, keeping roughly a five-foot distance. I froze in place, my hand shooting to my bare collarbone as Ada unlocked and opened the door. Cobwebs stretched across the frame and broke apart, and then the lights turned on.

My heart skipped a beat when I caught a glimpse of books. Caspian craned his neck inside, and I jogged to the front, nudging him out of the way. An audible gasp escaped me.

The building was two floors joined together by a staircase that spiraled along the walls, which were made of fully stocked bookshelves. It was airy and open with a cathedral ceiling, and it felt like my eyes could never catch all of it. The scent of old books permeated the air, heavy and rich like fog. A ladder leaned against one wall on a track that allowed it to move horizontally. Despite the amount of dust, newer novels mingled with classics, so the place wasn't completely abandoned. A table and two chairs rested at the center, and I sat down before my knees could collapse.

"This... this is amazing." My voice cracked, and I covered my mouth with my three fingers. Caspian's defensive countenance shifted to amusement. Our eyes met, and his face illuminated.

"You can spend as much time in here as you like, any time you want," Ada announced. "The Guardians are usually too busy training in combat and weapons to spend time reading for leisure. But I take it you're more brains than brawn, aren't you?"

I held my face in my hands and nodded, smiling from ear to ear to the point it hurt.

"I'll get some people to clean it up in here," Ada said. "I'll leave you two alone to enjoy it."

"Thank you so much, Ada!" I called out as she stepped over the threshold.

"Sure thing, darling!"

Caspian swiped his finger over one of the shelves and rubbed it against his thumb. "Yeah, she wasn't lying about them not using it much."

"I don't care, this is incredible! I can't remember the last time

I've been able to read in peace. Plus, I lost all my books in the fire." I finally gathered the strength to stand and browsed. After about ten minutes, Caspian still stood in the same spot, watching me more than the books.

"You can go ahead... I don't want to bore you," I said with a nervous chuckle.

"No boredom. I'm glad to see you in your element. I didn't know you loved to read," Caspian said with a soft grin. "Take all the time you need."

Heat rose throughout my face, and before I knew it I had a whole stack of books in my arm and one on the table. I organized the stacks by fiction and education. Caspian took the heavy medical textbooks to spare my wrist, but it still twinged from the strain. The pain was still worth it. I grinned at a classic romance novel I'd always craved to read but never got around to with my studies. I traced my fingers over the beveled title, and gazed at him.

"Have you ever been in love before?" I asked suddenly, my voice cutting through the stagnant air. These were dark times, and he lived his life in the shadows, but... having gotten to know him, I knew light still remained. His eye flicked to the book I examined and his lips stitched together in a line.

"Once," he replied in a hushed whisper, as if saying the answer too loud would dredge up a horrible memory. I hoped that what I thought was a harmless question didn't put salt in any open wounds.

"Oh—"

"It was a long time ago. I had to choose." He lowered his gaze to the floor and his blank face twisted into anguish.

Choose what?

I stood there in silence, blinking. I resisted the urge to ask, to accidentally scare him away and build more walls.

"I vowed to never feel again after that," he said, lifting his eye to mine once more. "It's been difficult keeping that vow as of late."

The pit of my stomach warbled, but I brushed it off as a reaction to all the danger we'd faced in the past several weeks. Out of all the emotions he had buried, perhaps fear rose from his grave.

"Can I..." I swallowed drily, smacking my lips. I couldn't hold it in anymore. "Can I ask what the choice was?"

"No," he said sharply, and like a switch, his face ironed back to numbness. I bristled at his tone, then eased into one of the dusty chairs and switched my focus to the textbooks.

"Sorry," I muttered, and opened one of the patient care books. I might've overstepped, but I hadn't expected him to react that way. I guessed I'd been spoiled with how gently he always spoke to me. I stared at the words in the book, but didn't read a single one.

Caspian's shoes barely scraped the floor as he stormed out of the library.

32
BRIAR

It might've been a placebo effect, but when I took those pills, I didn't so much as look in Astoria's direction, or at any of the humans we passed as we left Vyrn's house.

Astoria and Caspian ran off together somewhere. By morning, Draven and I were taken by Vyrn to start our first round of training. We piled in Vyrn's truck, its blue paint invaded by rust. It took a few tries on the ignition; nevertheless, it got us to where we needed to be once it got started.

Vyrn took us outside of Avant Garde, ten miles away from the caverns until we emerged onto the shore.

"This is where we're going every day until you two are comfortable with your abilities. The sand will prevent any wildfires as long as you face the water no matter what."

I raised my hand hesitantly. I dreaded opening my mouth.

"We already got questions?" Vyrn pulled out his flask with an agitated sigh. My eye twitched at his annoyance, but I waited for him to take a swig before speaking.

"I don't have any abilities. I just wanna learn how to control my cravings without depending on those pills," I said, folding my arms.

"Don't listen to her, man. The whole house started shuddering when I fought Uriah. Remember?" Draven nudged my shoulder.

"We don't know if I did that for sure." I rolled my eyes and waved my hand dismissively.

"Well, I know your eyes turned orange, your veins turned black, and smoke came from ya at White Fang. It was like lava tried to break through the floors," Draven said, and turned to Vyrn with his thumb pointed at me.

"I don't remember that," I droned.

"Ya ain't gotta. I saw it."

I frowned. Maybe he did, but the main thing I remembered from White Fang was Draven losing his mind and forgetting who I was. But that wasn't the worst part.

It was the bones he left behind after devouring the Keepers. Even if they were Sun Dwellers, a Vampyre would've never done that. We survived on blood. Nothing more, nothing less.

I need to talk to him about that...

"Hey!" Vyrn snapped his fingers. I flinched, spine locking in place. "Pay attention, girlie. Ya ain't getting out of this training. Sounds like you definitely have something going on. Draven had a head start on his but we'll be starting from scratch with you. Being a fledgling makes it a lot harder because you're so busy trying to control the cravings. Those pills should help for now."

I shifted my weight on my feet.

"You two must have some temper issues, right?" Vyrn asked, tucking his flask into the sand.

"I gue—"

My head snapped to the side as he struck my cheek, and Draven tackled him to the ground. I reared my fist back while Draven held him in place.

"Control it!" Vyrn shouted in a strained tone. Only then did it occur to me that this was part of his training.

"Draven, let him go." I groaned. "That's not gonna work. Have you really done this before, Vyrn?"

The man laughed, panting once Draven finally released his headlock. Vyrn stood, grabbed his flask and dusted the sand off it. "Yeah, but only with Oren. You kiddos are gonna be a little more difficult."

"A slap to the face might make me angry, but not ball-of-fire angry. If what Draven saw really happened, then..." I trailed, biting my lip as I tried to remember. It was a fog except that one moment seeing Draven rip those Keepers apart.

It must've been a life or death situation.

"Then you both need to search within and figure out what you're so angry about." Vyrn rubbed his neck.

"That's a lot of things," Draven said as he crossed his arms and spread his feet shoulder-width apart.

"No, no." Vyrn wiggled his index finger. "You both have one core issue that feeds everything else. Right now, it's what's controlling *you*. Flip the script, and you'll wield your flames in no time."

"What makes you think that's what the connection is?" I asked, staring at the calm waves beyond his shoulders.

"Because Oren figured his out, and went from creating small puddles to toppling a ferry boat without strain." Vyrn said. He tossed his head back under the flask, but frowned with a dejected sigh when only a drop landed on his tongue.

"Jeez, maybe Oren needs to be the one to train us," I grumbled. Draven gave me a warning look.

"Kidding," I said with a nervous laugh.

"I suggest we come out here every morning for meditation, therapy, combat training—the whole nine yards. We'll start tomorrow, when Caspian decides to show up. Today, we need to get you clothes," Vyrn said, then trekked through the sand back toward the truck.

I crouched over the sand, scooping it up and letting it sift through my fingers until Vyrn was out of earshot.

"When are you going to ask him?" I whispered.

"Ask him what?" Draven frowned, sliding his hands in his pockets.

"About how you went cannibal at White Fang," I said, and instantly regretted the way it came out. I couldn't think of a gentler way to say it. Draven winced, and stared at the water with wide eyes as if it were happening again right in front of him.

"That was a fluke," Draven said.

I stood, brushing my hands off on my pants. "I haven't heard you complain about being hungry in a hot minute. Not to mention how you spit out the human blood in Samara's car."

The red flags were there, but it was easier to look away for the time being. Draven opened his mouth with a sharp breath, but closed it again. His face fell slack, shifting from aggravation to apprehension.

"You need to tell him," I pressed, and trudged forward through the sand. He lagged behind, and when I looked back, he was watching the ocean like he yearned to drown in it.

✳

It took no time for our eyes to adjust to Avant Garde's dimly lit cavern when we returned. Vyrn dropped us off at the marketplace, where Caspian was already walking out of a shop with layers of black clothing draped over his arm. As if he sensed our presence, he turned toward us, and I saw he had a fresh, black eye patch with green stitching covering his damaged eye. We jogged to him, and I peeked through the small circular window of the quirky store trimmed in purple and teal. I smiled, eager to head inside. I was starved of shopping. Of normalcy.

"How are you doing, man?" Draven asked him.

"The usual," Caspian replied coolly.

"Where's Astoria?" I peeled my gaze from the store and turned back to him. I was surprised to see them apart.

"Still in the library," he said curtly.

"I want to talk to you about something," Draven told him, his hand pausing over the store's door knob.

"Yeah, me too," Caspian said. "I'll be in our cave."

I frowned.

Why is he being so short?

Caspian didn't bother taking off in a supernatural sprint. Instead he walked every step of the way toward the quarters Ada assigned us, as if he were stalling. Perhaps he wanted to see the fields since he hadn't gotten the opportunity yet.

Draven pushed open the door to the shop and I followed behind him.

"Welcome in," a girl with heterochromia—one red eye and one brown—greeted us. I stared at her a lot longer than I intended. Without a doubt, she was a Lightstalker, and the variation in how everyone's genes manifested was fascinating. How could Mundus Novus want to wipe that out?

"'Sup," Draven grunted, and roamed toward the men's section. I followed him.

"Ada said to grab whatever you want, it's on the house!" the girl called to us with a soft smile.

"Thanks!" I shouted back with a wave so she could see me. The top of my head barely poked above the racks.

"What was his problem?" I dropped my voice. Draven shrugged as he picked up a pair of dark sweatpants and flipped the tag over to see their size.

"Probably everything, Sunny. He woke up in a completely different place, found out he's a Lightstalker, and lost one of his eyes. I doubt we're gonna see sunshine and rainbows from him any time soon. Not that he ever had any to begin with."

I guessed he was right, and I was stupid to ask what could've possibly put Caspian in a sour mood, all things considered.

I broke away from Draven and moved to the women's section, wishing Astoria were with me. Loneliness threatened to creep into my chest, and the tense atmosphere closed in like a coffin.

33
DRAVEN

Briar and I left with five outfits each, plus something to lounge in. It felt wrong walking out of there without paying, and it felt strange doing so without a mask on my face and a gun in my hand.

We walked in silence, with my thoughts stuck on the points Briar had raised on the beach. She was right. I needed to tell someone. Especially before my hunger worsened.

No one was left sweeping the fields for harvest when we crossed the area. Lightstalkers, humans, and Vampyres alike were shut in their homes, and it made me wonder if the Lightstalkers had the ability to sleep.

Maybe some did, and others didn't.

I wasn't sure which was worse—to be born a Vampyre and guaranteed the flaws, or a Lightstalker who *could* have the best of both worlds but was dealt a bad genetic hand, like Caspian with his higher-than-average sun sensitivity.

Astoria suddenly burst out of the library, carrying a book. She pushed the bicycle kickstand up and mounted it with one hand.

"Vyrn! Where's Vyrn?" she shouted, her voice echoing.

"Shh! People are probably sleeping, Ria," Briar hissed. Astoria panted, looking around frantically.

"What's wrong?" I mirrored her movement, shoulders tensing as I prepared for danger.

"I think—I found—I got an idea for a cure!" She sped past us. I sprinted after her, the bags crackling in the wind. Briar stayed close as we raced to Vyrn's house.

I didn't ask questions—I wanted to know what she'd found in those books.

"What did you find?" Briar whispered as I banged my fist against Vyrn's door.

"Well... they might've already tried it before." Astoria held the book tightly to her chest, lowering her gaze to her feet.

I shook the door with harder knocks.

"Who the hell is it?" Vyrn yelled from upstairs.

"Draven! Astoria's got somethin' to say!" I shouted back. He stomped across the floorboards, kicking cans and storming down the stairs. Vyrn yanked the door open, sending a gust of wind over himself.

"This better be something important," he snarled, tightening the band around his robe. He stalked away from the door and we filed inside behind him.

"I-I'm sorry for waking you up, sir, but—" Astoria stepped between Briar and me, setting the heavy textbook over a pile of junk on his living room desk. "—I think I have an idea for a cure."

Vyrn snorted, stepping up to the decanter on his coffee table to pour himself a drink. Briar tilted her head, drawing in a breath to spit a venomous retort, but I stilled her with hand on her shoulder.

"Go on," he said, and brought the glass to his mouth. A subtle smirk played across his lips, as if he were waiting to laugh at whatever suggestion Astoria gave simply because she was young, and far from being a scientist.

"W-well, um... the virus presented itself as an aggressive form of anemia, right? I remember in college that it was caused by an iron deficiency. It's already established that a Vampyre's blood dependency essentially stems from that. The virus traded ice cravings for blood." Astoria flipped through the pages of the textbook where it explained its virology.

"Sideropenia," Vyrn asserted.

"What if iron supplements helped? Maybe paired with the blood donations of Lightstalkers? If they have human genetics combined with Vampyric DNA, they could have higher iron levels, which could supplement the lower dosages in the pills."

His face flattened, replaced with intrigue. Vyrn set his drink down and walked to the desk. He put a finger on the page and flipped to the cover of the book with a grunt, then opened it back up.

"This... this is actually worth trying." A spark of hope flashed in his watery eyes.

"What do you need to do it?" Briar asked eagerly.

"Well, for starters... I need iron supplements. And I'll talk with Ada tonight about getting some Lightstalkers to donate their blood." Vyrn patted Astoria's shoulder with a proud grin.

Then he added, "If this works, girl, you're gonna make history."

⁕

Caspian was in our room, on the bed diagonal to mine. He held a small dagger, running its blade at a slight angle against a piece of slate.

"Ada wants me to go on a blood supply run," Caspian said flatly, without moving his focus from the knife work. "Suggested we start building trust with her people by earning our keep."

"Sounds like someone complained," Briar grumbled under her breath.

"Perhaps after Draven's little tantrum." Caspian finally lifted his gaze from the knife to give me a pointed look.

"Oh, that *tantrum* was for your safety. I thought they were experimenting on ya," I said, crossing my arms. Caspian rolled his eye and shrugged, then stood from his bed. He holstered the knife at the small of his back.

"Are you coming with me?"

"Sure, it'll be like old times. I need to grab some stuff for Astoria and Vyrn too."

Briar briefly closed her eyes with a nod, showing she was fine staying behind. It had been a while since Caspian and I had gone on any sort of run alone, and I could tell he had just as much to get off his shoulders as I did.

I sifted through the duffel bag, barely hanging by a thread now with everything we'd gone through, and removed two pistols and extra ammo. I passed one of them to Caspian. He checked the chamber and magazine, and approached the bag to load it as I did the same for mine.

"You guys be careful out there, please..." Briar said, and reached for the pills Vyrn gave her.

"We will. And try not to use those as a crutch, okay? You were already getting a lot better without them," I said, and leaned to kiss her forehead.

"If I don't come back..." Caspian hesitated before reaching in his pocket. He handed a folded piece of paper to Briar. "Give this to your sister. Don't read it, if you can."

"I'll try," Briar teased with a chuckle, but her smile faded. "I thought this was just a blood run."

"It'll never *just* be a blood run. Not with the Onyx Sentries out there and two clans against us," Caspian droned, and slipped out of our cave. Briar wrapped tight arms around me, and I felt a hot tear soak through my t-shirt. My heart ached for her. Not because she was crying, but because I knew it ate at her to be benched in so many situations.

"Please come back to me," she murmured against my chest.

"I'll always find my way back to you," I promised, and we shared a tender kiss.

I might've made some empty promises in the past, but this one was far from it.

*

Ada loaned us one of her trucks. She offered a team of three more people, but we insisted we'd handle it ourselves. Besides... we didn't want to have to watch our backs. We always worked best without anyone else.

Caspian drove with one hand on the steering wheel and his elbow propped on the window with his head in his palm.

"What did you want to talk to me about?" I figured if he went first, I could stall as long as possible.

"Have you ever felt like you were losing yourself? Like everything you've ever known... was a lie?" A subtle crack appeared in his usual stone-cold demeanor, his chilled eyebrows knitted together. I blinked, having never heard him ask a question like that before.

"Yeah, I guess. I ain't feel the same since my parents died and Wraith bit me."

The truck wobbled over the uneven cavern floor until we finally exited Avant Garde and were outside among the trees. Golden-hour light filtered through the canopy, but the dimness of the forest was already triggering my Vampyric night vision.

"I don't know who I am anymore." Caspian tightened his grip on the steering wheel, straightening in his seat. He drove with two hands now.

"Why?"

"Everything was cut and dry with the Nightshades. I... I made peace with my life there. But after I saw how they treated you, even after all the things you did for the clan, I questioned their values. My own values. And Astoria—" He swallowed. "She makes me feel things I haven't felt in a long time, and it... scares me."

Coming from a Vampyre, that could've meant anything.

"What do you mean?" I frowned.

"I've run all sorts of scenarios in my mind for when everything hits the fan, and I'm having trouble imagining one where we all come out alive."

I turned my head toward the window to watch the massive trees streak by. I wouldn't admit it aloud, but I felt the same way. I had the sickening sense of everyone dying around me, surviving alone to grieve for an eternity. Or maybe I died instead, and it was Briar who had to mourn.

"I can't help but think it's all my fault. I'm sorry... for everything I put ya through after that promise," I said.

"You became my best friend, the closest thing I ever had to a brother. Here I was worried about losing my place with the Nightshades, never realizing I already had a family right in front of me." Caspian released a wavering breath. I braced for tears that I'd never once seen escape. "I always thought you were crazy for cutting so many breaks for people who owed Uriah money, especially the Sun Dwellers. And sparing Briar's life? I thought you'd *really* lost it. But... after getting to know Astoria, I-I think I understand now."

"So... what exactly are you afraid of?"

"Losing her, and turning into my father."

The forest ended, and we were greeted by a twisting road. Caspian flicked the headlights on as the sun plunged below the horizon, and we curved around a cliff overlooking one of Helios' several beaches.

"You could never turn into Cyrus, man," I said with a dry laugh. Inky shadows curled around Caspian's hands over the steering wheel, and for a second I thought they'd take control of the car. He took a deep breath, and they crawled back under his sleeves.

"What did you want to tell me?" he asked. I briefly closed my eyes with a sigh, wishing he hadn't remembered me bringing it up.

"There's something wrong with me, and I don't know if I

should tell Vyrn or not." I let my claws extend, and lightly dragged my thumb over my inner wrist. The copper taste filled my mouth from merely thinking about it.

"Tell him what." Caspian's impatient tone was far from inquisitive.

"I can't drink human blood anymore."

I didn't want to say it. *God, I didn't want to say it.*

"And that's a bad thing? You get to manipulate fire, walk in the daylight, and still keep your other strengths? You're an enhanced Sun Dweller now, every Turned and Vampyre-born's dream."

If only.

"No, I still need blood. It's just… Vampyre blood now."

The truck decelerated as Caspian's spine went rigid in his seat. His lips parted and closed repeatedly, as if he were typing a sentence in his mind and backspacing over and over. We accelerated again, and he opted for silence.

I was left sitting there, imagining how much he regretted referring to me as his brother just moments before.

✳

Caspian stopped at the front doors of the Lunar Mart. I leaned over the center seat to read the signs plastered all over the boarded windows. They were permanently closed.

"How is this possible?" he asked.

"Mundus Novus." I narrowed my eyes with a low growl, straightening in my seat.

"Don't they realize that taking away blood access will *force* Vampyres to hunt Sun Dwellers?" Caspian's usual monotone voice rose in irritation.

"Maybe they decided they weren't going to keep peace anymore," I said.

A loud pop against the car's metal bumper rang out. We ducked our heads, eyes darting in multiple directions to pinpoint where the source of the gunfire was. I caught a glint on the rooftop of a plaza strip across the street.

"Snipers!" I exclaimed, and Caspian slammed his foot on the gas. The tires screeched against the pavement, leaving black streaks on the ground. The next gunshot pierced the leather single-bench seat, near my shoulder. I flinched forward, yanking my pistol out of its holster and swinging my arm out the window to return fire.

"Drive, man!" I snapped as I reloaded the magazine.

"The pedal won't go any lower, Draven!" Caspian retorted, jerking the wheel to turn down a new street. The gravity held me against the door as more shots pierced through the back window and ricocheted off the truck's frame. I sucked my teeth after another bullet shattered through the windshield, then leaned half of my body out the window. I twisted to look behind us. Five Onyx Sentries rode sport motorcycles, similar to Briar's old one. I took a deep breath, gripping the edge of the window to hold my balance. I aimed, exhaled, and fired.

One Sentry fell back, becoming a speed bump under his colleague's wheel behind him. He tumbled off, but the remaining three still gained on us, and one of them raised a fist in my direction. Two small metallic wings unfolded from their forearm, and a panel at the top slid open to reveal a miniature arrow with a tiny blinking red tip.

My heart jumped, and I screamed, "Get out of the truck!"

Caspian didn't question my judgment. As I leaped from the

window, his door flung off and he lurched to the opposite side of the street. The truck kept speeding forward, veering off to the left without its driver.

The moment that arrow kissed the truck's tailgate, it burst into flames.

Sure, I would've survived it. But Caspian wouldn't have.

I darted across the street in a flash and unintentionally dug my claws into Caspian's shoulder as I dragged him to his feet. I let go when he fell into stride beside me.

His blood on my hand wafted to my nose, and I rang out more shots behind us to mask his scent behind the gunpowder. The three Sentries dodged every bullet, riding nimbly on their bikes. It was hard to believe they were human behind those full-face helmets.

Then again, Sterling had been a Sun Dweller cop and he'd held his own countless times.

We ran up the wall of a nearby building and vaulted over the railing. I tumbled to my knees and rolled onto my back while Caspian's boots slid gracefully across the roof. The rumbling whirs of the bikes faded, as though the Sentries had decided to keep driving forward despite watching us ascend.

Caspian extended his hand and I grabbed it, swiftly back on my feet. I patted the chalky dirt and dust off my pants while I caught my breath. He nudged my arm with a proud chuckle.

"Like old times, huh?" he asked breathlessly.

"Yeah, except that was the closest call we've ever had." I scratched my head and crouched, leaning against an air conditioning unit. "What are we gonna do about the blood run?"

"If that Lunar Mart is closed down, we should assume they all are around Helios." Caspian hesitantly stepped to the edge of the roof and peered below. He reached in his back pocket for his phone and glanced back at me to say, "I'll call—"

His voice was ripped right out of his throat when a glowing, electrified rope lassoed over his head from below. He tipped backward over the edge.

"Cass!" I shouted, lunging forward to catch his flailing arms. I swiped the air, an inch too short to grab him. I staggered and caught myself on the edge. Two ropes shot over my head before I could react.

It was a different kind of electricity, a different heat. So hot that it felt cold. I couldn't feel anything below my neck as the air instantly rushed from my lungs. The wind only held me for a second as I plummeted right next to Caspian, who writhed and gasped for air against the rope.

"Two suspects secured," one of the Sentries said through a cackling radio on his wristband. I reached for my neck and the rope scorched my fingertips. It sent a rush of energy through my veins, and Caspian's twisted face urged me to do *something*, but I couldn't.

I lay there with raspy breaths, watching their motorcycles return to them remotely. A van followed.

They can't know. I can't give them incentive to study me and build tech to use against me.

"Returning to base," another announced. They mounted their bikes while two Onyx Sentries exited the van and dragged us around the back.

As the doors shut us off from the outside world, I wondered...

Had I made a promise to Briar I couldn't keep?

34
CASPIAN

I'D NEVER SEEN ANYTHING LIKE IT BEFORE. THE ROPES tethered to our necks robbed us of our voices. We were thrown in the back of the van like sacks of potatoes, diminished to animals in the dark, and all I could do was glare at Draven for refusing to use fire to get us out of here.

And all he could do was stare back at me with a resolute, yet apologetic look. For the life of me, I couldn't read him. Of all our silent communications during Uriah's countless missions, where we were always on the same page, I couldn't understand his inaction.

Maybe Draven still didn't know how to consistently control the fire?

Maybe he wanted to see what the Onyx Sentries were up to from the inside?

Maybe he was waiting to use his power to take them all out at once?

My temples throbbed.

It wasn't a long drive. When the doors swung open, the Sentries jerked our ropes, forcing us out of the van. I ignored the pain to survey our surroundings. Electrified barbed-wire fences surrounded the compound, where Vampyres shuffled in shackles, carrying boxes from one end to the other. Their shoes scraped against the concrete with a level of exhaustion I never thought Vampyres capable of. They blinked slowly, as if they were on the verge of falling asleep in the middle of walking. But of course, that would be impossible.

Right?

The Sentries pulled us forward to a semi-circular insulated fabric shelter. Two Sentries were posted on either side of its entrance with automatic rifles. They wore full-face masks that only exposed their eyes.

Inside the shelter, white folding tables lined along the far wall with other Vampyres in a similar predicament. They had illuminated ropes around their necks as well, and they were being led down the line as Sentries then passed supplies. The Vampyres at the front held folded sets of jumpsuit uniforms, with a toothbrush, a roll of toilet paper, and a bar of soap placed on top.

I wheezed at the rough tug of my rope as we were brought to the back of the line. The silence was like static until the line moved.

The system they had was nothing compared to what I'd seen at White Fang. Then again, Draven might've seen more similarities given that he'd spent more time in their clutches. When I glanced at my friend, his chest was heaving with thick breaths. I waited for the smoke to roll, but I supposed he clamped down on it.

We passed through the line. I recalled the Vampyres outside without ropes, so I clung to the hope that these cursed things would soon be removed.

"Make the announcement," one of the Sentries ordered another, and he about-faced and marched out of the shelter. I frowned.

"We got the last of them. Helios is now contained."

The gears turning in my mind whirred louder, and the rope felt like it squeezed tighter. I didn't know how Mundus Novus' goons operated, and I could already see that it was nothing like the Vampyre clans in Neoterra. I couldn't predict their behaviors to make any calculations.

For once... I didn't have a plan.

Draven, still and compliant, shuffled down the row. He joined the second line by the front door. A vein bulged in his forehead. He appeared to be holding his breath for an unbearable amount of time, like he was fighting against demons not to unleash his power.

Or rather... fighting against sinking his fangs into one of the many Vampyres surrounding us. I still hadn't been able to digest that.

I took my place behind him, and a Sentry led us outside. Another walked down the line, removing the ropes from our necks. Sighs of relief and painful whimpers filled the air as they marched us across camp to another tent.

"Alright, bats." The Sentry stopped in front of a hundred-man tent framed in silver, snapping his heels together at attention. "These will be your quarters. There are bunk beds inside in numerical order. Find the bed with the matching number on your uniforms. You have five minutes to claim your bed and change your clothes."

I couldn't understand why they'd provide beds if we didn't sleep, but I kept silent. I moved the bar soap and toothbrush out of the way and took note of the white thirteen on the back of my charcoal coveralls. With Draven's number being fourteen, he was left with the top bunk. It groaned in protest as his bulky frame climbed on it. In any other scenario, I would've chuckled... but I thought humor had abandoned me for good.

The clock was ticking. Most of us were changed except for two Vampyres, who were still getting tangled up in the bulky sleeves. One of them struggled to button the front of their coveralls. Everyone—except for Draven and me—flinched at the abrupt sound of a metal baton clanging against the tent's silver frame when the doors swung open.

"Time to get to work," the faceless Sentry demanded, and scanned the room. He paused on the two Vampyre men who were still fumbling with their appearance. Before any of us could blink, he unholstered a pistol and shot them both in the head.

Silver bullets, no doubt... because they instantly dropped to the floor.

"Clean up at bay twenty-seven," the Sentry droned into his watch, and turned to the rest of us.

"Let's be clear. Any resistance will result in termination, whether or not it's intentional. Keep up, and don't be an idiot if you care to live." He marched out of the tent, and everyone rushed to get in line to follow.

The gunshots still rang in my ears.

One of the Vampyres lunged at his back, fangs aiming for his shoulder. The Sentry threw him down and shot him between the eyes.

"You all think you can still take us," he announced with a dark laugh, and said into his watch, "Deploy fog."

White smoke filtered through the vents in the ceiling, filling every square inch of the tent in seconds. It became opaque, and everyone—including Draven—dropped to the floor.

I understood the game now. I felt no different, and he probably didn't either. So I played my part and let my body fall limp.

※

"How did we manage to get captured in one of these camps?" I grumbled to Draven as we dug aimlessly. They didn't give us time to process after everyone came to before putting shovels in our hands and telling us to get to work, tethered together by silver shackles at our ankles. The silver didn't burn me, and I had a wavering speck of hope that the sun might not hurt either.

We were ordered to work through the night to excavate a rectangular space for construction. They didn't tell us what they planned to build. Dirt smeared across all of our faces from constantly wiping the sweat off our foreheads.

"They outsmarted us with their bikes," Draven replied, and sniffed the air. His stomach audibly growled. I cleared my throat, adding a foot or two of distance between us with that indicator.

I never thought I'd ever ask this question, but—

"What are we going to do?" I dropped my voice to a lower whisper when an Onyx Sentry roamed closer to the edge of the site. It was a silly thought, maybe even childish... but I hoped we could return to Avant Garde before Briar gave that note to Astoria.

"We might as well see what this is before we make our escape," Draven said. I begrudgingly nodded, and stabbed the dry soil with the tip of the shovel before prying up a chunk of earth. Rinse, repeat.

"I don't think they know about White Fang's experiments," I whispered.

Draven shook his head. "Me either. Let's keep it that way unless we seriously need to use it."

"I don't understand what I have. I *drank* the serum, you had it injected and Briar was bitten." If shadows were a part of me, I couldn't imagine what use I'd have for them. I couldn't complain though. If the sun became easier to handle and the Onyx Sentries couldn't use silver against me, then it was still a win, and White Fang was one serum short.

"We all had different reactions to it... but the same result. Be patient, and hope it doesn't manifest to the point *they* find out." Draven's digging became more aggressive with each jab, the mound of dirt at our perimeter growing by the second. Perhaps it was a distraction from his growing hunger.

"I just want ya to know I ain't worth saving. If there comes a time where we both can't get out, don't look back. The others findin' out about this place is more important." Draven spoke past parted lips, barely moving them like a ventriloquist.

"I wouldn't leave you behind," I said curtly, and continued to dig. "But if we get split up, don't come looking for me. I'll figure something out. You and Briar need to train."

"You're the smartest guy I've known my whole life. Don't start actin' stupid now for my sake," Draven said, and moved away from me with his chains rattling. He could only go so far, but it was the end of our discussion.

I supposed I could've reacted better when he told me about his side effect. But after having spent my entire life at the top of the food chain, how else was I supposed to react after being told I could be prey?

Draven was known among the Nightshades as having one of the strongest wills against blood starvation. I only hoped that still applied with his new appetite, because I couldn't watch the Sentries in front and my best friend behind me all at once.

35
LYRA

THE TATTOO WAS PAINFUL. NOT BECAUSE OF THE TINY needles repeatedly stabbing my skin, because that pain healed within ten seconds. But because I was committing the ultimate betrayal to Kiegan by getting the lion skull with the nightshade mane. It took everything I had not to cry in the chair. I had to look away, staring instead at the various bottles of inks on Wraith's cart. I pretended I was getting a tattoo of something else, like Kiegan's name or even something stupid like a slice of pizza.

"What's wrong?" Wraith asked without taking his eyes off my forearm.

"Nothing, I'm just not a fan of needles." At the very least, I could pick the colors I wanted, and I chose light red, hoping no one would notice the crest immediately.

"Ah, you'll be fine," he said, wiping away excess ink with a paper towel for the millionth time.

"So why red? Everyone generally goes with the standard black and white or getting the flowers colored," Wraith said. I shrugged with the arm that wasn't being held hostage.

"Purple was never really my color."

"A close cousin to blue, if you ask me."

"But not a sibling."

He unleashed short burst of laughter.

Our words ceased, replaced by the tattoo machine's buzz for the rest of the session. I peered down at it, watching the redness in my skin fade back to calcite as it healed after every stroke.

Healed. *Permanently.*

"Welcome to the Nightshades, Dawn." Wraith smiled, flashing those ghastly teeth as he peeled the black latex gloves from his hands.

"Thank you." It came out raspier than I intended. "I guess I'll get back to the party."

I wanted to run up the stairs, but instead I calmly strutted back to the main floor. I scanned the crowd, searching for Oren. After digesting the initial information he'd given me, I felt more comfortable asking him more questions.

But I couldn't find him anywhere. I even went upstairs and checked the doors, from bedrooms to linen closets to the final door with two white lion statues flanking it. At this point, I wasn't looking for Oren anymore... but rather an office space.

"Lost?" A rich, husky voice rang out behind me, raking ice down my spine that sent me flying out of my skin. I whirled around with a gasp, jerked Sterling by the wrist, and yanked him into a bathroom.

"What are you doing?" I shouted in a whisper. "Do you have any idea what you've done?"

Sterling raised an index finger over his lips.

"I tracked your scent here, and when I saw a party going on, I figured it was the best time to try to break inside. Maybe find that folder you told me about."

"Yeah, well, that's the whole point of *me* being here. I don't need your help, now get out!" I swatted his shoulder.

Through the muffled music downstairs, I heard footsteps shuffling upstairs. I pointed at the moonlit window behind Sterling, but instead he grabbed me by the waist and pulled me into a kiss, drawing the breath from my lungs. The ice melted from my shoulders just as the bathroom door swung open and a random Nightshade Vampyre staggered into the doorway.

"Whoa, my bad!" he slurred with a lazy laugh. "Carry on!" He slammed the door shut and moved on.

Sterling pulled away, but held intense eye contact with a puzzled look, almost as if *I* had kissed him first. I focused on his lips, my limbs diminished to water after the electric shock.

"I, uh..." His voice came out gruffer than usual, and he cleared his throat. He continued in a low tone, "I heard him coming. I didn't know what else to do." He finally let his palms fall to his sides.

"Go home," was all I managed to say, despite feeling the ghost of his lips on mine. The surge of loneliness returned.

The door trembled with more knocks. Sterling flicked the latch open on the awning window and proceeded to climb out of it. I waited until his second leg disappeared before flushing the toilet and washing my hands for good measure. I double checked my lipstick, then swung the door open with a flinch.

"Oh, I'm sorry, did I scare you?" Uriah peered at me with the corner of his mouth quirked.

"I—no, I didn't expect you there," I stammered, pushing a piece of hair behind my ear.

"I just got done telling people to use the bathroom downstairs, I wasn't expecting anyone up here."

"Is it too invasive? I'm sorry, the one downstairs was being used," I said. It could've been empty all night for all I knew. I just hoped that wasn't the case. Uriah's smirk stretched into a mirthless grin.

"Let's take a look at your new tattoo, hm?" He grabbed my wrists and turned my arms outward, exposing my inner forearms.

"Wraith never disappoints," Uriah mused, and stepped in stride with me.

"This is pretty big for a housewarming party," I said, gripping the railing as we descended the steps.

"Well... because it's actually going to be the last one for a while. I wanted everyone to celebrate like they'd die tomorrow because a lot of them probably will." He shrugged nonchalantly, and peered over his shoulder once he reached the first floor. I paused in the middle of the staircase.

"What's going on tomorrow?" I frowned.

"Come to the meeting tomorrow night and you'll be briefed. I won't discuss it right now." Uriah grabbed a glass of champagne from a girl walking around with a gold tray, then disappeared into the crowd. "Go have fun."

How many of them knew it was their last dance?

I didn't bother warning anyone as I slipped out the door.

✳

Since Delilah had picked me up from the town square, I had to catch a cab. The Vampyre driver tried to make conversation, but quickly got the hint when I gave him short answers. I wanted to warn him to leave Neoterra with his family, but I didn't want the news to reach Chief Duncan.

Crap. I have work tomorrow.

If Chief Duncan was working with the Nightshades, I couldn't let him find out that I'd gone undercover.

I wished I had Draven's contact information. If anyone knew how Uriah operated with the police, it was him.

I should've gone into that room with the lion statues. That was probably a study, and the file could've been in there. Better yet, I should've let Sterling go in the study while I distracted Uriah.

I sank into the back seat, rubbing my forehead as I fought tears. I wanted to blame the kiss for distracting me, but at the end of the day it was all my fault.

I passed the driver a tip through the plexiglass divider and trotted quickly to my car, snatching the heels off my feet to drive home barefoot. Sunrise was still an hour or so off, but the birds had already begun their morning songs.

The shower was running when I walked in. My first instinct was to reach for my gun stowed in the fireplace, until I remembered Sterling was here. I coached myself into not being awkward when I saw him again.

The shower shut off, and he walked into the living room a

few minutes later. His chin-length, wavy copper hair was combed back, dark and shining like fresh pennies. A few pearls of water still dripped onto his shirt. *Kiegan's* shirt. I averted my gaze when I felt a wave of nausea grip my throat. The quiet was more uncomfortable than an itchy Christmas sweater.

"Hey, sorry about before," he said, and shuffled into the kitchen to poke his nose in the refrigerator. "Hungry?"

"I'll pass." I leaned over the counter, burying my face in my arms. "We were so dumb."

"How?"

I propped my chin on my forearm and watched him drink a blood pouch.

"It would've been a golden opportunity to investigate that room upstairs. I could've distracted Uriah, you could've gone to look."

"You mean the office?" Sterling's scarlet eyes flipped to mine, and a cocky, lopsided grin played across his face.

"You've been in there?" I straightened.

He tossed the bag in the biohazard trash and shrugged nonchalantly.

"I checked it out. It wasn't in there."

I sighed and ran my hands through my hair. He moved closer to the counter with a squint, grabbing my arm to stretch it out. He stared at the tattoo, and the shame that washed over me was insurmountable.

I braced for the rain of insults, and prepared to kick him out of my house.

"Red ink. Smart," he said, tracing his rough fingertips over Wraith's linework. "Easy to cover up, but not as easy as blue."

"If that's true, then blue would've made it obvious that I didn't plan on keeping it," I said, although getting a coverup as a solution had never crossed my mind. I doubted it would help, considering the crest would always be underneath it.

"This isn't who you are. Don't forget that," he mumbled, and moved his hand away.

I tilted my head as I fidgeted with my nails. "Why are you doing this all of a sudden?"

"Doing what?" He crinkled his nose with a frown.

"Being nice to me. Who are you and what have you done with Sterling?"

A laugh escaped and he leaned against the counter, palms resting over the edge.

"Don't flatter yourself, Lyra. The kiss was strictly business, and the compliment was coming from a friend," he droned.

I loosed a scornful breath and slid off the barstool to shower and change into casual clothes. My phone buzzed in my back pocket, and I paused at the edge of the hallway to check it.

My heart dropped to my knees.

Everyone at the bar tonight, nine sharp. Dress appropriately.

Uriah. I'd hoped the meeting he mentioned was empty talk, and the "dress appropriately" rubbed me wrong. It might've been code, but no one told me about it.

"What's wrong?" Sterling folded his arms and flanked my side, peeking over my shoulder. I turned off my phone screen, debating whether I should keep him updated on what I was doing. After last night, it seemed like he'd follow me regardless, so it might be pointless to keep him out of the loop. Plus, I had been trying to get out of the habit of doing everything on my own.

"I have to go to The Nightshade bar tonight... for a clan meeting," I said hesitantly.

Maybe I could find Oren again.

"Okay... and? That's expected. What spooked you?" Sterling wiped water dripping from his hair off of his forehead.

"Nothing. I never been around that big of a Nightshade crowd in a long time, that's all."

Sterling continued to watch me, his chin dipped but his eyes peering from under his brows with skepticism. I sighed, my shoulders slouching in defeat.

"Uriah is planning something big tonight. The folder is the least of our problems now, but there's a guy."

"A *guy*?" Sterling loosed a caustic laugh, leaning against the wall at the edge of the hallway. "What, he's gonna save the day now?"

"Will you *stop* and let me talk?" I snapped. The kind and gentle Sterling Shaw was fleeting, and my heart already ached for those moments to return. I didn't have the energy for this.

Sterling blinked slowly, waiting.

"He said his name was Oren. He told me that Briar and Draven weren't there, as though he saw right through my cover and assumed they were the ones I was looking for."

Sterling pushed himself off the wall, his arms falling slack and his eyes widening at the mention of his sister. I didn't condone his idea of revenge, but that was a problem for later.

"So did he say where they were?"

My exhale was audible.

"Helios."

Sterling was quiet, gazing down at the floor with his irises darting side to side ever so slightly like he was reading the wood grain.

"Don't go to that meeting," he said.

"Why?"

"If he recognized you, that could mean he told the others. It could be a trap." Sterling shuffled into my living room and plopped on the couch.

"Or he could be undercover too, but for a group of his own."

"Did you bother to ask if Draven and Briar are there of their own free will, or if they are being held captive by one of the clans?"

"The Nightshades aren't based in Helios. They're all over the mainland. If anything, White Fang would be on that island, and Draven has already handled them once before."

I flinched when my phone rang, and my veins turned to sludge at the sight of Chief Duncan's name. My face remained placid as I answered.

"Officer Hart," I rasped, and swallowed what felt like cotton wedged in my mouth.

"Sorry to bother you on your day off. Governor Donovan would like to meet with you and Sterling today within the next hour." The chief's usual upbeat tone was gone. It was empty, maybe even held a tinge of guilt—but I could be biased after witnessing the file hand-off to Uriah.

"*Governor Donovan* wants to meet with me and Sterling?" I repeated, and Sterling sat so far on the edge of the couch that he might as well have been squatting. At that point, I put my phone on speaker and set it on the coffee table, kneeling across from Sterling.

"Yes, I recommended you two for advice, given your experiences with the Nightshades and White Fang clans. If Sterling refuses due to no longer being employed with us, there is a handsome compensation at work for his compliance. Showing up is mandatory, so refusal will automatically cancel the money." I wanted to ask how much, but I didn't want to pry into Sterling's finances.

"You'll be compensated too. Maybe even promoted," Chief Duncan added. Sterling and I exchanged an uneasy look.

"Advice for what, sir?" I asked.

"War."

36

LYRA

When the phone call ended, the silence was charged with white noise. For the first time *ever*, I was certain meeting with the Nightshades later tonight was a lesser evil than seeing Governor Donovan and Chief Duncan.

"I think *that* is a trap," I said. "Especially if they want us to meet in daylight. We'll be weakened by the time we get there."

"Yeah, probably. But if I had to choose, I'd see Governor Donovan because she has authority to deploy Onyx Sentries if she's in a bad mood. I don't think we can take them on like the Nightshades."

Or you just want whatever money she's trying to bribe us with.

I felt a stab in my forehead and rubbed it as I stood. I finally managed to leave and take a shower, dressing in a business casual grey sweater over a button down blouse with dark slacks. Sterling didn't bother asking if I had any more formal clothing for him to wear. I guessed he didn't care how he appeared in their presence.

I forced myself to drink the last bag of blood for sustenance, and with Sterling close behind, we piled into my car and drove to the Neoterra Police Department in grim silence.

✳

The police station building appeared foreign. I couldn't remember the last time I spent time here.

I was a feral cat being thrown into a cage. After spending so much time in the wild, it'd be a miracle if I behaved correctly in front of the woman who could destroy hundreds of Vampyres by uttering a single word. I sucked in a breath, and buried my anxiety deep.

She's only human. She can't hurt you.

I told myself those sweet lies long enough to walk inside with confidence. I checked my watch and sat on a bench in the waiting room while the burns healed around my face and ears. Sterling, however, still glowed like a Sun Dweller.

"Are you immune now?" I asked, peering up at him while I winced. He shrugged.

"I guess it finally kicked in, I don't know." He shuffled to the elevator and pressed the button, sliding his hands in his pockets as he waited for the door. I didn't stand until it opened, and scanned my badge for the floor we needed.

It was empty. Papers were strewn across every desk aside from Sterling's and mine, but no one was present. Not even a rookie suffering through paperwork, as though everyone had to drop what they were doing and clear out. The hairs on my neck stood straight up, because it was either ordered by the governor herself, or chaos in Neoterra had forced every bit of manpower Chief Duncan to hit the streets.

Either way, the lack of officers on our floor was a bad sign, and I ignored the vague instinct to grab Sterling's arm for emotional support like I used to with Kiegan.

Someone swiveled in the chair behind the frosted window that had Chief Duncan's name engraved in it. Sterling and I shared a tense glance. I stepped forward first and knocked without skipping a beat. Ripping off the bandage was better than standing there waiting for the hour to tick by and risk being perceived as late.

"Come in," Chief Duncan announced, and we filed inside. He stood next to his own desk, with Governor Elise Donovan taking his place behind it. She wore a crimson skirt suit with nude lip gloss, her charcoal hair pulled back into a chignon bun. Her makeup was so thick that it emphasized her pores rather than masked them. Governor Donovan crossed one knee over the other, both hands placed on the chair's armrests. Every movement she made was careful, as though the slightest movement would crack the mask she plastered over her face.

"Lyra Hart and Sterling Shaw." Her voice had an allure to it, like a snake charmer, and her smile—it was hollow.

"Governor," Sterling and I said in unison, dipping our heads in acknowledgment.

"How did it happen that two lone wolves began working together?" Her steely blue eyes shifted to Sterling's, and she tilted her head gracefully with a squint.

"Red becomes you," Governor Donovan purred. "Tell me, how did you Turn?"

I expected Sterling to fold in the presence of authority and tell her about Briar.

"White Fang," he responded tightly.

She straightened her neck with a simple, "Hm."

An unreadable response.

"Did you hear my announcement about the new curfews?" Governor Donovan leaned forward to grab a stress ball off of the desk and tossed it between her hands.

I shook my head, opening my mouth to speak.

"Yes," Sterling interjected. "I saw your announcement this morning."

"And yet... you two came here without a thought," she said.

"As essential personnel, yes. We had to break curfew however we saw fit to fulfill our duties," Sterling said with a frown. I bit my inner cheek, trying to calculate if this was a test. Were we *not* supposed to show up?

"It was our understanding that when the governor summons you, it overrides all law," I finally said, hoping she didn't perceive the bite in my tone. I wasn't very fond of tests.

"And it's my understanding that you like to cut corners for your own agenda, Officer Hart," she bit back. I bridled, silently fuming.

"Was there a reason you called us here, Governor Donovan?" Sterling asked. He clasped his hands in front of himself and shifted the weight in his shoulder-width stance. He wasn't the respectful, uptight detective I knew him to be, who would've stood at attention at either of their presences. Rather... he appeared to be challenging her with his chin up and chest poked out.

Perhaps the real Sterling was still at the hospital, and this was a doppelganger.

"Yes, actually." She caught the ball in one hand, and squeezed it. "I don't take too kindly to your species, but I see the merits. Given your connections to the clans, and Lyra's little undercover project with the Nightshades, I want all the intel you have."

I thought my heart would shatter my sternum.

"How do you—"

"I have eyes and ears all over this city. Mundus Novus didn't delegate me to clean this mess up for nothing," she said with an arrogant smirk, and resumed tossing the ball. "Anyways, you each would get one hundred thousand dollars for every piece of intel that proves useful."

The amount of information I had would've made us both wealthy. It definitely would've helped Sterling find a new home, which was probably something Governor Donovan was banking on.

"If I refuse?" Sterling angled his head. I blinked at his question, forehead creasing.

"Straight to Camp Helix in Helios for Reconditioning, without pay. This offer is only on the table for the next ten minutes."

She was also playing on his recent hold at the hospital. My eyes narrowed, and her smirk stretched wider.

We were backed into a corner, and she enjoyed watching us squirm.

"We might even consider letting you rejoin the force." She stood from the chief's chair, leaning over the desk with her slender hand held out.

"Fine," Sterling said through a tight jaw, his forearm muscles flexing with the firm handshake. I gave her a stiff nod, half-heartedly shaking her hand.

"Draw up reports on what you know and have it back to Chief Duncan by midnight," Governor Donovan ordered, then added with a dismissive wave, "Get back to your shelters."

We were on our way out the door when she said: "Oh, and another thing!"

"What?" Sterling snapped.

"I'd stock up on plenty of blood if I were you." She smiled deviously. Neither of us bothered to ask why, because we knew she wouldn't give a straight answer. Definitely a veiled threat.

Sterling and I didn't speak until we were back in my car.

"So you want to get back on the force, huh?" I asked the second my tires touched the street.

"No, I don't care about any of that. I'm just buying us time."

"For what?" I propped my elbow on the window sill, and felt the sun attempt to burn through my sweater with fiery frustration.

"To leave Neoterra and go to Helios," he said. I raised my eyebrows, resisting the urge to look at him while I dealt with the energetic traffic.

"I've had it with everybody. I dedicated my life to keeping the Vampyres under control. After Cyrene's death and Chief Duncan taking me off my cases, I realized that they weren't going to reciprocate, no matter how glowing my reputation was. My sister went missing, and even if I reported it, they wouldn't have let me work my own family's case. And I'm not going to talk about how she attacked me after," Sterling continued. "I don't know about you, but Chief Duncan is a small fish I'm not interested in catching anymore."

"The governor is technically a small fish too; she's working for Mundus Novus," I stated. We slowed to a stop at a traffic light, and I watched the Sun Dwellers move at much slower paces as they milled about, as though it were a Sunday afternoon.

"Yeah, I know. We can't do this by ourselves. After we check on my mother, we need to find Draven."

"You do realize that if we go to Helios, I'll be on a hit list with the Nightshades *and* the Onyx Sentries will be looking for us, right?"

"My sister's got the whole country after her, so those two don't scare me." Sterling reclined his seat back with a sigh, resting his forearm over his eyes.

"This isn't some ploy to find Briar and hurt her, is it?" I narrowed my eyes. With how much hate Sterling carried for Vampyres, going *against* Governor Donovan didn't make sense. Even as a Vampyre now, his heart was undeniably human. It would stay like that for an eternity.

"No, of course not," Sterling replied with a dry laugh.

I thought he'd just lied to me for the first time.

⁕

Sterling helped me pack once we got home. I laid out the clothes from Kiegan's side of the closet, and let him pick the ones he would be comfortable in. I expected to break down bawling, hiccupping so hard it made me nauseous. A dull pain like a fading headache instead filled the space.

I returned to the dresser, where my miniature photo of me and

Kiegan lay untouched. I returned it to my wallet, but my mouth went sour. I didn't deserve it, keeping him with me. Not after getting that tattoo and letting Sterling wear his clothes. I should've helped him buy some of his own.

"Are you okay?" His voice cut through my thoughts and I snapped my wallet shut.

"Yeah, I'm fine. Let's just get to it."

"Are you still going to the Nightshade meeting tonight? You might not get out of Neoterra in time," Sterling warned.

"I will. Uriah isn't abiding by the curfew. I need to find Oren, because he knows *exactly* where Briar and Draven are," I said as I rolled the suitcase to the door.

"In that case... I'll wait for you outside the bar," Sterling said, and moved on to the weapons I had laid out in a separate section of the bed. I watched him for a moment, wondering if he really meant it.

✳

I didn't put on a dress or heels, or wear makeup. My French bob was combed, but that was the extent of it. I focused on wearing stretchy bootcut jeans, a t-shirt, and sneakers, with a pistol at my hip and ankle in case I had to evade trouble. If Uriah was planning to trigger something tonight, I needed clothing I could be agile in.

There wasn't a line going into The Nightshade bar. Most Vampyres respected Governor Donovan's orders if it meant keeping the Onyx Sentries at bay. Unlike a normal night out, the entrance was closed. A narrow window slid open as I approached, and the bouncer's sunken eyes squinted. I didn't say anything except roll my sleeve up to show the new crest, and he opened the door with a grunt.

The first thing I noticed was that every Vampyre held a rifle, shotgun, machete, or pistol.

They were a lot more organized than I thought.

Their chatter was low among hundreds. The stage was empty, with five minutes left until the meeting officially started.

I wove through the crowd, searching for Oren's distinct platinum coils and trichrome skin. The club was so crowded, it felt like searching for a needle in a haystack. I couldn't catch his scent the other night past all the alcohol, so I had nothing to track.

I pushed through until I reached the back of the club, near the bathrooms. Every time I set foot near here, I remembered the night Draven tried to stop Wraith, his brother, and Delilah from hunting Sterling and me. It was a miracle that they didn't remember who I was.

Or maybe they did, and I was being strung along until they found the right time to strike.

My heart skipped a beat when I finally caught Oren stepping out of the bathroom. He smirked at me, spinning a machete in his hand nonchalantly.

"I thought you wouldn't show up," he said.

"I wanted to talk to you," I whispered. "Where's Briar and Draven?"

"First tell me who you really are and then *maybe* I'll tell you." Oren tilted his head with a mischievous glint in his eye.

I shifted my weight uneasily.

"I need their help."

"The Nightshades need them dead."

"I'm not here for them."

"You're a cop, aren't you?" Oren's voice almost became inaudible. I squeezed my eyes shut with a grimace, and gave him a short nod.

"Thank you all for coming early." Uriah's voice shot from the stage and spread from wall to wall like a firework. "Are we ready?"

The entire room rumbled in unison, with several punching the air proudly. I frowned.

"Yeah... the meeting was actually at eight-thirty and they're about to spill blood. Aaaand... I think you're first in line." Oren jutted his chin toward the back door exit in the short hallway where we stood.

I tracked his gaze over my shoulder to Delilah and Wraith glaring at us, machetes in hand.

37
STERLING

It felt weird wearing a dead man's clothes—like a bad omen. I reached in Kiegan's jeans' pocket and found gold lighter with his initials carved into it. I flicked it open and closed while I waited for Lyra across the street where Sundance used to be.

A new frilly and pompous sign labeled "Bethany's Corner" now graced the window.

With the new curfew in place, the streets were swollen with humans who hadn't been able to enjoy the night's allure in decades. Bethany's Corner was alive inside, revealing a pink and blue renaissance decor style, and every booth was filled with patrons while the waiting area remained at max capacity.

I felt a tinge of guilt—a tiny prick behind my sternum for having reported Sundance for hiring a human apprentice. At the time, even though Samara gave me information that could help me track

Briar, I wanted them to sink. I blamed them for her disappearance, but the reality of it was that she would've been taken no matter where she worked.

We didn't have the best upbringing. Briar, Astoria, and I only had each other, and it had been the first time I'd seen her in a better mood. She almost glowed, and I smothered her light by trying to keep her safe. Worst of all, I'd robbed her of a sanctuary when she escaped White Fang. She probably could've turned to them for help, and maybe... *maybe*... would have had more self-control.

And I would still be human.

I closed my eyes, clicking the lighter shut.

Stop it. I glanced at my watch, then across the street at The Nightshade bar. I tried to decide at what point I could assume Lyra was in trouble, and what I would do if she was.

"Come on..." I mumbled, pushing away from the car and standing next to the driver's door.

Then the ground rumbled, and I crouched as every muscle in my body coiled. I ducked when a nearby fire hydrant exploded like a geyser. People nearby gasped and shouted, then laughed playfully.

But who *wasn't* playful was Lyra as she burst out of the side door and darted across the street with another Nightshade, who I assumed was the guy she was looking for. Oren's eyes glowed greyish blue, and he stretched his palm toward the fire hydrant. The water froze in place for a moment, and as if it had developed a mind of its own, whipped at the stampede of Nightshades spilling out of the building behind them.

"*Go!*" Lyra shrieked, swinging her arm in a pitching motion.

My mouth gaped, but I snapped out of watching the impossibility of it all when Lyra and Oren bolted for the car. I ducked into the driver's seat and swerved out of the parallel parking space as gunshots rang out. I drove toward the Nocturne District, where we hoped we could reach the ferry before it shut down again. I sat at the edge of my seat, focused on weaving between cars until we were far enough away from the shooting.

"What happened?" I finally asked as I decelerated to a normal speed limit.

"Uriah told Dawn the wrong time of the meeting and they tried to kill both of us," Oren said.

"Dawn?" I scrunched my nose with a snicker. Why would she have chosen such an ironic name?

"What did you do to piss Uriah off?" I asked, and glimpsed at him through the rearview mirror. He couldn't have been a police officer, otherwise I would've recognized him.

"Nothing, but they saw me talking to Dawn, so I guess they assumed I was undercover too. Thanks for that, actually," Oren deadpanned, rolling his eyes and leaning across the back seat.

"What are they planning? Why were they all carrying guns?"

"The first phase will be feeding on some of the humans, Turning most of them. The next phase will be overpowering them, forcing them to fight. Tonight, the targets are the police department and the hospital," Oren explained.

"*What?*" I shrieked, and nearly flipped the car over in a spontaneous U-turn.

"There's nothing we can do about it now, trust me. We need to go to Helios," Oren said. That already went without saying, but how could we leave the humans out there defenseless?

"They can't protect themselves," I said. My grip on the steering wheel tightened until I thought I'd rip the whole column off. As I careened around a corner, I tried to maintain control of my strength.

"They can protect themselves plenty," Lyra countered in a bitter tone. *"They* decided to shoot up defenseless Vampyres while you were in the program."

Her words reverberated. I didn't—couldn't—respond.

"I know what you're thinking, man. It wasn't just criminals either. It was a group of ordinary people that had children, worked, paid their taxes. They got guns, and decided to kill Vampyres of *all* ages on their own volition," Oren added. "A group called the Skinwalkers."

"How could they possibly—"

The interior of our car flashed red and orange, as if the sun had suddenly broken through the night sky.

Fire blazed in my rearview, followed by a portion of a corporate skyscraper crumbling. I slammed on the gas.

"Sterling!" Lyra gasped, and clung to the door handle and the center console. Oren did the same in the back seat as their eyes glued to the sunroof.

The skyscraper's shadow eclipsed the street. I swerved between boulder-sized debris plummeting faster than the rest of the building. Cars collided in the streets as people abandoned them to scatter, as if their human legs could carry them faster than the engine.

I finally turned down a street perpendicular to the skyscraper as it landed and blew an acrid cloud of smoke and dust in every direction. The explosion of wind pushed us further and I slammed on the brakes before we collided into a street lamp.

We all sat there for a moment, our ragged breaths the only sound between us. A high-pitched ringing plagued my ears, and all I could see was my life flashing before my eyes. I backed off the curb and drove at a slower pace with trembling hands.

Lyra twisted in her seat and peered out the back windshield. "Oh my God!"

I checked the rearview mirror again, and the sight triggered an audible gasp.

Everything and every*one* in the skyscraper's path was flattened to nonexistence.

※

The ferry slip was dead. Our only option was the six jet skis a mile down the shore that needed refueling. The three of us stood around them, and the last crumb of my hope dissolved. Lyra's phone hadn't stopped vibrating since the explosion downtown. It wasn't rocket science to assume it was Chief Duncan. I hoped he'd assume we'd died.

"This could work," Oren said, and reached for a jet ski.

I snorted. "How?"

"Me," he said, his eyes flashing with that strange translucent blue. The tide stretched across the shore, beyond the swash zone, crawling toward us. Lyra mounted one of the jet skis, and I did the same.

Gunshots pierced the air, with one of them deflecting off the metal rack housing the jet skis.

"Do whatever it is you have to do!" I shouted, and pushed off. The water raced toward us like a storm surge, then recoiled, dragging us with it. Once we were on a steady course into the bleak horizon, I twisted around. I had hoped the Nightshades would be too occupied tearing the city apart, but it appeared Uriah had delegated a small group to go after us.

Two of them were the same macabre guy from that night at the club and a familiar woman who'd accompanied him. They both watched us helplessly from the shore with twisted scowls.

I laughed, and took the liberty of flipping them off with both hands.

Part 3

Hurricane

38
BRIAR

Vyrn thought it was the perfect time to train me on shore while Draven and Caspian were gone. If I distracted my mind with Vyrn's instruction, I could bury the reckless urge to go after them.

They were probably fine.

It's just a blood run. They've handled much worse by themselves and together.

Astoria was still in the library, and the corners of Caspian's note poked my leg through the thin fabric of my pocket—an annoying, constant reminder. I had an infuriating temptation to read it.

But... I couldn't invade their privacy like that, and I wasn't supposed to give it away unless he didn't come back. How long before I called it? How was I supposed to know the difference between them being in danger and them taking a lunch break?

The uncertainty was unbearable.

"Briar!" Vyrn kicked sand at my feet and snapped his fingers in front of my face. I jerked my head upward to meet his eyes.

"Can you chill out?" I barked.

"Can you pay attention? If you're worried about your friends, you need to at least be able to do *something* with your abilities to help." Vyrn threw his hands up and rubbed his face. I waited for him to reach for his flask. To my surprise, he didn't.

"Draven said he'll come back to me," I replied in a resolute tone. I had to trust that.

"With the Onyx Sentries in town, he shouldn't have said that," Vyrn replied, and dug his shoe in the sand until he found a seashell. He picked it up, tossed it between us, and stepped aside.

"What are you so angry about?" he asked randomly.

I scoffed and shook my head. "Where do I start? I've been life's punching bag, and the hits just keep getting harder." I locked my gaze on the seashell below, wondering what stupid assignment Vyrn had hidden up his sleeve.

"Let's start with your childhood, then."

"No," I growled. The corner of Vyrn's mouth ticked upward, but it was fleeting.

"You don't have to tell me. But start there, reach inside your heart, find the issue and use it to burn that seashell. Don't come back to Avant Garde until it's blackened." Vyrn weighed his flask and sighed at its emptiness, then began shuffling toward the forest behind us.

"Wha—you're just gonna leave me here?" I shouted.

"Yeah, you're a strong girl. You got it!" He waved dismissively without breaking stride.

I plopped in the sand, pulling my knees to my chest as Vyrn's truck engine stuttered, then faded into the distance.

I stared at the tiny seashell, remembering a time when I used to collect shells as a kid to make bracelets. Of course, that was only when I was with my father, because Vivian would've thrown a fit if we brought any back home. I kept a secret box under my bed, and sometimes Astoria and I pretended to be magical mermaids with them.

Our imaginations allowed us to wield magic, but in real life I can't even light a candle like Draven.

Everyone claimed I had some sort of power, but I didn't see it. I was a useless waste of everyone's time.

I kicked the shell with a hiss, then stomped it deeper into the sand.

My mother pushed from the stove with eyes of radioactive lasers. A deep gash leaked from my palm after I'd frantically attempted to pick up the cookie jar shards. It wouldn't have shattered if I hadn't stood on my toes to sneak a sugar cookie instead of finding a chair to stand on.

"Look at the mess you've made!" She stormed into the kitchen as I inched backward until I hit the cabinets. I shrank in the corner with nowhere to run. Vivian reared her palm back and—

I slapped my cheek with a scream. Why, of all times, did my brain dredge that back up?

A couple kids snuck a pack of strange cigarettes to me in seventh grade. Vivian always smoked, and they made her sleepy. I hadn't slept in days and my grades were dropping, so I took them. For a short while, they helped me escape the constant arguments and beatings. Until Vivian found them and the seashells. Next thing I knew—I was lying next to a heart monitor, hardly able to see past swollen eyelids. Every breath sent a sharp pain in my ribs. Protective services was convinced that bullies had done it. The escape I got from the cigarettes wasn't worth the risk, and I hadn't touched drugs since. They repulsed me.

"Get out of my head!" I screamed, picking up the shell and chucking it at the ocean. It plopped with a sizzle, and I gasped, darting toward the water to sift it out before the next wave swept it away. I scooped wet sand, searching the various pebbles and shells mixed in the grains before chucking it to sea. I splashed around, searching for that cursed shell until I accepted defeat.

I can't even do Vyrn's assignment right. Go figure.

I decided to pad along the shore, allowing the balmy breeze to dry my clothes. I watched the soft, wet sand break with every step, and the waves crawl to heal the cracks I left behind.

If only something could heal the cracks that still lingered in my chest.

I was a mile down the shore when the wind picked up. The waves grew in size, towering at six feet. Further out, they were twice that height. They billowed toward the shore, but never went beyond the swash zone. The ocean swelled, then deflated, revealing three jet skis bobbing in the distance. My steps faltered when I recognized *who* rode them.

The engines were silent, yet they moved straight for the shore as though the water brought them home. I tucked my hands under my armpits, slouching as I picked up the pace to walk back to Avant Garde. I wasn't ready to face him. Not after what I had done. Wasn't there supposed to be more time before he was released from the hospital? I could've sworn I had more time.

The jet skis shifted across the sand and they dismounted. I swallowed roughly, increasing the width of my strides until I broke into a light jog.

"Hey!" Sterling shouted in the same sharp tone he reserved for perpetrators, demanding them to freeze in place. I flashed into the tree line without looking back.

"Sterling!" Oren and Lyra shouted for him in unison, but I didn't bother to see if he listened. My feet barely touched the ground as I whipped between the thickets. Wide monstera leaves slapped me in the face like leather whips.

"Get back here!" Sterling roared, now only a few feet behind me. I cursed under my breath and leaped into a tree, the brittle branch snapping with the sound of thunder from my weight. I hurtled to the ground, and before I could recover, Sterling pinned me down and clasped both hands over my windpipe.

"Sterling, get off her!" Oren demanded, and lunged behind him. Sterling elbowed him in the face and swung his arm at Lyra when she attempted to flank him. For once, I didn't fight back.

Kill me.

I stared at him, stars dotting my sight.

It doesn't matter how many times I apologize, I know it won't fix it.

My wheezes lost their sound.

I deserve to die.

"You're gonna kill your own sister?" Lyra screamed in a rasp, and suddenly oxygen rushed back in. My body jolted with uncontrollable heaves. The black dots turned into rainbow stars. I rolled over when I felt bile resurface to the base of my throat. I didn't know if Lyra had shoved him off or if he'd decided to spare me.

I pushed up on my hands and knees, my arms overwhelmed with violent quivers. If Sterling showed me mercy—was it because I'm his sister or was it because he didn't want Lyra to despise him?

"She's not my sister," Sterling sneered, and spat on the ground.

"Nice seeing you too," I snarked hoarsely, brushing the grass and dirt off my pants. I leaned against a tree with a sigh, waiting for the tremors to wane.

That was the life-or-death moment I'd hoped would trigger a fire response, but nothing came.

Sterling scowled at me, clenching his fists at his sides. Lyra watched him warily, poised to get in his way if he decided to finish what he started, and Oren... he admired the forest as if seeing it for the first time.

"Where did you guys come from?" I asked.

Lyra blew her bangs out of her eyes. "Neoterra. It's... not in a good condition right now."

"We should get a move on to Avant Garde," Oren said, and continued to trudge up the gentle slope through the forest. Surely, Vyrn didn't mean it when he said I couldn't come back until I burned the seashell. But...

"I'll hang back. I'm not supposed to return until I burn something," I said.

"Is that what Vyrn said?" Oren lifted an eyebrow with a small smirk. "He ain't mean it literally. Besides, he's not in charge of the guards. Ada is."

"Yeah, well, I'd hate to disappoint him," I rubbed my arm. "I'll head back a little la—"

"You can come back out here later. Come on." He reached for my wrist and pulled me along. I resisted at first. The aura surrounding my brother pushed against me like an invisible force field. But... I supposed Astoria would prefer all of us together after having been split up for so long.

"So what is this Avant Garde?" Lyra asked as we all stepped over a fallen tree trunk.

"A place where dreams are born," Oren replied with a proud smile—an odd look on a guy who often had a blank face. He and Caspian had that in common.

"Cut the bull. What is it?" Sterling growled, and snatched a branch off a bush. He scowled at me as he snapped it in two. I was certain my presence caused him internal decay.

"No bull. It's better to show you guys than try to explain, because you're just gonna call me crazy."

When the forest sloped downward, revealing tire tracks cutting through the grass below, and a small plateau covered in trees and moss appeared, I knew we'd made it back. It wasn't as far on foot as I thought, but then again, we were Vampyres.

"What, you have werewolves there or something?" Sterling laughed. Oren rolled his eyes.

"No, but we have Lightstalkers," he said with an exhausted sigh, and sped to the mouth of the cave. Sterling and Lyra paused at the top of the hill. They didn't follow him until I continued forward, and I was surprised my brother trusted my judgment enough to do so.

The cave stretched for two miles in narrow darkness. At the back of my mind, I knew Sterling was waiting for the trap to spring. When a small pin light appeared at the end, and the cave expanded into a vast cavern teeming with life, he and Lyra both gasped.

I stepped aside, letting them walk forward in a trance—the same reaction I'd had when I first reveled in Avant Garde's beauty. I didn't say a word. I let them enjoy every moment, wishing I could experience it for the first time again.

While they were distracted, I noticed a flicker of dim light in the library windows. I broke away to visit Astoria, stuffing my hands in my pockets. When my fingertips met with Caspian's note, I pulled my hands back out and shook them. Up until I reached the door, my mind ran several laps around the concept that something horribly wrong had happened to Draven and Caspian.

I lightly tapped my knuckles against the door before I entered with a tight smile. Astoria's head was buried in books, three of them splayed out while her notebook was covered in jumbled notes. Her cheeks were flushed, her eyes haggard.

"Ria?" I called, and took a seat across from her with a concerned frown.

"Huh?" Astoria jerked her head up, blinking hard like she hadn't done so in hours.

"How long have you been in here?" I scrunched my nose.

"I don't know, that clock doesn't work." She pointed at the dusty clock above the door with her pen. The hands were stuck ticking at three-thirty.

I sucked in a breath, deciding to hold off on telling her about Draven and Caspian leaving for a blood run. There was still enough time for them to return without either of us freaking out. Astoria returned to writing frantically in her notebook like she had a time limit to get all the information down.

"Sterling is here." My voice was clipped and dry in the stale library.

Astoria popped her head from the notebook and jumped from the desk, darting for the door. I flashed in front of it, holding her back by her shoulders.

"Bri, get out of my way!" she yelled, pushing forward. I locked my elbows in place.

"Wait, slow down! He's not the same! He tried to—"

"Of course he isn't! *You* Turned him!" Astoria interjected, and shoved me aside with her shoulder. She yanked the door open. I chuckled derisively, frozen in the doorway while she ran across the stone.

"Sterling!" she squealed, snapping him out of his trance. She leaped into his arms and he spun her around in the same tight hug they'd shared the day I bit him. An embrace I hadn't felt from him since he took me and my sister out of foster care when he was eighteen. Not even after I escaped White Fang's captivity.

She's not my sister.

I wasn't sure why I was so surprised. I attacked him in broad daylight right in front of her. I guessed I just didn't expect Astoria, of all people, to throw it in my face.

Maybe I'd finally realized that he'd never considered me to be his sister—even before my mistake.

I balled my fists at my sides, deciding it was the perfect time to check on Draven and Caspian. It wasn't like I would be missed if anything happened to me anyways.

39
DRAVEN

HUNGER AS A FLEDGLING IS WORSE THAN WHEN YOU'RE human. I remembered being a teenager, skipping breakfast and waiting hours until lunch at school or dinner at home, and knots forming in my stomach. It was a simpler time when a pizza commercial made me salivate.

Then I became a fledgling, and the hunger intensified to the point where the skin on my arms crawled, a bitter copper taste stayed in my mouth, and I could smell the Sun Dwellers' aromas for miles. I couldn't think about anything else, especially when I was alone with my thoughts in a dark cell in Uriah's basement.

Now, I felt like I'd taken a step back in time after enduring White Fang's experiments. The Vampyre prisoners surrounding me in Camp Helix were a buffet. Every pulse, heartbeat, and breath was a pull on the chain bound at my ankles. It tugged harder, and harder, until—

"Draven!" Caspian hissed in a hushed whisper next to me, clenching his fists over the wooden table we sat at. Cold rain pelted us, lightning occasionally flashing beyond the barbed wire. The Sentries forced us to eat outside, the rain mixing with our plastic cups of blood and trays of raw meat. I'd forgotten it was dinner time after we spent the night digging. We only had an hour left before day would break and everyone could finally retreat to the bays.

"Smoke," he warned in a mumble, and brought his cup to his lips. With my forearms braced on the table, I noticed the steam rising from my pores against the frigid rain. I concealed my hands in my lap and stared at my tray, knowing full well it would taste disgusting.

"Five minutes!" one of the Onyx Sentries announced. He walked between each table with his hands behind his back, holding the same electrified baton the Keepers had used at White Fang. He clicked the button repeatedly, activating the electricity like it was a pen.

"You need to eat, man," Caspian whispered after the Sentry passed us for the third round. Each lap, he lingered over my shoulder a few seconds longer.

I gnashed my teeth, digging my claws into my knees as I avoided Caspian's eye. Too close, everyone was too close.

"I... can't..." I spoke in a pained growl. I shut my eyes tightly, trying to calm the tremors.

"Something wrong, kid? Rain too cold? Food isn't good enough for you?" The Onyx Sentry returned, flicking my temple. I yanked his wrist. I caught a glimpse of his badge next to a key ring at his hip. The baton met with my chest, knocking me off the bench.

I writhed on the ground, heat rising at my fingertips. I dug my fingers in the mud to smother it.

The Sentry jammed his boot into my side and shouted, "I'm sorry, was that earlier lesson too hard to understand?"

I coughed, but immediately recovered. I stayed down.

"Take his food away," the Sentry spat.

I stifled a laugh. Like *that* was a punishment. I stared at the prints his boots left behind as he stormed off. Caspian peered at me, his frosted hair plastered against his forehead. His eyebrows and lips were pinched—that same miserable look he made whenever Uriah had me in the same predicament. Except this time, I didn't feel as much pain from the baton.

It was a shock. The energy knocked me from the table, sure, but...

It felt like a defibrillator giving me life.

I sat up and cracked my neck. Most of the other prisoners' jaws hung open. Some shook their heads in disappointment, and others nodded proudly.

"Alright, back to work!" the Sentries demanded, and everyone else stood as one unit to return to the site.

"Did you see those keys?" I whispered to Caspian.

His mouth quirked in a proud grin as he dangled the key ring and badge before tucking them away in his coveralls' pocket. I nudged him with my elbow and followed the others. At least I could always count on his stealth.

✳

The pit became a muddy mess, melting along the walls of the site. Nonetheless, we were expected to keep digging since we never grew tired. A group of Onyx Sentries sat on upside-down buckets under an awning and played cards with their backs facing us, and the one that was supposedly standing watch was on his phone with his rifle propped over his shoulder.

Further ahead, a Sentry scanned his badge over a keypad and the holographic gate opened for a flatbed truck packed with boxes on its tailgate. I tapped Caspian's arm.

"There," I whispered. "We figure out which key unlocks these shackles for the others and use that badge to open the gate."

"Hey!" The same Onyx Sentry from dinner burst out of a hundred-man tent, kicking mud with every stomp.

"Which one of you maggots took my keys and badge?" He jerked his gun from his holster and pointed it at Caspian and me with one hand. We both dropped our shovels and held our hands up. I knew those bullets couldn't harm me, but Caspian… we couldn't be so sure. Especially with him being a Lightstalker.

"I'll kill you and search your corpse if I have to!" he threatened, spit flying from his lips. He brought his second hand to the pistol's handle for further stability.

"We ain't take your keys," I shouted over a crack of thunder. "Maybe ya lost them. It's only human, right?"

I smirked, and the veins on his neck bulged so violently I thought he'd have a stroke.

The gun sang, and the bullet pierced my chest with a dull pinch.

I took a step back with a grunt from the force. A second shot rang and hurtled toward Caspian.

Black clouds curled around him, then dispersed like ink in water.

When the air cleared, he was gone.

40
BRIAR

I left Caspian's note on top of Astoria's textbook in the library. When he gave it to me, the paper was folded with perfect creases, as if he'd spent hours just doing that. Now, it had wrinkles from being stuffed in my pocket. I laughed drily, grumbling under my breath as I left the library. At this point, I was used to messing up the smallest things.

But helping Draven and Caspian... I was determined not to screw that up.

The intuition I experienced about Sterling during that arson wasn't as strong as this one, and he technically could've been hurt if the circumstances were slightly different.

The number of armed Avant Guardians indicated that there *had* to be some sort of armory nearby. I might've been self-aware of my stupidity, but I wasn't *that* stupid. Fire manipulation or not, I wasn't leaving without a gun.

After bathing in the spring and changing clothes, I searched for Ada. I found her in the center of the markets, her mouth running a mile a minute, gesturing to her surroundings while my brother, her son, and Lyra trailed behind her. I shrunk into the clothing shop that Draven and I had gone to before.

"Welcome in—" The girl frowned at the sound of the lock clicking. "What are you…"

"Where do you guys keep your weapons?" I asked, cutting to the chase.

She frowned deeper. "Why?"

"My friends are out there on a blood run and I think they're in trouble." I leaned over the counter, briefly scanning the wall behind her for a shotgun she could have stashed. The girl's face softened.

"Oh, that's okay! Sometimes it can take days for the scouts to come back with supplies. Especially now with the Onyx Sentries being in Helios."

My face was unflinching.

"Where?" I asked in a lower tone, nearly failing to keep the growl at bay. The rose-gold left her cheeks, and she shrunk against the wall. She peered at the door as if a hero would appear at the last minute.

"It's guarded. You'd have to ask Ada."

"I don't have time."

"Then take mine." She reached under the counter, and as I expected, presented a shotgun and a box of shells.

"Thanks," I grabbed them before she could change her mind. "One more thing. Where can I find alcohol?"

⁕

The glass clinked with every shift of the duffel bag slung across my chest. No one questioned the fledgling newcomer as I waltzed right out of the mouth of the cave. As far as anyone knew, I was taking supplies to the beach to continue my training. With unlimited stamina, I ran along the path through the forest toward Helios' mainland. My first instinct was to check both Lunar Mart grocery stores.

I expected humans to be out and about, reveling in their freedom without the worry of fangs around their necks. Instead, Helios was a ghost town on all fronts. I wondered if everyone had been forced to evacuate.

The first Lunar Mart I visited was the original one built years ago. The windows were boarded up, and faded paint and weeds growing in the cracks plagued the parking lot. Draven and Caspian's scents were also nonexistent.

They didn't go to this one.

As a human, we could only go to Sun Valley Grocers and other human-only stores. I had never been to Lunar Mart, but I knew it was the Vampyre counterpart. So it made little sense that when I approached the newer one, I saw it was *also* closed. Aside from overpriced local convenience stores, Lunar Mart held a monopoly on the blood supply.

I stood in front of the doors, staring at the sign announcing their permanent closure. The smell of burnt rubber and gunpowder vaguely clung to the air, and I finally pulled away from the sign to examine the rest of the lot. Curved tire marks were printed into the pavement a few feet away. Bullet holes pierced the brick, and while I was far from a ballistics specialist, it was safe to assume they'd been here.

The real question was if they got away, and where they ran off to.

I scanned the roofs. The tire tracks led into the street, arcing left. I darted across the parking lot to the next strip of stores. The tracks didn't line the road, but skidded in patches as the vehicle made sharp turns.

Gunshots popped in the east. I paused my trace.

My breath hitched, and I changed course, heading straight for the center of Helios.

✳

The sky had opened up and wept, sending heavy droplets at slow intervals. I held my arm tightly against the bag to steady the clinking and jogged across the street. A brown sign with bland white lettering hung in front of a holographic gate stretching around the barbed-wire perimeter.

Camp Helix.

I leaped to the second flight of stairs on the fire escape bolted against a nearby apartment building, then crept to the rooftop. The wind was heavier here, and the cold rain pelted my face. Every breath rushing from my lungs was forced back in, and I couldn't seem to catch it.

Below, olive-green and white tents sprawled among shipping containers. Onyx Sentries marched strings of shackled Vampyres toward a construction site at the center, where a small group dug through sludge.

Except... no one was actively *digging.* They all stood frozen with fear plastered on their faces, shovels scattered across the ground. One of them held his hands up in surrender while a Sentry aimed his gun. My heart skipped a beat when I recognized the dangerously arrogant smirk across Draven's face. A faux surrender to the gun he knew wouldn't hurt him. I noted a bloodstain on his coveralls.

A malicious whisper brushed through my mind. The same one that had demanded I drink from Moses.

Kill them. Kill them all.

I crouched behind a utility box, and kept an eye on the skies for helicopters or drones that could be patrolling the area. The duffel bag shifted and clinked as one of the bottles rolled. I removed the alcohol, followed by a rag and a lighter.

The Sentry demanded Draven not to move. His voice didn't carry the authoritative bass from before. I wished I'd witnessed what Draven had done to trigger such fear in an elite Onyx Sentry. The whole camp appeared shaken to the core, even the other prisoners.

But... where was Caspian?

I glanced at the Molotov cocktail in my hand, hesitant to chuck it into the camp. What if the rain instantly doused it?

I peeked over the edge again. The Sentry marched up to Draven with a wide stride, and slammed the barrel of the gun against his forehead.

I hurtled the bottle at a pair of trucks before he could shoot.

It spiraled in the air, the flaming rag whipping behind it like a flag. It crashed against one of the tents, the fire flashing and spreading over the canvas. The threads broke apart, forming a medium hole before the flames quickly died out. The small explosive alerted the other Sentries to begin searching the area.

A storm roiled within my chest, a vortex forming in the pit of my stomach. Heat spread across my skin, and before I knew it—I was racing across the roof and lunging off the edge, far above the fences and into Camp Helix like a shooting star.

322

41
DRAVEN

THE BULLET SHOT THROUGH MY CHEST AND EXITED OUT OF my back. The dull ache was already gone, and everyone in Camp Helix stared at me.

I guess the cat's out of the bag.

I raised my hands again with a soft chuckle.

"Don't move!" The Sentry demanded, raising his gun again. His colleagues surrounded me, with a couple patrolling the area searching for Caspian. "What are you?"

"A magician," I finally answered with a recovering smile, my palms warming. "Wanna see another trick?"

"Get on the ground!" The Onyx Sentry stormed toward me with the gun trembling in his hand. He jabbed the barrel against my forehead, but my knees refused to buckle.

Where did Caspian go? What sort of power is that?

The Sentry clenched his teeth, pressing the gun so hard against my head that it'd probably leave an indentation. "Something wrong with your knees, boy?"

From the corner of my eye, a flash shot through the sky, barreling toward the camp like a meteor. Beyond that ball of fire, I could distinguish a woman's silhouette.

But not just *any* woman.

The Sentry snapped his head in that direction, swinging the barrel toward the sky. I knew his aim would be impeccable.

I let go of the reins and unleashed the flames from my palms like a blowtorch, fusing his uniform to his charred body.

Briar crashed into a tent, leaving a large hole. Its edges in the roof still glowed, threatening to spread.

Bullets spewed at all angles until the Sentries' triggers clicked on hollow chambers. I sucked a breath through my teeth, charging up for another strike.

Frozen air engulfed me, taking the oxygen right from my lungs. My skin *burned*—taut and swollen—as if I'd jumped into a snowbank. I thrashed my arms around, palms numb as I tried to shoot more blazes, and writhed against what I realized was the foam from a fire extinguisher.

I collapsed to my knees, trembling and gasping as the Sentry scowled down at me, breaths heaving.

Then, I was back in that frozen chamber at White Fang, chained to the wall with the icy cuffs fusing to my wrists.

"Go, go, go!" Several voices commanded, and a drove of Onyx Sentries charged in Briar's direction. I cracked my eyes open, barely able to make out the blurry figure emerging from the tent. Black veins spread all over her face, arms, and legs. They pulsed with a magmatic glow with every ragged breath, like a chimera ready to ignite.

The ground shook as Briar barreled through the Sentries. Their bullets were as useless against her as they were against me. Their demanding shouts turned into those of anguish and fear. Some of the fallen bodies were seared—rock solid like cooled lava. Briar cleared a path, her palm reaching for me. I grabbed it and a bolt of energy jolted through my body.

I leaped to my feet, the skin on my arms replaced by blazes as though she were a match reigniting my dying fire. Briar wrapped tight arms around my waist, completely unharmed by the flames. Our eyes locked, and I noticed hers were completely white like the sun. I caressed her face, tracing the black veins across her cheek with my thumb. We ignored the bullets bombarding us.

After a moment, I finally lifted my gaze. Heat waves quivered around us, melting the bullets before they could pierce our bodies. I gasped at the heated force field she'd created around us.

But my smile was fleeting. The Sentries were ducking into their tents.

"What?" Briar finally tore her focus from me. Her flames sputtered out, her rose irises reappearing in the negative space.

I jerked my gaze skyward—at the red mist dropping from the helicopter sweeping over Camp Helix.

"Run!" I gripped her wrist and pulled her with me as I scurried toward the barbed fence. If a fire extinguisher had brought me to my knees, that red fire retardant might kill us.

Briar dug her heels in the ground, yanking me backward.

"What are you doing?" I roared. The black veins in her skin cracked open to reveal fiery rifts as though she were a volcano splitting open. She sprung her palms up, spewing lava with a roar. The blades' whirring rhythm slowed. The aircraft dipped, and the Onyx Sentries scrambled frantically out of the way as it crashed through the fence. A blackened mushroom cloud erupted.

By the time the smoke cleared, Briar and I had already escaped.

✳

Briar rammed her elbow through the window of a nearby car and jumped in the driver's seat. I didn't question it. She hot-wired it, then slammed on the gas. The vehicle lurched forward. We sped back to the forest. We were halfway to Avant Garde when the gas gauge needle plunged. The engine sputtered and we were forced to continue on foot.

The silence was heavy. I couldn't decide if I wanted to be angry with her or elated. She'd gotten me out of Camp Helix, and hopefully Caspian was somewhere safe—wherever those shadows had taken him.

If we get split up, don't come looking for me. I'll figure something out. You and Briar need to train.

I needed to trust Caspian knew what he was doing, even with the strange anomalies. He was right—if we were to stand any chance against Uriah King, Dr. Ivanov, or Mundus Novus... we needed to be prepared.

Briar clasped the duffel bag strap across her chest, staring intently ahead with a subtle frown.

"I told ya I'd come back for ya," I finally said.

"And now you don't have to," she droned, kicking a dead branch.

"What would ya have done if your powers didn't work back there?" My brows cinched at her nonchalant shrug.

"Died, I guess? I don't know. It didn't happen, so why does it matter?" Briar stopped, sifting through the duffel bag for the pills Vyrn had given her. She shook the bottle and released a bitter sigh when the last one fell in her palm.

"It matters 'cause ya can't keep doin' this. I can't keep worrying about you every second of the day," I snapped.

"Then don't," Briar barked, and picked up the pace along the path. I cursed under my breath, realizing I might not have taken the best route to address her rescue mission. I broke into a short trot.

"Why are you acting like this?"

Briar scoffed, rolling her eyes.

"I could finally do something, and the first thing you do is treat me like I got in the way," she said. "Or maybe it's your fragile ego talking."

"Wha—" My voice caught in my throat. The words jumbled together, and my train of thought seized. The temperature rose in my neck, and I shuttered my eyes with a deep inhale. "You weren't in the way at all. I just don't want you in my world any more than you already have been."

"It's far, *far* too late for that." She peered over her shoulder, her cherry blossom eyes wilting to a deep orange, then flickering out like a dying flame. My shoulders sank, and I slowed down so she could be a few feet ahead of me.

I'm sorry, I wanted to say. *I'm proud of you for showing the strength I knew you had.*

Instead, I let my fragile ego keep my mouth shut.

42
BRIAR

ADA'S GUARDS STOOD AT THE MOUTH OF THE CAVE WHEN Draven and I returned. They pointed their rifles at the rustling of our movement over the hill, but promptly lowered them when we emerged. They split off to check the perimeter to make sure we weren't followed.

Draven and I plodded through the darkness until Avant Garde's dim lighting greeted us.

"I'm sorry, Briar." Draven's gravelly voice echoed through the chamber. "I'm really proud of ya. Seriously."

"I'm not weak," I replied bitterly. He'd never said that, but he didn't have to. It clung to his thoughts like musk.

Heat emitted from him like a furnace, but I couldn't tell if it was from residual adrenaline or suppressed anger. I didn't bother to look back to find out.

I feared seeing Astoria's face once she noticed Caspian wasn't with us.

"Bri!" Astoria shrieked from the library, dashing fifty yards to meet us. She tackled me, squeezing my neck in an embrace similar to what she shared with Sterling earlier. I staggered back, my body going rigid. *Now* she cared?

Sterling and Lyra followed behind Astoria, flanking Draven and me within seconds. My brother remained withdrawn. Perhaps he worried about me, or maybe he was disappointed I'd made it back alive.

"We heard what happened! It's all over the news. Thank God you guys are okay." Astoria's voice went brittle. She pulled away with a sniffle, eyes darting between Draven and me. "Where's Cass?"

There it was. The dreaded question.

"We dunno," Draven said.

Astoria's thick black eyebrows fused into one. "What do you mean you 'don't know'?"

"They almost shot him, but then that weird black stuff appeared, and he disappeared with it," Draven explained in a softer tone. A lot gentler than when he chastised me for saving his tail. "Maybe that's what the serum gave him. Some kind of built-in flight response."

"So... where did he go?" Astoria's voice rose in pitch, her breath hitching as it always did seconds before the waterworks.

"We don't know, Ria." I sighed, and kept my eyes glued to the town beyond her shoulder. I wished we could've stayed back to find him too.

"For what it's worth... he ain't get shot. He's smart. He'll find his way back to ya," Draven added.

"Or he's dead," Sterling drawled. "There's a trend of people's lives getting ruined when Briar's around."

I laughed, because I had no defense.

Lyra slapped his arm with a disgusted groan. Draven released a threatening scowl, and I shook my head so he'd let it go. Sterling wasn't wrong. There was no honor for Draven to defend.

I continued forward, leaving them in their circle. While I was still frustrated with Draven, I appreciated that he stayed behind to comfort my sister.

✳

I returned to our cave, dropping the duffel at Draven's bed and shuffling to the nook next to his. I gathered fresh clothes, soap, and a towel, then made my way to the spring to bathe.

I stopped in the middle of the swaying suspension bridge that stretched across the chasm. I peered below, the void so opaque that even my Vampyric sight couldn't see the bottom. Wind passed through, as if the center of the earth breathed from there.

Jump.

I flinched at the voice. The same one that echoed my own. The one that'd been in my corner this entire time, waiting for me to trip and fall. The cursed voice that pushed me into the things I'd done to Moses, Sterling, and Camp Helix.

I gripped the rope.

Everyone would be so much better off without you.

I leaned forward, raising one foot.

How is it that the world lost someone like Moses, but now it's stuck with the likes of you?

Tears filled my eyes.

Even Draven thinks you're a burden. His love will only go so far.

"No," I whimpered, and let go of the rope to continue the crossing. Even if I jumped, my body would heal anyway.

Stars glittered above the skylight, mirrored in the spring's surface. I descended the sweeping stone steps, looking around to make sure I was alone. I sniffed the air for good measure, then undressed. I felt disgusting—inside and out.

I scrubbed my skin to the point that it split and mended back together. It would never be enough.

✳

The coolness of my damp t-shirt clinging to my back was somewhat of a relief as I returned to the sleeping quarters. A soft melody trailed from the tunnels, echoing through the fields. They'd completed the harvest for the day, but many Vampyres, humans, and Lightstalkers alike stayed to listen anyways.

The melodic chords ushered in humming, a voice so rich that I didn't feel worthy to step into the tunnel. I stood in the field with the rest of the Avant Guardians.

The humming turned into soft singing. It didn't take long to realize it was the same song from the time Draven and I visited The Hole. My feet were moving before my mind could process it.

I leaned against the archway of our cave, observing Draven as he slouched over the guitar, the strings dancing beneath his fingers. For the first time in a while, he was relaxed, drinking up the moment to cope with the years of having nothing to wash down his worries.

I stayed there until he finished, closing my eyes and pretending I was human again. My stomach growled, and the guitar went silent.

"Briar?" Draven lifted his head and blinked. I shuffled to my nook to set my stuff down.

"Sorry, I just got back from the spring. I, um... I'm gonna go find some blood." I took a long stride to step away, but he caught my arm. His lips parted as if he had something to say, but nothing came out.

"Vyrn wants us to train every day starting tomorrow morning," he said.

"Is that what you really wanted to say?" I raised an eyebrow. Draven shook his head and stood, now towering me. I craned my neck, only to look down again. His scarlet eyes pierced keenly into my soul, and I feared what he'd find there.

"No, I wanted ya to repeat some things after me." He cradled my head, forcing me to look back up at him. I felt like my skin had turned clear, and he could see and hear my thoughts.

"I am strong," he said firmly.

"No." I frowned.

"Vampyres can't sleep. We got all night." One dimple appeared as his lips tugged in a lopsided grin. I rolled my eyes.

"I am strong," I deadpanned. *As if.*

"I am powerful," Draven said, leaning forward until our foreheads met.

"I... I'm powerful." My voice splintered.

"And... I am loved." He brushed his nose against mine.

The words caught in my throat. My lips trembled as I stifled a sob.

He's only being nice to you because he feels guilty. Astoria might be forgiving, but she'll never forget.

"Say it, Briar," he said in a quiet demand.

"I'm..." Tears welled in my eyes until his face was unrecognizable. "I am loved."

Draven closed the remaining space between us with a tender kiss.

"Ya see that mirror?" He pointed across the room to an oval mirror mounted next to where Astoria slept. I wiped the back of my hand across my damp cheek and nodded.

"I want ya to promise me somethin'," Draven said, and I waited expectantly. I had an inkling of what he'd suggest, but I didn't want to agree to it.

"Say those words to your reflection every day before training."

I let my head flop backwards with a groan.

"I know it's cringe, whatever. Just try it, alright? Promise?"

"Fine, I promise." I rolled my eyes. "Are you coming with me to get food?"

"I ain't gonna eat but I'll tag along," he said. I faltered for a moment. How long could he wait before his hunger took complete hold?

⁕

Draven and I reached the coastline thirty minutes before Vyrn was set arrive. Per my promise, I chanted the three affirmations in the mirror before we left. I only felt lighter for two seconds before the bitter taste in my mouth returned.

We sat on a giant square towel in the sand, watching the sunrise. I poked at the sand lumps under the towel, creating divots. My mind had been running a mile a minute since I'd stood in front of the mirror, and I was already exhausted.

When we went to a cafe to get blood, he'd watched my every move while I drank. It wasn't a gaze of endearment, but that of a predator waiting to pounce on his prey. The image still haunted me.

"I want you to promise me something too," I began.

"Sure." He scooped up sand, creating a mound that he then stabbed his fingers through.

"Tell Vyrn about your problem today."

The air was so still that for a moment I thought the ocean would turn stagnant. Draven's Adam's apple rolled, his nostrils flaring. He nodded stiffly.

At that moment, Vyrn's truck rumbled through the trees and parked at the edge of the sand dunes. He hobbled toward us with his thin hair tousled and the buttons on his shirt lopsided. Liquor permanently clung to his breath, and the saline breeze brought it right to our faces.

"I did some studying last night," he said by way of greeting, pushing his glasses up his nose. He pressed his palms together in front of his nose with a deep breath, then pointed all ten fingers toward us. "I know why Uriah, Oren, and Caspian's powers manifested so fast."

Could we trust his findings were accurate if he was always drunk or hungover?

"Lightstalkers' DNA is entirely different from Vampyres *and* humans. You know, the two-strand spiral? Well, they have three and—"

"Hold on, are ya tryin' to say Uriah is a Lightstalker too?" Draven laughed dubiously.

Vyrn threw his hands up. "I need some of his DNA to confirm but I have good authority to say he could be."

"Then... why would he want to cause so much destruction? Why not just—" I tilted my head, cutting myself off as my mind buffered.

"Because if he conquers Mundus Novus, he'll never have to worry about his secret getting out and them executing him for it. He'd rather die for his crimes, not for his species."

Draven scoffed drily, shaking his head.

"Now, I ain't saying for sure. I'd say... hmm... sixty percent chance I'm right." Vyrn ran a hand through his greasy hair and swatted an invisible gnat. "Ada's comin' later to teach y'all firearms. Today, we're focusing on combat."

Draven snorted.

"I want y'all to spar so I can get an idea of how bad you are," Vyrn said with a pointed glance in my direction. I grimaced at him, and repositioned myself to stand at the center of the towel. Draven stepped in front of me with a sigh.

I set one foot back and raised my fists in front of my face in an attempt to mimic the fighters from television. I swung, and Draven dodged, then nudged the back of my head. I staggered forward with a gasp. Heat crept to my cheeks, and I swung again with a left jab. Draven jerked sideways, grabbing my wrist and spinning me around, effectively locking me against his chest like a straightjacket.

"Let me go," I growled.

"Make me," he purred in my ear.

"Okay then," I smirked, and headbutted his nose. He cursed, grip loosening. I lurched forward. Blood dribbled from his nose before it stopped entirely. He chuckled, wiping it from his upper lip with the back of his hand. His eyes flashed bright orange, like the sun hanging above the periwinkle horizon. He lunged, my knees locked in place, and the wind rushed out of my lungs as I was slammed on my back. Draven growled, baring his fangs. His grip around my wrists tightened, claws digging into my skin until blood broke free. Draven's pupils dilated, making his eyes appear black. His nose crinkled with a snarl, and he angled his head toward my neck in a feral jerk.

"Draven! Get off!" I screamed, fear corroding my core. "*Control it!*"

"Whoa, whoa!" Vyrn shouted, snatching Draven by the back of his shirt collar. "Snap out of—it ain't that serious, boy!"

Spit flung from Draven's mouth and I wriggled against his palms. His fangs inched closer, and my heart inflated with panic because I didn't know what a second bite from a Vampyre could do to me. Vyrn pulled out a gun and shot into the air, but Draven didn't so much as flinch.

My arms glowed white-hot like a star, and he flinched his hands away. He pushed off me, face contorted in unfiltered terror.

"What the hell was that?" Vyrn demanded. Draven scrambled to his feet, on the brink of hyperventilation. Vyrn shoved his chest, but he didn't budge. Draven moved off the towel, running his trembling hands over his face with a deep breath.

"Draven—" My voice cut off, and I reached for him before placing my hand back over my chest. I couldn't decide if I should give him more space or hug him tightly.

"I'm sorry, I-I ain't mean it," He stammered. "I ain't..."

I decided the latter, taking a step forward. Draven held his hand up, stepping back.

"No, don't. Please..." His voice cracked, and my heart fissured.

"What was that? This was supposed to be a *friendly spar.* Not some lover's quarrel! And did you really just try to bite her? What's *wrong* with you?" I'd never heard Vyrn yell, and for once his eyes were clear.

"I..." Draven scratched his cheek, stuffed his hands in his pockets and rocked on his heels. "I ain't drink no human blood in days."

"Tell him, Draven..." I mumbled. He sighed, dropping his head.

"Tell me *what*?" Vyrn growled.

"I crave Vampyre blood." Draven finally lifted his gaze to meet Vyrn's, and all light dissolved from his eyes. Heavy stillness lingered between us, and I clung to the sound of the waves to ease my nerves while I braced for Vyrn's reaction. He rubbed the back of his neck with a drawn-out exhale.

"How long has this been going on?" Vyrn's tone softened. Crisp, like that of a doctor.

"I dunno, a week, maybe two?" Draven shrugged. "I ain't realize how bad it was until... uh, we got Astoria back from White Fang. Right before we ran into y'all."

Vyrn scratched the stubble on his chin with a nod. I caught myself chewing on my thumbnail, eyes darting between them.

"Alright, um... okay. We're gonna table the fighting for now and do individual training until I figure out what this means." He reached in his pocket for the flask, and drained it to the last drop. It was the longest time I'd seen him go without it. "I'm gonna need a blood sample from you later."

"Yeah, sure." Draven chewed on his bottom lip. "I, um… I think I'm gonna sit this one out. I need a smoke."

He flashed across the beach, kicking up a cloud of sand in his wake, before either of us could convince him to stay.

43
CASPIAN

— Two Weeks Later —

Life always played sick jokes.

For the last two weeks, everything had been in black and white, as if the shadows had pulled me into a noir film I couldn't escape. Somehow I ended up in Neoterra moments before Camp Helix was painted red—in Uriah's old backyard, the King Estate in ruins. I roamed the neighborhood, where dogs barked at me and their human owners couldn't see me.

It didn't take long to realize I'd turned into the very thing everyone called me—a ghost.

I wondered if I was truly dead.

I forgot what color looked like. It was as if I'd *become* the shadows that pulled me from Camp Helix before the bullet could reach me, and I was stuck in their witness protection program. But being a shadow had its perks.

I didn't know how to get back to normal, but I did discover how to phase through walls, manipulate light, and walk among the Sun Dwellers undetected. With the nocturnal grocery stores shut down, I resorted to hunting. I had Cyrus to thank for prior experience. I wasn't proud of it; half the Sun Dwellers I drained had Astoria's face. I was always plagued with guilt afterwards.

I swept through downtown, where they'd replaced every billboard and screen with security footage from Camp Helix and news outlets covering the attack. Traffic lights were shut down, converted into checkpoints for Onyx Sentries to examine all vehicle passengers. Traffic was infuriating, but no one resisted except for the occasional Vampyre, who they caught and sent to another camp.

I walked under a streetlamp, and its light flickered when I sat on a bench. Across the square, Sun Dwellers attended a bluegrass concert in one of the few parks untouched by the Nightshades' terrorism. The grass was hardly visible among the blankets and towels laid out. Fireflies danced with their candles and glow sticks, seemingly in rhythm with the music. The soft melody slowed as their lead singer stepped up to the microphone.

"I wanna thank everyone who still came out tonight. It's scary out here, but thanks to Governor Donovan, Neoterra is sixty-five percent contained and we're a step closer to reclaiming the night!"

The Sun Dwellers erupted in applause, clapping and whistling and raising their beers.

"So, this next song is our anthem. Our freedom from the Red Plague virus and the monsters that spawned from it!"

I observed the flyer next to me on the streetlamp. A man flanked by two others with automatic rifles stood at the center, with a caption in all caps: RECLAIM THE WORLD. TAKE HUMANITY BACK. JOIN US.

I stood, ripping the flyer off the pole, and continued my trek up the sidewalk, away from the humans who proudly condemned my kind. The thought of being a Lightstalker almost sickened me.

Something glinted in the corner of my eye. Behind a display window, resting on a black velvet mannequin, was a white-gold necklace with an elegant teardrop moonstone, its ridges carved like a cockleshell. Thoughts of Astoria's hand reaching for her neck danced through my mind. Her spine would stiffen at the emptiness of her collarbone, shoulders subtly hiking to her jawline.

I stared at the necklace. I wished I could see its colors, but I still found myself captivated by the charcoal and silver swirls, like a storm cloud was trapped inside. Sure, it wasn't jewelry passed down from her late father, but...

I surveyed it a moment longer, imaging how it'd look on her. I reached my hand through the window and took the necklace. It wasn't an opal, but I hoped she'd like it.

I stuffed it in my pocket and continued moving forward.

I passed a group of four high schoolers standing outside a sandwich shop.

"The candidates this year should, like, withdraw from the race 'cause everyone's gonna vote for Governor Donovan." Vampyres and politics were all anyone discussed these days.

"Yeah, she's literally a hero."

I froze in place, clenching my fists in my slacks' pockets.

"I'm waiting for her to give everyone the green light to kill them all."

"Who cares? The Skinwalkers already do that for us and she's not going after them."

"Yeah, well, maybe I want to pitch in."

"Then just join the Skinwalkers."

"Nah, becoming an Onyx Sentry is way cooler."

I leaned in his ear and whispered, "You need to know how to do a push-up first."

The boy flinched, looking around. "Who said that?"

I waved my hand over the shop's sign. The neon light hummed louder, burning brighter until it burst. The students shrieked and ducked from the thin glass shards, and sprinted carelessly across the street. I loosed a low, ominous laugh, and continued my journey to Uriah's house. Hopefully, he still had the key to Mr. Barnaby's armory in his safe.

I needed a way back to Avant Garde. Ideally, I'd bring the key and we could take control of Uriah's access to the weapons. At the very least, I needed to tell them how much worse Neoterra had gotten... and show Astoria I was still alive.

God. I hope she hasn't read my letter.

✳

Uriah's new mansion wasn't quite as big as his previous one, but it wasn't far from it. He lived down the street from his original address, but I'd never had the privilege of seeing the interior of his new home. I was a traitor by then.

As expected, the driveway was empty. Everyone probably was sharing White Fang's headquarters in Helios for the time being, lying low after the terrorist attack on one of the corporate buildings.

Unfortunately for me, Uriah was smart enough to remember to empty his safe and take its contents with him.

I darted to the garage, closing my eyes and allowing my body to dissolve into a black cloud, penetrating the wooden fibers of the door until I was on the other side.

The cars were gone too. I left the garage the same way I entered, then moved on to the house itself. I went through the side wall adjacent to the dining room.

Whatever boxes Uriah might've had when he first moved in were gone. I flashed through the first floor, and was met with only a pool room, dining room, a couple bedrooms, and a door to a basement. I bolted up the stairs, surmising his study would be on the second floor as it was in his previous home.

And there it was.

The same ivory lion statues flanking the sides of the door. The statues that Draven and I always dreaded approaching to give report of our missions, because we knew that what resided on the other side was nothing but pain.

Even if he was here, he can't see you, I reminded myself.

I stepped forward, reaching for the door knob. I could've gone through the wall, but I was stalling. I still expected to see Uriah at his desk, smoking a cigar with a glass of wine, admiring the Neoterran map behind him.

Dust fell as I cracked the door open.

Uriah's study was as still as the rest of the house, and I relaxed my shoulders. I rounded his desk and crouched to peer beneath it. The same safe was there, but Uriah changed the combination every day.

I vaporized my hand, seeping through the metal door and intricate parts within the safe until I felt the shelf inside. Mr. Barnaby's phone wasn't there, but sharp cardstock poked my index finger. I pulled it from the safe and allowed my hand to solidify.

I frowned at a red folder and flipped it open. Names, social security numbers, addresses, species, and their respective blood types were listed alphabetically in the chart. The Neoterra Police Department's seal was watermarked on each page. The rows were endless, Neoterra's database of the entire population.

A lower-level cop could never have access to this information. *We* couldn't have it even with the amount of money Uriah paid the department.

Unless...

Uriah had connections with the chief of police, which was worth more than anything money could buy. Chief Duncan had a reputation for being as by the book as they came, so there had to be something Uriah possessed that the chief desperately wanted. Or needed.

With this information, Uriah didn't need to hunt for anyone with Briar's blood type. They could march right to their doorstep...

And make as many serums as they want.

My throat went dry. I took pictures of the pages, shoved the file back in the safe, and phased through the outside wall to get out of that cursed house as fast as possible.

⁕

The ferry was permanently inoperable. Planes were grounded. No one could get in or out of Neoterra, and the smaller surrounding cities like Eclipsis shut down their bus routes. It didn't help that Helios was miles across the ocean.

Swimming was out of the question.

The only option I had left was to find a boat and sail to Helios with the hope of landing on the side of the city unmonitored by Onyx Sentries. I wasn't sure what state the island could be after what Draven and Briar pulled at Camp Helix. I couldn't imagine it getting any better.

The problem with finding a boat was that all of the ports were guarded. The influx of Onyx Sentries in Neoterra had been ten times worse than Helios, partially because it was twice its size. I couldn't walk a mile without running into one, and I feared the day my shadowed cloak lifted before I was ready for it. That is... if it could lift at all.

I sat on the edge of the fountain in the center of the town square, brainstorming. My mind kept rubber-banding back to Chief Duncan.

Until it finally hit me.

✳

The Neoterra Police Department building was desolate. It was hard to determine if it was because of Uriah's hit list or because they were stretched thin to help the Sentries enforce the new curfews. I doubted their chief was in the building at this point, especially during Gloaming, despite Governor Duncan's curfew extension.

Sun Dwellers may have been exploring the night more after the flood of Vampyres forced into camps, but a man like him wouldn't fall for the false security. Most of the Vampyres captured had no part in the Nightshades or White Fang. They were civilians just like the humans, torn from their homes because of their species. Clan members were usually too slippery to get caught.

I swept through the precinct until I found his name on a plaque next to the door. I smiled at the camera perched in the corner, angled directly above the door like it could see me. After phasing through the wall, I was greeted by an office filled with family portraits, medallions, diplomas, and a military uniform immortalized in a shadow box. I ignored it all and went straight for the filing cabinet. Surely, his office had paperwork with his address on it somewhere.

I crouched in front of the bottom drawer and raked through the surnames starting with "S" out of simple curiosity. My fingers brushed over Sterling's file. I sat on my heels as I flipped through it.

Sterling appeared ten years younger in his photo. Despite the glowing reports listed in his jacket, a red stamp in bold letters covered his photo: "Compromised."

I snickered. I wondered if that status came before or after he Turned.

I put Sterling's file away and combed through the files under "D" in the top drawer, then went through each individual file.

And just like that... I found Chief Duncan's file sandwiched in an unassuming rookie's. His position, rank, species, address, and banking information were all laid out on the first page. I took note of it, and snapped a picture for insurance. I winced at the camera flash. Green, blue, and red static infiltrated in my vision. For a moment, the office appeared dull beige and maroon before it all faded back to greyscale.

I rubbed my eyes and waited for the color to return. It didn't.

I shook my head and put everything back the way I found it

before I left, heading straight for Chief Duncan's home in a Diurnal Zone across Neoterra.

※

For a man in a respected position playing devil's advocate for both the Nightshades and the governor, I expected more. His house was a quaint, unassuming Tudor with moss and vines growing across the front. The grass had already slipped into slumber for the encroaching winter. Oak leaves overflowed the gutters, and pine needles invaded the shingles.

I walked up the front porch and paused at the door. Banging erupted against someone else's across the street.

"By the order of Mundus Novus, we demand you to step out of the house right now!" Five Onyx Sentries crowded around the neighbor's front porch. The first two were clad in riot shields and helmets, the others armed with weapons standing behind them. A raid I'd seen one too many times.

They must've found another Vampyre living among the Sun Dwellers. One that was probably Turned, who either couldn't afford to move to a Nocturnal Zone or refused to leave their family.

I passed through Chief Duncan's door the second they burst the neighbor's off its hinges. I blocked out the screams erupting in the residence.

"Yes, they're raiding as we speak. They're probably getting sent to Camp Brutis."

I inclined my head toward the ceiling.

"No, I still haven't been able to get ahold of Shaw *or* Hart."

I crept up the stairs, homing in on the voice on the other side.

I would've assumed he was talking to the governor, but it was a breathy male's voice on the line.

I rounded the corner to a cracked door leading to Chief Duncan's bedroom. He paced back and forth in front of the window, occasionally peeking through the blinds to observe the raid across the street.

"Draven and Briar are at large in Helios *somewhere*. If Sterling and Lyra did run off, it's possible they made it to Helios. If you don't get a hold of either of them, it won't matter if Mundus Novus falls. You'll never see *her* again."

"You need to give me time, Uriah."

"You told me that if you forced Lyra and Sterling to work with you and Elise, then you'd be able to find out Draven and Briar's whereabouts. Now, I'm wasting my own men to track them down before we take Camp Cerberus. It's been two weeks, and you're out of time."

The line went dead, and Chief Duncan rammed his fist into the wall with an agonized roar.

"Quite a predicament you got yourself in, Andrew."

He flinched, fraught eyes sweeping over every corner of the room. I refused to give him the satisfaction of using his title.

"Who's there?" he demanded, and yanked his pistol off his nightstand. "Show yourself!"

I ran my fingertips through the dust on his dresser. He shot in my general direction, but all he managed to do was fray his wallpaper.

"You're playing a dangerous game. I hope you have enough

moves to keep going." I perused his room, taking note of the portraits he had with a young woman in a graduate gown.

"Who are you?" Chief Duncan growled through tight teeth, jerking his pistol in various directions.

"I'm the one standing between yourself and your grave." I stood a foot in front of him, examining the beads of sweat pearling over his brow. I jammed my shoe into his stomach, knocking him into the nightstand. Chief Duncan gasped for air, coughing and holding his hand over his abdomen with a wince.

"What is Elise planning? How does she have so much authority in the war?"

"Go to Hell," Chief Duncan rasped, scowling in the wrong blank space.

"I prefer the cold, but you can take my place there," I retorted coolly. "You know that file you gave to Uriah? I can easily show Governor Donovan what a two-faced snake you are. Uriah doesn't take too kindly to traitors either."

"What's in it for you?" Chief Duncan observed every direction, scooting to lean against the nightstand with a pained grunt.

"Get me a boat, and a direct route to Helios to a port that's unmanned by Onyx Sentries. I won't say a word to anyone."

"That's *it*?" He loosed a rough guffaw.

"I expect to be gone by midnight," I said plainly.

"Fine." Chief Duncan winced again. "Meet me in Nocturne at the marina at two in the morning. I'll have a boat for you."

"That's not midnight," I hissed.

"Take it or leave it, whoever you are. That's the window for the Sentries' shift changes."

For the first time in two weeks, I grinned. It was only a matter of time before I saw Astoria, and this time, I would never let her go.

44

ASTORIA

I learned about the five stages of grief in college, but what they didn't teach us was how long each stage was supposed to last.

Maybe I'd missed that day.

I hadn't read the letter Caspian left behind, because it felt like accepting his death. It didn't sit right with me that he would die in *any* situation, let alone one where Briar and Draven used their powers to break out.

I carried the note everywhere with me as if it were the necklace I'd lost—as if his heart still beat within the paper, and opening the folds would let his soul escape.

Two weeks passed, and Caspian still hadn't returned, and Sterling couldn't find our mother. She wasn't at the hospital or any surrounding prisons within a hundred-mile radius.

Briar spent hours on the beach training alone well after Vyrn's lessons for the day. She was distant with me and Sterling, and Draven was distant with everyone. He never wanted to tell me what was going on, much like how Sterling loved to keep me out of the loop.

They all seemed to think I'd fall to pieces.

I hid Caspian's letter under my pillow in our sleeping quarters, then pulled my hair into a high messy bun. I draped a towel over my forearm and gathered clothes to sleep in and some soap, then shuffled across the tunnels. When I reached the suspension bridge stretching over the gorge, my stomach wrenched back and forth until I reached the other side. It didn't matter how many times I crossed it. I never got used to the height or the abyss below.

I paused at the top of the stone steps and peered at the spring. Briar drifted on her back in the aquamarine water with her eyes closed and her arms floating at her sides. She was still, like a corpse. She embraced her pixie haircut, but she never dyed it again. The short, wispy strands swirled around her head like ink.

"Don't worry, I don't bite anymore," she droned without opening her eyes. I paused, sucking a breath. She more than likely heard me coming before I even crossed the bridge, but her Vampyre senses still startled me at times.

"I'm not afraid of you, Bri," I said, and shifted the towel and clothes to my other arm before descending the steps. "I wish you'd stop that."

"Stop what?" She finally opened her eyes, the water subtly rotating her body clockwise.

I scoffed lightly. "Acting like you're some sort of monster."

I remembered what I'd said to her before she left Avant Garde. I still blamed myself every day for her reckless act, and the only thing that helped me was knowing she'd returned in one piece.

Sometimes I worried that I made her feel like she needed to punish herself for what she did to Sterling. I'd since apologized for it, taken my words back, but the wounds were still there.

"Aren't we all?" Briar asked with a dry chuckle. She let her legs sink then swam to the edge of the spring, climbing up. She adjusted her swimsuit straps after the water's weight tried to pull her back in.

"Maybe, but... I recently learned the humans are capable of much worse than Vampyres."

"I used to think that too." Briar ruffled her hair with her towel, then wrapped it around her shoulders. Water dripped from her nose and she sniffled.

"How's Draven?" I set my stuff down once I reached the bottom.

"He's... um... he's okay." Briar forced a grin. "What did Cass write to you?"

Changing the subject. She was an expert at that.

"I haven't read it yet." I sat at the edge of the spring, allowing my legs to dangle in the water up to my calves.

"Why not?"

"Because I don't believe he's dead."

"He said to read it if he doesn't come back, not if he dies. What if he had a backup plan in there, or what if he wanted you to know how he felt?" Briar's voice echoed as she climbed the steps.

She had a point. Caspian was always ten steps ahead of everyone. If he thought for any reason he wouldn't come back, he could've had a plan in place to help him get back home.

Oh god. What have I done?

Once Briar was gone, I undressed and bathed quickly, racing against a clock that had long stopped working.

⁎

My feet slapped against the stone, leaving a trail of water as I sprinted back to the cave. I wiped my hands over the towel to make sure they were dry and threw everything in a pile at the foot of my bed before snatching the paper from under the pillow. All that rushing... just to sit on the edge of the makeshift bed and stare at his handwriting on the fold.

Please don't be a death letter.

My pulse pounded louder in my ears as I reversed every fold.

Please don't be dead.

His handwriting was slanted and precise. Surgical, as if he took every stroke into careful consideration as he wrote.

Astoria:

You asked me if I'd ever fallen in love before. I know it was an innocent question, but it terrified me. The last time I ever uttered that word, two brothers forced me to make a choice. You asked what that choice was... and it was her, or the Nightshades.

Everyone's initiation into the clan is different. Uriah seeks out our weaknesses and exploits them, to test if we are capable of overcoming them for the sake of the clan. Letting him into my mind was a fatal mistake, but it turned me into something unrecognizable. Something dangerous and apathetic. A walking corpse.

I never understood why Draven risked so much for your sister. From the moment he came into contact with her, he seemed more human. When I promised to help him save Briar, I thought you would be nothing but a pawn in my schemes. A mindless, helpless human who would sooner rather than later reach her limit.

But... I felt my heart beat again with you. The first time: when I took you to the beach in the Nocturne District, and you didn't balk at my touch when I brushed your tear away. The second time: when you found out what I was on the rooftop, but still gave me the chance to explain myself. The third time: when I visited you in the hospital after Delilah hurt you. Finally... when I thought I'd lost you to White Fang for good.

I have seen and caused a lot of death in my life. I spent my years building walls of stone, but in reality they were made of paper. The thought of losing you put those walls through a shredder. I didn't realize it until I spent time with you. I became so obsessed with finding a family to belong in that I didn't know I had my own right here with you, Draven, and Briar. A family who never forced me to kill for them, but a family worth dying for.

I think about you all the time... and if I were human, I'm certain I would dream of you too.

I told Briar to give you this letter if I didn't come back. I want you to know that I'm trying my hardest to get back to you. If I don't return within a year, I'm dead. After a year, tell Draven he was the best brother anyone could ask for. Live your life. Survive. You deserve the world and everything outside of it, and I wish I were there to give it to you. I'd risk it all with the Nightshades a hundred times over if it meant meeting you every time.

Thank you, Astoria, for bringing me back to life.

-Cass

I clutched the paper to my chest and released a quiet whimper.

A tear dropped over his name, spreading the ink in a distorted blob. I lay down and curled into a fetal position, facing the wall. I wasn't sure whether I felt relief or despair. I wanted to convince myself that Briar had forged it to make me feel better, but her handwriting was as chaotic as her personality. Not to mention I'd never told her or Draven about our moments on the rooftop or at the beach.

Helios was only so big. If he really was alive, why was it taking so long for him to find Avant Garde again? Camp Helix was the only one on the island, and it was destroyed. Mundus Novus never came back to rebuild—they recaptured the Vampyres that escaped and transferred them to the mainland.

The more I thought about it, the more I feared he truly wouldn't come back.

I pulled the paper back, rereading the line where he warned that if he didn't return in a year, he was dead. It hasn't been a full month yet.

"Ria? Are you okay?" Briar's raspy voice sounded through the chamber. I froze in place, refusing to turn around and reveal the shiny, ruddy face I most definitely had.

"Yeah," I muttered with a sniffle. A rush of wind passed over me before Briar's cold hand rubbed my arm with comfort.

"Did... did you read it?" she asked hesitantly.

"Yep..." I trailed, my throat constricting.

"Is..." Briar took a deep breath. "Is he dead?"

"N-no. He... he said to give him a year to come back before we assume he's dead." I rolled onto my back, throat burning with another wave of tears threatening to surface. Briar squeezed into the narrow space at the edge of my bed.

"Then we trust him," she said with a thin smile. I nodded and rubbed my nose with a sniffle.

"How's Draven?"

Briar's smile fled at the mention of his name. The muscles around her eyes went slack, and the light in them dulled.

"He worries about Caspian every day. He blames himself for it." Briar leaned her head back against the wall with a somber sigh. "He thinks Caspian chose to stay away because he told him about his side effects."

"That doesn't sound like him," I said with a frown.

Briar shrugged. "They know each other better than either of us combined."

I flinched at the shuffling gait echoing through the tunnel. Briar sniffed the air, and her eyes hardened to an icy glare. I propped myself up on my elbows and peered over my shoulder at the mouth of the cave, where Sterling stood with Ada and Lyra.

Like two territorial predators, Briar and Sterling stared each other down, daring the other to make the first move.

Ada's eyes bounced between both of them, then she cleared her throat.

"Is everything alright?" Briar broke contact first, her eyes shifting to Ada warily.

"Oh, yes! I come bearing good news, actually. One of my recon women found your mother."

I sat up straight with a gasp. Briar's body went rigid, and she gripped my ankle tightly before I could stand.

"We're going into town to meet up with her," Sterling said coolly, and raised his chin. "Either of you are welcome to tag along."

"Absolutely not," Briar growled.

"Why?" I jerked my ankle out of her grip. She scoffed.

"Are—I'm sorry, am I the only one who remembers what happened before we got here? You couldn't even last a supply run without getting abducted!"

I winced at the memories. Being tied in the van, getting punched in the face. My wrist broken, forced into a chair to be a test subject. And worst of all—watching Cyrus try to drown Caspian in shallow water.

I pulled my knees to my chest.

"Nothing's gonna happen to her with Lyra and me there," Sterling insisted.

"Yeah, well *Caspian* was with her last time and she still got taken, so forgive me if I don't trust you with her safety," Briar hissed.

Sterling erupted into laughter. "*You* don't trust *me* with Astoria's safety?"

"Shut up!" I hollered. "Stop talking about me like I'm not here!"

Ada blinked with a nervous laugh. "Alright, guys, let's calm down..."

I jumped from the bed and jabbed a finger at Sterling.

"You need to get over it! Briar isn't a fledgling anymore! She has control now!" I pivoted back to Briar, my hair snapping like a whip. "And you need to stop treating me like a kid!"

"Yeah?" Briar tilted her head with a sardonic smirk. "Then you need to get stronger so you can take care of yourself." She stormed out of the cave, knocking her shoulder against Sterling's as she passed. He growled, but all it took was Lyra touching his arm before he quieted.

"We're leaving in ten minutes. Come or stay, I don't care," Sterling grumbled, then stalked away. I pursed my lips, stifling more tears. I still hadn't recovered from reading Caspian's letter.

"I'm sorry, dear," Ada said, and stepped up to my bedside. She crouched in front of me, taking one of my hands in both of hers with motherly warmth. "Don't take it personally. They still have a lot of wounds to mend too."

"I know," I croaked, glancing at the mouth of the cave.

"And if you want to see your mother... that's a risk only *you* have to be willing to take." She spoke in a whisper, as if she sensed my siblings eavesdropping.

I took a deep breath.

Vyrn found comfort in alcohol. My mom found hers in drugs. Draven smoked his cigarettes. Briar was an adrenaline junkie.

For me... it was fear. It made me avoid risks and kept me safe. For the most part.

As much as I wanted to see my mother, I couldn't bear the thought of setting foot outside of Avant Garde.

45

STERLING

My breath fogged up the side mirror of Ada's truck as I leaned closer, pulling down my lower eyelid with one hand and inching a brown contact lens toward my iris with the other. I couldn't stop my hand from shaking, and I couldn't decide if it was rage after dealing with Briar or anxiety to see Vivian.

"What's the point of wearing contacts anymore? The Onyx Sentries test for temperatures now," Lyra droned from the hood. She leaned against it, occasionally checking her watch and looking toward the tunnel where Astoria might appear from—should she decide to accompany us.

"I don't want her to know what I've become."

"I thought you were estranged?" She picked underneath her nails.

"We are, I just—Lyra, let me focus," I griped, and cried out when I poked myself in the eye. I cursed under my breath and threw the contact to the ground, stomping on it until it blended in with the dirt.

"Why don't you be yourself? It's your mom."

"Trust me, you don't want that with her," I said. I still hadn't told Lyra that my mother was a criminal, or the things she'd done to me and my sisters growing up, or that she'd caused my father's murder. As far as Lyra knew, she was a staff member at Black Bay Prison who hadn't seen her son in years.

Lyra sighed, her shoulders sinking. "I don't think Astoria's coming. Let's just go." She mounted the passenger seat, and I stood next to the driver's door for a few more seconds. It finally hit me what Briar had said.

You couldn't even last a supply run without getting abducted!

When did Astoria get taken? If Caspian was as lethal as they made him seem, how did my little sister get taken in the first place?

Maybe they were outnumbered... but with Lyra by my side, we could protect her better out there.

I shook my head, dismissing the thought. Whatever happened to Astoria couldn't have been good considering Briar's overprotection.

I climbed in the driver's seat and started up the truck. I paused in the middle of shutting the door as Astoria darted toward us with a gun at her hip.

Ask for forgiveness later.

I slammed on the gas, the tires squealing as we sped out of the cave before Astoria could reach us. I looked at her in the rearview mirror. She slowed to a stop, arms falling slack to her sides as she watched me dejectedly.

I just wanted confirmation that Vivian was alive and well. I hadn't been planning on it, but I'd have to convince her to come back with us so Astoria could see her. Maybe that would make up for my abrupt exit.

*

We were halfway through the forest, white noise crumbling through the radio to occupy the silence.

"Why'd you leave her like that?" Lyra asked.

I fumed at the bite in her tone.

"Briar's right. She's a liability," I replied with restrained irritation.

"You offered for her to come with us." She frowned, glancing at me with knitted brows.

"I know, and I changed my mind. I'm sure my mom would love to see her." I spoke flatly, but was unable to fully suppress the sarcasm. The ball of her jaw feathered, but she opted to look out the window instead.

Shortly after Briar and Draven destroyed Camp Helix, the Onyx Sentries orchestrated a mandatory evacuation for all humans in Helios. It was the last time the ferry ran before they shut it down. Until they knew where my sister and her boyfriend went, they considered them armed and dangerous, and the island entirely inhabitable. In a perfect world, Avant Garde would've reclaimed it, moved to the surface, and minded their business.

But Mundus Novus would never let this place go.

Any time Lyra and I went out on a supply run with Ada's people, or by ourselves, I kept my eyes to the skies for drones. Silvery, overcast days like this made me the most unsettled, because Mundus Novus had the technology to see us through the clouds.

We drew closer to a desolate park. The clouds hung low, and the wind rustled dried leaves across the street.

I left the truck running as we both dropped out, our doors slamming shut in unison. We moved like soldiers, our boots in sync as we decimated the dead leaves in the mulch. The swings swayed subtly, as if ghosts of children still rode them.

I staggered over the curb, breaking the rhythm in our harmonious stride.

Vivian sat on a wooden bench with her legs crossed and her hands resting on her knee. She wore a black-and-white polka dot dress with a red scarf, mauve lipstick, and white gloves, her honeyed hair styled in a retro pinup.

I couldn't remember the last time I saw my mother cleaned up. As a kid, she was always unkempt, and for most of my adulthood... her attire was exclusive to the Black Bay Prison's fashion.

"Sterling!" Vivian beamed, rising from the bench with her arms outstretched. I stared at her, and she closed the gap with a hug before I could process if she was real.

"Mom," I mumbled, pulling away shortly. Her eyes bounced between me and Lyra, and then the color left her cheeks.

"You—oh, no... not you too," she gasped, taking a small step back. I inhaled deeply, bracing for the fallout as she noticed our irises.

"Did Briar do this?"

"No," I blurted. I'd buried my story so many times that it became second nature to deny anything implicating Briar, no matter how much I hated it. Vivian always blamed everything on her anyway. I didn't want to add to it.

"Who is this, then? Did she?" Vivian tilted her head, sizing up Lyra, who scoffed in response.

"This is Lyra, we worked together on the force. She's helped me through a lot," I explained, before Vivian formed a complete opinion of her.

"Well, she's a much better choice than that creep Briar's with." Vivian smoothed the back of her dress before easing onto the bench again.

"You look good," I said, desperate to change the subject. "What happened?"

"The Onyx Sentries tracked all the inmates that escaped and transferred them to Cedarwood. Since they had limited space, they decided to let all nonviolent charges get dropped. So." She tilted her head with a curtsy and added, "Vivian Shaw is a free woman!"

"What were you in for?" Lyra folded her arms, sliding a sharp glare in my direction. She wasn't the type to judge, especially for those with nonviolent backgrounds... but I knew that look. One of betrayal, since I hadn't opened up to her about my family.

"Possession," she said, rolling her eyes with a dismissive wave. "My dear son loved me so much that he personally handled my arrest." A saccharine, venomous smile stretched across her lips.

Lyra whipped her head at me. "Are you serious?"

"Yeah, after she got my dad killed breaking curfew. I'd say we're even, don't you think?" I fought the urge to clench my fists, tell Vivian to go to Hell, and drive off.

"Hardly," she mumbled, and tugged at the bottom of her gloves. "So, where are you staying? I have nowhere to go, honestly. I found this lovely outfit in one of the stores that closed."

"Avant Garde." I spoke flatly. "I was actually going to ask if you wanted to come back with us. Astoria wanted to see you, but I thought it would be better for you to come to her for once."

Vivian's eyes lit up and she jumped from the bench.

"I would love to!" She grinned, then frowned. "Where is Avant Garde? That sounds far, I never heard of a place like that."

"It's still in Helios. You'll see," I said, and returned to the truck. Lyra was already three paces ahead, climbing into the back. I guessed she considered it respectful, but I would've preferred her to remain in the front. Vivian would've been less inclined to critique my driving from the back seat.

✳

I didn't think Vampyres were capable of headaches. At most, I thought it was something fledglings suffered from while we transitioned away from humanity. That theory got debunked during the drive back to Avant Garde. By the time I parked the truck at the edge of the market, my temples were throbbing. Vivian wouldn't shut up on the way back, and her talking kicked into overdrive at the sight of the cavern.

"This is insane! How is it that I never knew about this place?" Vivian asked as she picked up various fruits at a stand. "It's so big!"

"They had to hide from Mundus Novus. That's how they wanted it," Lyra explained. I nodded in agreement, surveying the array of booths. The Avant Guardians even had their own currency of copper coins.

In the time I'd spent in Avant Garde—albeit short—I couldn't wrap my head around Lightstalkers. A life without curfews, the humans and Vampyres living in harmony without fear of being drained. They had a mutual blood donation agreement, but most of the Vampyres here willingly lived off of animal blood.

Vegan Vampyres. I snorted aloud at the thought. Had I known that was an option, I wouldn't have broken my strike at the hospital. Matter of fact, why didn't the hospital try to train fledglings on animal blood to begin with? Then human donations wouldn't have to be mandated.

Lyra frowned. "What's so funny?"

"I had a random, funny thought." I tossed an apple in my hand, measuring its weight before placing it back in the barrel.

"Where's Astoria?" Vivian asked.

"I'll go find her." Lyra glowered at me before flashing out of sight to retrieve my sister. Then bells jingled, followed by a door slamming shut with a loud *thwack*. Briar stood frozen in front of a cafe door, holding two bags. I assumed one was for Draven or Astoria.

"You brought her back here?" Briar's voice rose with every word until it was loud enough to briefly pause the din in the marketplace.

"For Astoria, yeah." I frowned. "She had nowhere else to go."

"It's great to see you too, Briar," Vivian sneered, placing a gold necklace back on a hook at a jeweler's booth. "My ankle is a lot better, thanks for asking."

Briar's eyes scanned Vivian from head to toe, much like how our mother had observed Lyra. There was no denying they were related.

"Make your visit quick," Briar hissed, and stormed toward the residential area, up the hill to where Vyrn lived. I sighed, pinching the bridge of my nose as lightning struck behind my eyes.

"She hasn't changed a bit," Vivian mused.

"Oh, she's changed plenty," I countered in a low growl. "I'll find Ada, she'll make arrangements for you to stay here."

Briar would just have to deal with Vivian staying. It wasn't my call to kick anyone out, and my feelings for our mother were nothing short of indifference or maybe mild disdain. Astoria still cleaved to the idealistic concept of a real mother, and Briar still clung to hate. Granted, she'd gotten the worst treatment out of all three of us, but she needed to get over it. Vivian couldn't physically harm us anymore.

"It's nice to have the whole family together again, don't you think?" She grinned as if Briar hadn't expressed scorn toward her seconds ago.

"Just wait here," I drawled, and began my search for one of Ada's guards on patrol.

I hoped I didn't regret bringing Vivian back, judging by Briar's reaction. The tension between them was at an all-time high. They must've spent some unwanted time together at one point.

46
DRAVEN

The cold concrete bit into my palms, microscopic sediment digging into my skin as I pumped out pushups.

I lost count at two hundred and fifty.

Condensation dripped down the stone walls in the cell, a pocket buried deep in one of the tunnels near the residential area. After what had happened in training, I'd volunteered to be put here until Vyrn figured something out about my side effects. Of course, we all knew the cell wasn't enough to hold me back if I truly wanted to get to anybody. That said, one of Ada's engineers rigged a sprinkler as a fire extinguisher to douse me if I tried to break out. Only humans were allowed to deliver messages, water, and animal blood.

Since Astoria's iron supplement suggestion, Vyrn had been running tests with a few Lightstalkers and Vampyres. He started me on a regimen of iron pills, but stayed away from blood transfusions to avoid using too many variables.

Two weeks passed, and I didn't feel much different. I didn't know what progress he was making for the others, though. Perhaps they still had hope since they weren't tainted by White Fang's experiments.

I didn't stop my pushups until the usual black mud-stained boots approached the bars. I sat on my knees, greeted by a beaming Briar.

Of course, rules were always suggestions for her. I gave up trying to push her away. She made it clear that no matter what I became, she wasn't one to balk.

I eased to my feet and ambled to the bars with a half-grin. "Ya know the guards only have ten minutes left on their break, right?"

"I know their schedules like the back of my hand by now," she said, and stood on her toes to peck my lips through the bars. I traced the sound of crinkling in her hands and arched a curious brow. Briar dangled a white bag in front of me.

"I don't suppose you find donuts bitter, right?"

"Nah, that's one thing I'm allowed to keep," I said with a small chuckle, and maneuvered the bag through the bars. Briar sat on the floor, crisscrossing her legs. She pulled out a donut, and I did the same. I watched her fangs sink into the pastry, my gaze trailing to her neck, taking note of the subtle pulse of her carotid artery—

"My mom's here," she said.

My forehead crinkled as I stuffed half of the donut in my mouth.

"Vivian?" I mumbled around the thick bread. Briar gave me an incredulous look like I'd asked the world's most idiotic question. I finally swallowed and reached for the half-empty bottle of water.

"Obviously, yeah, but *how* is she here?"

"One of Ada's scouts found her, and then Sterling went out to meet with her and brought her back. He claims it's for Astoria, but he doesn't understand that Vivian's the reason for half of the mess we were in." Briar balled a napkin in her hands after she finished, whereas I wiped my hands on my pants like a heathen.

"Did ya ever take the time to explain it to him, or are y'all just gonna keep being mad at each other?"

"Neither of us is the forgiving type."

"Well, maybe you should start. If not for him, do it for yourself." I swiped the sweat from my forehead and leaned back on my palms.

"I ruined his life," she muttered, words subtly wavering.

"It ain't ruined. Not really. You could've killed him," I said.

Briar visibly recoiled. I winced.

"I ain't mean—"

"No, it's okay. You're right, he could've ended up like Moses. I think about that every day," she said, hugging herself. "I should go before the guards get back."

"Sunny..." I slipped my hand through the bars, but she was already out of reach. Her shadow stretched and bobbed against the sconce-illuminated walls in the tunnel.

I hit my head against the iron bars with a frustrated groan, then resumed my pushups. I started over at one.

Without the skylights in the main cavern, it was impossible to tell time. An hour or two could've passed, or an entire day. High-pitched ringing plagued my ears, possibly from the many servings of animal blood that offered zero sustenance. I had moved on to crunches and various calisthenic exercises to keep my mind off of Briar and every other Vampyre in Avant Garde.

Ada's guards had dropped off two buckets of plain water, one with soap, and fresh clothes. I was in the middle of redressing when I recognized a foreign yet vaguely familiar scent. I straightened out my t-shirt and turned to see Vivian, her lips spread in a dark, reptilian smile.

"I guess I can see the appeal," she purred, tapping her chin in observation. "You don't stick out like a sore thumb behind bars like this."

"Yeah? Well, you certainly do being out of that jumpsuit," I retorted. "What do ya want?"

"Oh, nothing. I was just exploring Avant Garde." She examined her nails with a sheepish shrug.

"Really? Have ya seen the exit yet?" I sneered.

Vivian flashed a deadly look underneath her brows.

"I've seen enough," she said lowly. "I heard through the grapevine that you're a danger to Vampyres now."

I released a sardonic chuckle, rolling my eyes. I slicked my damp hair back, the ends curling around my ears.

"If it isn't true, what did you do to wind up in here?"

"Ain't none of your concern."

"It is if you're gonna be dating my daughter."

"Ain't much datin' these days." I folded my arms. "You don't have to pretend to care now. There ain't no audience to impress."

Vivian laughed, her voice a cacophony of allure and venom. "Maybe not here in Avant Garde."

I cocked my head with a suspicious squint. "What are ya after?"

"Self-preservation. Something you should've been after a long time ago," she said, and strutted away with her heels sharply clacking against the uneven ground.

"Sorry! Excuse me, miss," Vyrn's voice drawled down the tunnel, shortly followed by a giggle.

"Oh, you're fine, sir," Vivian replied before her footsteps faded into the cavern. Vyrn appeared at the mouth of the tunnel, still peering over his shoulder.

"Who was that?" He asked with a broad grin. "I've never seen her around here before."

"Briar's ma." I kicked the pile of dirty clothes into a corner. "Ya find anything that can help me?"

His veiny hand angled a red vial under the lantern. The liquid was transparent, so it wasn't blood.

"Something to buy us some time, I think." He passed the vial through the bars, but I didn't take it.

I was sick of being a guinea pig. I wanted one guaranteed answer for once. Was that too much to ask?

"What's wrong, son?" Vyrn asked, curling his fist over the vial.

"What are we doin', Vyrn?" I lowered my gaze to the floor. "What am *I* doin'?"

"That depends..." Vyrn furrowed his brows. "What do you want?"

The ground suddenly shook with a loud boom, dust and pebbles spilling from the ceiling. Vyrn staggered, catching himself on the bars with wide eyes. My shoulders tensed, and I sniffed the air.

Gunpowder.

"Vyrn, let me out!" I demanded.

He straightened, sifting through his cargo pocket for a key ring. His hand trembled as he fumbled with the lock. I burst through when he cracked the door and flashed toward the sound, leaving Vyrn in the dust.

I stopped at the edge of the tunnel and peeked around the corner. My eyes widened in horror at the sheer number of Onyx Sentries rappelling through the skylights, shooting from above at the Avant Guardians.

47
CASPIAN

After the Nightshades' first terrorist attack on downtown, isolated events such as hate-fueled mass shootings and vicious brawls occurred daily. So frequently that the media labeled it the "Second Crimson War." I'd always imagined conflict at this scale as two sides in bulletproof vests and helmets, going head to head in tanks and fighter jets on a designated battlefield.

I guess war put on many faces, and Elise had the power to decide which one it would don.

I had six hours to burn—a pretty short time to gather as much intel about Mundus Novus, the Nightshades, and White Fang as possible before I sailed to Helios. I only hoped Briar and Draven had trained enough to put an end to the pandemonium before there was nothing left to fight for.

A rarely used amphitheater was located at the edge of downtown. Wide concrete slabs arranged in half circles were embedded in a hill sloping downward in a valley. Narrow strips of vivid green turf divided each row.

Today, the amphitheater was filled to the brim. Every Sun Dweller in Neoterra in one place. Without the Vampyre population, the city was dwarfed to something similar to Eclipsis. Governor Donovan stood at the center in her usual skirt suit, opting for emerald green rather than red or navy.

A *lifelike* version of Governor Donovan. I wouldn't have even realized if it weren't for the occasional flicker or bird flying through her hologram.

Smart, but not smart enough.

I roamed the top edge of the theater, surveying the surrounding buildings. Holograms were fussy tech. They began to present issues once the user went beyond their range, and most models—even the most expensive and advanced ones—only allowed for up to three hundred yards.

"I believe in complete and utter transparency. It is with much regret that I must say the Vampyres can't be saved," Governor Donovan announced, and lowered her head with a quiet breath for a moment of vulnerable silence. I rolled my eyes at her theatrics and continued to saunter around the perimeter. For optimal connection, windows and blinds needed to be open.

"The Reconditioning process isn't working. Camps Brutis, Celeste, Cerberus, and Nox are failures. So we must cleanse and start anew with the incinerators at Camp Cerberus. It is a bittersweet moment, but after all is said and done, the country will be reclaimed entirely, given a name, and your true leader from Mundus Novus will reveal themselves.”

Clapping crackled across the seats.

I launched across the bowl, landing on the closest roof.

It can't be this building, the hologram wouldn't be flickering.

I jumped to the next one, and scaled across the opened windows. Nothing but a bunch of shoddy apartments ranging from immaculate to disgusting. A waste of time.

I leapt to the next one.

Then the next.

As suspected, I went to the furthest building—City Hall.

A little disappointing that the governor would choose such an obvious location if she was going to hide behind a hologram.

“Two Vampyres of inexplicable strength still walk among us. We don't know how many more are like them, but our honorable Onyx Sentries are doing an intensive investigation in Helios to find their hidden community as we speak,” she declared.

She cleared her throat as she carefully swept a loose strand of hair behind her ear.

“Normally, I don't condone taking the law into your own hands, but we do what we have to do for peace. With that being said, I permit the Skinwalkers to do whatever it takes to help the Onyx Sentries achieve their goal,” she continued.

I paused on a narrow grotesque jutting from the corner of the City Hall building, slowly turning my head back toward the amphitheater while I smoldered at the gross audacity.

She had to be referring to Draven and Briar. If what she said was true, then I had a lot less time than I thought. Those Sentries never left a stone unturned, and that meant they'd inevitably venture into the forest.

"We need to act fast, because we have reason to believe the Vampyre race is evolving, wielding elemental abilities that will surely bring the world to nonexistence."

I jumped from the grotesque carving and landed on a narrow windowsill. I phased through, entering a conference room overlooking the city, and followed the smell of expensive perfume. Governor Donovan's voice echoed, harmonizing with her own as she spoke through a microphone in a room down the hall.

"I don't mean to scare you, but like I said before—I believe in transparency. We need to stay united in these dark times... more than anything. I bid you all a good night. Stay safe."

Her voice was loudest behind the wooden door with filigree relief carvings. Several pairs of feet shuffled on the other side. I passed through it to see five bodyguards and an assistant packing up the camera and hologram equipment.

"Governor," her assistant began. "Your flight to Mundus Novus is being pushed up to one hour. They're in need of your next orders."

The governor scoffed, stalking to a mirror to reapply her lipstick.

"What do you *mean* they pushed it up to one hour?"

"They found out that Draven Hawthorne survives off of Vampyre blood. They need to know if you want to use him, or kill him like the rest."

"Really?" Governor Donovan raised a tamed brow with a sly grin. "Hm. That *is* interesting. Tell them to hold off on him for the time being."

The phantom leader... it's her.

I pulled a dagger from my belt.

The assistant immediately dialed a number on her phone. I tightened my grip around the hilt and crept a foot behind Governor Donovan. Goosebumps prickled along the back of her neck from my breath and she visibly shuddered. Something in my gut kept the blade from kissing her skin.

It wasn't smart. If she held that much sway over Mundus Novus, while disguised as a governor over Neoterra—they would level the entire city if I killed her. I closed my eyes with a restrained inhale, then sheathed my dagger.

One bodyguard gathered the equipment in his burly hands, with two behind the governor and two in front. They filed out of the room, walking right through me as if I didn't exist.

I hated every fiber of my being as I watched her go.

※

Night unfurled, illuminated only by the stars as the new moon remained hidden somewhere above. I arrived at the docks in the Nocturne District ten minutes early.

The pit of my stomach hollowed out at the sight of the churning ocean. I watched the murky water lap up the posts hungrily and imagined how many bodies it had claimed.

Sails whipped as the crisp breeze passed through. Boats of all sizes bobbed in the water, with the largest barely moving. Seagulls, even at this ungodly hour, scrounged trashcans and swept the skies above along with the crows.

Chief Duncan stood on the pier, looking around and occasionally glancing at his watch, unaware that I stood three feet from him.

"I'm here," I announced. "Where's the boat you promised?"

Chief Duncan flinched, and pointed across the water at a three-tier yacht nearing the docks. I furrowed my brows at the familiar striped hull.

"Who is this for?" I demanded.

"Why does it matter? You're invisible."

Chief Duncan's stubbled face stretched into a mischievous grin. He began walking down the pier as a rowdy crowd of men and women came pouring out of the marina's service building. I growled lowly, fighting the urge to crack the chief's skull open.

The crowd walked through and around me. My eyes darted across their exposed skin. A Nightshade crest on an ankle, forearm, hand, neck—

I watched them board the yacht and my heart seized.

I should've known. A man like Chief Duncan playing both sides wouldn't think twice about playing a man he couldn't see.

The yacht began to undock. I ignored the cotton in my mouth and the clamminess in my palms as I ran and hopped over the railing, landing on the helipad at its bow.

Then it sailed to where only the stars lived.

The wind was stronger standing directly above the water. My breath kept running away from me, growing sharper and thinner.

I grabbed a fistful of my shirt in front of my chest, sinking to my knees as I tried to force deeper breaths.

Is... this a heart attack?

I shook my head at the irrational thought. Vampyres couldn't have heart attacks unless they were medically induced.

The world flashed from greyscale to color every time I blinked.

I can't breathe.

I tried to focus on the sounds behind me—glasses clinking, guns cocking, laughing, talking, whispers, *anything*. I couldn't grasp any of it over the roaring waves. The Nightshades' voices faded to muffled murmurs as they all piled inside the cockpit.

"I thought I smelled you." The low, menacing growl was barely audible.

My eyes shot open. The wooden helipad below me was no longer charcoal, but oak. I turned to see Wraith baring every single sharpened fang as he aimed a pistol at me.

"Long time no see, friend," he sneered. "You look just like your old man with that one eye missing."

I can see color.

He can see me.

My chest was still caving in on itself.

Wraith took slow, prowling steps up the bow. I took an unsteady step back.

"I don't know how you managed to get on this boat without getting caught, but you're out of your element now." His teeth flashed in a sly, sharp smirk. "Now... what was it you said to me when you killed Larkin again?" He racked the slide.

I forced air through my nostrils with a shrug, and played off the exhale with a nonchalant chuckle.

"*He had it coming,*" Wraith snarled.

"He did," I insisted, and eyed the barrel. "Didn't you say that whenever you'd find me, you'd kill me?"

"Yeah, I did. That promise still stands."

His finger twitched over the trigger. I dodged and unsheathed a dagger, flinging it forward. Wraith ducked, and the blade lodged itself into the cockpit's wall.

"One eye or not, you still got those annoying reflexes," he growled.

"Or maybe you're a bad shot," I said, lips tugging into a crafty smile, and flashed across the helipad. I leaped in the air and the sole of my boot crunched against his chest. Wraith grabbed my ankle and twisted, and we both tumbled down the steps. I swung my elbow into his ribs before he could sit up. His knuckles met with my nose and I staggered into the railing. I gasped, peering over my shoulder at the foam bubbling over the sloshing water.

The air was cut off from my throat as Wraith wrapped his hands around my neck. His claws dug into my skin, and I reached up until I grasped his index finger and snapped it sideways. He roared, but it was cut it short as I jumped, wrapping one leg around his head, and slammed him on the ground. Wraith writhed in the triangle choke hold.

"Tell Larkin I said hey," I strained, and grabbed his chin and the back of his head. Wraith rammed his free fist into my ribs. One hit cracked against the bone, and I lost all the breath I had left.

I yanked Wraith's head from his shoulders, ligaments ripping and snapping like rubber bands. Red coated my face and seeped into my clothes. The Nightshades poured out of the cockpit. They crowded around and struck me with their fists, slashed claws through my skin. I coughed, blood spattering across the wooden floor as Wraith's head gaped back at me.

"Enough!" Uriah's thunderous voice ripped through the entire yacht.

The Nightshades pulled away. I wheezed as my rib bones glued themselves back together. They split a path as he stalked by and yanked me up by my shirt collar. Pure hate, rage—worse than anything he felt toward Draven—bore into my soul. I swallowed the remaining blood in my mouth, the bitter tang of it burning my throat. I chuckled.

"I gave you money, power, a home, a *family*—" He shook me like a rag doll, each word more furious than the last. "—when your own father thought rats had a higher purpose!"

"Kill me, or don't," I said coolly, and swung my elbow at a ninety-degree angle to snap his arm away from my shirt. Instead, I hit something solid, and he shoved me into the railing. I caught the lifelines stretching between the stanchions, pulling myself back to a stable stance. From head to toe, Uriah's body became chrome. I blinked, in denial of what stood before me.

"I think you should go for a swim one more time first."

Uriah shoved me again, and before I could react, I was flying over the edge.

48
BRIAR

I sat with Astoria in her nook, consoling her while she ranted. The last time we had a moment like this was well before our house had burned down, long before I worked up the nerve to break curfew that first time. It took my mind off of the sting I still felt from my conversation with Draven.

"He offered me to go with them, and then burned rubber to get out of here as soon as he saw me. What was that?" Astoria's voice was brittle, eyelids neon red as she balled a tissue in her fist. "What if—what if she doesn't want to come back here, and…"

She rambled on, and I chewed my inner cheek to keep from telling her that Vivian wasn't even worth the tears. She wasn't worth risking Astoria's life for a second time.

But now wasn't the time for that. I had to be the big sister, there to listen and comfort. I wrapped my arms around her in a side hug, resting my head on her shoulder.

Was it so wrong of me to pretend Vivian wasn't already here?

"I'm sure Sterling will find her. That's what he does, remember?" I assured her.

Astoria sniffled loudly, leaning her head against mine. "You're right. Even if she's not at their meeting place, I'm sure he can track her down. Plus he has Lyra."

"You think they're a thing?" I asked with a smirk.

"I doubt it since she's a Vampyre," Astoria grumbled. My smile faded and I pulled back from her shoulder.

"Yeah, well, he is too. They spend an awful lot of time together... joined at the hip, basically," I said. She shrugged and opened her tissue to blow her inflamed nose for the millionth time.

"I would be very surprised," Astoria said, and got up to toss her tissue in a small bucket across the room. I smiled pensively, imagining Sterling finally being with someone that made him happy. He had been in love with Cyrene for the longest time, but she never truly gave him the time of day—probably because of his bigotry. When she finally promised to give him a date, she was slaughtered right in front of him. If Lyra filled the void in his heart, maybe he'd learn to forgive Vampyres in general.

Forgive *me.*

Gunshots echoed throughout the cavern like fireworks. I flinched, and Astoria jumped out of her skin with a yelp. I jogged out of our pocket cave, through the tunnel, and stopped at the edge of the exit. I swung my arm out to block Astoria from stumbling too far.

Onyx Sentries dropped from the skylights, shooting at everyone—humans, Vampyres, Lightstalkers... it didn't matter. One of them torched the wheat fields, instantly filling our side of the cavern with black smoke. Avant Guardians shot back, and Oren was actively summoning water from the springs to put out the fire. Sterling and Lyra stood back to back, firing at the horde of Sentries who managed to make it to the ground. Some held cameras and their phones, recording the onslaught with no regard for their own lives.

"We need to get Draven out!" I exclaimed, then crouched, prompting Astoria to jump on my back. Ada shouted through a bullhorn, ordering everyone to evacuate. Unarmed citizens with children funneled through a secret door built beneath a rocky slope. Astoria coughed violently, and I veered left toward the string of evacuating people.

"Mom!" Astoria cried hoarsely and pointed. My shoes squealed to a stop.

Vivian, smiling ear to ear, shook a Sentry's hand and allowed two others to escort her to the rappels, where they then ascended to the surface.

Cracks erupted across my face, arms, and legs. Astoria yelped, lurching from my back with a wince.

"You better run," I growled, everything shifting to shades of red. Bullets sprayed at us, and I sent a heat wave to block them while Astoria bolted across the open space to the evacuation line.

"You sold us out?" I roared, arms glowing white-hot as the ground began to tremble. With my claws and fangs lengthened, I broke into a dash while everyone else ran in the opposite direction.

I charged a ball of fiery light in my palm, reared back, and hurled it in Vivian's direction.

It missed Vivian, but seared through a descending Sentry's rope. He screamed as he plummeted to the ground, and instantly splattered. I sent another sphere of blazes and it singed the Onyx Sentry's chest. His body hung limply from the rope. Vivian shrieked as she caught onto his boot. She swung her legs, and looked down at the distance in horror.

The boot slipped. Vivian wailed as she plunged to the ground. Her legs and spine crunched. I flashed forward to her body and watched her struggle to breathe with her body contorted.

"Br-Br-Briar," Vivian wheezed, "Th-they... made... me..."

"No, they didn't. Your price was always cheap. You would've done this if they offered you a free dinner at the Silver Dollar," I spat.

Vivian choked, releasing gurgling sounds as blood leaked from her nose and mouth. She could barely raise her hand, reaching for me. My tears evaporated the second they hit my cheeks, stinging my skin. Just when I thought this woman couldn't make me cry anymore, she proved me wrong yet again.

"Die knowing you destroyed hundreds of lives." My voice was calm. "If any of them show up in Hell with you, I hope they torment you for eternity."

"Please... I-I'm... sorry—"

I stepped on her reaching hand, my lip curling with disgust.

I crouched and leaned forward so she could hear me among the chaos. "Your apologies never meant anything before, and they don't mean anything now."

The rise and fall of her chest ceased, and the tears halted at her ducts. The muscles in her face relaxed.

"Briar!" Draven's voice rang out, and my fire dissipated. He was carrying Vyrn, but released him so he could run for the tunnels with the others. I caught up with Draven, pausing in front of an apple cart. I had to push Vivian's betrayal out of my mind and focus on the issue at hand—but a sadistic part of me was still upset she'd died so quickly.

"You need to go help the others evacuate," Draven shouted over the gunfire. A Sentry charged from behind him, rearing back an electrified baton. I shoved Draven out of the way and swiped my claws through the Onyx Sentry's helmet, melting it on contact. He screamed, dropping the baton and writhing in agony. Draven shocked him with it until his body stilled for good.

"I got this, Sunny," he said, and jerked his chin toward the tunnels. "They need someone with our strength. There could be others waiting on the surface."

"Be careful, *please*!" I pleaded, and he laughed in defiance as another Sentry approached with a flamethrower. Draven caught the barrel, bending it backwards. He smashed his palms against the Sentry's chest, hands glowing until the Sentry's armor erupted in flames. The Sentry screamed, flailing wildly and spreading his blazes to the booths.

"Briar, go!" Draven demanded, seamlessly fighting a crowd of ten Sentries at once. I nodded, forcing my legs to move. I refused to look back, because if I saw even the slightest hint of resistance, I would stay behind to help him.

Ada stood by the entrance, reloading her rifle before shooting at distant Sentries.

"Hurry up, girl! They're gonna get ambushed up there!" she shouted.

I picked up the pace, pushing past the string of citizens walking through the tunnels.

"Y'all know the drill!" Vyrn shouted from the front, and like soldiers, everyone—even the very young and very old—crouched in unison. The pitch-black tunnel opened into the forest. At Vyrn's signal, the citizens exited the backside in stealth sprints, heading north of the cavern. I stayed behind, noticing that most of the trucks idling around the main entrance to Avant Garde were vacant while their occupants laid waste to the city.

If any of Onyx Sentries survived, I intended to make sure they couldn't follow us through the forest.

I went through every truck and jabbed my elbow through each driver's side window. I stood on the running boards and leaned in, ignoring the glass shards slicing my stomach as I tore the steering column apart. I could've slashed the tires, but I wouldn't waste time checking if they had spares, which I was certain they did.

I found a couple cans of ammo and slung a rifle over my back, then broke off in a sprint.

A branch snapped. I hid behind a tree, sniffing the air. Sea salt, petrichor, and citrus was all I could manage—the same scents Helios always gave. I pivoted on my heel to return to the evacuees, assuming it an animal was fleeing the sound of gunfire.

Then something solid caught my ankle.

I bit my tongue and tumbled forward, dropping the ammo. A woman loosed a deep, sinister chuckle.

I pushed to my feet and turned in a slow circle. Everything—down to the bone, to my very soul—burned hotter than the sun itself. I balled my flaming fists, huffing hot air through ground teeth like a brazen bull. I uttered one word in a low, monstrous growl.

"Delilah."

49
CASPIAN

Sinking was like falling in slow motion. My arms stretched above, reaching for the bubbles floating from my nose and mouth. My chest burned—panic gripping me while I clawed for the surface—until the pain waned into serenity.

Cyrus wasn't crushing my collarbone to hold me under anymore.

I felt weightless, what I imagined a mother cradling her child would feel like.

I didn't fight it.

My heart's rhythm in my ears slowed, and my eyelids grew heavy. *Could this be... sleep?*

A chain floated by my face, its teardrop moonstone still attached. I swung my arm to catch it, allowing the chain to wrap around my fingers like a web.

Astoria's voice echoed through the water like a siren, beckoning.

If you know how to conquer and respect it… then you can't fear it.

Images of her floating on her back, swinging her arms in confident freestyle and backstroke, flipped through my mind. She remained elegantly poised and patient when I resisted her instruction. I remembered the way she dove underwater and kicked her feet, tucking her elbows in before spreading her arms outward to push herself back to the surface. She overcame the water, became one with it, as if she were indeed a siren after all.

I tightened my fist around her necklace, mirroring her kicks. I cupped my free hand, swimming upward. Black spots crowded my vision with neon streaks wriggling across as if someone had flashed a camera inches from my eyes. I could feel myself fading as my chest ballooned—

Until cold air iced over my hand.

I threw my head above water with a sharp gasp. I thrashed my arms, forgetting how to tread.

If you're ever tired from swimming, you can relax and stare at the stars.

I trembled violently from the frigid ocean, but allowed my limbs to fall limp as I leaned back. I imagined Astoria's hands at the small of my back as we trained in the still spring waters. The ocean waves were calm, rocking me like a giant cradle.

I'd always feared the water, but I had also always wanted to learn how to swim. I wanted to experience the beach like the Sun Dwellers, but disguised the fear of my father behind a concern for sharks. Memories still scratched at the back of my mind, tugged on my soul—still wanted to drag me down into the ocean's depths and swallow me whole, but for once... I remained above water.

The stars twinkled in celebration, despite the moon's absence. I sniffled with a relieved chuckle, tears bubbling.

Shadowy smoke curled around my arms and legs before submerging me entirely, and I didn't panic. Instead I welcomed it.

One moment I was floating on my back, and the next—shadows dispersed, and I found myself staggering through sand. But it was tan, not pale grey.

Distant cracks echoed through the forest in rapid succession, like popping bottles.

I knew better than that.

Slicking my drenched hair out of my eyes, I stuffed Astoria's necklace in my pocket and hurried through the trees. I desperately hoped I wasn't too late.

⁎

The tunnel flashed with gunfire, occasionally highlighting silhouettes wielding weapons. I unsheathed the only knife I hadn't lost in the water, and wielded the shadows to send me back into their noir world. I held the dagger upside down, blade jutting past my fist, and sped past Onyx Sentries, slicing through the soft sections of their tactical uniforms. They dropped dead in my wake, but once the tunnel opened up to the cavern, many more appeared. They crowded around Draven, some taking hits from his fiery power and others prepping to unleash fire extinguishers.

"Draven, behind you!" I shouted. He rammed his fist straight through one of the Sentry's helmets and made a 360-degree turn, sending a column of fire into the group, reducing them to ash.

Draven's breaths heaved as he leaped from another crowd of Sentries and landed on the roof of one of the mud-brick buildings. He circled with a puzzled frown, trying to pinpoint the source of my voice.

I made the shadows lift the cloak.

"Down here!" I called, and backflipped over a silver bullet whizzing by. I watched it pierce a neighboring Sentry's shoulder, knocking him back. Draven's eyes lit up, fangs gleaming in the widest smile I'd ever seen.

"You're alive!" he exclaimed in a guffaw.

"More alive than I've ever been!" I shouted back, and veiled myself again, raising my hands. The dim lights throughout Avant Garde flickered. Smoke from Draven's fire churned and darkened into the obsidian shadows I wielded, then began swallowing each Onyx Sentry. Agonized, bloodcurdling screams filled the cavern. Draven finished off the rest with whips of orange and crimson lashing from his palms.

Then we were surrounded by darkness. The cavern ceiling crumbled with thunderous groans.

"Let's get out of here," Draven said, and sprinted toward a tunnel on the side of the cavern underneath the houses. I followed closely behind as jagged icicles of stone began collapsing at a faster rate. We flashed through the tunnel until a blast of smoke and air pushed us the rest of the way out. I phased through a tree to avoid the impact while Draven crashed into a thicket.

The forest went still, as if giving a moment of silence for the tragic fall of Avant Garde.

Draven grunted before emerging, brushing leaves and grass

from his short, midnight hair. I rolled my neck and sheathed my dagger at the small of my back.

"Where's Astoria?" I asked, dreading the answer.

"She should be with the others," he responded, and sniffed the air. "I think they all headed north."

We began our trek through the trees and thickets, following the various sounds and scents. I couldn't track Astoria's among them, and I wondered if it was because of the number of people or because I'd been away for so long.

"What happened to ya?" Draven asked.

"The serum finally worked," I said with a shrug. "I can become a shadow."

"English, man," Draven grumbled.

"It's hard to explain. It's like I become darkness itself and I can see the world in black and white, phase through walls like a ghost. *Teleport*, even. I accidentally ended up in Neoterra before they shot me in Camp Helix, like my body protected itself before I could react." I held up my hand, surveying the black veins that always appeared whenever the smoky wisps curled around my knuckles.

"That sounds cool." Draven grinned. "Ya master it yet?"

"For the most part, yeah. I was stuck as a shadow for a while, until I got on a boat and ran into Wraith."

I refused to admit that it wasn't Wraith who triggered the shadow veil to lift, but my irrational fear of water. I slid my hands in my pockets.

"So can you switch back and forth at will?"

"As long as I remain calm," I said, and rubbed my thumb over

Astoria's moonstone in my pocket. I told myself I wouldn't have made it without those brief lessons. I clung to them amid the panic.

She was my lifeline.

"Ha, yeah, you mastered it then," Draven quipped, but his smile faded when his stomach growled.

I took a couple steps to the side to widen the gap between us, not that it'd help much.

"How's your, um... eating habits?" I didn't know what other way to put it. It could've changed for the better or worse in the past couple weeks.

"I still got issues with it." He pulled out a pack of cigarettes and grabbed one that was virtually crushed from the fighting. He snapped his fingers, triggering a soft flame on his thumb, and ignited the end of the cigarette.

I raised an eyebrow. "You're smoking again?"

"Best way to ignore the blood I smell on ya," he drawled.

I cringed, but understood. At least he was making an effort to make temptations easier to handle. I wasn't sure if now was the time to tell him that Mundus Novus had found out about his issues, and that they intended to use him as a weapon of sorts in their war.

In the new quiet between us, distant weeping, low chatter, and leaves crunching became louder.

"Some Nightshades made it to Helios," I warned, surveying the distant torches lighting the way for the Sun Dwellers among the Avant Guardians. "I think some are White Fang too."

"Yeah? I'll tell Ada and Briar then." Draven became a smear of color as he fled to the front of the line. I picked up the pace, walking among the humans to examine each face for Astoria.

But I didn't need to do that. She had the longest hair out of everyone there—a roaring waterfall cascading down to her mid-thigh. Her soft, round face was the moon on a starless night. And her smile...

"Astoria," I said as I touched her shoulder. She whirled and gasped, eyes instantly flooding. She stepped out of line.

"Cass—"

I grabbed her face, and planted my lips on hers. Her voice caught in her throat, shoulders tensing until she finally melted and wrapped her fists in the hem of my shirt.

We should've been trekking along with everyone else, but I didn't know how many minutes or seconds we had left with each other. Danger lurked in the trees, the sea, the sky... and I refused to die with regret.

We parted, our foreheads resting against one another. I sifted through my pocket for the necklace.

"You're alive," Astoria murmured, tears raining down her cheeks. There were too many to catch.

"Only because you were my lighthouse," I whispered, and clasped the necklace around her slender throat. She tucked her chin to examine it, lips stretching into a dazzling smile as she angled the pendant to see its various colors.

"I read your letter." Astoria finally tore her gaze from the moonstone, meeting mine.

"It was pretty wordy, wasn't it?" The anxiety warbled in my stomach and iced over my palms. I dropped my attention to my shoes with a wince.

"It was beautiful." She blushed. "No one ever writes letters any-more."

"Saying 'I love you' didn't feel sufficient," I admitted, briefly grabbing her chin with my thumb and index finger before letting my hand fall. I lifted her into my arms and cut through the air in seconds to catch up with the others. Electricity sparked through my veins; I could run to the ends of the earth with her in my arms.

50
BRIAR

Delilah circled me like a wolf herding its prey. I tracked her movements, rotating in tandem. As much as I wanted to know how she'd found this place, I didn't have time to talk.

I swung my arm, releasing a fireball in her direction. Delilah swiftly dodged, clicking her tongue and wiggling her index finger.

"Just because you're a Vampyre now doesn't mean you're stronger," she crooned. Frost spread across her arms like the air had dropped twenty degrees. She smirked, eyes flashing a silvery blue similar to Oren's.

"Uriah gave you the last serum? What a waste," I sneered.

"I think it's more of a waste that Draven threw his life away for you." Delilah darted forward, knocking me into a tree. I winced at the frostbite burrowing into my chest from her touch. The cold spread from my ankles up my legs, locking me in place against the tree. I watched thick blocks of ice crawl up my body.

"Uriah's plan to destroy Neoterra will work whether or not the Vampyres are immune to the sun. Once the Sun Dwellers are decimated, it's nothing but time to perfect the sun immunity."

"Yeah?" I rasped, shutting my eyes with a grimace. My legs burned with a different sensation, from my own fire. I jerked against the ice, trying to will myself to melt it. The numbness crawled up my hips and core. "What are you going to do without a food source? Has he thought about that?"

"Farms, of course." Delilah's fangs stretched into a sinister smile.

"I'm... I'm not gonna let you win," I said with erratic breaths, fighting through chattering teeth. "Y-you can't keep winning."

"Too late," she intoned, and tapped my nose. "I'll be sure to tell Draven your last words." The cold spread across my face, seeping through my skin and raging through my bones. I couldn't blink. My vision iced over like frosted glass, her silhouette behind it rippling.

All I could see were her diamond-white teeth gleaming as she took a proud step back. She watched me, admiring her handiwork before sauntering off.

Walking away... just as she did in my house fire. Astoria had been upstairs on the brink of death, and Delilah had given me that same gloating grin before disappearing through the back door.

I couldn't reach her. The flames lapped up the walls and closed in on the archway to the kitchen.

Astoria had minutes—no—*seconds.*

You let her go.

I couldn't feel my body anymore. The numbness I craved from the pain of my past had finally been gifted to me.

And I *hated* it.

A crack in the glass appeared.

"What are you so angry about?" Vyrn once asked.

A self-preserving, abusive mother.

A crime lord with a thirst for power.

Another crack.

His lackey hellbent on destroying my life and the people I love.

A mad scientist with the dream to create immune Vampyres, no matter the cost.

A society taught to hate and fear the many because of a few.

Steam forced its way out of the fissures, and the ice block shattered.

My throat ripped itself apart as I roared and barreled across Delilah's path. I left charred earth in my wake. She dashed through the forest toward the Avant Guardians. I leaped in the air, drawing a clenched fist backward.

Delilah stopped in her tracks, raised her palms, and shot sharp icicles in my direction. A vibrating aura of heat surrounded my body, and the icicles vaporized before they could touch me. I continued to descend, tightening my fist before slamming it through her wall of ice.

Dirt, grass, leaves, and branches spat upwards. A crater formed around us. Delilah splayed her fingers, sending blades of ice at my face. I mirrored her movement, sending caustic waves of red heat. My muscles barked as the pressure built between us, and we pushed forward. The ball of energy grew larger—fire and ice battling for dominance. I leaned into it until the earth shuddered and the flames intensified.

Delilah fell to a knee, crying out. Her elbows buckled as she leaned back, gasping for the air my fire devoured. I stepped forward, pushing harder.

A blast of light exploded between us, knocking me back against a boulder.

My ears rang, and for a moment everything was blurry. I blinked until clarity returned.

Smoke clung to the air, concealing the trees left standing in the surrounding area. I forced myself to stand with a labored grunt and walked across the crater. Delilah's body was charred and shriveled, some of it fused to the ground. Her mouth stretched open, fangs fully formed and frozen in a perpetual shriek. I tapped her leg with my boot and ashes flaked off it.

Delilah was completely unrecognizable, yet as I stared at her corpse... the horrific memories still lived.

Cold air brushed over my skin. Goosebumps rolled across my arms and the hairs stood on my neck. For a moment—I thought Delilah's ghost was still around, waiting to strike back.

Rapid footsteps beat the ground, and I let the blazes engulf my palms once more.

"Briar!" Draven appeared in a blink and tackled me in a tight, bear hug that stifled my hands. I sank into his embrace with an unstable sigh.

"You weren't with the group and the explosion and—" He inhaled sharply, resting his chin on the top of my head. "I don't know why I ain't think you could handle yourself."

"Me either," I teased, and patted his back before pulling away. "I'm sorry, I know I was supposed to be with everybody, but I didn't want any Sentries to follow so I stayed behind to destroy their trucks and then... Delilah showed up."

"Delilah?" Draven echoed, and observed the crater and splintered tree trunks. "Whoa... did you do this?"

"Yeah," I laughed nervously, scratching my head. He scanned the crater once more, eyes landing on the lump of coal that was once Delilah's body.

Draven's eyebrows climbed to the top of his forehead. "Was that her?"

"What's left of her," I said with a nonchalant shrug, although the calm exterior was a façade. I was still recovering from the shock of my capabilities.

"Sick." The dimples resurfaced on his face. "Well... I ain't gotta tell you that if she was here, the others can't be too far off."

"Right. So we should get going." I looked at her corpse once more. Draven held out his palm, and I laced my fingers with his before we jumped over the three foot crater wall and sped away.

✳

After trailing the Avant Guardians' scent, we found ourselves at the edge of a runway at a condemned airport. Patches of turf dividing taxiways, ramps, and runways grew to three feet tall, conquered by weeds and wildflowers. The airport itself was dark—windows covered in dust and cobwebs. Everyone stood in a circle with Ada and Vyrn at its center, heads hanging low in prayer. Draven and I slowed our pace to avoid interrupting the moment of silence for the fallen. His jaw feathered, fingers curling into lethal fists.

"Those were good people," I mumbled. The words "Until Equinox" burned into the cavern's ceiling flashed through my mind, along with the devilish smile on Vivian's face as she shook hands with the enemy.

"Where day and night meets at equal length. Until equality and equity is given to Vampyres and humans, we won't give up," Ada once said. It pained me that so much blood had to be shed for a dream to be accomplished, without a guarantee that it ever would.

My heart fluttered at the sight of frosted hair across the circle. I stood on my toes, craning my neck to see over the varying shoulder heights until Caspian's face emerged. His arm was draped over my sister's shoulders, and Astoria toyed with a new necklace around her neck while she leaned into him. To their left, Sterling and Lyra stood side by side, stained in blood and dirt. I grinned, shuttering my eyes with a silent *thank you.*

We were all together again, in one piece.

"Hank and a few of his other aeronautical engineers restored, rebuilt, and maintained one of the old commercial jetliners here, in the event that Avant Garde was compromised," Ada announced, and pointed at the greying hangar, its doors barely holding together.

Draven snorted.

"I *know* she ain't expectin' us to get on no plane that's been sittin' here for decades," he grumbled with a wry chuckle. I rocked on my heels, chewing on my lip ring.

"These gentlemen conducted countless test flights. We'll be fine. But now's the time we link up with our sister community, Oleander Valley."

Everyone murmured indistinctly, and judging by their reactions—they hadn't known the place existed either.

"Shh, shh, I know. I know you're all confused," Ada said. "I haven't been completely transparent, but I couldn't afford to let anyone in Avant Garde know about them unless I knew for certain we didn't have any double agents among us." Her coal-black eyes passed over every face as she turned in a small circle. When they met mine, I sank behind Draven's shoulder. My *beloved* mother had been the double agent. In the short hours she'd visited, this lovely community had been destroyed.

The hangar doors lifted with an alarm, revealing an aircraft with pristine white paint and chrome accents on its jet engines, as if it had been delivered straight from the factory the day before. Four men watched with their chests poked out and their chins raised. It was safe to assume they were the ones that had made flight possible.

"Don't worry, friends. Our fallen people haven't died in vain. They made it possible for us to get to this evacuation checkpoint. While Avant Garde may have been a place of hopes and dreams, Oleander Valley is a place of reality. When we get there, we will discuss ending the war between Mundus Novus and Vampyres once and for all."

We all waited patiently to board the plane, eager to strike back.

51
STERLING

In all my years, I never thought I would fight alongside Vampyres. If anything, I imagined myself on the other side of the battlefield. Of course, I never *dreamed* of combating Onyx Sentries, or so much as even being near them. They were only deployed in times of war or rebellion, and the country had been at peace since the first Crimson War.

Watching the Sentries descend from the skylights in Avant Garde, shooting down at the citizens with no regard for their species...

Vivian did horrible things in our childhood, but I never thought she'd offer our heads on a platter. Was it revenge because I arrested her? Was it just pure evil?

As I stood in a circle with the Avant Guardians, bowing our heads in mourning for their friends and families, a bitter taste filled my mouth.

All those years I spent on the force keeping Vampyres in line, I'd been perpetuating Mundus Novus' values of hate without a second thought, because my heart was already blackened by it.

And then I brought bloodshed right to their doorsteps by bringing Vivian to their sanctuary.

I wanted to strip out of my body and become someone else.

✳

The pilot, Hank, rolled the jet onto the tarmac and everyone began to board. Draven, Briar, Astoria, and Caspian stood in the middle of the line, but my feet fused to the asphalt.

Lyra nudged my arm with her elbow. "What's wrong?"

I swallowed, staring at the plane and its might—the massive wheels, the powerful jet engines, and the vast wings. I thought about the impossibility of a metallic bird soaring thousands of miles above the earth's surface, and the huge chance of it crashing.

"Have you ever flown before?" She angled her head before moving in front of me. I blinked, snapping out of my horrified trance.

"No," I rasped, then cleared my throat.

"It's not that bad," Lyra promised, and reached for my hand. She tugged lightly. "Come on, they're waiting on us now."

Indeed, Ada stood at the top of the steps with her arms folded and shoulders squared. I chewed my inner cheek and willed my feet to move.

"I'm right behind you," Lyra soothed, as if the wrong tone would send me running for the hills.

It might have.

My knees wobbled with every step. I ducked under the frame then straightened, my head barely brushing against the ceiling. Everyone stared at me, already settled in their seats. I scanned each row, finally catching an empty spot toward the back. I allowed Lyra the window seat, then settled next to her. I'd always appreciated the sky, but I never wanted to be in it.

I flinched at the sound of the heavy passenger entry door shutting in the front.

"It's going to be about thirty minutes to get there," Ada announced from the front. "Buckle up, everybody!"

Hank spoke over the intercom, running over safety measures. Typical instructions he'd probably gone over a million times before he found a home in Avant Garde.

High-pitched fans sang throughout the cabin as the jet powered up and moved across the taxiway. Once we reached the main runway, the whirring grew louder. We pushed forward, picking up speed until the tarmac's resistance vanished and gravity pulled me further into my seat. The cabin slanted and I slammed my palm on top of Lyra's hand, squeezing my eyes shut. The plane trembled and groaned, and a mortifying yelp escaped my throat.

"It's only turbulence," Lyra said with a light chuckle. "Totally normal."

"You fly often?" My voice was strained.

"I took vacations every now and then," she said.

An eternity passed before the plane finally leveled out. I made the mistake of glancing out the window. The clouds were enormous up close. The land below was a giant grid in shades of brown and green, and then it turned into infinite blue. Lyra giggled under her breath, leaning her head back against the seat.

I scowled. "What's so friggin' funny?"

"You. I didn't think you were capable of fearing anything," she said. I released a short, sardonic laugh.

"I don't think it's a fear. It's common sense. We weren't born with wings." I rolled my eyes.

"Yeah, okay," Lyra laughed. I didn't let go of her hand. She was my anchor—my parachute.

✳

Fifteen minutes into the flight, the plane began its gradual descent. I felt the subtle shift in gravity, but refused to open my eyes until Lyra nudged my arm and pointed at the cluster of single-floor buildings and houses below. There were no glittering skyscrapers or lush woodlands. Rather, red mountains scribbled across the landscape with patches of dried grass, succulents, and Russian thistle scattered throughout. Wind kicked up dirt from the alpine desert—a drastic contrast to Helios' coastal paradise.

I held my breath until the wheels slammed into the ground and the jet finally slowed to a stop. The plane's mechanics whirred at a lower pitch as it powered down. Hank opened the door, and everyone immediately began to deplane.

"Welcome to Oleander Valley. Their population is diverse with humans, Lightstalkers, and Vampyres. They took shelter at an abandoned military base, in the underground missile silos—away from the sun, and from the Mundus Novus drones. The settlers in Oleander Valley dreamed of a society that would heal yet again," Ada explained as she led the group across the sparse terrain. Jagged peaks pierced the sky; it was a miracle we could land at all with how uneven most of the ground was.

The fact that not one, but *two* hidden communities existed in fear of Mundus Novus made me wonder how many more could be out there.

The missile silos were in view across the desiccated plains—disguised as single-story houses—but were farther away than we anticipated. After thirty minutes of walking, Ada suggested that the Vampyres and Lightstalkers lift their human companions and carry them across.

Ada led us to a house with cracked vinyl and a white flower spray painted over its weathered front door. The interior was covered in dust, cobwebs, and chipped paint. The ceiling and baseboards were bowed like it'd collapse at any moment. Ada led us through the kitchen and opened a creaky door that led to a basement.

The basement stretched into an endless spiral staircase descending into the earth's depths, down a cylindrical tube. Life teemed below—a calm din of hundreds of voices. Lyra's steady breaths became more erratic the deeper we went.

"Are you okay?" I whispered to prevent my voice from echoing through the chamber.

"Yeah, I never liked tunnels or tight spaces. Avant Garde was a lot more... open." She took a deep breath and tucked her blonde hair behind her ears.

Once we reached the bottom, a man with thick salt-and-pepper coils wearing round glasses, a t-shirt, and ripped jeans swung his arms open for Ada. Oren joined their embrace. Standing side by side, I could see they shared the same deep complexion and similar facial features.

"Everyone, this is my twin brother, Andre. He oversees Oleander Valley and used his former military experience to train everyone.

They're a hundred strong," Ada explained, throwing her arm over her brother's wide shoulders.

"I always knew if I saw any Avant Guardians here, then the worst has finally happened. I wished we had a chance to meet under different circumstances." He spoke with a rich timbre that projected itself in the far reaches of the silo. "Come, follow me to the chow hall. We're all ready to discuss the next moves."

The remaining fifty of us trailed behind Ada and filed into the vast chow hall. Long, rectangular banquet tables stretched along the length of the room. Oleander Valley residents crowded every table. Crumbs and balled napkins piled on most of their trays The second we entered, their chatter ceased, magnifying the sound of our shuffling gaits. The Avant Guardians stood in the back, some sitting on the cement floor.

A small wooden platform stood at the front, and Andre led Ada, Vyrn, and Oren to it. To my surprise, Draven, Briar, Caspian, and Astoria joined them. I hid among the crowd, weaving through until I reached Lyra, and hoped I wasn't expected to be on the stage as well.

"I need to tell you something before they start." I barely moved my lips as I tilted my head, keeping my eyes glued to the stage.

"Not now," Lyra whispered.

"If anything happens—"

"I don't do goodbyes," she interjected sharply. I winced at her reaction, the words swelling inside my chest while I attempted to bury them deep.

Andre introduced his sister and the others, explained Avant

Garde's existence and why it was also hidden from his people, and then gestured for Ada to take the floor.

"Sterling and Lyra, you two up here." Ada pointed at us directly. I seethed as we made our way to the front.

"It has come to my attention that Mundus Novus decided to take drastic measures to regain control. Caspian Bishop here has spent the last couple weeks in Neoterra and would better explain it himself."

His skin waned further, and he shook his head with a grimace. Draven attempted to be inconspicuous when he nudged his arm with his elbow... but we all saw it.

A restrained exhale puffed through Caspian's nose as he turned to the crowd.

"They're activating the incinerators at Camp Cerberus and Governor Donovan gave the Skinwalkers the privilege to kill any Vampyres that haven't been detained yet," Caspian said as if reading off a bulleted list. He didn't pause at the gasps or murmurs, or let them digest the news.

Andre held up his hand, a simple gesture that instantly silenced the hall. Everyone on stage, except Ada, watched him with disbelief.

"When was this?" someone demanded.

"Yesterday," Caspian droned.

"This is genocide!" someone else exclaimed.

Memories of my own rage unfurled before my eyes, blurring the riled audience. How many sleepless nights did I suffer through, craving a killing spree of all the bipedal creatures with fangs? How many days on the force did I let that rage drive my ambition?

How many times had I spat my hate toward Lyra, a Vampyre

with more humanity in one fingernail than the entire Sun Dweller race?

"I suggest that's the first place we hit." Caspian turned to Ada and Andre. "There's no telling how many lives we've already lost standing here talking about it."

"We've had scouts get as close as they could to the camps. They're fortified. No matter what point of entry we take, there will be bloodshed regardless. We need to hit the Nightshades' headquarters, and finish off White Fangs' while they're still weakened. At least then we'd have one enemy left." Andre folded his arms, raising his chin in challenge. "What do you propose we do with minimal casualties, Bishop?"

"I need two groups—attackers and rescue," Caspian said. "I'll pave the way for entry at Camp Cerberus. Attackers will hold the Onyx Sentries at bay while the rescuers evacuate the prisoners."

"I can lead the attack group," Draven added.

Caspian shook his head. "Actually... I think you'd be better elsewhere."

"What?" Draven laughed wryly, glancing at the crowd as if to verify he'd heard correctly.

"The governor found out about your... predicament," Caspian whispered, then faced the audience and projected his voice when he added, "If Draven allows them to capture him, he can destroy Mundus Novus from the inside."

"Are you crazy?" Briar erupted.

"I'll do it," Draven said, ignoring Briar's outburst. I clenched my fists at my sides, swallowing the hard pill I could never get down. I had to start making things right.

"I'll join an attacker team at White Fang," I said, and stepped forward with resolve. "Dr. Ivanov won't stop making those serums and putting it in the wrong hands."

"Me too," Lyra declared, and took her place beside me. Caspian nodded with newfound respect.

We spent the rest of the evening discussing the next strategies and backup plans if and when things went awry, and planned to strike before first light.

52
DRAVEN

There were a few times when Ada and Andre had to calm the crowd as everyone erupted in disagreement, but we eventually reached a compromise every time. We all had our roles.

Briar, however, never agreed with the concept that I'd allow myself to get captured. She wanted to go with me, but Ada tasked her with being on camera with Oren to add more footage to the flash drive. She had already gathered the videos from the Avant Guardians, who recorded the recent violence and evacuated with the rest of us. The "final ingredient"—as Ada put it—was a testimonial from Briar and Oren.

Everyone dressed in tactical gear, armed to the teeth with the weapons they specialized in—ranging from sniper rifles, pistols, knives, longbows, and various explosives. Vampyres and Lightstalkers had their fill of blood in the chow hall while I numbly watched.

I switched my focus to Briar, who wore the same uniform as the rest of us. Her face was cold, eyes bleak and jaw set while she watched some of the recordings Ada already had on her phone. Oren wasn't far from her side, helping a couple people set up cameras.

Vyrn emerged from the crowd with a sheet of paper, sober eyes darting until they found their target—me.

"Draven! Son." He was breathless as he approached. "Look!"

A lot of numbers, a chart with zigzagging lines—something that easily sent a lightning strike through my temple.

"You're gonna have to translate that mess," I said after a brief glance.

"I finally finished putting together the data from our experiments. Of the hundred Vampyres Astoria and I tested on, sixty percent no longer have cravings."

Great, but it still didn't work for me.

I forced a smile and patted his shoulder.

"Keep up the great work, man. Maybe tell Ada. She can put that in the video too."

"I already told her. She wants to keep it quiet, doesn't want to trigger too much excitement." He pushed his glasses up and instinctively reached for his cargo pocket, but it was empty. "I wanna tell you kids good luck."

"Thanks," I grumbled. I leaned against the wall, crossing my arms and ankles, and patiently waited for Briar. I groaned under my breath when Sterling approached, completely blocking my view.

"Hey." Sterling hooked his hands on the collar of his bullet-proof vest. I didn't respond, only stared at him irritatingly from under my brows.

"You and I clashed a lot, but you always had my sister's back. You could've been like any other Nightshade, but you weren't. I just wanna say I'm sorry for everything. You're not a bad guy, and I hope you make it through this." He ran through the words as if each one burned his tongue.

I pushed off the wall with a blink, rerunning his statement through my mind.

Is any of this real?

Sterling held out his hand stiffly. I stared at it for a heartbeat before giving it a firm shake.

"I don't think you're so bad yourself," I said. Of course, there were countless times I'd imagined choking him or slashing his face, but loving Briar had been the leash I needed. There were also times where I pitied him. "If ya ever need someone to talk to about bein' Turned, don't hesitate to give me a holler."

Sterling smiled thinly, then returned to the small group of people assigned to infiltrate White Fang.

"Alright!" Andre shouted, commanding the hall to go still. "Let's move out!"

Everyone fell in formation, running up the staircase in two lines. Their rhythmic marching echoed through the chamber like a drum as we ascended to the surface. Briar stood from the table, waiting for the end of the line. I sauntered to her side and grabbed her hand with a light squeeze.

I inhaled sharply, my heart caving in on itself the more reality set in.

"This is it, Sunny," I said, inclining my head to observe the string of Oleander Valley and Avant Garde fighters. "It might be a minute before we see each other again."

"The important thing is that we *will* see each other again." Briar wrapped her arms around me in a tight embrace, then stood on her toes to plant a tender kiss on my lips. She pulled away, dabbing the corner of her eyes to avoid messing up her mascara.

"I love you," I said, and fell in line.

"I love you too," Briar croaked behind me, and we broke into the steady jog to begin our fight for freedom.

✳

A string of humvees and trucks waited for us outside. I joined Caspian and a few others in a convoy to Camp Cerberus. There were twenty of us, with four piled in each truck. A Vampyre woman sitting in the passenger seat wore a full face helmet, and the ballistic body suit sleeves extended into gloves, tailored exactly to her size. There was no space for her skin to get exposed unless there was a tear. I noticed that was the uniform of choice for the Oleander Valley Vampyres and Lightstalkers with sun sensitivities.

"Where did y'all get all this stuff?" I asked.

"What stuff?" A Sun Dweller called from the driver's seat.

"Your weapons, gear, trucks... all of it."

A proud chuckle. "Scouts stole some from junkyards, bought some of the vehicles from auctions, and we built the rest with raw materials ourselves. We've got a few killer seamstresses and blacksmiths."

"Impressive," I said, and shifted my focus to the window, flipping through scattered memories like a poorly arranged scrapbook.

Mundus Novus' oppression was a real thing, but I never bent

to their laws. Not as a Vampyre, and I certainly never planned to as an evolved one. My main concern remained with the Nightshades and White Fang. I couldn't kill Uriah with my fire, and even if we exposed our government, Uriah would probably try to take their place.

On top of that... what if I fell into a frenzy and attacked innocent Vampyres during the rescue mission, inadvertently giving Mundus Novus what they wanted?

"What are you thinking about?" Caspian asked, eyebrows subtly raised.

"A lot," I grumbled, and patted my cargo pocket for the flash drive. While the videos were still being compiled, Oleander Valley programmers had built drives that could be accessed remotely, without directly plugging them into a computer to download or upload files. All I needed to do was make sure the live feed was activated in Mundus Novus' tower, and plug the drive into their console.

"We got this," Caspian reassured me.

After twenty minutes, the convoy slowed to a stop on the side of the road, just beyond the treeline that concealed the camp from traffic. I took the liberty of swallowing the flash drive, and gagged as the metal scraped against my esophagus.

Camp Cerberus was thirty miles from Oleander Valley and seventy miles out from Neoterra, in unclaimed territory. It was eighty miles from Mundus Novus, which meant we had about eight minutes to get as many prisoners out before the Onyx Sentries' backup arrived in their fighter jets.

Black smoke wrapped around Caspian's body until he vanished entirely. With that signal, we all got out and crept through the trees.

Vampyres were snipers posted in the trees while the humans and Lightstalkers remained on the ground with their rifles. I opted to not carry a firearm due to my abilities, especially since I didn't want to instinctively shoot at the Sentries when I needed to let them capture me.

I'd have to swallow a lot of pride to let them win.

Beyond the barbed wire, there were five bone-white cube buildings lined up in a grid, similar to barracks. Each had a single narrow pipe jutting from the corner of the roof.

We watched a Sentry lead a string of Vampyres to one of the doors. Another Sentry stood at the back of the line with a rifle pointing at their heads. The Vampyres dragged their feet, heads bobbing back and forth as if they were inebriated.

The wind didn't carry the stench of alcohol, and the Onyx Sentries would've never provided that for prisoners. But they had to have given them something.

They'd never willingly march to their deaths.

The Sentries slammed the door shut after the last Vampyre entered the cube. My stomach twisted and I took a step forward, ready to intervene.

"What are you doing?" an Avant Guardian hissed.

"They're about to burn them—"

"Not until Caspian's signal!" someone else whispered harshly. I scoffed, shaking my head as I stormed to the fence and melted a hole through it. Grass blades sizzled against the bright red metal that dripped on them like acid rain.

I wasn't going to spend the rest of my life knowing I let twenty Vampyres burn alive while I stood behind a fence.

A monotone, robotic voice spoke through a PA system across the camp. "Cleansing in three... two..."

A shot rang out as a red flare cut through the sky. I jumped through the fence, Sun Dwellers running through the hole I'd created behind me. Everyone else with enhanced capabilities jumped over the fence. Sharp, percussive pops filled the air in rapid succession. Onyx Sentries poured out of buildings at every angle, rolling out cans of tear gas.

The Sentries surrounding the incinerator building dropped like flies, their throats striped in scarlet. Blood soaked into the mulch and sprayed the bushes flanking the front door. A dozen more circled the building and fired at the air as if they could penetrate Caspian's shadow.

I shot a ball of flame into the sky above, and it dropped in a heated circle like falling stars. Some of the Sentries fled, some thrashed as their uniforms caught ablaze, and others frantically aimed their weapons until one of them spotted me. He alerted his colleagues.

Their feet thundered as they barreled in my direction. I stood in place, watching Caspian reappear. He opened the door and a chain of prisoners darted out of the incinerator. The rescue squad approached from around the back of the building and formed a shield around the Vampyres, opening fire on additional Sentries emerging from the tear gas.

I ignited my arms, ready to strike at the first line of hostiles—

A loud boom. Dirt and debris flung in the air, sending a shock wave that hurled everyone back and crumbled the side of the nearest buildings. For a moment, Onyx Sentries, Avant Guardians, Oleanders, *and* prisoners alike stood still as we regained our bearings. Fifty people dressed in black and white body suits similar to the Onyx Sentries ran through the blasted barbed wire fence in flashes.

I caught a glimpse of several hand tattoos depicting two different crests—the lion skull with a nightshade mane and the four fangs roaring over an ace of spades card.

The Nightshades and White Fangs had not been considered as a possibility.

This wasn't part of the plan.

I aimed above the Onyx Sentries' heads and sent a wall of heated fury to block the clans. They didn't break stride as they emerged from the flames, suits untouched as smoke swirled from the hexagonal fibers. Sterling and Lyra shot at them, ducking for cover to reload. Lightstalkers, Sun Dwellers, and Vampyre allies fired at the clans, but few bodies dropped on the enemy's front. The body suits glowed with every bullet as they absorbed the hit.

The work of Dr. Ivanov's genius, no doubt.

I charged with nothing but my claws and fangs exposed, and crouched to lunge at the nearest White Fang or Nightshade.

But something cracked against the back of my head. I whirled around, and a cloud of red fire retardant sprayed directly in my face, drawing the air from my lungs. I fell to my knees, gripping my chest collar as I gasped, and a burlap sack snapped over my head before I could see who'd attacked me.

53
LYRA

EVERY INCH OF MY SKIN WAS COVERED BY MY FULL BODY SUIT. I wore a helmet with tint so dark it triggered my night vision.

Hank flew us back to Helios, where Sterling and I joined a modest team of four Lightstalkers with sun immunities. We were posted behind sand dunes spilling into the street, guns in hand, and were surveying the ivory building overlooking the ocean. A plastic sheet over a hole in the second floor whipped in the wind. There were no vehicles, and the windows were devoid of activity. Sterling held his palm up and swept it overhead, gesturing for us to move forward. We trudged through the sand, coming to stand beneath the hole. One of the Lightstalkers removed a blade and jumped, slicing the plastic sheet open before landing.

Sterling leaped through the hole, and we followed suit. Two Lightstalkers broke off in opposite directions, clearing the perimeter of the laboratory. The other two followed Sterling and me. We crept toward the door, holding our guns low.

I pulled the handle completely downward. The door's hinges were silent as it opened to the corridor.

It was empty, with only the crackling sound of a radio or television emitting from one of the rooms. Sterling peered at me over his shoulder, his copper eyebrows sinking low over his deep-set eyes.

Something didn't feel right, and judging by his look, he thought the same.

There should've been Keepers patrolling the halls—an increase of security after their attack. Unless they were fighting alongside the Nightshades in Neoterra... but there still should've been a skeleton crew ensuring the research was safe.

The Lightstalkers broke off to clear the other room while Sterling and I followed the crackling sound. We stopped at a plain door with a small window. We flanked both sides of it and I leaned across to peek inside.

The walls were stark white, and two sterile leather chairs with straps dangling from the armrests sat in the middle of the room. On the far wall, a television buzzed, then scratched like a record player before a video began to play. Sterling carefully opened the door and swung a hard left while I checked the right. The room was clear aside from a large spotlight propped in the corner. We lowered our guns, captivated by the video playing from the angle of a security camera.

A Vampyre man sat in one chair across the room. He didn't fight against his binds—rather he was smiling and squirming eagerly while hooked up to an IV attached to a blood bag. In the opposite chair, wan and frail and wriggling to get out of her binds, was Briar.

Sterling's face blanched.

"Are you ready, Frankie?" Dr. Ivanov's accent sounded over a speaker in the video. Shortly after, the spotlight flashed, turning the screen white. Everything was covered in red. Frankie was gone, disintegrated to the cellular level, and Briar shrieked at the top of her lungs.

The video glitched into a new one, this time with Draven in the chair across from Briar. He seized, foaming at the mouth while she was forced to watch.

Sterling's breathing grew rattled and he turned away from the horror on the screen.

"Is that what you call a contribution?" Sterling screamed at the speaker on the ceiling, as if Dr. Ivanov were still there.

"She's trying to get in your head," I said in an even tone. "Keep calm..."

"No, no, Lyra, that's what she did to Briar, that's—look at her eyes! She was human in those videos!" Sterling shouted, and bolted into the hallway.

"Show yourself, Ivanov!" he ordered, his voice echoing.

"Here I am," Dr. Ivanov drawled from behind us, and we whirled around with our guns pointed. Sterling's knuckles turned white around its foregrip. She raised her hands in surrender, but her coy smile never faltered.

"If you kill me, Mr. Shaw, you'll never be human again." Dr. Ivanov crooned with honeyed words. "And my Keepers will simply destroy you and the little mercenary group you brought here."

Sterling's tense shoulders relaxed as he lifted his head from his weapon's iron sights.

Don't fall for it.

Sterling narrowed his eyes. "Why should I believe that's possible? Eighty years of research and no one's ever found a cure."

Dr. Ivanov slowly reached in her breast pocket and removed a packet of white pills.

"Perhaps because I have been researching that entire time. I am one of the earliest Vampyres to rise from the grave." Her nose poked into the air proudly. "If you place your weapon on the ground, we can talk about giving you that life you yearn so much for."

"Sterling—"

"What're the side effects? Am I gonna explode like Frankie?" Sterling interjected, his rifle now dangling at his side.

There's no way he's seriously considering this.

"What do you have to lose?"

"You can't possibly think—"

"There's enough pills in here to change Briar too. Wouldn't you want your family to be whole again?" Dr. Ivanov tucked the pills back in her breast pocket.

"Alright," Sterling said. I inhaled sharply to plead otherwise, and he fired without warning. The bullets rained, and Dr. Ivanov's body shattered to pieces, as though she were made of glass.

"What the hell?" Sterling mumbled.

I gawked at the shards on the floor. What kind of tech was that? A new hologram variant?

Sterling howled in agony. Dr. Ivanov plunged a curved silver blade through his back and twisted. She kicked the back of his knees just before I shot her again. More glass.

Disembodied laughter swirled around me. The corridor filled with multiple clones of Dr. Ivanov. I cursed under my breath, turning in a small circle as I ogled them.

Why didn't we think of her taking the serum?

"Who needs Keepers when I have myself?" The doctors said in unison.

The Lightstalkers suddenly barreled into the corridor, blasting the first row of Dr. Ivanov's clones. Some of them dodged the bullets, flying around in blurs. Others dropped, seizing or instantly dying from the silver.

Among the clones, only one took off running to another wing. I pushed through the crowd, firing a clone between the eyes before I skidded around the corner. I smashed my fist through a glass case that housed a hatchet as Dr. Ivanov copied three more of herself. She bolted for the elevator, and I shot the clones as they charged at me. Dr. Ivanov slammed the button repeatedly, glancing over her shoulder as I advanced. I spun and let the hatchet fly.

Dr. Ivanov screamed. The silver blade wedged into her hand, and held it hostage against the panel. I slowed to a power walk the rest of the way with a satisfied chuckle.

"It's gotta really suck to be the one stuck with cloning while everyone else got cool traits," I said icily.

The elevator doors slid open, and she ripped her hand away from the hatchet. The skin around it blackened, necrotizing her flesh before her hand could fuse back together. I reloaded the pistol while I watched her desperately crawl across the threshold.

I shot her other hand, and cut her wail short with a bullet to the back of her head. I closed the rest of the space and crouched at her side—and heard her heart's final beat.

Reaching in her coat breast pocket, I removed the pills. I scoffed with disgust at the label.

Aspirin. Of course.

Distant gurgling made my ear twitch, and I beelined back to Sterling. I grabbed the corner of the wall to careen around without losing momentum.

Sterling lay in a puddle of his own blood, gasping.

"The knife had some kind of surgical-grade retardant on it," one of the Lightstalkers pointed out as she inspected the blade with a sniff.

"His lung is hemorrhaging faster than his body can heal," another said. "We gotta go, Lyra. Camp Cerberus is under attack."

For a moment, all I could see was Kiegan. Blood bubbled past his lips and escaped through his nose while he stared at me with hopelessness and agony.

It was like my heart became a stress ball, and a giant fist reached in to crush it. I closed my eyes—inhaling and exhaling through tight lips—and remembered my medical training at the Academy. I dropped to my knees and sifted through Sterling's cargo pockets until I found a pen.

"Go ahead. We'll catch up," I said. The Lightstalkers took off without hesitation.

"Leave... me..." Sterling strained. "Tell... Briar..."

I shook my head roughly.

"I told you..." I disassembled the pen for the empty barrel. I jammed it between his ribs, and a rush of air flowed through it. Sterling sucked a deep breath as if he had been held underwater for minutes. I waited for his breathing to stabilize as blood drained through the pen. His chest expanded and deflated in steady rhythm.

Tears streamed down my cheeks as I smiled. Running a trembling hand through his hair with a relieved exhale, I pressed my forehead against his and whispered, "I don't do goodbyes."

54

BRIAR

Oren and I stood in the middle of a destitute town formerly known as Lunacy that had been in ruins since the Crimson War. Camp Cerberus was five miles away—far enough to avoid getting involved with the raid, but close enough to be within earshot of the chaos.

Ada stood with three other women while they set up a tripod and camera. I turned in small circles, stuck in a trance as I surveyed the historical destruction. A place in forgotten history where the earliest Vampyres and Sun Dwellers had done fine without harming each other. One might think it was lunacy to even suggest a thing.

"Do you know what you're gonna say?" Oren asked, gazing across the flat plain at the treeline. Beyond it lay Camp Cerberus. His eyebrows were knitted together, lips pursed with subtly flaring nostrils. I knew he worried about his people as much as I did mine while we listened to the rapid gunshots and tracked the columns of smoke stretching to the heavens.

"I've never really been the public speaking type," I grumbled. "But... I got an idea."

"Then you lead," he said, hooking his thumbs in his belt loops.

I didn't like speaking to people, let alone on camera, but I had plenty to say. I just didn't know where to start.

"We're ready to roll," one woman announced. I combed my fingers through my hair, stiffened my back, and raised my chin. My inhuman irises bore into the camera lens as one of the women, Hannah, silently counted down from three with her fingers.

"My name is Briar Shaw, and before I Turned, I broke curfew. Actually, more than once," I explained with a nervous chuckle. I winced at the thought of blatantly confessing to a felony on video, knowing it would play on every screen and echo across the news.

I released a shuddering exhale and added, "They taught us that the Vampyres lacked restraint, that if you went outside even a second after sunset, you would be killed. But that's not true! Before I Turned, I made friends. I found a place that accepted me as a person, not just for my species.

"I've been held at gunpoint by a human. My mother treated me like her own punching bag. But I've been attacked by Vampyres too. The point is... it doesn't matter what the sun does to your skin. There's evil in everyone."

Oren nodded in concurrence.

"My name is Oren Jacobs, and I'm a Lightstalker. You've probably never heard of that term before, but that means I'm a half-breed. Yes, my mama's a human and my dad was a Vampyre. I'm one of the rare few whose mama survived birth." He gestured around him and turned in a slow circle. "The sun doesn't bother me. And I'm not the only one either. A whole city was built underground and named Avant Garde. My people had to go into hiding, because Mundus Novus doesn't want you to know we can live in harmony. They found out where we lived and destroyed everything."

"A united people means one common enemy, and *they* would lose their authority," I added.

"And there's a potential cure for blood dependency," Oren blurted. Ada's face went wan. I bit my lip, glancing at Oren. That wasn't meant to get out yet.

"We've been doing trials with iron supplements and blood transfusions, and sixty percent of Vampyres no longer crave blood, and their bloodwork remains stable in nutrition. Those terrorists? The clans wreaking havoc? They found a way to create sun immunity too. Imagine what could happen with both? There's hope for a life without fear."

"Remember who the real... enemy..." I trailed, raising my gaze to the sky. A fighter jet caught the sun's glint, cutting through the sky with the stealth of an owl. The door in its belly opened, revealing two missiles.

I dove into the camera, grabbed Ada and Hannah, and flashed in the opposite direction as one missile hurtled into Lunacy.

Blinding white light ripped through the world like a second sun. Buildings with caved roofs, peeling paint, and cracked brick erupted up and outward, pushing everything back with a force that ripped nearby mature maple trees from the root. Ada and Hannah wheezed from my iron grip around their waists. I sank to my knees at the edge of the field near the treeline, barely far enough to miss the impact. The brittle buildings rumbled as they crumbled to nothing.

Ada screamed, tears streaming down her cheeks. Hannah looked pallid, a gash in her forehead. I finally let them go and turned to face the damage.

Ada clutched her chest with one hand and beat the ground with the other, shrieking as veins bulged in her neck and forehead.

"No—" My voice finally broke through.

The two other videographers and Oren were still in town, and the fighter jet was already on its way to Camp Cerberus.

Where Draven and Caspian were.

But I couldn't just *leave* Oren and the other two—what if they were dead?

Maybe Oren ran in a different direction?

The fighter jet rapidly shrunk in the sky.

My voice escaped me once again, and I took off at full speed without another thought.

I left embers in my path as I accelerated beyond anything I ever thought I was capable of. My skin melted, revealing the molten rock beneath, and I shot into the air with a ball of light and flames churning in my palm. I hurled it through the sky and continued running when I landed on the ground. I kept my focus on the jet, watching the missile drop a second before my fireball made impact at its tail. The jet broke apart in a burst of orange and charcoal.

Then came the mushroom cloud rising above the general vicinity of Camp Cerberus.

My ankle rolled when I skidded to a stop with a gasp, hands

shooting over my mouth. My heart evaporated with everything else when the missile's nose made impact.

I heaved, each breath growing heavier and hotter than the last. I pulled on my hair, shaking my head.

No. They got out. They saw that jet.

They heard the first explosion. They had to get out.

The fire couldn't hurt Draven. Surely, Caspian survived. Surely.. the prisoners were already rescued.

But Oren—

I stood again, returning to Lunacy's simmering ruins in a burst of energy. I paused at the three charred bodies sprawled among the rubble. Ada was already kneeling in the ashes beside the taller body. His teeth were stark against the singed skin, frozen in a permanent grimace.

Hannah roamed around with the camera, filming the new destruction.

Something cracked inside me. This was all my fault. Why didn't I say anything? Why did I assume he had the same reflexes as me, grabbing the other two girls in each arm and bolting for safety? I should've made a warning call.

Cotton wedged itself in my mouth. I licked my lips and attempted to swallow.

"Ada... I-I'm so sorry," I said, voice hoarse. I knelt on the other side of Oren's body, across from his mother. The tang of burnt skin and hair seeped in my nostrils.

"I should've never let him get involved," Ada whispered, and held his rigid, warped hand.

"I don't think Oren would've been comfortable on the side-lines," I said. "He... he'd still be here if I'd said something."

"Don't do that. Blaming yourself will eat you alive," she chided gently.

"Isn't that what you're doing to yourself?" I asked. From the corner of my eye, I noticed Hannah recording.

"The difference is I'm his mother, and I put this cursed world before my only son." Her voice broke, and she used the back of her hand to wipe the tears from her cheeks. I wished we had the time to bury him.

"If you could be a dear and..." She sniveled and stood, brushing the ashes from her knees and shins. "Put him to rest."

Bile crept up the back of my throat, but I nodded and held my palms inches above his body. Heat waves rippled around him, and his existence crumbled among the ashes. While Camp Cerberus melted behind us, Oren's image etched itself into my mind and eroded my soul.

Part 4

Dissipation

55
DRAVEN

Being hog-tied was a new low. Being hog-tied with an oxygen mask over my face that produced mild fire-retardant fumes was even lower, but it helped the nausea swirling in my gut from the flash drive I'd swallowed. It also helped me ignore the instincts to murder every Sun-Dwelling Onyx Sentry in the armored truck they'd stuffed me in. However... it was also a new form of torture. They made me go a full minute of oxygen deprivation before switching the vapors emitted through the mask. Each desperate gasp was harsher than the last in a vicious cycle of catching, then losing, my breath.

It was a long drive to Mundus Novus, and it gave me enough time to think about everything that could go horribly wrong. The Nightshade and White Fang clans raiding Camp Cerberus at the same time as us was the first thing. The Onyx Sentries being equipped with various forms of fire retardant to specifically subdue me was another thing. It might not be as simple as Ada made it seem to plug flash drive in and expose Mundus Novus' lies.

"Our solution to everything can't be arson, Draven," Briar once said. Boy, did I want it to be. For the longest time, it *was* the Nightshades' solution to everything. Arlo's house wasn't the first one that had caught the match. But even if I had the strength to do it now, I couldn't. Destroying the tower with every Mundus Novus politician in it would only fuel everyone's fears, and confirm the propaganda they'd spread about Vampyres. Ada wanted the public to turn against them of their own volition.

With a little nudge, of course.

The truck finally came to a halt, and the Onyx Sentries grunted as they lifted me off the metallic floor. The action ripped the small amount of air I'd tried to conserve before they switched the vapor back to oxygen.

⁎

The burlap sack and mask ripped from my face, a rush of cool air washing over my skin. I gasped loudly, drinking up the air with goosebumps prickling along my arms. Energy flooded my limbs, the blood in my veins boiling. My claws shot out, gouging the wooden armrests my hands rested upon. I snarled, fangs at full length as my eyes darted like heat-seeking missiles around the room.

My rage distilled into confusion.

I wasn't in a cell, handcuffed, or in some sort of elaborate restraining device to suppress my fire abilities. A wide window overlooked the city and vast land. Rolling hills and the distant ocean faded into a misty horizon. The city below was grim, arranged in rigid grids with short, stocky buildings surrounding the tower—in contrast to Neoterra's organic roads, bridges, cliffs, and coastline. The sky was overcast, some of the clouds hanging low in a fog that appeared close enough to touch.

I sat at the head of a rectangular banquet table made of sturdy cherry wood that held six places on each side. The table was set with gold dinnerware, a pale-blue floral runner trimmed in gold, and blue cloth napkins. The seats were empty except for Governor Elise Donovan, who sat at the other end. She idly swirled a glass of white wine. The fire in the marble fireplace crackled behind her, outlining her mahogany chair in gold. An oil painting depicting a man in dress blues from one of the military branches in the old era rested above the mantle. His eyes were cold, his back rigid, his lips tight. However much blood he'd spilled, it was hard to determine if he regretted any of it in the portrait.

"Welcome to Mundus Novus," Governor Donovan greeted. The shadows filled the hollows of her face.

"What is this?" I double-checked my wrists and ankles. Nothing could stop me from leaping across the table and carving ribbons out of her face.

This has to be a trap.

"I was hoping we could negotiate, Mr. Hawthorne. I'm sure you'd be less inclined to do so if you were in a cell." She leaned back in her seat, taking a sip of her wine and crossing a leg over her knee.

"Who told ya I had the authority to take any negotiations?" I shot back.

"Every statesman knows you could wipe that underground militia out with a flick of your wrist. Why on earth would they deny you any authority?" Governor Donovan's voice was cool, as though it hadn't felt the warm touch of spring since birth.

"Then what makes ya think I'd wanna negotiate anything after your goons kept suffocatin' me on the way here?"

She looked up from her plate and gave me a thin smile that didn't reach her eyes.

"Hopefully, we can make amends. The Onyx Sentries, you see… they despise Vampyres. That's one of the qualities they get screened for when they enlist. I told them to make sure your transport here was as smooth and comfortable as possible."

No, you didn't, lying witch.

A door slammed down the hall outside the dining room. I jerked my head in the general direction with a growl.

"Calm down, it's just one of our servers bringing you something to drink," the governor said with a dismissive wave.

I stifled a laugh. I wished I knew what look on my face gave her the impression I was an idiot.

The door swung open, and a server dressed in a tuxedo placed two glasses filled with blood in front of me. I sensed one was of human origin and the other was from a Vampyre. I tucked my hands under the table, digging my nails into my palms to resist the glass on the left. If I had so much as a *drop*, Ada's plan would disintegrate.

"What do ya want?" I forced my attention away from the glasses.

"It is my understanding that you don't crave human blood anymore. Is that correct?"

I stared at her. Caspian had already said they knew, so I couldn't lie. But I didn't want to give her the satisfaction of an answer either.

"We could put an end to this war entirely if you agree to use that against the Nightshades and White Fang." She scraped up the remaining food on her plate. I gritted my teeth at the screech of the fork.

"We're already fighting them too," I said, narrowing my eyes. "Why would I ally with y'all when you've done nothing but alienate and destroy us?"

"What if I told you we had a cure for blood dependency?"

I slowly rose from my seat, palms flat on the table as I leaned forward.

"I'd say you're a damn liar," I growled. "Where's it at, then?"

"I'll let you in on a little secret." She dabbed the corner of her crimson lips with a cloth before tossing it on the table. "We've had it from the start of the Red Plague."

My claws dug into the table as I stifled my boiling fury.

"Why... wouldn't you people... release it?" I demanded through a clenched jaw.

"Overpopulation turned the former United States into a third-world country. Other countries kept fighting each other for limited resources due to... guess what? The same problem. So... someone came up with the genius idea of a bioengineered virus to thin the population. Of course, we wouldn't have released it without a cure. The one thing no one expected was the dead reviving as Vampyres, but it didn't affect how the treatment worked."

"You're still not answering the question."

"You're a smart guy, Draven. Come on." Governor Donovan laughed. "Why would we release a cure for a decades-long problem when it's *so* much easier to maintain power over a divided people?

Overpopulation would never be an issue again when the police have the green light to put down Vampyres who step out of line. And that happens often."

I scoffed, closing my eyes tightly. If what she was saying was true, this wasn't a negotiation. This was my last meal before execution. She'd never let me out of this tower alive with this information.

"Where is it?"

"Not here."

"If I help Mundus Novus fight the Nightshades and White Fang, then you'd need to release that cure. That's the only way I'd agree," I said, straightening with my chin raised.

For the first time, the ice queen's eyes lit up with excitement, and her wicked grin crinkled the corners of her eyes.

"I'll pitch the idea to the statesmen," Governor Donovan stated, and rose from her seat.

"You're not the phantom leader? I thought you made the calls on your own," I challenged.

"I'm not a tyrannical monster," she responded, rolling her eyes.

"Course not. Where's your can? I gotta use it," I said.

She paused with her hand on the knob, eyes twitching to a subtle squint. "Last door on your left down the hall," she said. "Keep in mind, you're on the hundredth floor."

Ha, as if that'd stop me.

"I ain't gonna leave. I'm curious to see what your beloved statesmen will say," I cajoled her. She gave me a wry chuckle before jerking the door open. We both knew they would never agree. If she claimed otherwise, it would be yet another lie.

Governor Donovan's heels clacked against the marble floors as she strutted down the hall. I listened for her footsteps to fade behind another door before flashing to the dimly lit bathroom in the opposite direction. I locked the door and checked the stalls.

I hunched over the sink and shoved a finger down my throat, triggering a gag strong enough to regurgitate the flash drive. After drying it off with a paper towel, I washed my hands with my lip curled in disgust. I swished water through my mouth before spitting it back out in a poor attempt to erase the tang of bile in my mouth.

Now when you get to the tower, there's gonna be a control room on the one hundred and fifth *floor.*

Vyrn had explained it to me after everyone left the briefing in Oleander Valley. He had the blueprints spread over a table in the chow hall. Briar stood next to me, and Caspian, Sterling, and Lyra flanked his other side. We all hunched over the map, studying the lines. Vyrn was the only one with previous Mundus Novus experience; he knew the tower like the back of his hand.

I peeked outside of the bathroom, looking down the hall before I followed the fire evacuation exit sign.

It'd be quicker to take the stairs with your speed instead of the elevator. Once you find the room, there will be a ton of screens and panels. Find the supercomputer, and plug this into the USB at the top row next to the blue and red button.

"Blue and red button," I mumbled to myself repeatedly as I shot up the stairwell for five more flights. I cursed under my breath once I entered the carpeted hallway. It was like a penthouse on this floor, and I wondered if all the alcohol Vyrn drank had fried his memory.

I opened every door, growing more frustrated when all I kept seeing were expensive office spaces. Unlocked, because I assumed they never had to worry about security breaches with elite soldiers and a docile population.

I pushed forward, bumping my head into a door when it didn't budge.

"There you are," I muttered with a satisfied grin, and rammed my shoulder into it. The frame splintered, and an Onyx Sentry hidden behind the usual full-face helmet swiveled in a chair with a gasp. He slammed a button on the console, triggering an alarm. I flashed to him, grabbing his jaw and snapping his neck with one hand. He buckled at my feet, and I grabbed the weapons off his belt before jogging across the room to the vertical supercomputer. Behind a glass door, there were various wires, plugs, panels, and buttons. I wrenched it open, cracking the glass.

"Top row... blue and red button..." I whispered once more, lifting my gaze to the top of the computer.

"I ain't nobody's weapon but my own," I growled, and shoved the drive into the open port. I smiled, turning to the screens mounted above the console. They went black before finally turning back on, showing Briar and Oren standing in the middle of a dilapidated town.

I tore my attention from the television when Onyx Sentries flooded the room with Governor Donovan right behind them, as well as several elderly statesmen in suits.

"What have you done?" she screamed. I shot a wave of flames at them, and sprinted toward the windows. The governor and her colleagues wailed in anguish, scattering in the hallway. The blazes caught onto the walls and the ceiling. I caught a glimpse of an Onyx Sentry raising a fire extinguisher on the other side of the doorway. I sprinted toward the windows and jumped, crossing my forearms in front of my face—and broke through the pane.

And fell down, down, down.

56
BRIAR

The checkpoint everyone was supposed to meet at was a mile off from the Mundus Novus tower, at a condemned mall in a southern city named Orion. I stood in front of a dried, cracked fountain, searching every face that appeared in the main atrium. Those faces warped into Oren's—pink and black flesh like wrinkled paper, torn and melted onto exposed gums and teeth.

What if Sterling and Lyra had died at White Fang too?

My knee bounced as I chewed on my thumbnail. None of the men resembled Caspian or Sterling—neither of them possessed average facial features that could be mistaken. None of the women looked like Lyra, either.

As much as I wanted Draven showing up to be a possibility, he was supposed to be in the tower. I could only hope he made it before the airstrike. The only person's absence I appreciated was Astoria's.

She was safe and sound in Oleander Valley, hidden from the bloody violence on the surface while she focused on research with Vyrn.

It should've been you in Oren's place.

I flinched at a hand resting on my shoulder as my mind began its spiral.

"It's just me, Bri," Sterling said, his chin and torso covered in dried blood. I gasped and wrapped my arms around him securely.

"I'm so sorry. I'm sorry. Oh god, I'm so sorry," I repeated, burying my face in his chest. Sterling strained against the constriction.

"What are you sorry for?" he asked with a grunt, and pulled away. I didn't want to let go. It was already hard enough to believe he was standing before me.

"For everything," I whimpered with a sniffle. "I didn't... I know a lot of this is my fault, especially Turning you, and I worried if you didn't make it out then I'd have to live with—"

"I almost didn't." Sterling lowered his gaze with a wince. "Lyra saved me."

I flopped on the edge of the fountain and buried my head in my hands with a shuddering sigh.

Sterling joined, cracking his knuckles as he leaned over his knees.

"I, uh... I should be the one saying sorry," he said.

I froze, holding my breath.

"I know what happened to you at White Fang. I disregarded the level of trauma you endured and only focused on what you became. I shouldn't have called you a monster."

I became a statue, on the brink of crumbling.

"I spent my time in the hospital dreaming of killing you after what you did to me. But... when I heard about the airstrike in

Lunacy, all I felt was crushing despair. It was the same kind that hit me when Dad died, when Cyrene was slaughtered, when you were abducted, when I learned what they'd done to you, and when I thought Astoria had burned alive. I realized that deep down, I wasn't angry anymore. I finally understood you didn't mean to hurt me. You've been hurting, and I failed you as a big brother."

I exhaled sharply, palms slick with the tears I tried to suppress. I finally lifted my gaze, and for the first time in ages, his lips stretched outward in a soft smile. He tossed his arm over my shoulders and ruffled my hair.

"No hard feelings?" he asked with an anxious chuckle. I nodded, feeling one of the wounds in my soul stitch itself back together. Sterling gave my shoulder a light squeeze before pulling away.

"I need you to forgive yourself too..." he trailed for a moment, peering down at his woven fingers. "For what it's worth, I don't think I would've learned how wrong I've been about everything if you didn't Turn me. I would've been fighting on the wrong side of the war. So in a sense, you helped me."

"I don't think so. I'm sure Lyra would've steered you the right way regardless," I countered.

Sterling's eyes dulled at the mention of her name, his lips retracting into a thin line. His gaze swiveled around the atrium before he stood, walking into the growing crowd of Vampyres, Lightstalkers, and Sun Dwellers arriving at the mall.

Moments later, Lyra emerged with most of her platinum blonde hair matted in dirt and blood smudged at the top of her head. Her solemn face lit up like a firework when her gaze locked on Sterling's, and they hugged each other like no tomorrow.

Judging by that reaction, they'd gotten split up at some point.

Just a year ago, my brother would've never wanted to breathe the same air as a Vampyre.

Now, it was as if he couldn't breathe without her presence.

I rose from the fountain's edge, deciding to wade through the crowd to find Caspian. It was possible he was here, just invisible. I cupped my hands around my mouth and drew in a breath—

The mall shook, dust and pebbles falling. Everyone immediately unholstered their weapons, pointing toward the doors and windows, and some at the ceiling. I peered up at the Mundus Novus tower through the glass ceiling.

A ball of light descended from the top floor like a falling star.

Draven's arms extended over his head as he left a trail of flames against the side of the tower as he dropped. Onyx Sentries stood in the flames, shooting down at him regardless of the cost of their own lives.

My feet moved before my mind did. I was outside in a desolate shopping center in seconds, greeted by clusters of clan members filling the parking lot and streets as they passed through to get to the tower. Mundus Novus must've been next on their target list.

No one stopped to notice me standing outside the mall. They were too busy watching Draven's descent like deer in headlights.

Draven fell past the fiftieth floor. He didn't scream or roar. Like a satellite breaking through Earth's atmosphere, he ignited. Except he didn't break apart.

I shot across the lot, landed on a roof, and bounded again. Power surged within, hurling my heartbeat into my ears. Heat crawled from the soles of my feet to the top of my head, building until I had no choice but to purge.

I ran along the side of the tower and pushed off the side, snatching him out of his extreme acceleration as gravity dragged him down. Our flames morphed for a second, turning bright blue.

The ground split open at our impact as we tumbled across grass and concrete. The whiplash didn't stop until our bodies burst through the brick wall of a nearby building.

I lay on a pile of rubble, panting and staring at the paneled ceiling and the flickering light fixture that dangled on a thin wire above me. Live wires snapped and popped. My skin, arms, and legs fused back together piece by piece.

Draven grunted, and the pile of debris shifted as he pushed up to his hands and knees and climbed out. He straightened, coughing and waving the dust away. His inky hair was coated in a chalky white substance, turning it grey.

"Briar!" he exclaimed, and staggered to my side. I squinted and blinked at the sudden shift of light as he blocked my view of the fixture.

"I'm okay," I replied hoarsely, and coughed. "What happened?"

"I-I don't know if the video's still p-playing 'cause I set the room on fire. They were gonna kill me, so I jumped out the window. They got stuff that can actually hurt us." His words came rushed, his pupils dilated, his pores leaking sweat, and his heart roaring.

Helicopter blades whipped above us in a crescendo, before fading again. I pushed myself to sit up, neck and back finally cracking into place. Draven held out his hand and pulled me to my feet. I slid down the mound of rubble and jogged to the gaping hole in the side of the building. Helicopters rushed to spray the fire on the top floor and the few beneath it as Draven's blazes spread. He stepped beside me, watching the black cloud roiling like waves from the structure.

"Did you kill them?" I asked.

"They ain't have much time to run," Draven mumbled. He turned to me with his eyebrows furrowed and lips pinched as if he still had bad news to give.

"What else happened?" I folded my arms.

"They had a cure this whole time," Draven said lowly, like he couldn't believe his own words. He stepped through the hole, squinting at the silver sky. I followed him, the hairs on my neck rising at the screams, war cries, gunfire, and the tang of blood on the wind.

My heart jumped in my throat.

"They're here," he mused, and dusted off his shoulders. Clustered in the streets, it was difficult to see who stood on which side. Machetes slashed, guns spat, claws swiped—a cacophony of savage chaos.

One person stood out, though... and he was headed our way.

Uriah's lips tugged in a malignant half-grin as he prowled toward us in a cocky swagger.

"Thank you, son. You've done us a great service taking out Mundus Novus. Raiding them was the whole reason we made the trip to this beautiful city. I'm sure many people are loving your little performance too, Miss Shaw." Uriah projected his voice until he got close enough. "I can't wait to set up shop in that tower now that they've put the fires out. I heard the views are breathtaking."

Draven growled, leaning with one foot forward and palms

aglow. I allowed my hands to warm with soft flames, waiting for the moment to raise the temperature.

"Draven, wait—"

"Don't help me," he snarled. "He's mine."

Then he lunged.

57
DRAVEN

Uriah's skin hardened to steel the second my claws met his bodysuit. Sparks bounced, sizzling through the air. He delivered a right hook. I dodged. He caught me by the ears and rammed his knee into my nose, sending lightning strikes through my vision. I dragged the back of my hand across my upper lip with a snarl.

I glared at him from under my brow and reset my nose before the bones could fuse together crooked. The crunch mirrored the sounds erupting from the clans clashing violently behind him.

Uriah had always overpowered me. From the time I was an early Nightshade to the time Briar and I fought him at his estate, he was always two steps ahead.

"What's the matter, son? Still haven't learned to fight for yourself?" Uriah sneered.

I roared, the flames lapping up my arms as I delivered a left jab, followed by a cross. I dodged, then slammed my forehead against his in rapid succession. My skin split and I staggered backward, holding my head until the gash closed.

"You're weak! Give it up, Draven! You and your people lost!" Uriah's metallic skin glinted as the clouds parted above. "Give it up now, and I *might* spare you and your friends." He reared back and his arm shifted into a curved blade. He crooked four fingers on his other hand with a smug grin, as though this were a sparring game.

"Draven, get back!" Briar shrieked. I backflipped onto a roof, narrowly missing the jagged edge. It grazed the ends of my hair, the strands floating in my place.

"Go help the others fight the clans!" I barked at her.

"No!" Briar retorted.

She lashed a whip of lava at Uriah. I matched her strength with a wall of fire. Uriah crossed his forearms, morphing into a shield like liquid mercury. Our blazes burst outward, breaking into wisps of sapphire and emerald. For the first time, a loud grunt escaped Uriah's lips as he pushed against our fire. My muscles tightened as I stepped to the edge of the roof, pushing against a force that even I—an *enhanced* Vampyre—struggled against. Sweat pearled and ran down my face, only to evaporate in the surrounding heat waves. Uriah's shield glowed and warped, but he reinforced it by transferring extra metal from his legs to his upper body.

Briar screamed, knees and arms trembling as they threatened to buckle. Black veins bulged in her arms and neck while she strained against Uriah's might. I dropped from the roof, our pillars of fire combining into one.

The burnt orange deepened into indigo, eliciting a bloodcurdling cry from Uriah as it bore a hole through his shield. Our force launched him across the street and into a high-rise office building, pulverizing its walls and windows on the bottom floor. The shrapnel embedded in several Onyx Sentries' and Avant Guardian's backs and throats—wiping out a dozen who fought too close to Uriah's landing.

As if we had entered the eye of the storm, the dust settled and the structure fell quiet. I sprinted through the rubble before Uriah could gather his bearings—if he was even alive. Briar was close behind me, her breath brushing against the back of my arm.

Uriah's skin smoldered, eyes rolled to the back of his head. His breaths were so shallow, his chest hardly moved.

"What are we gonna do now?" Briar asked, running a hand through her hair.

"We're gonna do what we do best," I said, and picked him up.

The remains of the building groaned. We dashed outside, and I threw Uriah's limp body in the middle of the street.

He moaned, cracking his eyes open. His scorched skin gradually began to mend itself.

All it took was one Nightshade to notice us standing there, triggering a domino effect where everyone stopped fighting each other within seconds. I kept my hand ignited, and they took it as a warning to stay put.

"Y'all can stop killin' each other now. Your enlightened Alpha decided to retire," I called out with a gloating grin, and crouched next to Uriah's body.

"You were like a son to me," he mumbled. "You're gonna kill me, after everything I've done for you? After I molded you?"

"Yeah? You were never like a father to me. Ya ruined my life. But no worries, I'm gonna make the best out of it now." I glanced at Briar. She knelt next to me with a deep inhale.

Uriah chuckled and said, "I hope you're still able to make the best of it without her."

I released a dry laugh. "What?"

"Draven—!"

Uriah palmed my face, smearing his own blood across it. I shouted, frantically wiping my sleeve across my face while my mind threatened to shatter.

"No, don't! Focus, Draven! Fight it!" Briar's pleas sounded a mile away.

Then I couldn't hear them anymore.

My shouts deepened to wild, animalistic snarls. White Fang Keepers and Nightshades barreled toward us in Uriah's defense, with Avant Guardians and Oleander Valley villagers failing to intercept them because of the Onyx Sentries attacking their other side.

I ripped away from Briar's desperate grasp and fell to all fours, charging at the crowd. The first hostile to approach raised his machete. I caught his arm, claws plunging into bone. His cries reached a new pitch as I sank my fangs into his shoulder, tearing through his bodysuit's fibers. A rush of energy flooded my body, and the starvation clawed awake. I didn't realize how blunt my fangs had become until they grew sharper, and I sank them into the next victim, and the next—

Hunger departed me. I left piles of bodies in my path as greed consumed me instead. Fire broke free from my palms, weakening the structures around us until the smoke choked the sun.

I missed the part when they stopped attacking and instead scattered like crows.

The fight became a hunt, and it was exhilarating.

Another prey stumbled over the curb and dropped his rifle. He crawled backward and grasped a knife from his ankle. He brandished it wildly, slicing the air as I dodged each swipe. I pounced—

A heated blast flung me through the window of a nearby building and into a granite countertop. The fog in my mind thinned. Nausea replaced the raw wrath in my core. I coughed in the smoke, cracking my eyes open to look around with newfound clarity. I landed in a hotel lobby, and my impact had taken out the receptionist's desk. I belched, and that only made my nausea worse. Had I eaten an elephant?

A petite, dark silhouette framed by the harsh sunlight stepped over the rubble and entered the lobby. I retched across the broken stone, and gawked in horror at the blood and bones that came up.

Steps crunched over glass shards, pausing five feet away from me. I sniffled, wiping my mouth. I leaned my head back, prepared for whatever fate stood before me.

"Briar." I released a relieved exhale. "What happened?"

A shaky sigh escaped her lips, and she inched closer.

"I... I'm sorry. I had to." Briar's eyes welled with tears. "You were about to kill Sterling."

I pushed myself up with a grunt and stood, sweeping a hand through my hair. Beyond the hole in the front doors, corpses were strewn across the street and buildings had been laid to waste. Fighting still ensued, but a few blocks over. It didn't sound as calamitous as before, indicating significant casualties on all sides.

Casualties that I'd blindly caused. I stared at the bodies, hoping that our allies hadn't fallen at my hands. Governor Donovan's voice slithered around in my mind with a wicked laugh. I shut my eyes, jaw tightening as I buried the thought of inadvertently helping Mundus Novus.

I turned to Briar, who still kept a wary distance. "Where's Uriah? Did he get away?"

"I dragged him in between a couple dumpsters and fought off as many as I could. I don't know if he's still over there at this point. He might've healed by now or someone could've gotten him out." She rubbed her arm.

"Show me," I said, more urgent. Briar flashed outside, and I followed. We paused at the dumpsters. The space was empty, with only his scent left behind.

"You two almost had me," Uriah called from above, rolling his neck. "I'm impressed."

He sat on a balcony railing with his ankles crossed. A cigar dangled from his mouth. Amid the chaos, he'd found time to light it as if celebrating a victory.

"Ya think it's over?" I called out. "That trick back there will only work once."

"You think I only have one?" Uriah's skin hardened to steel. "I'm giving you two one last chance to join us before my people bring the Sun Dwellers to their knees."

"Mundus Novus is done now. They were our common enemy, manipulating the Sun Dwellers to fear us. We fixed that," I insisted. "*You* have one more chance to make your people stand down."

"No!" Uriah dropped from the balcony in a furious roar, leaving a shallow crater. "I was there! I lost my arm in the Crimson War. They dropped that bomb on us like we were nothing! They didn't care about us then, and they certainly don't care about us now. It's our turn to make them kneel!"

"No," Briar cut in. Her eyes burned white, the skin around her sockets splitting to expose the magma beneath. "You're no different."

Briar swung her arm, slinging a string of blazes. Uriah crossed his arms again, blocking with another makeshift shield. Several daggers born from his own metal shot from his hand, and I shoved Briar out of the way. She held her hands out as she tumbled, sending a wall of heat waves in front of me. The knives warped and turned blunt, bouncing off my chest.

Uriah released a wry chuckle.

"What a dynamic duo," he said in a snide tone.

I looked at Briar and flicked my eyes toward Uriah. She nodded, shooting to her feet and snatching my hand.

Uriah turned both of his arms into curved swords and swung in sharp left and right hooks. I yanked Briar closer, his blades only nicking her shoulder. We didn't break contact as our combined fire shifted to emerald. His shield warped at our flames' contact, until he reinforced it. I lifted Briar by her waist, and she kicked his chest. He staggered back and swung, the serrated edges catching my stomach. I grunted and used my rage to fuel a stronger blaze in his direction.

We pushed forward together. Uriah dug his heels in, the force dragging him across concrete until his back hit the brick wall. His grunts escalated to a desperate cry as his arms of steel glowed, melting away to show the skin and bone beneath. The ground shook and the tower swayed, groaning under the pressure.

Blue embers crackled across our skin, spreading through the rest of the fire until it flared into bright sapphire flames. Uriah's wails shredded into tormented screams as we torched the man of steel into ash.

58
BRIAR

IT WAS A MIRACLE SO MANY OF US CAME OUT UNSCATHED. Well, *physically*. There were some days when I felt splintered, torn between joy and terror. I still saw Oren standing behind me when I looked in a mirror and still smelled his flesh and hair whenever I lit a candle. I could hear the horrified screams from the Avant Guardians and Oleanders as they fled from the Onyx Sentries.

It was a shame that as a sleepless Vampyre, being awake didn't protect me from the nightmares. But no matter what—whether I hurled my guts out over the toilet, trapped in the fetal position as I hyperventilated, or turned our high-rise apartment upside down in a blind rage—Draven was there. He was *always* there to bring me back, even if it took hours.

Draven would often sing to me during my panic attacks. I'd get lost in his voice, and remember that we survived. Now, we lived together without fear of someone trying to capture or kill us.

Work helped, as well as sitting on the rooftop terrace. I escaped there often to clear my mind and listen to Neoterra's white noise below.

I sat on the edge of the terrace now, dangling my feet over and swinging them back and forth. I kept an eye on my watch, waiting for the time I was supposed to meet Draven at The Hole.

Ada took on the role as president, instituting some age-old traditions. Her first order of business? Transparency and starting from scratch.

The country lost its name after the Red Plague, absorbed into a single government that oversaw what remained in the world. Several countries never returned after the virus, and global leaders at the time decided it was best to streamline authority—through statesmen representing each continent and subregion, with a hidden phantom leader that no one could plot to assassinate. They never named the country to prevent nationalism from resurfacing. Nonetheless, we voted on live television to name our nascent country Equinox, and for a small morale boost, held a competition for a flag design.

Ada lifted the curfews and assigned Draven, Caspian, Lyra, and me as Enforcers in Neoterra. We helped the communities heal and rebuild trust, but our main purpose was dealing with issues beyond the police force's capabilities. One example: the Skinwalkers. They were still spreading their propaganda, aiming to recruit the traumatized Sun Dwellers who still feared Vampyres. The Enforcers would sweep in to stop any public attacks initiated by their order. Ada still had hope that they'd heal one day too, but that level of optimism escaped me.

Many of the Nightshades and White Fang clan members were still being arrested for their war crimes. Draven and Caspian were in charge of tracking their whereabouts since they were familiar with clan operations. It was therapeutic for them—working together again. This time, they worked toward the greater good.

Former Mundus Novus employees came out of hiding to reveal where the cure was. It turned out that it had been in an underground vault beneath the tower. It took six months to clean up the debris above it, one month to unlock the vault, and it would take years to run trials and ensure it was truly the cure Governor Donovan had claimed—without side effects.

Astoria was back in school. Not for nursing, but for microbiology and pathology. Working with Vyrn to create a temporary solution for Vampyre cravings until the cure could be released inspired her to pursue a career in that field.

Astoria and Vyrn's iron pills helped with Draven's barbaric frenzies, but they weren't strong enough to get rid of his new Vampyre-blood dependency. Until they worked out the kinks, I donated my Vampyric blood once a week for him.

A week after Mundus Novus fell, it had me thinking about the fleeting characteristics of life. So, I asked Astoria if she'd ever Turn.

"Hey, Ria... can I ask you something?" I spoke around a mouthful of cake Draven had ordered to celebrate our victories. I sat on the floor while she opened boxes of furniture I had yet to tackle. Draven was satisfied with sitting on the floor, but I didn't want us living like barbarians anymore.

"Shoot." She sucked in a breath as she put all her strength into ripping tape apart.

"Have you ever thought about Turning?" I whispered while the guys were outside on the balcony. Astoria paused with a pensive smile. She reached for the necklace Caspian had given her, twisting the moonstone between her fingers.

"I have, and I think I will at some point. But... I want it to be on my own time," she said. I nodded, and left it at that.

Astoria clung to her humanity like I once had, but in a different way. She admired the beauty on both sides of the fence, and never once thought the grass was greener. She just wanted to be happy, near her friends and family. She always had my utmost respect for that. I was proud that the violence hadn't destroyed her light. At this point, I was convinced nothing ever could, and I was excited to see what her future held.

My watch beeped, and I hopped off the edge. The amber string lights illuminated the terrace, gilding the sectional, grill, and pool in gold. Ordinarily, I would've jumped off the edge to get to my motorcycle faster, but I didn't want to mess up my hair. This was the first date Draven and I had gone on in months, and despite everything we'd been through together, I still felt butterflies in my stomach.

✳

Seeing the skate park and all its complex, detailed street art was refreshing. The ground thrummed rhythmically from below. I sighed at the sight, reminiscing when I'd first seen this place. I was just a girl without a purpose, celebrating an apprenticeship I'd landed at a Vampyre-only establishment. Now, I returned as a hero.

I followed the music to the trapdoor and dropped down without using the ladder. Draven was on stage, deftly strumming his guitar and filling the space with his coarse, husky timbre. It never failed to send goosebumps over my skin. His eyes locked on mine and he winked before shutting them again. He always sang with his eyes closed, as if keeping a part of his heart hidden from the world while he performed. I paused in front of the crowd, observing his black button-down blouse and slacks. Either Caspian had acted as a fashion advisor or Draven had somewhere else to be after our date, because I didn't think he'd ever trade the baggy hoodies, t-shirts, and jeans or joggers for anything. His sleeves were rolled up to his elbows, exposing half of his dragon tattoos. For a moment, I swayed to the music, forgetting the mission I'd had to grab a drink.

The grungy, fast-paced tunes slowed to a ballad, morphing into a new song. I finally broke away, watching him from the bar while I waited for the bartender to return with my daiquiri.

I found a rose I should've crushed.
Instead, I cut myself on her thorns.
I was the moth to her flame,
And set myself ablaze.

I homed in on the lyrics, heat rising up my neck when I recognized they were about me. The bartender tapped my drink on the counter and I sipped through the tiny straw as I wove through the crowd. I caught a glimpse of a couple Sun Dwellers down here, having the time of their lives as I once had. Hopefully, they didn't share my experience of an inebriated Vampyre attempting to bite them. Several of them slow-danced until the song entered the last verse.

Even the sun isn't bright enough
To take your place in my life.

You helped saved the country,
But you saved me first.
You've been stifled by thorns,
So let me adorn you in roses.

Draven's eyes opened and the guitar chords stopped, but the piano continued softly in the background. He pulled the strap over his head and propped the guitar against the piano before jumping from the stage. He reached in his pocket, sinking to one knee.

I choked on my drink, spitting it right back in the cup. Sweat glistened across his forehead as he opened the maroon velvet case, revealing a raw diamond ring shaped like a kite. I could only see it for a second before everything became warped behind my tears.

"Will ya marry me, Sunny?" He raised his eyebrows with round, crimson eyes, as if he still doubted a positive outcome. I sniffled, shoulders heaving with hiccups. I nodded and tackled him in a tight embrace while everyone in The Hole erupted into applause.

I didn't take my eyes off that ring for the rest of the night.

59
STERLING

I paced across the beach in the Nocturne District. Every now and then, I got close enough for the water to submerge my feet before it withdrew into the ocean. For the tenth time, I inspected the large square blanket held down by lit candles at each corner. The plastic wrap covering the food glinted under their light. I checked my phone, eager for Lyra to show up.

Six months... and so much had already changed. After Ada took over, she appointed me as an ambassador. I never understood why. My reputation as the greatest detective always carried the blemish of my hatred with it. Everyone knew how much I'd despised Vampyres throughout my career. Humans praised me, Vampyres loathed me.

But that hate had since left my heart and mind. Remembering that praise left a bitter taste in my mouth. Ada's justification for the role was exactly for that.

"Briar favored the Vampyres, and Draven favored the humans. But you, Sterling... you're a success story where knowledge transcends hate and fear to love and understanding." Ada spoke passionately with her hands, pacing with caffeine-induced energy. Her smile never faltered despite the loss of her only son a week prior, though I was certain she mourned when no one was looking.

It's your job to bridge the gap and show that it's okay to have an open mind.

I watched the waves rise and crash, matching my breathing to their rhythm. It only settled a fraction of my jitters.

Tonight was the first time I could manage to break Lyra away from the constant work as an Enforcer, and purge the words that had been smoldering inside me for too long.

"You know, usually when it's a date, I get asked first and then I can actually look nice," Lyra called out as she descended the steps from the boardwalk. She grinned, pale cheeks pinching at the scene I'd begged Briar to help me set up. I was certain she and Draven were somewhere watching. Close enough to listen and watch, but far enough where the ocean's brine masked their scents.

"Wow," Lyra breathed once she finally approached. She hooked her long bangs behind her ears and crossed her arms with a nervous smile. She wore her usual maroon blouse and black tie underneath a charcoal trench coat with dark wash jeans.

"You look beautiful," I blurted. It felt liberating to finally say it aloud without feeling guilt or disgust. Lyra's snapped her gaze to mine, eyes rounded.

My heart raced as the words inched their way past my teeth.

"Back in Oleander Valley... I wasn't trying to tell you goodbye."

I took another deep breath and grabbed her hands.

"You led with 'if anything happens' which is literally what my late husband *always* said whenever we had a dangerous case," Lyra said, a subtle edge to her voice. "And... the day he was killed."

"I'm sorry, but... I'm not Kiegan. If you let *me* finish..." I dialed down my tone with a sigh. She could be unbearable, but I couldn't imagine living without her.

Lyra rolled her eyes, but didn't pull her hands away. "*Say it,* then."

"I wanted to apologize. I haven't been the easiest to deal with." I paused with a deep inhale and continued, "I've said a lot of terrible things, and you stuck around to help me find my family regardless. Even when I was in the Transition Program, you were there to visit me when you could've cut me out of your life. Why?"

Lyra peered down the shore.

"I guess... you struck me as a fox caught in a snare. You needed someone to help you get out and learn that everyone isn't the hunter." She returned her gaze to mine, eyes glimmering like rubies.

I forced a swallow and squeezed her hands gently—I was too afraid to say it directly. I pulled her close to break the lingering eye contact. Lyra rested her cheek on my chest, eyelashes shuttering. I breathed in her bergamot perfume and the world slowed to a stop.

"I want to be more than friends," I whispered. "I-if you'll have me."

Lyra pulled away. I braced for the gut-wrenching response.

My chest ached as my heart tried to claw its way out. A wide, alluring smile stretched across her face as she lifted her gaze and exhaled like she'd been holding her breath this entire time.

"Finally." She cupped her hands around my face, and closed the gap between us. It was invigorating, like drinking ice water after spending years in a desert. A rift closed. The puzzle pieces finally clicked together. This was real, and suddenly everything made sense.

For once, I had high hopes for our future.

***

Thank you for reading!
If you enjoyed this book, please consider leaving a review on Amazon and/or Goodreads. Reviews are golden for us indie authors and they encourage more exposure. It would be very much appreciated!

***

AUTHOR'S NOTE

If you are interested in monthly updates for bonus content, upcoming projects, and events, you can also sign up for my newsletter for free on my website at www.taliawall.com!

ACKNOWLEDGMENTS

Wow! You've made it! This has been such a crazy year. Starting a debut series rather than a standalone was a huge risk.

Until Equinox was inspired by infamous historical events such as World War II and the Jim Crow era. In a dark world, I wanted to give readers hope. I pray I achieved that for you.

I give my deepest thanks to God for giving me the strength to push through the trilogy. The last book had many challenges through the year with short writer's block periods.

I want to thank my line/copy editor, who provided such amazing insight. Without her, I wouldn't have been able to grow as a writer. I can now go into my next projects with more confidence.

Thank you to my family, who have supported me since day one by not only reading, but also spreading the word to their friends. My husband had endless patience for the long hours I spent isolated in my office, typing away.

As always, I thank my readers. Your support goes beyond purchasing my books. Reviews, joining my newsletter, or even a shoutout to your friends helps tremendously. I hope this series inspired you.

I can't wait to bring you more adventures!

ABOUT THE AUTHOR

Talia spent most of her life in North Carolina and had the lifelong dream of becoming an author since she was five. She not only loves to write but also to draw and paint. She has a loving husband and Persian cat named Thor who often interrupts her writing sessions. She writes young and new adult, paranormal, urban fantasy, and dystopian genres with the intent to send powerful, relevant messages and warnings through fiction.

Social Media Handles

TikTok | Threads | Instagram

@fromdreamstopaper

Website:

www.taliawall.com